Peggy
Sue

Doug L. Hoffman

ISBN 978-0-9884588-5-7

Published by
The Resilient Earth Press
www.theresilientearth.com

Preface

Peggy Sue is the second book of the T'aafhal Inheritance series and the sequel to *Parker's Folly*. It should come as no surprise that there is a sequel to my first book, since the epilogue of *Parker's Folly* hinted that the dark ones took exception to the actions of Captain Jack and his crew (and the preface said that this book was already finished). The first part of *Peggy Sue* has its roots in questions from readers of its predecessor. Specifically, what happened when the Peggy Sue returned to Earth?

The stage for this book is also expanded, including many new worlds and new alien races, as the characters from the first book stretch their wings and travel into the wider Galaxy. Relationships deepen and bonds between crewmembers grow stronger as the intrepid band of explorers face a future that they did not ask for. Indeed, the mysterious T'aafhal will finally be revealed—raising even more questions about the ancient war between warm life and the Dark Lords, and naturally setting the scene for book three.

Again I would like to thank my early readers: Brandon Willis, Clayton Ward and Rik Faith in particular for their useful and in depth critiques. Thanks to my family for putting up with my obsessive prattling about trisexual, hermaphroditic, intelligent plants and other oddities. The book was written using OpenOffice and the cover art done using the GIMP. I hope you enjoy Peggy Sue.

Doug L Hoffman
20 January, 2013
Conway, Arkansas

i

Prologue

AFTAC, Patrick AFB, Florida

Senior Airman Robinson was manning AFTAC's sensor array when he was roused from his daydreaming by an alarm. AFTAC, the Air Force Technical Applications Center, is a not quite secret organization that monitors Earth and nearby space for nuclear detonations. A burst of gamma rays had been picked up by several satellite detectors. Slight differences in arrival times, combined with the positions of the satellites in space, allowed the source of the radiation to be pinpointed. "Man, that is way out there. It's also off the plane of the ecliptic by quite a bit," he said to himself.

This triggered a memory regarding the recent Texas spaceship brouhaha. Three weeks ago, a spaceship, supposedly built in the wastelands of West Texas, blasted off from Earth and rendezvoused with the International Space Station. According to the deep space tracking network it then visited the Moon. That was followed shortly by some kind of lunar eruption and the appearance of a moving source of radiation that headed away from Earth.

The Texas ship followed and, at a point approximately 665,000 km from Earth and 322,000 km above the ecliptic plane, both tracks ended. It was as though both objects vanished into thin air—well, thin space. At first, Robinson had entertained the wild thought that one of the objects might have returned, but this new point was more than 50 million kilometers away from the point of disappearance.

More alarms sounded as the particle detectors provided confirmation of the radiation source's location. Whatever caused this was a long way away. *I guess I'll just log it under the strange readings category,* thought Robinson, *the last thing I need to do is stir up a hornet's nest like last time. I think the Colonel still blames me for that one.*

What SrA Robinson did not realize was that the burst of radiation his instruments picked up had, in fact, occurred at the same point where the two objects had disappeared twenty two days ago. Robinson was judging the distance relative to Earth, and that was the wrong frame of reference. Earth travels in orbit around the Sun with a mean orbital velocity of 29.783 kilometers per second. Since the initial incident, humanity's home moved almost 57 million kilometers along its orbital track.

The location in 3-space where these comings and goings were taking place, however, had remained fixed in a different frame of reference. This was because it was the terminus of an alter-space transit line between the Sun and a distant star nearly 30 light-years away, Beta Comae Berenices. While Earth's position within the solar system had changed, the relative positions of the stars varied little during the brief interval between incidents. The burst of radiation SrA Robinson dismissed marked the return of humanity's first and only starship.

* * * * *

TK Parker, an oil billionaire in his late 70s, was at his ranch in West Texas. He was maintaining residence not because he liked the place—it consisted of flat scrub and a now partially demolished WWII era dirigible hangar. He was staying at the ranch to aggravate the authorities. The government had tried to seize the property three weeks ago, after the launch of his pride and joy—a spaceship secretly built in the old hangar.

In the final stages of testing, the ship's reactors emitted enough radiation to draw the attention of the Air Force's monitoring satellites. Thinking they had uncovered a nuclear plot against the nation, the authorities sent all manner of law enforcement officers to seize the ranch and whatever equipment was emitting the radiation. They even sent a squad of Marines to capture the hangar.

This forced Parker's hand and he ordered the ship's crew to take off, even though they were not ready. That was more than three weeks ago, and there had been no word from the ship since. So TK and his housekeeper, Maria, occupied the ranch house to keep federal agents from having free access to the property while Parker's phalanx of lawyers blocked the government in the courts.

"Maria. How about rustling up some more coffee?" TK called over the intercom. Maria had been his cook and housekeeper for more than two decades and was the only real family he had. At times they argued with each other like a couple long married, though there was no physical intimacy involved in their relationship.

2

"Si, Senor Parker," came the reply, "I will make another pot."

Thank God for Maria, TK thought, *at least there is one person left on the planet I can trust.* He had kept himself busy getting the ranch house fixed back up after the spaceship's unexpectedly energetic departure, that and prodding his lawyers to file more suits and injunctions against every agency from the DOD to the U.S. Marshals to the Texas Rangers. Still, worrying over the fate of the crew on board Parker's Folly kept him up most nights.

Parker's Folly was the name the construction workers had pinned on the spaceship. Secretly, TK was rather proud of that name. The workers thought the ship was a joke, but they all stopped laughing after the ship actually flew, reaching orbit, the Moon and beyond.

At first the news media couldn't get enough of the spaceship story, clamoring for interviews and filling their broadcasts with uninformed speculation. But since the media has the attention span of an untrained puppy, the spotlight soon faded. Now the only ones left interested in TK and Parker's Folly belonged to the government bureaucracy.

The satellite phone on TK's desk chirped, a sound he had not heard before. It was not one of the ringtones he had programmed. Picking the phone up, he looked curiously at the display, trying to figure out what caused the strange audible signal. There on the display was a text message:

WE R BACK. SHIP & CREW OK. MEET SOON. JACK

TK's eyes misted over as he read the message from his captain. "I knew you were the man for the job, Jack my boy," TK said out loud. Then, shouting to his housekeeper, "Maria! Start packing. We gotta make a trip to Australia."

Part One

Keep Your Friends Close, And Your Enemies Closer

Chapter 1

Bridge, Peggy Sue, Earth Orbit

Jack Sutton sat in the captain's chair, pensively watching the blue and white globe turning slowly beneath his ship. After a week in alter-space, they had spent the following month flitting about the asteroid belt storing antimatter containers acquired while blowing up the alien refueling station at Beta Comae. Now the Captain could no longer put off the inevitable—he knew from the outset that some of the people on board the Peggy Sue would need to be repatriated.

As much as it pained him to see friends and colleagues from the last voyage scatter to the winds, the crew deserved some shore leave and some form of closure was necessary for those who participated involuntarily. He needed to return the squad of Marines that he had "borrowed" to the United States, and the two surviving cosmonauts, rescued from the International Space Station, needed to at least contact their countries of origin.

The first of the crew ashore was Lt. Bear, the ship's Master-at-arms. Bear was now up north for some R&R, mostly hunting and maybe an attempt at recruiting a few of his fellows to the cause. He also mentioned something about looking up his old flame, Isbjørn. *Hopefully he will find the food more to his liking in Norway,* Jack thought moodily.

The source of Jack's discontent was not Lt. Bear's epicurean preferences but the insistence of Ludmilla Tropsha, Russian ISS cosmonaut and acting ship's medical doctor, that she must report in person to officials of ROSCOSMOS, the Russian Federal Space Agency. Despite his argument that she might not be allowed to return Ludmilla would have none of it—she would report and then come back to the ship. The fact that she shared the Captain's cabin and held sole possession of his heart could not sway her.

"Permission to enter the bridge, Captain?" It was Lt. Gretchen Curtis, Jack's second in command. She had just returned from dropping Bear off and was set to transfer the Marines planetside. The tall red haired First Officer was wearing a standard, skintight spacesuit that showed off her trim athletic figure.

"Permission granted, Lieutenant, welcome back. Was Lt. Bear happy to be back on Earth?"

"Thank you, Sir. He certainly was, but I think he's starting to go soft in his old age. He actually hugged me before getting off the shuttle."

The three of them, Lt. Curtis, Lt. Bear and Captain Sutton, had been together for more than five years, working on the spaceship that they now voyaged in. Over that time the trio became as close as brothers and sister. Of course, being in combat together did tend to create bonds, even between the most unlikely souls.

"He'll have a good time, I'm sure," Jack replied. "I just hope he finds us some more recruits, we are certainly going to need them." On the ship's maiden voyage, after a brief stop to rescue a trio of stranded cosmonauts from the ISS, Captain Jack and company discovered the presence of hostile aliens on the Moon. Drawn to an anomalous cavern beneath a lunar crater in the hope of find an alien device left by ancient visitors, a surface party led by Lt. Curtis came across a hidden probe ship and a swarm of belligerent, spider-like cybernetic creatures.

After a short firefight and a harrowing escape from the probe ship's violent blastoff, Parker's Folly followed the fleeing alien vessel into the hidden dimensions of alter-space. This came as quite a surprise to all on board the Earth ship, since no one suspected the Folly could enter alter-space or that alter-space itself even existed. Another mystery revealed with suspicious timing by the ship's computer, which was interfaced to the ancient alien data storage device known only as "the artifact."

After catching and destroying the alien probe ship and then staging a daring raid on an enemy refueling station orbiting a devastated planet, Earth's lone starship returned home. Though their mission was a success the price they paid was high—four expedition members were lost while escaping and then blowing up the alien space station, five if the traitorous Col. Kondratov was included. That action led directly to the renaming of the ship, now officially christened the Peggy Sue.

"Did you talk with the Marines, Sir?" Gretchen asked. The next mission was going to be a bit touchier than simply dropping a single passenger off on the desolate shores of Norway. "They are all intent on returning, even though the Corps was throwing them out?"

Jack sighed, they had been over this ground before. When the Peggy Sue departed its construction dock in West Texas it had on board a squad of U.S. Marines. These Marines were not part of the ship's complement but rather, a boarding party sent by the government to seize the ship. With half of the squad incapacitated by injuries at takeoff—the squad's lieutenant among them—Captain Jack was able to strike a deal with Jennifer Rodriguez, the Gunnery Sergeant left in charge. During the voyage, the Marines fought heroically along side the crew against the threatening aliens, tragically losing two of their number in the process.

Jack offered to let the survivors stay with the ship as its detachment of Marines but Lt. Merryweather, the unit's commander, had regained consciousness on the trip home and was now back in charge. He saw it his duty to bring the squad back to the U.S. and the Marine Corps. As a former Navy officer, Jack had to grudgingly admit that Merryweather was doing the correct thing—not necessarily the right thing, but the correct thing. "I'm afraid that Lt. Merryweather is quite insistent, and I gave my word that I would return them to Earth at the end of the mission."

"If you got the squad alone, without the Lieutenant, you know that they would opt to stay with the ship," Gretchen said. More than anyone else on the crew, with the possible exception of Bear and JT, she had bonded with the Marines. Seeing them leave was like saying goodbye to family.

"The Lieutenant has his duty, and they are all Marines," Jack said resignedly. "I would expect nothing less of them than to follow their officer's orders." *As much as it pains me to see them go*, he added silently. "The Chief has them assembled in the cargo hold, wearing their original uniforms. Their weapons and ammo have been boxed up and can be dropped off with them."

No need to tempt Lt. Merryweather into doing anything rash, like try to take over the landing shuttle. The thought was unvoiced but understood by both of them. Gretchen nodded her assent, "Then there's nothing for it, except to take them home."

"I'm afraid so, Lieutenant. Take them back to Earth and drop them where they got on, at TK Parker's ranch. When you are clear we can contact the authorities."

"Aye aye, Sir."

Astronomy Department, University of Padua, Italy

It was another glorious summer day in the north of Italy, replete with golden sunshine, verdant foliage and singing birds. Dr. Lucrezia Piscopia, Professore Associato in the Departimento di Astronomia, Universita degli Studi de Padova, was staring wistfully out of her office window overlooking the Riviera Paleocapa. Flowing slowly beneath her third floor perch in the Astronomy Department building the waters of the Bacchiglione river moved unhurriedly as they had for centuries. Lucrezia, or Elena, as she was known to her colleagues in the department, was frustrated and dissatisfied with her lot in life.

Being an Associate Professor at one of the oldest and most prestigious universities in the world would have been a crowning achievement for most scholars. After all, Elena performed research and taught astronomy at the same university where Galileo Galilei once taught. Indeed, the University of Padua is credited with being the second oldest university in Italy, generally dated to the year 1222 AD. It was founded by a large group of disgruntled students and professors from the University of Bologna, Italy's oldest university. Evidently, disagreements among scholars are nothing new.

Though her office was in a relatively new addition, that building was adjacent to the original university observatory, known as La Specola. The Specola itself was a tower, part of the old medieval castle of Padova, which dated from the 13th century. It was a famous landmark in a city of famous landmarks.

Close to the renaissance city walls surrounding the old town of Padova and in the heart of modern Padua, the old building sets on a point of land where the Bacchiglione river splits into two. The left branch, called Tronco Maestro, travels along the medieval walls towards the ancient Carmine Church and runs under Molino Bridge, just down stream from the Astronomy Department.

In the 18ᵗʰ century, the Venetian republic decided to give Padova's university an astronomic observatory. Dedicated by the University as the seat of astronomical studies, the Observatory started its activity in 1779 after a renovation of the tower was completed. The Observatory continued its academic activity until December 31ˢᵗ, 1923, when it was separated from the University and established as an autonomous institution attached to the INAF, the Istituto Nazionale di Astrofisica.

Elena had worked closely with scholars from INAF over the years and there was a lot of crossover work between the Department and the Observatory staff. The main telescopes and other instruments belonging to the Observatory and to the Department of Astronomy were located in Asiago, on a 1000 meter high plateau 90 km from Padua. But here, next to the old Observatory, one could really sense the history of the place—nearly 800 years of teaching and scholarship. Elena was proud to be a part of that tradition, and that was why she was feeling depressed.

In recent years the Italian economy had been terrible, the nation barely able to avoid defaulting on its financial obligations. Since Italy's universities were all state run, with students paying little or nothing to attend, the University had fallen on hard times. And though she loved her job, both the research and the teaching, there was no possibility that she would ever become a tenured full professor in the foreseeable future.

Not that prospects for astronomy professors were good anywhere in Europe these days. She should have made a move several years back, when she was something of a minor celebrity. Standing five foot nine in three inch stiletto heals and partial to short cut, clingy dresses, Elena did not look like a typical astronomer. With a tawny main of thick unruly hair, deeply tanned olive skin and blazing dark eyes, Elena more closely fit the image of an Italian starlet—at least she did a decade ago.

At that time she was the host of a science show on Italian TV called *Cacciatori di Stelle,* the Star Hunter. While she was trying to promote astronomy, the network was trying to make science sexy, and for a while it had worked. But nothing lasts forever, and once the novelty of a smart woman in a real short skirt wore off the ratings plummeted. Still, it had been an intoxicating experience. Now nearing the end of her fourth decade, Elena could still stop men in their tracks when wearing a skimpy bathing suit. But she had no illusions, time and nature affected everything and everyone —even stars grow old and die.

Elena's building funk was interrupted by a lively Baroque tune from her cellphone. The snippet of Scarlatti ended abruptly as she answered the call, "Departimento di Astronomia, Professore Piscopia."

"Dr. Elena Piscopia?"

"Si?" Then, realizing that the caller had a foreign accent she switched to English. "Can I help you?"

"Yes, hello Elena. This is Rajiv Gupta. You may remember me from CERN two summers ago."

Two years ago Elena attended a month long workshop at the CERN Laboratory, which sits astride the Franco-Swiss border near Geneva. Also visiting, but for a different program, was Dr. Gupta, a renown particle physicist from America. Their paths had crossed at a number of social functions held by the Lab.

"Si, ciao Rajiv, how have you been?" She could not recall what institution he was with or where he was from in the U.S., limiting her conversational response. Moreover, she could not think of a reason for him to be calling her, though they were both physicists they worked in different fields.

"Good to speak with you as well, Elena," the mysterious scientist continued. "I was wondering if you would be attending the conference in Melbourne next week?"

"Melbourne? Australia?" she replied, even more confused.

"Yes, I was hoping to talk with you there, if you were going to be in attendance. I have a line on some work that is right down your alley."

"*Vi chiedo scusa?* I beg your pardon? Down my what?"

"Oh, I'm so sorry, American slang. I have an opportunity that you might be interested in and it appears to be a good fit with your areas of expertise and recent research. Specifically, the search for habitable exosolar planets."

Ah, now that made more sense, Elena thought, much of her recent work had centered on detecting potentially habitable worlds circling other stars. "Really? What type of work would it be? Consulting, a visiting scholar position?" *Or possibly a longer-term opening?* She pleaded silently. *Would that be too much to ask for?*

"The project is a long-term one, but we could use your expertise on whatever terms you could offer. It really is too complicated to describe over the phone, which is why I was hoping to see you at the conference. I can say that we have some top notch people and a unique observation platform."

Elena had not planned on attending the Melbourne Astrophysical conference but she knew there was still some travel money in her research budget. And getting an Australian visitor's visa for such events could be accomplished via the Internet. *Come on, girl!* She chided herself, *this is a sign. Seize the day!* "Yes, I am going to attend the conference. I will look for you there, Dr. Gupta."

"Excellent! I look forward to talking with you then. Good bye."

"Arrivederci!" *What a timely happenstance!* Even a temporary position for a semester or two would be a welcome break from her normal schedule. And even if the job does not work out, a trip to Australia was just what she needed to erase her gloomy mood. Italian immigrants arrived down under in large numbers during the decades immediately following World War II, and were now the fifth largest ethnic group in Australia. Melbourne in particular attracted many immigrants and as a result, Lygon Street now boasted the biggest selection of Italian restaurants and cafes of anywhere in Australia. In Melbourne, she could leave home and never feel homesick.

Happily humming to herself, Elena grabbed her bag and headed out of the Department, stopping by the administrative secretary's office to arrange reservations for the trip. Then she headed home to begin packing. Walking past the ancient walls of the Specola, across the arched stone bridge from the Ponte dell' Osservatorio to the Piazza Accedemia Delia to wait for a shuttle bus back to her apartment, her conspicuously short dress attracted admiring glances from a number of men—both students and older. Elena didn't even notice them.

Parker's Station, The Australian Outback

Rajiv Gupta ended his call to Dr. Piscopia and turned to face his colleagues. Among them were Dr. Yuki Saito, astrophysicist and formerly an astronaut on the International Space Station, Dieter Schmitt, a brilliant if somewhat eccentric chemist, and most importantly, TK Parker, the money and driving force behind the whole enterprise. They were in the ranch house of Parker's Station, a gigantic cattle ranch located in the Australian Outback.

Australian cattle ranches, called stations, are by far the largest in the world. In fact, some Australian stations are bigger than entire countries. Anna Creek Station, well known as the biggest Australian cattle ranch, covers 6,000,000 acres in the Outback of South Australia. By comparison, the biggest American ranch is the famous King Ranch, located in south Texas between Corpus Christi and Brownsville. It claims only 825,000 acres. That a Texas billionaire had to come to Australia to buy a really big ranch was a matter of considerable mirth locally.

The Australian style of farming cattle is also very different from that used in America and other places around the world. The Outback is so dry and the vegetation so sparse that large amounts of land are needed to support enough cattle for the economics to work. Because the areas involved are so large, Australian cattle are essentially "free range." Meaning they are basically wild animals, often being born and growing up without ever seeing a human. Raised on grass and rarely given any chemical supplements, Australians claim their beef is the best in the world.

Arguments between Texans and Aussies over whose beef is best aside, the main attraction of Parker's Station was its privacy. Life on any station is isolated, with the nearest neighbors often a full day's drive away. Most contact with the outside world is by radio and the mail planes that also deliver supplies to the widely scattered station houses. Even medical emergencies are handled by the RFDS, the Royal Flying Doctor Service.

This lack of outside contact was exactly what TK Parker had in mind when he bought his station in the Outback. TK was less interested in raising cattle than he was in building a small fleet of space shuttles to complement his spaceship. In the decade that TK had owned the station, he never once told the local Jackaroos, as

Australian cowboys are called, what to do. He was a strictly hands off owner, letting his hired manager run the place for a share of the profits.

What interested TK most lie under the land near the station house. A vast complex of laboratories and construction areas lurked just beneath the hot dry surface scrub. There, safe from prying eyes and the occasional spy satellite, Parker had slowly built up a staff of highly skilled workers. There were scientists—physicists, chemists, biologists, geologists, material scientists, etc.—along with information theorists, linguists, code breakers, computer scientists and engineers of all stripe.

The excavated rubble from Parker's mad scientist's lair had been carefully graded into the surrounding landscape, though no one would have thought it strange to have piles of excavated dirt scattered about. At the town of Coober Pedy, several hundred kilometers to the south, there were piles of dirt everywhere. There everyone lived in houses underground, converted from working opal mines. Even so, TK was a cautious man, and nowadays it was unlikely that anyone would remember when excavation work was going on at Parker's Station.

Hidden within the labyrinthine installation were bays that held two completed large shuttles, plus another still under construction and a pair of smaller craft. The large shuttles were 16 meters long by 10 wide, blunt arrowheads with lifting body shapes. Between their shape and hull material they were inherently stealthy, very difficult to spot using conventional radar. Each could carry 42 passengers in a 2-2-2 first class seating arrangement within a 6 meter wide cabin. Alternatively, the seats could be collapsed into the deck, resulting in a 10 by 6 by 2.5 meter cargo area.

A rear stairway could be lowered for passenger loading from the runway underneath the craft, similar to the airstair arrangement on some old Boeing 727s. When docked flush against the hull of the Peggy Sue, the same stairway extended into a purpose built airlock on the spaceship's upper deck. The windscreen of the flight deck and the entire top of the passenger compartment, from armrest height upward, was constructed much like the nose of the Peggy Sue—large sweeping transparent panels framed by thin silver strips where the panels met. Under normal conditions the panels in the passenger area were kept opaque, but they could be turned transparent in an instant, providing a breathtaking overhead view. Those who experienced the ride to or from orbit with the cabin in transparent mode described the experience as Disnyesque.

Each smaller shuttle, referred to as a pinnace or Captain's launch, was built on a similar planform shrunk down to a 10 meter length. With a cabin area roughly equivalent to a corporate jet, they could carry eight with a crew of two. Both types of shuttle were equipped with small fusion reactors, gravitonic drive and acceleration compensating deck gravity generators. Full coverage repulsor arrays were mounted to ward off space junk—a real problem near the incredibly trashy lower Earth orbits—plus the repulsors could turn away small arms fire if the occasion warranted.

Though the Peggy Sue was fully capable of landing on Earth, doing so and then returning to space required a great expenditure of energy. Even running on muon catalyzed fusion power, such a wasteful use of energy was expensive. Besides, bringing the whole ship to the planet's surface to embark or disembark passengers and supplies offended TK's engineering sensibilities. When the Peggy Sue quietly made orbit a few days ago, instead of landing at Parker's Station—an event that might not have escaped notice—it was one of the large shuttles that flew up to meet the returning starship, bringing up new additions to her crew and ferrying much of the existing crew planetside for some well deserved R&R.

Among those crew members were Rajiv Gupta and former ISS astronaut Hiroyuki "Yuki" Saito. Since returning to Earth they had been working feverishly on plans to improve the efficiency and output of a number of the ship's systems. Aiding in their efforts was the estimable Dr. Schmitt and a gaggle of engineers. The other thing the returning scientists concentrated on was an effort to recruit more scientists to the project. Hence Rajiv's call to Dr. Piscopia.

"Well it looks like she will be coming to the conference in Melbourne after all." Rajiv smiled at his colleagues. He had checked the preregistration for the conference, or more precisely he had one of the staff computer hackers do it for him. Elena was not on the registration list, prompting the phone call. "And I do believe that she is interested."

"Und how do you know that, Rajiv?" asked Dieter. Dr. Dieter Schmitt was a tall man, close to two meters, thin with pale icy blue eyes. Stooped shoulders, sharp features and a prominent nose topped by a shock of untamed black hair gave the chemist a markedly vulture like appearance.

"She was not planning to attend the conference, or at least was unregistered. But she immediately decided to attend when I mentioned we might have some interesting work for her."

"That's great, Rajiv," said TK, "I hope we have as much luck with the others on the list."

"Rajiv, my friend. All of this secret project work has rubbed off on you," said Yuki, smiling to show that the remark was intended in jest. "Dr. Piscopia will be an excellent addition to our group if she accepts the offer."

"Yes, her reputation is outstanding and though I don't know her all that well, she seems to be an adventurous type. And as we both know, a thirst for adventure is a definite asset on board the Peggy Sue."

"Bah, most of my friends would gladly battle space aliens for a chance to travel among the stars," Dieter scoffed. "But then they are mostly physical scientists. Let's see how good a reception Ludmilla gets when she calls Olaf."

Sickbay Office, Peggy Sue, Earth Orbit

Dr. Ludmilla Tropsha, formerly of the Russian Federation Air Force and ROSCOSMOS, was sitting in her office in Peggy Sue's medical section. She had been putting off calling her friend and colleague, Dr. Olaf Gunderson, since the ship made orbit. Ludmilla had known Gunderson for more than a decade. He was a large man with shaggy dark hair and a bushy beard, reflective of his Norwegian ancestry. No doubt, a thousand years ago, some of his ancestors sailed the Baltic and North Sea raiding any village they came across. Olaf, however, was generations removed from pillaging Vikings. Directly descended from Wisconsin farming stock he was one of the gentlest souls Ludmilla had ever met.

He was also a world renown evolutionary biologist, with a reputation for challenging convention. An iconoclast who took endless delight in debunking consensus science and those who would not, or could not, think outside conventional theories. One of the things he was adamant about was that the accepted evolutionary story of *Homo sapiens* was total bunk. If there was anybody on the planet below who would welcome the news that humans had been genetically manipulated by ancient alien visitors, it would be Professor Gunderson.

Well, here goes nothing, Ludmilla said to herself and placed a call to his university office number. On the fifth ring someone picked up. "Hello? Gunderson here."

"Olaf? Hello, this is Ludmilla Tropsha."

"Oh really? You are supposed to be dead," came the reply, slightly delayed by the satellite link. That delay was just enough to throw off the normal rhythm of conversation and they both tried to speak at once.

"If this is a joke it is in bad taste," Gunderson said on the second try. "But I'll be damned if you don't sound like Ludmilla."

"That's because I am Ludmilla," Dr. Tropsha snapped, instantly regretting her quick temper. "Olaf, what is that American saying? 'The reports of my death are greatly exaggerated.'"

"Well, I'll take this call as preliminary evidence that you are still among the living, but I'm not going to tell anybody else without more solid proof. They said you were going to die on the ISS when that big solar storm arrived month before last," Olaf paused to chew on his mustache, a habit long established when he was deep in thought. "And then there was something about a mysterious spacecraft and an explosion on the Moon. For someone supposedly dead twice over you sound quite alive. Wait a minute...tell me about your husband."

"My ex-husband is Yuri Tropsha, I divorced him ten years ago," she replied, somewhat miffed that asking about her ex was the best test he could devise to establish her identity. "That information proves nothing, it is a matter of public record that anyone could have looked up. Better to have asked about the conference in Stockholm four years ago when you passed out from drinking too much beer at the reception and several of us had to carry you to your room."

"Now that is the Ludmilla Tropsha I know," came the chuckling reply. "You always have had a very high standard for evidence."

"Now that we have established my continued existence, I need to talk with you about something," Ludmilla replied. "I know you have a more open mind than most, so you may be more willing to believe what I am about to tell you than I was when I first heard it."

"Wait a minute, before you start telling me any tall tales, where are you? The last known location I have for you was in Low Earth Orbit."

"Olaf, I don't want to stay on the line any longer than necessary, for reasons that will become clear later. But to answer your question, I am once again in Earth orbit, though a bit higher up than the ISS. I have been to the Moon and to another star system. I have samples of tissue taken from alien organisms." Ludmilla paused to be sure he had not hung up on her.

"OK, go ahead," came Olaf's cautious reply.

"I am still on board the 'mystery' spaceship, which is called the Peggy Sue. I have seen things that a few months ago I would never have believed, so I can understand if you find what I am saying farfetched." Again Ludmilla paused. Now she understood how Jack felt the first time he had tried to explain all this to her. *Jack, my love, I owe you yet another apology.* Swallowing hard, she continued, "Olaf, I have information that implies humans were genetically modified by an outside party, and that our evolution was altered to suit their purposes."

Silence.

"Olaf? Are you still there?"

"Yes, I'm still here." A pause. "And you say you can prove this?"

"I can show you the records of the experiments, detailing the modifications made and when—the records go back 4 million years. I'm not experienced in evolutionary genetics to judge the veracity of the records. That is why I am calling you, I would like you to come and examine the 'proof' before we tell others about it..."

* * * * *

At the receptionist's desk outside Dr. Gunderson's office, his teaching assistant, Kimberly Lawson, was listening on the extension phone. While it was not Kim's habit to spy on her boss, when she heard "you are supposed to be dead" through the open office door curiosity got the better of her. This was her second year of grad school and her first as Dr. Gunderson's assistant, a job that mainly consisted of grading papers and keeping his calendar up to date.

Before the supposedly dead caller hung up, Kim overheard Gunderson agree to take a trip to Australia to meet with her. Carefully hanging up the extension she quickly shuffled a pile of homework papers and acted like she was busy grading them. Dr. Gunderson stuck his head out of his office and said, "Kim, I'm going to need a flight to Adelaide, Australia. And a hotel near the University of Adelaide."

"Yes, Professor," Kim replied, looking up from her papers innocently. "Is there anything else?"

"Yes, I'll need a rental car," then adding, "I will need to call Dr. Mary Sun and let her know I'm coming." *It would look suspicious to travel all that way and not stop in on a colleague,* he thought. *I don't think I'm going to be very good at this sneaking around stuff.*

"What should I put on your calendar, Professor?" Kim asked, "and who will be covering your classes?"

Damn! I hadn't thought about that. "Put that I'm going to Kangaroo Island to have a look at some interesting genetic divergence among western grey kangaroos. I'll get Dr. Phillips to cover, she owes me for last semester. You can teach the undergraduate section, and thanks for reminding me." *Kim is a good girl, I don't know what I'd do without her.*

"Yes, Professor." Kim turned to the computer on her desk and began checking flights to Australia. *I don't know what this is all about,* she thought, smiling a private smile, *but I'm not going to be left behind. Daddy never checks the charges on the credit card he gave me to come to graduate school and besides, I've always wanted to go to Australia.*

Shuttle Dock, Third Deck, Peggy Sue

Lt. Curtis had Chief Zackly send the assembled Marines up the companionway from the lower deck to the third deck shuttle airlock. Third deck was seldom visited by the crew with the exception of Melissa Hamilton, the ship's horticulturist. Most of the space on the ship's highest deck was taken up by equipment bays and more of the hydroponic gardens that seemed to be wedged in nooks and crannies all over the vessel.

The Peggy Sue's hasty initial departure left neither the time to wait for the shuttles to be completed, nor would they have been useful on that hectic jaunt to Beta Comae. Lurking in Earth orbit and needing to move personnel around the globe changed that outlook—this was precisely what the shuttles were intended for. Now that the shuttle craft were operational, the third deck would see a lot more traffic.

The ship could carry a pair of shuttles, which docked back to back atop the Peggy Sue's hull. Amidships there were a pair of airlocks built specifically to mate with the underside of either sized shuttle. Once in place, a docking collar is extended to seal around the shuttle's built in stairway. After a good seal is confirmed the shuttle's airstair is lowered into the airlock providing access.

After climbed up the three decks to the open airlock, the Marines were ushered into the large shuttle's passenger compartment. Bobby Danner, one of the ship's helmsmen, was forward at the shuttle's controls, and Lt. Curtis was standing at the front of the passenger compartment to instruct the boarding Marines. "Please move forward and find a seat, as you can see there is plenty of room."

Not fully recovered from his terrible injuries, suffered when the ship launched suddenly nearly two months ago, Lt. Ernest Merryweather was slightly out of breath from the climb and feeling pains in his limbs. This, along with the fact that he spent most of the mission unconscious in sickbay, put him in a cranky mood. He felt like a teenager who passed out early at a party and missed all of the fun, only to awake with a hangover in time for parental punishment. "You're not planning on flinging us around the cabin on launch again are you?" he groused.

The ship's initial takeoff had subjected all of those on board to significant gee-forces, which caused injuries to half of the Marines and several of the crew. This was because the deck gravity system could not be calibrated while in Earth's gravity well. Once in orbit, the final gravitonic circuitry was grown and the system became operational. The system not only provided adjustable gravity throughout the ship, it compensated for acceleration imposed by the vessel's movement.

As with the ship's deck gravity system, the shuttles had to be taken into orbit without any acceleration compensation the first time. Since then, with their own deck gravity operational, passengers on board the shuttles felt no sense of motion, even under violent acceleration. All of these facts ran through Gretchen's mind as she looked at the scowling Marine lieutenant. She took a step forward and stood, looking down at the Marine officer.

"You will experience no unwarranted acceleration on board the shuttle, just as you have not since the ship's gravity became operational," she said, adding in a quiet, icy tone, "and the proper form of address for a Naval officer of superior rank is either Sir or Ma'am."

Despite himself, the Lieutenant stiffened, came to attention and replied, "Sorry, Ma'am." In truth, Merryweather didn't hold anything against the ship's First Officer, she had always treated him with proper courtesy. It was apprehension about what lie ahead that fed his ill disposition.

While the inter-officer drama was playing out in the front of the cabin, the remaining Marines and one Navy Corpsman climbed on board and found seats. All except Gunnery Sergeant Rodriguez. She paused at the foot of the boarding ladder and turned to the Chief. "Take care of your self, Hank," she said, offering her hand.

"You too, Jennifer," the weathered old Chief Boatswain's mate replied, clasping the proffered hand. "Don't let 'em jack you around down there."

"Hell, what can they do but throw me out of the Corps? And they were already doing that before this mission started." With that the Gunny turned and climbed up into the shuttle.

The Chief stepped out of the airlock and sealed the inner door. "Yer all clear to undock, Lieutenant," he called over his collar pip.

"Roger, Chief," came Gretchen's reply. "Beginning departure procedure."

Chapter 2

Melbourne, Australia

It was Elena's third day at the Astrophysics convention, which was being held at Victoria University's City Convention Centre on Flinders Street. She was staying in the Langham, a very ornate and rather expensive hotel on the south side of the Yarra River. That meant every day she had to cross the Yarra on the pedestrian bridge, walk through the tunnel under the old train station and then dodge the streetcars and other traffic to reach the convention center on the north side of Flinders Street. Elena didn't mind the walk, but Melbourne's uneven sidewalks, appropriately called footpaths by the locals, were definitely not friendly to high-heeled shoes.

On the first night there was a reception and cocktail party where she bumped into a number of colleagues and acquaintances—the international astrophysics community was not really all that large. The next night she went to dinner with some friends at one of Melbourne's trendier bistros. When she got in late that evening she found a message waiting for her that said to meet in the morning at one of the outdoor eateries along the south bank promenade. It was now 9:30AM and the morning fog was still burning off, the temperature struggling to get into the teens. Elena was sipping a cappuccino and picking at a croissant while trying to fight off the late winter chill.

A slender, dark complected man wearing a dark blue jacket and aviator sunglasses walked down the wide promenade carrying a slim briefcase. He entered the bistro's seating area and came to her table. "Elena?" the man asked, a hopeful smile on his face. "Si. Is that you Rajiv?" she replied.

"Yes, I am Rajiv Gupta," he said, happy relief showing on his face. "It was so good of you to come. I hope that I haven't kept you waiting long, all of these little riverfront bistros look the same and I had a hard time finding the correct one."

They shook hands and Elena motioned to an empty chair. "Please, set down and have a coffee. The cappuccino here is quite good. Of course, Melbourne is a remarkably international city."

"Thank you," he said, taking a seat, "and you are right about the multicultural flavor of the city. Aside from the original English, Scots, and Irish settlers there are Italian, Chinese, Indian, Indonesian and, of course, native aborigines. There was an oriental young man behind the counter of my hotel this morning and I expected him to sound like either a Californian surfer or a Chinese grad student. Instead he said "G'day, how ya goin' mate?" He really scrambled my cultural expectations."

The waiter came over and Rajiv ordered. Then, once the waiter had departed, he opened the briefcase and took out a slim folder. Opening it revealed a collection of large photographs, all shots of a dun colored planet with prominent icecaps. "Would you please look at these and tell me what you see?"

Elena picked up the photos one by one, carefully examining each in turn. The waiter returned with Rajiv's coffee and another cappuccino for Elena, who murmured "grazie" without glancing up from the pictures in front of her. After several more minutes, she looked up and said, "This would appear to be a terrestrial planet, but it is not in this solar system. I would suspect the image of being computer generated, but somehow I think you will tell me differently, no?"

"Correct. What would you say if I told you that the world in the photos before you circles a star almost 30 light-years from here?"

"I would say that there are a number of star systems that are within that distance which might have an Earth or Mars like planet. Which one is this?"

"Beta Comae Berenices."

"Ah," the astronomer said, "and just how did you get these pictures? The resolution is quite high, I would have guessed they were taken from close by, perhaps in orbit—but how would that be possible?"

"We thought that showing you some pictures would be easier than trying to explain in words." Rajiv smiled warmly and took a sip of his cooling coffee. "Those were taken a little more than a month ago by a spaceship from Earth."

"But that is impossible!" Elena sputtered. "Even with today's technology, the ship would have had to have been launched thousands of years ago! And then, transmitting using radio or lasers, the photographs could not be received back on Earth for another 30 years—Einstein's cosmic speed limit is strictly enforced."

Rajiv grinned a Cheshire cat grin. "What if I told you there were ways around Dr. Einstein's inconvenient speed restriction? What if I told you I viewed that planet with my naked eyes?"

"I would say that you are either delusional or playing a very elaborate hoax on me, or both."

The slender physicist continued to smile as he took out a cell phone and dialed a number. Waiting for someone to answer, he held one hand over the phone and spoke to Elena. "I believe that you know Yuki Saito?"

"Si, but Dr. Saito was reported dead on board the ISS. This joke is rapidly becoming not funny."

He held up a hand to forestall more angry comments as someone picked up on the other end. "Yes, this is Rajiv. I'm with Dr. Piscopia. Could you put Dr. Saito on the phone? ... Thank you." Without saying another word he handed the phone to Elena.

"Hello, this is Hiroyuki Saito, can I help you?" came a familiar voice on the phone. It was a voice that Elena recognized as her colleague Dr. Saito. "Yuki? Is that you?"

"Yes, Elena, it is me. As you can tell, I did not perish on board the ISS and too many things have happened since our rescue to tell you over the phone. Please trust Dr. Gupta. He will bring you to a place where we can explain everything."

"It is you! *Grazie a Dio!* You are alive!" A million questions swirled through Elena's head. How could this be? Yuki alive, closeup pictures of alien planets, claims of faster-than-light travel—it was too much to take in all at once. Rajiv gently took the phone from her hand and told Yuki "Thank you, I think she believes us now my friend. See you soon."

Hanging up the phone he looked back at the stunned woman sitting across from him. "Elena? Are you all right?" Focus slowly returned to her gaze, she looked at the diminutive physicist and asked "what happens next?"

"Next, you can enjoy one last day at the conference and then meet me at the train station in the morning. We are booked on the Overland to Adelaide departing at 7:35AM."

"The station across the river?" Across the river, on the north bank of the Yarra, was a beautiful old Victorian train station that she passed under walking to and from the conference center.

"No, that's Flinders Street station. The train to Adelaide departs from Southern Cross Station on Spencer Street. Don't worry, just tell the desk at the hotel you need to catch the Overland to Adelaide in the morning and they will arrange a shuttle bus. Pack enough clothes for a couple of days, we will overnight in Adelaide before continuing on by plane the following morning. I have a few more errands to run and will meet you at the station."

"Si, I will be there," she affirmed, again staring down at the pictures of the alien planet in front of her. She had hoped a trip to Australia would bring a bit of adventure with it, but this was taking things to an extreme. She looked up and Rajiv was gone, the only proof that they had talked was an empty coffee cup and the glossy photographs she held in her hand.

Parker Ranch, West Texas

The shuttle dropped silently from the dark night sky, after a careful stealthy approach. Bobby Danner, one of the Peggy Sue's helmsmen, was at the controls with Lt. Curtis acting as copilot—an experienced helo pilot, she had not yet found time to be checked out as pilot in command on the new shuttles.

Their reentry had been over the Pacific, well out of sight of land. For a few brief minutes the shuttle was enveloped in a fiery shell of plasma as atmospheric friction slowed the craft from orbital velocity. Outraged atoms shed their electrons, which joined their naked nuclei to form a charged particle soup, blanking out communication and painting a glowing streak across the night sky.

Gretchen had set the entire cabin ceiling to transparent, giving the Marines a spectacular show. Still 50 kilometers high and traveling Mach 15 when they crossed the west coast of Baja, Mexico, the shuttle made a shallower descent than the old

American space shuttles. Below, off the left side of the craft, the coast of California was outlined by lights, like a spray of jewels on black velvet.

Then, dropping quickly through commercial airspace, the shuttle went subsonic crossing over the Texas-New Mexico border. The few lights below reflected the sparse population of West Texas. Now flying at less than 500 meters, Bobby circled TK Parker's ranch once to ensure that no one was around to witness the shuttle's landing, though the thought of purposefully creating a UFO sighting was tempting.

Almost without sound, save for a low thrumming caused by its repulsors, the shuttle came to a hover above the parched West Texas scrub. Landing struts deployed and the craft settled softly to the ground behind the old dirigible hangar. There were no signs of life from the huge dilapidated building, originally built during World War II to house Navy airships. It was inside that hangar that the Peggy Sue was built and it was her hasty, overly energetic departure that wrecked the building.

Gretchen unfastened her shoulder and lap belts, worn as a precaution even though the deck gravity eliminated all sense of motion. Before opening the door to the passenger cabin she turned to Bobby and said, "I don't expect any trouble deplaning our guests, but if I shout get us into the air fast."

"Aye aye, Ma'am," the slightly chubby helmsman replied. Bobby was a couch potato, addicted to science fiction movies and video games. But his greatest pleasure in life was flying. While combat maneuvers in the Peggy Sue were the best, flitting about in a hypersonic shuttle did not suck either in Bobby's book.

As Lt. Curtis stepped into the passenger cabin the transparent upper fuselage became opaque and the cabin lights blinked on. From the rear of the cabin came the hum of electric motors as the stairs lowered to the ground beneath the rear of the craft. Gretchen looked at the Marines one last time. Most of them had fought beside her, either on the Moon, on the alien space station or both. No getting around it, sometimes duty sucked.

"This is the end of the line, people. Look around the cabin and don't forget anything, then move to the rear and down the stairs," she announced. "After disembarking the shuttle get well clear so our departure doesn't injure any of you."

Then in a quieter voice she addressed Lt. Merryweather. "Lieutenant, it is BMNT," using the Navy acronym for Begin Morning Nautical Twilight, the beginning of dawn. "Sunrise should be in less than an hour. We will contact the authorities as soon as we are airborne and let them know you are here."

"Thank you, Lieutenant," he replied, "for the uneventful flight. Your captain is a man of his word." With that the Marine Lieutenant turned and headed for the rear of the compartment. Lt. Curtis paused and then followed him aft. By the time she reached the top of the boarding ladder the only one left was Gunny Rodriguez.

The Gunny turned to Gretchen and offered her hand. "We've seen some amazing things together, Lieutenant. And I'm sorry we have to go."

Accepting the handshake, Gretchen replied, "That we have, Gunny. We all hate to see you and the squad go, but you gotta do what you gotta do. It was an honor serving beside you."

"Same here, Lieutenant." Then the Gunny came to attention and saluted the Lieutenant, saying, "I request permission to leave the ship, Ma'am."

The ship's First Officer returned the Sergeant's salute and said, "Permission granted Gunnery Sergeant, and Godspeed."

* * * * *

The Squad was assembled 30 meters to the west of the shuttle. They were all standing in their combat gear looking at the now sealed shuttle in the growing dawn light. Without warning, two containers dropped from the shuttle's belly, bouncing slightly as they landed on the ground. "Hey look!" shouted PFC Sanchez, "the shuttle just took a dump."

"Nice imagery, Joey," remarked PFC Kwan. "That must be our weapons and ammo." Beside Kwan, LCpl. Reagan was rummaging through his vest pockets, from which he pulled a cell phone. The face of the phone illuminated and he smiled, "It still works! I think I got maybe two bars."

A low thrumming from the shuttle announced its imminent departure. Dust scattered in all directions from the press of the repulsors. The craft rose 10 meters into the air as its landing struts retracted into the hull. Then it slid quietly forward, rapidly gained speed and ascended into the morning sky.

Sanchez shook his head sadly and said, "ain't nobody going to believe we was on a trip into outer space, or that we was just dropped off by a flying saucer."

"They just might," replied Reagan, who was holding his phone up in front of him. "I just caught the departure on video and sent it to my sister."

"Great, but you better not tell the LT, bro. Now call someone to get us the hell outta here before the Sun gets too high. Standing around the West Texas scrub in the summer is not my idea of a fun time."

Frederiksted, St. Croix, U.S. Virgin Islands

James Taylor and Billy Ray Vincent were bellied up to the bar in one of Frederiksted's seedier dives. There was no shortage of seedy bars in the smaller of St. Croix's two towns. They grew in wild profusion in the rabbit warren of old buildings, back alleys and passageways between Strand and King Streets. Off the normal tourist circuit, Frederiksted was less glitzy than Christiansted on the other end of the island. It was also considerably more laid back, with the west-end Cruzans, as the local were known, more interested in having a good time than hustling visitors.

The two men were an odd couple. JT, as Taylor preferred to be called, was tall, black and built like an NFL running back, while Billy Ray was even taller, slim and very white. "Fish belly white" was how JT described his friend. Both were Texans, but more importantly they were shipmates, both serving on the spaceship Peggy Sue.

Billy Ray was one of the Peggy Sue's two helmsmen, along with his pal Bobby Danner. Dressed in jeans, cowboy boots and hat, he was nursing his third Heineken. Next to him, JT was resplendent in shorts, sandals and a bright orange tee-shirt that read "I ain no tourist, I ban ya."

JT was a former Green Beret who had gone to graduate school when he got out of the Army to study Astronomy. He had been working as a camera man for a West Texas TV station when he accidentally joined the crew of the Peggy Sue. In fact, it was his partner, Susan Write, aka Peggy Sue Whitaker, who the ship was named for. She had heroically sacrificed herself on the alien refueling station in Beta Comae. Waiting alone in the antimatter repository, she gave the ship time to escape before setting off the fuel dump, destroying the station.

That memory still pained JT, but it was even worse for Billy Ray —he and Susan had been lovers and her loss had devastated the normally outgoing cowboy. Initially, it was the shared loss of Peggy Sue that helped forge the friendship between the two shipmates. JT was now a permanent part of the ship's science contingent and also worked as navigator on the bridge. Since Billy Ray was usually manning the helm when anything important happened, they saw a lot of each other.

"Tell me again what that tee-shirt of yer's says, pardner?" Billy Ray asked, after taking another sip of his beer.

"It says 'I ain't no tourist, I was born here' in the colorful local patois," JT replied. "Isn't that right, Jessie?" This last question was directed at the barmaid, busy washing glasses behind the dark wood bar.

"Don't ask me, mon, I Jamaican," she shot back with a big smile. "Dis ain' my Island, I only work here." Though St. Croix was officially part of the United States, it was populated by a mix of folk from all over the Caribbean. A local resident was just as likely to have come from Antigua, Barbados, Jamaica, Montserrat or some other similar spec of land. As David Crosby wrote, "From here to Venezuela, nothing more to see, than a 100,000 islands flung like jewels upon the sea." Almost all of those jewels were populated and, compared with most, St. Croix was the land of opportunity.

JT took another pull from his rum and coke. The rum was made locally and was incredibly smooth. It also had a way of sneaking up on the unwary. This had been discovered the hard way by any number of Navy sailors, who woke up after a night of shore leave "screwed, blued and tattooed." The Navy had an intermittent presence in Frederiksted, submarines and surface ships often docking at the long pier that the local government once hoped would attract cruise ships to this end of the island.

The Navy vessels came to calibrate their sensors and fire practice torpedoes and rockets on the test range that lay in the deep water just off the west end of the island. Though the schedule of ship arrivals was kept secret by the Navy, the local beer trucks were always on the pier to greet the arriving sailors. The tattoo parlors and brothels were also open and ready to service new customers as, of course, were the bars.

There is something special about a sailor's bar. The furniture is heavy, in order to survive the inevitable fights, stained by years of spilled booze and cigarette burns. The walls are always covered with memorabilia, posted by the sailor's themselves. Pictures of ships, uniform patches and the occasional purloined shipboard sign chronicled the comings and goings of the fleet. Such places have not changed much since the fathers and grandfathers of today's sailors went to sea.

Of course, the purpose of being in a bar is to drink, but there are also some requisite accompaniments for the beer and booze. Amazingly, these seem to be the same around the world, at least where ever American sailors are frequent visitors. As one sailor described it, behind the bar there must be "at least six Slim-Jim containers, an oversized glass cookie jar full of Beer-Nuts, a jar of pickled hard boiled eggs that could produce rectal gas emissions that could shut down a sorority party, and big glass containers full of something called Pickled Pigs Feet and Polish Sausage."

That sailor, whose initials were JFK, warned, "Only drunk Chiefs and starving Ethiopians ate pickled pig's feet, and unless the last three feet of your colon had been manufactured by Midas, you didn't want to get anywhere near the Polish Napalm Dogs."

It was in such an establishment that JT and Billy Ray found themselves on a sunny late Caribbean afternoon. They had, in fact, been searching for this particular bar for the past two evenings, because they were looking for some sailors. There was no Navy vessel in port, but these sailors were actually ex-service members who were plying their skills as divers on the island. Moreover, they were past acquaintances of Captain Sutton and Chief Zackly.

It didn't matter that the sailors in question were no longer in the Navy, once a sailor always a sailor—at least when it came to frequenting sailor's bars. The Chief had assured JT and Billy Ray that their quarry would sooner or later make an appearance at the establishment they were currently drinking in.

As the Chief had foretold, just as the Sun was setting, which it does with startling quickness near the equator, three large men with short cut hair and sunglasses walked through the bar's open portal. It was not that the men were overly tall, the shortest was around 5'7" and the tallest maybe 5'10". It was more an impression of mass, of solidity that made them seem large and imposing. A closer inspection revealed them all to be heavily muscled with sloping shoulders and impressively thick necks.

This is not the trio to pick a fight with, thought Billy Ray, who was leaning with his back against the bar, facing the entrance. He elbowed JT and said in a low voice, "I think our targets just walked in."

As their sunglasses came off, the three made eye contact, first with JT and then Billy Ray. Billy Ray, who had been in his share of bar fights, knew when he was being sized up. To these three, he appeared a lesser threat than the muscular JT. For his part, JT was staring back at the three sailors in what he hoped was a non-belligerent way. In the end, the tension was broken by the barmaid.

"Now boys, ya ain even had no 'ting to drink yet," Jessie said with a big smile that showed off several gold teeth. "It's too early to start fightin' but if ya goin' ta tussle take ya asses out to da alley."

"Oh now Jessie, you know me and the boys don't ever start any trouble," said the biggest and probably senior of the three. "I was just wondering how a cowboy and his boyfriend found their way into a real navy bar."

"Damn," JT shot back, "that's what that smell is!"

The three sailors spread out a bit in anticipation of the impending brawl.

"Now JT, you've been hanging out with sailors for the past two months and you never complained about the smell before," Billy Ray drawled in his best cowboy argot. "Besides, the Chief said that these fellers were supposed to be housebroken."

This comment brought perplexed looks from the trio of belligerent sailors. Again the biggest one spoke. "Which chief told you what about who?"

"Whom," Billy Ray corrected.

"What?"

"You use *who* when you are referring to the subject of a clause and *whom* when you are referring to the object of a clause."

"Ignore him," JT suggested, "he was an English major."

"I'm not believing this conversation," the bewildered sailor remarked.

"If you're who we think you are," Billy Ray continued, "we've got things to talk about, friend." Reaching slowly into his pocket, he retrieved a small silver object. "Chief Zackly said you would recognize this." He tossed the silver object to the sailor who had been doing all of the talking.

The sailor snatched the object out of the air with a meaty hand and peered at it. The object was an old fashioned cigarette lighter, the type that took flints and liquid lighter fluid. On one side there was an engraved and enameled crest showing the bow of a ship throwing a wake, surrounded by stylized cording, anchors and other nautical stuff. "Would that be Senior Chief Hank Zackly?" the sailor asked, looking back at Billy Ray.

"It would be indeed," the cowboy replied. "The Chief sent us here to talk to you fellers about a little employment opportunity."

Adelaide, South Australia

Dr. Olaf Gunderson was sitting in the lobby of his hotel, enjoying a second cup of coffee. It had been a hectic trip so far: he flew Qantas to Sydney and then changed to a smaller plane for the hop to Adelaide. This left him in a strange city in mid afternoon with his internal clock completely scrambled. Rather than waste the day, he went to the local University and looked up his colleague, Professor Sun.

She was happy to see him and they ended up having a nice, relaxing dinner at a restaurant he never would have found on his own. On the down side, once he told her about his supposed interest in looking at the Kangaroo Island greys she insisted on making some calls to ease his way with the local authorities. This meant that he actually had to make the short trip to the island and spend two days acting suitably interested in the large marsupials.

Having established his cover story at a level of detail he never intended, Olaf had returned to his hotel late last night. Now, after his first good night's sleep since arriving down under, he was lazing around the lobby reading the latest edition of the Journal of Evolutionary Biology and wondering when he would be contacted by Dr. Tropsha.

"Dr. Gunderson?" A woman's voice asked.

Olaf looked up to see a pert young woman, perhaps in her mid twenties, about 5'6" with medium brown hair cut in a pageboy and hazel eyes. "Yes, I am Olaf Gunderson," he replied cautiously. *Now what? This woman most definitely is not Ludmilla Tropsha.*

"G'day, Professor. I'm Sandy McKennitt and I've been sent to collect you and some other arriving visitors." The voluble young woman stuck out her hand and smiled. Olaf stood up and shook hands with the girl. "Other visitors?" he asked, puzzled.

"Yes indeed, I've already collected Doctors Gupta and Piscopia and dropped them at the FBO. I left them having brekkie but we need to shake a leg, or they're going to wonder what happened to us. And I still have to pick some things up at the market for Mrs. Reilly." She stood there, looking at him expectantly.

"Who is Mrs. Reilly? And what's an FBO?"

"Now don't worry about that, you need to go pack up and check out. Then we can go to the airport where the plane is. An FBO is a Fixed Base Operator, an aircraft service center. That's where I parked the Caravan." She took him by the arm and led him toward the front desk and the elevators. "Come on Professor, off with you, we've got places to be."

* * * * *

A half hour later, Dr. Gunderson found himself being hustled into a waiting car by the effervescent Sandy. She had been talking nearly nonstop since introducing herself, and was now explaining that they needed to get back to the Adelaide airport so they could continue their journey to someplace called Parker's Station, which was evidently somewhere in the wilds of the Australian Outback.

"Come on Professor, you're going to love it," Sandy was saying as she threw his bag in the back seat and shoved him into the front left seat of her rental car. This was a bit disorienting to Olaf, since Australian cars are right-hand-drive. "Australia is a really big place and you'll get to see a lot of ace countryside. It may seem that Parker's Station is beyond the black stump, but we'll be there well before dark, I promise."

With that she started the car and launched them into traffic. Olaf gathered that she was also to be his pilot for the next leg of the journey. If she flew like she drove, it was going to be an exciting flight, perhaps more exciting than he was prepared for.

As the pair departed, neither noticed the blond woman observing them from across the street. *Oh crap! Where did she come from,* Kim Lawson thought furiously, *and where is she taking him?* Kim had been following the Professor around for three days now and though the sneaking around like a spy was exciting at first, the Mata Hari act was starting to get old.

We better get to where the undead cosmonaut is soon or Dad's going to have a stroke when he sees the credit card bill, she fretted as she flagged down a cab. "Follow that car!" she told the driver, and then smiled. *I've always wanted to say that.*

Captain's Cabin, Peggy Sue

Jack was gazing out one of the large cabin viewports as Ludmilla finished getting dressed after showering. Among the nice things about the Peggy Sue's guest cabins were the private showers. And this cabin was the largest and most luxuriously appointed of all, intended as the owner's stateroom. Jack requisitioned it for his own use when TK Parker was not on board for the inaugural cruise.

The extra space made sharing the cabin with Ludmilla easy, though Jack would have gladly shared a storage closet with the ash blond ship's doctor. It had been a blissful month of cohabitation since they overcame their initial animosity and fell into each other's arms. At least it had been up till now.

I can't believe that we are having our first fight over this, Jack fumed. *She of all people should understand the danger in delivering one's self to government agents. But she is dead set on this, probably because Yuki is going back to Japan in a few days. But Japan isn't Russia. I'm not going back to the U.S. Not that I trust the American government either, but Russia! They have gone from being a communist dictatorship to a kleptocracy run by thugs.*

The computer display in his desk beeped and flashed a status update. Jack sighed. "Lt. Curtis is docking the shuttle now, Luda. It will be well after dark in Australia when we arrive, but we shouldn't delay."

"Yes, Jack," Ludmilla replied, brushing her hair in front of the vanity mirror. Overall, Jack considered Ludmilla pretty low maintenance—a quick shower, throw on a new jumpsuit and pass a brush through her hair and she was ready to go anywhere. As far as Jack was concerned, Luda was the perfect woman: smart, witty, beautiful, and libidinous. "Are the new scientists going to be there when we arrive?" she asked.

"Lt. McKennitt should have collected them a few hours ago and flown them to Parker's Station. Last I heard, Prof. Gunderson brought an aid, a young, female graduate student."

"Why that old goat!" Ludmilla said with a smile. "I'm sure that it is all very proper and aboveboard, but wait until I see Olaf. He is such a serious and proper gentleman, I can tease him for months."

"I've never seen this side of you before, Luda. How could I have fallen in love with such a sadist?"

"Pfagh! A little good natured kidding between colleagues is a good thing," she shot back unrepentantly. "Besides, it will keep him quiet about our sleeping arrangements. Trust me, Olaf would be scandalized to know that the ship's captain was sleeping with one of the crew." Ludmilla threw her hairbrush into the case on the bed and walked over to where Jack was standing.

"I'm somewhat scandalized myself," Jack said with a chuckle. He turned to find Ludmilla standing next to him. "You know how much I am going to miss you when..."

"Shhh," she said, placing a finger on his lips, "we said we would not talk about that anymore." Then she kissed him. A long lingering kiss.

"If they try to hold you, no power in the Universe will stop me from coming for you," he said in a raspy voice. "You are more to me than the entire planet."

"Trust me, my Captain, nothing will prevent me from coming back to you." Then she added with Russian practicality, "of course, if we do not leave I can't come back, so let us go to the shuttle."

"Yes, Dr. Tropsha," Jack replied, recovering his composure, "let's go to Australia and meet the new crew members."

Cessna Caravan, Somewhere Over South Australia

Sandy McKennitt, recently designated a Lieutenant Junior Grade attached to the Earth Space Ship Peggy Sue, was starting a descent to Willawog Station. Willawog was about two thirds of the way from Adelaide to Parker's Station and Sandy had promised to pick up some items for Mrs. Reilly, wife of the station manager.

Sitting next to her in the front of the big, single engined turboprop was Professor Olaf Gunderson. In the two rows of passenger seats behind them were Dr. Lucrezia Piscopia, Dr. Rajiv Gupta and Miss Kimberly Lawson, one of Gunderson's student assistants. It was still a bit of a mystery how Miss Lawson had gotten to Australia. How she came to be on the plane was less of a mystery.

A few hours ago, Sandy had parked the rental car and hustled Professor Gunderson into the Outback Air FBO at Adelaide International Airport. The small terminal, serving general aviation and a number of bush pilot outfits, was located about 100 meters west of the main International Terminal. Both Gunderson and Sandy were carrying bags of groceries, with Olaf having to juggle both the sacks of food and his own suitcase. "Come on, mates! We need to load the Caravan so grab your bags," Sandy called to Doctors

Piscopia and Gupta, who were seated in the lounge area. "No bludgers allowed here!"

Elena leaned close to Rajiv and asked in a soft voice, "what is a bludger?" To which the equally flummoxed Rajiv replied, "My dear Elena, I haven't the foggiest idea. My ears tell me that the young lady is speaking English but my mind cannot decode the words."

The talkative Aussie pilot led her charges out the front of the terminal to a large high-winged airplane sitting near by. The airplane was a Cessna Grand Caravan, a big fixed gear craft with a single propeller in its nose. Normally, a Caravan is powered by a single 675-horsepower Pratt & Whitney turbine engine. This one, however, was propelled by a 900 HP flat rated Honeywell TPE331-12JR engine. It also boasted an aftermarket co-pilot's door and 14 inch wingtip extensions. Sandy walked over to the big Cessna and opened a wide cargo door behind the wing, swinging it up like the hatchback on a car.

This was no luxury corporate aircraft. The interior was laid out with a combination of high density passenger seating forward and a sizable rear cargo area. Up front, behind the seats for the pilot and copilot, there were two rows of 2-1 split passenger seats. After storing their few pieces of luggage in compartments built into the large conformal belly pod under the plane, the pilot turned to her passengers and said "Go on, step up Dr. Gupta. We'll pass the groceries up to you. Just stack them all neatly in the center against the rear bulkhead."

When they were done loading the cargo, Sandy went on board and with Rajiv's help, secured the grocery bags with snug netting. "All right, in you go," the pilot beamed, hopping back down to the concrete apron. "Just work your way forward and take a seat. Prof. Gunderson, give Dr. Piscopia a hand up. Then you come up front with me."

Sandy turned to Olaf before closing the cargo door saying, "I've got to do a quick pre-flight. You can climb in the front through the door on the other side." Then she paused as something over the Professor's shoulder caught her eye. "What have we here?"

Running across the aircraft parking area was a young woman, frantically waiving one arm and clutching a small valise with the other. Behind her, several of the FBO's personnel were in hot pursuit. "Wait! Please, Professor! Please wait for me!" came the woman's plaintive cries.

"What? That looks like Kim," said a stunned Dr. Gunderson.

"And whose Kim, Professor?" Sandy asked, in a what-are-you-trying-to-pull tone of voice.

"Kim, my teaching assistant. But she didn't come with me on this trip, she should be back in Chicago."

"Well, it would appear that your little sheila followed you here, Professor," Sandy commented as Kim practically ran into Olaf with the airport personnel just steps behind.

"Oh please, please, Professor Gunderson!" the out of breath fugitive pleaded. "Please let me come with you. Don't let them arrest me, Daddy would never understand."

Seeing that Gunderson was dithering Sandy made a command decision. *After all,* she reasoned, *I'm the ranking officer on this little outing.* "It's all right mates," she shouted to the airport men who were just pulling up at the plane. "Young lady almost missed her flight is all."

"She weren't on the passenger list, Sandy. I ought to give you a gobful," the lead pursuer said with considerable heat. "Bloody seppo wacker making us run our arses off. I say we call the divvy van."

"Come on, Jimmy, she'll be right. Be a cobber." Sandy looked at the man with a mixture of innocence and pleading.

"Oh, All right," the man relented. "But just this once, and only because its you. OK, mates, false alarm, back to the terminal."

As the winded pursuers turned and started back to the FBO at a much slower pace than when they arrived, Sandy turned to her newest charge and in a much less friendly voice said, "Get on board Miss. I'll let Mr. Parker and the Captain settle you when we get to the Station."

With that she practically pushed the young woman inside the plane and slammed the cargo door. Turning to the still befuddled Dr. Gunderson she said, "You too, Professor. Climb on board and no more surprises."

That was more than an hour ago and things went much more smoothly once they were in the air. The big Cessna was a docile beast and the Garmin G1000 glass cockpit was state of the art for aircraft of this class—after takeoff, it quite literally flew itself. A quick exchange with Willawog Station to say she was landing and Sandy turned on approach to the Station's dirt strip.

* * * * *

Twenty minutes later they were back in the air and headed for Parker's Station. All but one of the bags of groceries had been off loaded at the last stop. While the other passengers were content to fly in silence, it was not in Elena's nature to remain quiet for long.

"If you don't mind me asking, Miss McKennitt, what was that last stop all about?"

"Well, Doctor, in the Outback every thing is a long way away, and when you're making a trip to the city it's only neighborly to ask folks on your route if they need anything. In this case Mrs. Reilly asked for some fresh vedgies. In fact, they looked so good I got some avos and rockmelons for us as well."

"Avos and rockmelons?"

"Avocados and cantaloupes," the pilot explained. "We try to keep a low profile at the Station, but out here not helping the neighbors would attract more attention than being sociable."

"I think that is very nice, neighbor helping neighbor," the Italian astronomer said. "The world could use more of that kind of thinking."

"Well I don't know about that, it's just the way I was brought up."

"Such a spirit of cooperation has all but disappeared in modern urban society. You should be proud of your upbringing," Elena replied. "Have you been flying in the Outback long?"

"My Da had me behind the controls of an old Luscombe 8A Silvair before my 12th birthday. I was flying long before he'd let me drive." Those memories brought a momentary smile to her face. "Anyway, we should be landing at Parker's Station in another 15 minutes. Check your seat-belts, please."

Chapter 3

Station House, Parker's Station

The band of travelers from Adelaide were standing in the main room of the station owner's house, each clutching a drink and all trying to talk at once. They had been joined by Yuki Saito and Dieter Schmidt. Also present were JT and Billy Ray, who were shadowed by a trio of muscular men with short haircuts and tight fitting tee-shirts. They were standing in a separate group, talking with Sandy and another young man with decidedly military bearing.

"Although it is very good to see you, Dr. Saito, I'm still wondering where Dr. Tropsha is?" said Olaf. Seeing one of the astronauts who supposedly died on the ISS a few months back did make him more confident that Ludmilla was alive. Still, he would not be satisfied until he talked with her face to face.

"Do not worry, Dr. Gunderson," the Japanese physicist replied, "Dr. Tropsha and the Captain are in transit from the ship and will be with us soon."

"They are coming from the spaceship, the Peggy Sue?" asked Elena. "I still find it hard to believe that there is a large spaceship orbiting the planet and nobody has reported it."

"Vell, I imagine that you will be invited on board after meeting the Captain," Dieter Schmidt said, in his pronounced German accent. "Zat assumes you accept our offer to join the project."

"And you are telling us that you have walked on other planets and traveled to another star system?" Elena asked the three project scientists. "*Per favore mi perdoni,* but I am still having a hard time accepting that you can travel faster than the speed of light."

"Oh believe me, Elena, both Yuki and I were skeptical as well, and we were on board!" replied Rajiv. "Sadly, I did not get the chance to leave the ship. Somehow Yuki managed to both walk on the surface of the Moon and then visit the interior of the alien space station."

"Alien space station?" asked Kim, no longer able to stand quietly by. "What alien space station? What aliens?"

"Do not worry, Miss," Rajiv said, "the Captain will explain everything when he arrives."

"I do hope so," replied Olaf, "I'm as anxious to hear this story as Elena and Kim are."

There was a soft chime from the hall, signaling that the elevator from the underground facility was arriving. All eyes in the room focused on the hallway entrance as the murmur of conversation faded to silence. There, side by side, appeared a tall, well built man with a neatly trimmed beard and a beautiful woman with ash blond hair. The man was dressed in a black jumpsuit devoid of decoration with the exception of a small pip on his left lapel. The woman also wore a jumpsuit, which highlighted her stunning figure, though her suit was pure white. Her left lapel also bore a pip and from the way they stood, their body language made it clear that they were a couple.

"Well, don't stop the party on our account," the man said, "we just dropped by because we heard there were free drinks to be had." He smiled and the woman playfully swatted him on the arm.

"Do not listen to him, his is just having a joke," the woman in white said, with a noticeable Russian accent, "he knows that, since he is the captain, everyone will laugh." At that everyone did laugh. Recognition lit in the woman's eyes and she headed for Dr. Gunderson, extending her hand, "Olaf, so good of you to come!"

"Is that you, Ludmilla? My goodness, you look wonderful for someone supposedly killed by a solar flare." Olaf stepped forward to meet her and warmly grasped her hand. "I truly did not know what to think after you called. Even after seeing Dr. Saito here, alive and well, I was afraid to hope. My God, this is wonderful!"

"Believe me, Olaf, I'm as glad to be talking with you as you are with me. Yuki and I had been beyond hope when the Peggy Sue rescued us from the ISS." Managing to reclaim her hand from Dr. Gunderson's grip she turned to Elena and said, "You must be Lucrezia Piscopia, it is very nice to meet you."

"*Grazie*," the Italian astronomer replied, shaking Ludmilla's hand in turn. "Please, call me Elena."

"And you must call me Ludmilla, since we are all going to be colleagues." Then Ludmilla spotted Kim, half hiding behind Dr.

Gunderson. "And who are you, young lady? I was not aware that Olaf was bringing a date."

Both Olaf and Kim blushed, while Kim managed to stammer, "I'm Kim, Kimberly Lawson, Professor Gunderson's assistant."

"Your assistants get younger and prettier every year, Olaf," Ludmilla said with a knowing smile and sideways glance of her eyes. This caused Olaf to turn even redder and Kim to look both confused and upset at the same time.

"This is all perfectly innocent, Ludmilla!" He managed to say. "In fact, I don't even know how Kim got to Australia."

"Hmm, so you say," she said, not letting him off the hook just yet. "Now you, Miss Lawson, what do you know of the purpose of this trip?"

"I," she started, "I overheard Prof. Gunderson on the phone, something about the ISS astronauts being alive somewhere in Australia. It sounded mysterious and dangerous and I didn't think he should be going alone. So I followed him."

"Well you are here now. We will just have to see what the Captain wants to do with you."

* * * * *

Meanwhile, the Captain had walked over to the cluster of crew, to be greeted by a chorus of "good evening, Sir," from those assembled there.

"Lt. McKennitt, I see you were able to collect all our lost sheep," Jack said to the young pilot, Then, turning to the young man standing beside Sandy, he said, "you must be Nigel Lewis, good to meet you in person."

"It's good to meet you, Sir," the man said, shaking hands. His accent was English, not Australian, his hair black and curly, eyes gray and complexion fair. He looked every inch a young Royal Navy Lieutenant, which is precisely what he had been up until a few months ago.

The Captain then shifted his gaze to the three muscular men standing beside JT and Billy Ray. "And these must be the Chief's acquaintances."

"Yes, Sir," JT replied, "may I introduce Petty Officers Bud Jones and Phil Kowalski and Chief Petty Officer Rick Morgan?" The three drew themselves up to attention and stiffly shook hands with the Captain.

"Welcome, gentlemen, I'm Captain Jack Sutton, commander of this three ringed circus," Jack said, smiling. "I wanted you all here together so I could meet everyone at the same time."

"Good to meet you in person, Sir," said Chief Morgan. "You gave us a lift to a job once off Somalia a few years back."

"Ah, Chief Zackly did mention something about our paths having crossed previously." The Captain nodded to the three SEALs. "Welcome aboard, gentlemen. Rather than force you to sit through an evening with a room full of scientists and officers, I've asked Mr. Vincent to take you below and explain what we are all about here. After that, since you will undoubtedly feel more comfortable in the canteen, Senior Chief Zackly will join you there and you can catch up on old times."

"Aye aye, Sir," the three replied as one.

"With your permission, Captain?" Billy Ray drawled. Jack acknowledged and Billy Ray led his charges away, headed in the direction of the hall elevator. Before they boarded the elevator it discharged two new passengers: a slightly pudgy young man wearing the black jumpsuit of an officer and an old man seated in a four-wheeled electric wheelchair.

"Jack!" shouted the old man as he drove into the room. Sighting his target, the man in the wheelchair headed straight for the Captain. As he did, the chair transformed itself, rising from four wheels to two and extending upward. The now standing old man shouted, "Jack, my boy! Let me get a good look at you!"

The gaggle of scientists stopped talking amongst themselves and turned to face the loud newcomer. As the scientists and ship's officers looked on they witnessed a sight few had ever seen—the cybernetic septuagenarian leaned forward in his gyroscopically stabilized wheelchair and enveloped the Captain in a bear hug.

C130 Hercules, Somewhere Over The Southern US

Gunnery Sargent Jennifer Rodriguez sat, eyes closed, in the uncomfortable canvas seat. Her head tilted back, she was running her tongue over the inside of her cut and swollen lip, trying to figure out just what sort of cosmic bunny hole her squad had fallen into. Her hands were in zip cuffs before her. Her head ached and her ears were ringing from the noise of the transport plane's four large turboprop engines.

Opening her eyes, the Gunny looked around the dark interior of the transport's cargo hold. Seated around the hold were the other surviving members of her squad of Marines—more precisely, five marines and one Navy Hospital Corpsman. Farther forward, isolated from the others, was the sad figure of the Lieutenant. The Gunny could not have predicted the type of reception they were to receive when the shuttle dropped them back at Parker's ranch, but this was not on the list.

After watching the shuttle disappear into the rising Sun, Lt. Merryweather used LCpl. Reagan's cellphone to report their whereabouts to his superiors. Little over an hour later, a pair of AH-1 Super Cobra's roared overhead, popping up from the far side of the dilapidated dirigible hangar to the north. This was followed shortly by a pair of MV-22 Ospreys, one landing to the east of their position and one to the west.

Each Osprey disgorged a full complement of 24 armed Marines, while their door gunners covered the puzzled squad of returnees. As the platoon sized force of heavily armed men quickly surrounded Lt. Merryweather's unarmed little band, a voice over a bullhorn ordered, "Stay where you are! You will all take a kneeling position with your hands behind your heads. Any resistance will be met with deadly force."

The LT raised his hands over his head and tried to asked why this was happening, only to draw a burst of warning fire. "I think they are serious, people," he said to the squad members, sinking to his knees. "We had all better do as they say."

The squad moved to comply as their captors moved in, weapons at the ready and pointed at the confused Marines. "Man, this is so bogus," said PFC Sanchez. This brought a quick command of "Quiet!

No talking!" from the man with the bullhorn, who appeared to be a Marine captain.

They kneeled before their captors for what seemed an eternity before a CH-53 heavy-lift helicopter flew in and landed with its tail toward them. Dust swirled around both captor and captive, as the big helo's single rotor spun down and its rear cargo ramp lowered. From the darkened cargo hold of the CH-53, an officer emerged with several men wearing flight suits displaying no insignia.

The Marine Lieutenant Colonel, who was evidently in charge, walked over to the still kneeling squad. Lt. Merryweather tried to stand up and report, saying "Sir, Lt. Merryweather reporting with a party of eight." This earned him a rifle stock in the stomach, which took him back to his knees.

"Damn it, we're Marines!" the Gunny shouted. For this she received a boot in the back that knocked her face down in the dirt and resulted in the cut and swollen lip she was still savoring. LCpl. Washington also tried to protest the treatment of the Lieutenant, or possibly the Gunny, earning him several blows that laid him out on the dirt.

"There will be no talking," the light bird said. "You will be zip cuffed and marched onto the helo. If anyone attempts to speak you will also be gagged." While he was speaking several members of the arresting party moved the two crates that contained the squad's weapons and ammo up the ramp into the helo's cargo area. Once this was done the zip tied Marines were marched in as well.

The helo took them to Goodfellow Air Force Base, where they were isolated in a remote hangar and interrogated individually by the men in civilian dress. The irony of their incarceration at Goodfellow was not lost on the Gunny, this was the first stop on the squad's ill fated mission to the San Angelo Airshow, more than two months ago.

After a brief head call, the squad was once again zip cuffed and marched on board a waiting C-130 cargo plane. The C-130 Hercules is a four-engine turboprop military transport that has been in use around the world for over half a century. It was built for neither comfort nor speed. The Gunny had no idea where they were being taken, only that things were probably going to get worse before they got better.

They had been aloft for over two hours and had not yet started a descent. With a range of better than 2,000 nautical miles they could be headed to Camp Pendleton, outside San Diego, or Camp Lejeune in North Carolina. For that matter, they could be headed for Gitmo, the still operational terrorist detention area on the eastern tip of Cuba. Regardless, after being manhandled by a platoon of motards and thrown on board a transport under armed guard, the end was not likely to a happy one.

Kong Karls Land, Svalbard, Norway

Lt. Bear was happily rambling along the northern shore of the largest Island in the Kong Karls Land archipelago, singing a Frank Zappa song. "Way up north were the huskies go, don't you eat no yellow snow," he sang tunelessly, slightly mangling the lyrics. Words to live by, as far as Bear was concerned.

Not that Bear was a big Zappa fan, but the hero of this particular song cycle was named Nanook. And since Nanook means polar bear in Inuit, the song was a good one in his book. This was because Lt. Bear himself was a 1300 lb polar bear.

Most of the 2,400 or so human inhabitants of Svalbard live on Spitsbergen, the largest island in the nearby Svalbard archipelago. More important to Bear, Svalbard and Franz Joseph Land share a common population of more than 3,000 polar bears. Moreover, Kong Karls Land is the most important breeding ground for polar bears in Svalbard and, as a consequence, it is completely off-limits to all visitors. This was fine with Bear, since the natives were required to go armed outside of the few settlements precisely because of possible polar bear attack. Nothing like a trigger happy Norwegian to ruin your day.

There was still sea ice in the water north of the island, though the climate in Svalbard was generally warmer than other areas of the high arctic. The Sun was getting low in the sky, but it would not be setting until the end of the month. In the spring, polar bear mothers brought their new cubs to the islands, but things were starting to thin out. Earlier, he had bagged himself a ringed seal, the first fresh meat he had feasted on in ages.

For variety, this morning he climbed a cliff and breakfasted on some seabird chicks and eggs. Polar bears, like other bears, are omnivorous and will eat almost anything, but they are more adapted to a carnivorous lifestyle than either brown or black bears. Having satisfied his yearning for fresh food, Bear was now working on his second objective—finding the company of his own kind.

Talking polar bears often figured in the mythology of native Arctic peoples and, as is frequently the case with legends, there was a basis in fact for such tales. Among the world's 25,000 or so polar bears only a small minority, a few thousand at most, can talk. According to his human friend, Captain Jack, both humans and polar bears had been genetically altered by aliens. The result of this evolutionary meddling was talking hominids and talking ursines.

Whatever the aliens' intent, talking bears were much smarter than normal polar bears, with a noticeable talent for learning languages. Bear himself spoke English, Russian, Sami, Norwegian, Finnish and a half dozen Inuit dialects, mostly picked up by hanging around human settlements or from listening to the radio at abandon research and hunting camps. Remarkable language skills aside, Bear was currently using a communication skill that had more to do with his primitive ancestors. Periodically sniffing the air as he walked the flat tundra along the shoreline, he caught the scent of something familiar and female.

Following the scent, he headed inland and traveled over a low ridge before sighting the object of his search. Down at the bottom of the hill were three bears: one large male, a half grown male and a female. The female and smaller male appeared to be squared off against the bigger male, a bruiser who looked even larger than Bear. No matter, Bear headed straight for the developing fracas.

* * * * *

As Bear drew near it became obvious that the large male was a normal, non-talking polar bear. That meant the situation would not be resolved with words. Close up, he could hear the voices of the two smaller bears. "I said run away, Umky," the female said to the adolescent male.

"And let you face this big dork alone? No way Mom."

The large male roared and charged. The younger male got between the male and female, leading to his being swatted down to the ground by his larger adversary. The big male was probably twice Umky's weight and proportionately taller—the smaller bear was going to take a mauling if someone didn't intervene.

Intervention came in the form of the female, obviously the adolescent bear's mother. She plowed into the larger male, knocking him off her cub. This caught the big male's attention long enough for him to throw her roughly aside. His intention was not to harm the female, he had more amorous designs on the she bear.

"Pardon me asshole," came a deep rumbling voice from behind the big male. "I know you can't understand this, but it would be best for all involved if you hauled your smelly carcass off over the next rise."

The big male, turning around to see another male polar bear about his same size, rose up on his hind legs and roared at the top of his lungs.

"I figured as much," Bear said, ducking down and to his opponent's left, raking the standing bear's stomach with his sizable claws in passing. This brought the brute back down on all fours, but before he could turn, Bear slashed his hindquarters. The non-speaking bear yelped and bounded forward, out of claw range before turning around.

Instead of standing up for another charge, the would be suitor ran at Bear on all fours. What happened next was hard to make out exactly—Bear grasped the head of the charging aggressor between his clawed paws and rolled backward, letting his opponent's momentum carry him up and over. From a position on his back and underneath his opponent, Bear kicked out with his rear legs, sending the big male soaring head over hindquarters. The belligerent male landed with a whomp on his back and rolled sideways, partially stunned.

Bear sauntered up to the still shaky disputant and began pummeling him on either side of the head with repeated blows. Finally, red blood starting to show on his coat, the desperate male rolled away and beat a hasty, if somewhat unsteady retreat toward the next rise. Bear rose to his full height and yelled, "That's right, run shithead! I know kung fu!"

Quite pleased with himself, Bear dropped back to a four legged stance and turned to the two smaller bears. "Hello, Isbjørn, how have you been?" he said to his one time mate. "You're still looking good, babe."

Station House, Parker's Station

The assembled group of scientists and ship's officers were just finishing an evening's repast, highlighted by local beef, salad with avocados and fresh cantaloupe with vanilla ice cream for desert. As coffee and brandy were being served the Captain stood at the head of the table and waited quietly for the group's attention. The crowd, highly animated during the course of the meal, quickly fell silent.

"Once again, I would like to say how pleased we are that all of you could come tonight," Jack began. "First, I would like to thank Maria for preparing this wonderful meal for us and Lt. McKennitt for thoughtfully fetching the fresh fruit from Adelaide." There was a murmur of agreement from the seated diners. "Earlier, I introduced the founder of this project and the driving force behind the construction of the Peggy Sue, Mr. TK Parker. TK, is there anything you would like to say before I begin?"

"Naw son, you go ahead," the old man said, seated in his electric wheelchair at the far end of the table. "I'd only confuse everyone if I tried to explain the situation."

"As you wish, Sir," Jack replied. After a brief pause to collect his thoughts he continued. "I'm going to start with the genesis of this project. It starts in the wastelands of eastern Saudi Arabia in the mid 1980s. A young Texan, prospecting for petrochemical deposits in the rocky desert of the empty quarter came across a man, half crazed by Sun and thirst, crawling along a wadi. After getting the man under cover and giving him some water, he proceeded to tell the strangest story."

"It seems that the man was an archaeologist, who had been investigating a dig somewhere in the surrounding mountains. According to the young scientist, he and his colleague had discovered a strange, ancient artifact in a mountain side cave. A huge structure with holographic writing etched into its metallic surface. Having devised a way to open the structure, the two archaeologists were accosted by Bedouins before they could unlock their find. The senior investigator was shot and presumably killed, but the younger man managed to elude the bandits by entering the structure at the last second.

"After spending an indeterminate amount of time inside the alien structure, the surviving archaeologist was expelled miles from the site of the dig. He proceeded to tell his rescuer a tale of strange visions concerning an interstellar war more than four million years ago, aliens landing on Earth and a desperate gamble by the original inhabitants of the structure, which was actually a starship."

This last statement caused a ripple of low conversation among the diners. Jack paused to take a sip of water, then continued.

"It would be logical to pass off the man's story as the Sun addled ravings of someone lucky to escape death in the desert. However, he had with him physical evidence that his story was not fantasy. Wrapped in the tatters of his jacket was a sizable object, a clump of amber-like material that he claimed was the memory of the ship's computer. This clump of translucent golden stuff supposedly contained the story of why aliens landed on our planet and why they took the actions they did."

"As the story was told, the ship's computer—an Artificial Intelligence, an actual sentient being—was the only one left of the ship's crew. It had been left by its organic companions with a mission to accomplish. The ship and its crew were involved in a great conflict, an interstellar war involving many different lifeforms. Evidently there were two sides in this conflict, a loose alliance of creatures from nearby star systems and an opposing force commanded by creatures referred to only as the 'dark ones'." With that the room erupted into conversation and shouted questions.

"Surely you must be joking with us, Captain," said Elena Piscopia. "You ask us to believe alien refugees landed on Earth four million years ago, fleeing a war with the forces of darkness?"

"Yes, Elena's right," added Olaf Gunderson. "This is science fiction, a Hollywood movie script!" Sandy McKennitt and Nigel Lewis had not heard this story either—both were sitting in dumbfounded silence.

After waiting for the initial shock to subside, Jack called for silence. "Please, I know you all have a multitude of questions, but if you will let me finish the story things may become clearer. Then I will attempt to answer your questions."

As ordered was restored, Jack cleared his throat and picked up where he left off. "As I said, the refugee from the desert told the tale of an ancient war that raged across the Galaxy, a war that was as old as the collective memory of all the races in the Milky Way. Supposedly, the alliance cause had suffered a significant defeat in our little corner of space. The aliens were dying, their ship damaged and their enemies trying to run them to ground. Desperate times lead to desperate measures and the aliens hit upon a scheme that defies the imagination."

Jack looked around the room at the faces—some anxious, some stunned, some showing open disbelief. "Bottom line: the alien plan was to have their ship's AI, its self aware computer, carry out a program of genetic manipulation on the local life forms. This manipulation was aimed at creating an intelligent, cooperative race that also possessed a sufficient amount of aggression—a martial spirit if you will—to eventually take up the struggle with the alien's ancient enemy."

"Once the breeding program bore fruit, the ship's computer was to reveal the truth to the new race. And in order to give their successors a leg up on preparing for war, the ship was to provide a repository of advanced knowledge and technology. In short, the aliens, knowing they were dying, arranged the forced evolution of their own relief. Ladies and gentlemen, we are the result of that breeding program—we are the ones who are supposed to carry on the struggle against the 'dark ones'."

"And you expect us to just believe this?" asked an incredulous Prof. Gunderson.

"No, Professor. I offer as proof what you see on the screen behind me," Jack said, stepping to one side. On the screen floated an image of the Peggy Sue. "That is the starship Peggy Sue. In it, several of us in this room ventured into space and traveled to another star system. If you will withhold judgment for a while longer, we will show you the video records of the first flight of the Peggy Sue, or Parker's Folly as she was known at the time. Once you have seen the chronicle of that voyage, we will offer as further proof a trip to the ship itself, where it will become clear that it was built with advanced alien technology."

"Why do you tell this to us?" asked Elena. "Why not tell the government, the United Nations? Surely this is something the whole world should know about."

"We intend to do just that, Dr. Piscopia. All of the video images you are about to see are going to be delivered to the Secretary General of the UN and to the heads of state of all the nations of the Security Council."

"But that still doesn't explain why you lured us here," Olaf said. "Why Elena and myself?"

"Because your reputations are impeccable. Prof. Gunderson, we would like you to work with Dr. Tropsha to analyze the timeline and description of the human genetic manipulation program described in the artifact's datastore. There are also alien tissue samples to be examined, though we have more biologists coming to help with that." Jack smiled at the biologist and then turned to Elena. "And you, Dr. Piscopia, we would like you to help us plan a next mission. A reconnaissance to see if we can find any remnants of the civilizations that are supposed to inhabit this end of the Galaxy."

"If you have a ship that can actually travel to other star systems I will be glad to help, assuming I get to come along." *I don't care what outrageous tales you tell,* Elena thought, *if you have a working starship I will do anything to be on that voyage.* "But tell me why you are so intent that the man's story be believed?"

"Because I was the oil prospector who found the archaeologist in the desert, young lady," TK said. "I smuggled the artifact back to the US and figuring out how to read that damned pile of amber has consumed me for nearly thirty years."

"And because," the Captain added, "once we did get a ship built and went to take a look around, we found more evidence that the archaeologist's story was true," the Captain added.

"That is correct," said Ludmilla, who had been quietly observing the others reactions up to this point. "Because at Beta Comae we discovered a world that bore the unmistakable signs of a global technological civilization." The image of Peggy Sue was replaced by a view of the same planet Rajiv had shown to Elena in the bistro in Melbourne. "Unfortunately that world was dead, devoid of any life more complex than simple bacteria. It appears that it had been purposely scoured clean of higher life."

"Moreover, what alien life we did encounter proved to be implacably hostile," Jack concluded. "What we are trying to tell you is that the war of four million years ago may still be raging, and if so, we are about to be drug into the middle of it..."

* * * * *

Several exhausting hours later, the meeting broke up with plans to reconvene after breakfast. Jack turned to Ludmilla and asked, "do you think we won them over?"

"Not entirely. But remember, Jack, it took you a while to convince me." A coy smile played across her lips. "Once Olaf starts to go over the records of the genetic program he will be hooked, I guaranty it. As for Elena, you could not drive her away now, not as long as she has a chance of getting on board the ship. She might even try to seduce you to make sure, I saw it in her eyes." Ludmilla raised a single shapely, ash blond eyebrow in an unvoiced challenge.

"That might prove interesting," Jack said smiling. "I'm already as seduced as I can handle."

"And do not forget that while I am away," she said. "I understand that Yuki is leaving early in the morning. I should depart myself the day after."

"We are sending the government information packets out tonight, which will also alert Japan and Russia to Yuki's and your respective survival." Jack turned to the woman he could not imagine living without. "So, we are agreed that you will meet with ROSCOSMOS on neutral ground, at the UN headquarters in Vienna?"

"Yes, yes," Ludmilla agreed. "The Chief will accompany me in one of the small shuttles."

"I also want you to take a couple of the crew along, just in case." Ludmilla began to protest but Jack cut her off. "They don't have to leave the pinnace if things go smoothly, but if something goes wrong you many need help."

Realizing that this was the best compromise she could arrange, Ludmilla grudgingly acquiesced. "Very well, my Captain. You treat me like some kept woman, a princess or a queen."

"You are the queen of my Universe, Luda," he said in a quiet voice. He only called her 'Luda' in intimate moments when they were alone.

"Da, of course, Captain of my heart," she smile and took his hand, leading him toward the hallway, "and now your queen has need of you in her bed chamber."

Haneda Airport, Tokyo, Japan

The pinnace dropped Yuki off on Okinawa, from which he took a flight to Tokyo's Haneda airport. As he rode the multi-story escalator down to the main lobby floor he marveled at the soaring glass, metal and concrete structure. After spending six months on the ISS and then two more on board the Peggy Sue, such large open spaces seemed an extravagance. He also thought how nice it was to be in a crowd of people where everyone was speaking Japanese. He had not realized that he was so homesick until he boarded the plane at Naha airport for the two and a half hour flight to the Japanese mainland.

His plan, as far as he had one, was to catch the monorail into the city, change to the Yamanote Uchimawari Line at Hamamatsucho and then take the bus from Ueno station to the University. What he was going to do once he got there was not clear, he was just making it up as he went along. Stepping off the escalator, he was looking forward to some home cooking and the hustle of Greater Tokyo. Distracted by his thoughts, Yuki did not notice the man wearing a dark suit, leading two uniformed airport security police.

"Dr. Hiroyuki Saito?" the man asked, stopping in front of him and bowing.

"Hai," Yuki replied, returning the bow. "I am Dr. Saito."

"I am Inspector Isamu Takashi, from the NPSC," the man replied. "Would you please come with me?"

Japan's police are a mostly apolitical body under the supervision of a number of agencies. At the top sets the NPSC, the National Police Safety Commission, an independent agency not directly controlled by the central government. Officials involved in the criminal justice system are, for the most part, highly trained professionals and are allowed considerable discretion in enforcing the nation's laws. They are kept in check only by an independent judiciary and scrutiny from a free news corps.

The police are generally well respected and rely on public cooperation to accomplish their work. Having been brought up under this system, Yuki had no reason not to trust Inspector Takashi. What Takashi did not mention was that he was with the NPSC's Security Bureau. The Security Bureau is responsible for keeping tabs on foreigners and radical political groups, including investigating violations of the Alien Registration Law and administration of the Entry and Exit Control Law.

"Do you have any luggage, Dr. Saito?" the plain clothes policeman asked, as they walked toward an unmarked exit, the two uniformed officers falling in behind the pair.

"No, I am traveling light. All I have is in this briefcase."

"Very good. We would like to ask you some questions downtown and then we will escort you to your apartment."

"Please, you do not need to bother taking me home"

"It is no bother at all, Dr. Saito," the police official said, "No bother at all."

Camp Lejeune, North Carolina

The C-130 carrying GySgt Rodriguez and company eventually touched down at a big Marine base. The plane was met on the taxiway by a bus and an armed escort, consisting of a pair of Humvees filled with armed Marines. Without explanation, the squad was hustled off the transport and onto the bus, which immediately departed. The Lieutenant was taken off separately and driven away in a staff car.

In the back of the bus, still bound but otherwise left to their own devices, the squad conversed in hushed tones. "Where are they taking us, Gunny?" Asked Sanchez, his voice masked by the noise of their ride.

"Don't know," the Gunny replied quietly. "This is definitely Camp Lejeune, but they can't be taking us to the brig, it was closed down a couple of years ago." The Marine Corps Base Camp Lejeune —properly pronounced Luh-JERN—is a 246 square-mile United States military training facility on the coast of North Carolina. The base's 14 miles of Atlantic beaches make it a major area for amphibious assault training, and its location between the deep-water ports of Wilmington and Morehead City allow for fast overseas deployments if needed. During their careers, most Marines end up spending time at Lejeune.

Maybe they're taking us to the Eastern Judicial Circuit, she thought. The Eastern Judicial Circuit is part of the Navy-Marine Corps Trial Judiciary, an independent military court composed of both active duty and reserve military judges. The Circuit includes all Marine Corps bases, air stations, camps, depots and logistics bases within the state of North Carolina but its judges preside over courts-martial conducted worldwide. If the squad members were to be tried before a general court-martial, an Article 39(a) hearing before a military judge would be a first step.

After leaving New River Marine Corps Air Station, the bus took the Highway 17 Bypass to Lejeune Blvd and headed east. Shortly, they turned south on Holcomb Blvd and then bore left onto Sneads Ferry Road, almost as though they were taking a tour of the base. Surrounded by the flat, pine and palmetto covered plains of down-east Carolina, the bus followed Sneads Ferry Road until turning off the highway and heading southeast on a secondary road.

"Hey," said LCpl. Ronnie Reagan, "this is the road to the Mockup." During World War II, Marines conducted amphibious landing operations using open-topped landing craft, which they boarded by climbing down netting hung from the sides of troop transport ships. Marines training at Camp Lejeune could not practice landing operations in the sea off Onslow Beach because of the threat from German submarines. Instead, a full-scale mockup of the side of a troop transport was built on the inland side of the Intracoastal Waterway.

On this wooden stand-in for a troop ship, sometimes referred to as "the movie set," a generation of Marines learned to climb up and down rope netting, carrying a full pack and rifle. No longer essential for assault training, the Mockup remained a base landmark.

Before reaching the Intracoastal and the Mockup itself, the bus turned off onto a side road that was little more than twin sandy ruts in the undergrowth. "Man, this is the asshole of nowhere," observed PFC Kato Kwan. "Why are they hauling us off into the boonies?"

"Because we are evidently not officially here," said the Gunny. "Otherwise we would be in the detention area or secure quarters at one of the satellite bases. No, people, we are being held in secret, where nobody will stumble upon us accidentally." *This just keeps going from bad to worse*, she added silently, *at first I was afraid of being court-martialed, now a court-martial doesn't sound so bad.*

"We are so screwed," moaned Sanchez.

"Shut up and grow a pair, Joey," replied LCpl. Washington.

Brakes squealed as they pulled up in front of a cluster of temporary structures, surrounded by fencing and razor wire. Armed guards with dogs walked the perimeter and the sound of a generator could be heard. *It looks like we have been slipped the big green weenie*, the Gunny thought silently, *and our future prospects look flatter than hammered shit.*

Chapter 4

Beneath Parker's Station, Australian Outback

In an office dug out of the bedrock beneath Parker's Station, Jack sat doing paperwork, the bane of all commanding officers. Round duct work brought in fresh air, which circulated out through a grate above the door to the hallway. Drifting through the grate, Jack could hear voices—a small crowd of people not in agreement about something. Then came a knock on the door.

"Come," the Captain called out.

The door opened and in marched the Chief, followed by the three SEALs and a large black woman that the Captain did not know. The Chief halted in front of the desk, came to attention and saluted, saying "Senior Chief Zackly, reporting to the Captain with a party of four."

This must be something serious, for the Chief to be strictly adhering to protocol. Normally the Navy does not render the hand salute indoors, unless under cover or armed—or when formally reporting to the commanding officer. The Captain returned the salute. "At ease. What is this all about, Chief?"

"Sir, I got a matter that needs your attention," the Chief began. "Our new SEAL contingent brought some extra personnel with them, specifically this lady behind me." The lady in question smiled, revealing dimples and several gold teeth.

"And you are?" Jack asked the woman.

"I be Jessie, Captain," she replied, with a strong Jamaican accent. "Jessie Lowe, da bar tender at de Flustered Virgin."

"I see," Jack said. "and how is it that you came to accompany Chief Morgan and these other gentlemen to Australia?" Chief Morgan and the other two SEALS, Petty Officers Jones and Kowalski, were standing at parade rest, hands clasped behind their backs and eyes focused on the wall above the Captain's head.

"Well ya see, Captain, des boys be comin' into da Virgin for a while now," the island woman began. "Some of my best customers, dey are."

"No doubt." The Captain looked at Chief Petty Officer Morgan, the ranking SEAL. "And you and the boys just couldn't bear to leave your favorite bartender behind, Chief?"

"Yes, Sir. I mean no, Sir," Morgan replied. "I mean that there is more to it than that, Sir."

"I'm listening, Chief Morgan."

"Well, Sir. It's like this," said Morgan. "When we first started hanging out at the Flustered Virgin there were some trouble makers there, a real bad element. Me and the boys, we sort of invited all the unsavory types to leave."

"And these undesirables all took your advise and vacated the premises?"

"Most of 'em, Sir. Though some had to be asked more than once. The thing is, Captain, some of the people we ran off blamed Jessie here for it."

Jack could see that Jessie wanted to speak, but Chief Zackly had obviously told her not to speak unless asked to. "Miss Lowe, did you have something you wanted to add?"

"Yes, Captain. Some of dem dat was trown out were really bad, rude boys and gangstas. I knew I can't stay if Rick and da boys go away."

"So you asked them to take you along?"

"Yes, Captain. Dat I did."

"And you thought this was a good idea, Chief Morgan?"

"Yes, Sir. Sorry, Sir, but I couldn't think of any good alternative on such short notice."

Jack sighed. Sailing a spaceship to other stars and fighting hostile aliens, that was the easy part of his job. The hard part was taking care of the crew. "All right, Miss. Here is what we can do. We can drop you back on the island of your choice, or we can probably set you up in one of the larger cities here—Sydney or Melbourne, for instance."

"No, please, Captain," the large woman said, a hint of pleading in her voice. "I been listening to da two officers dat picked us up, de good lookin' one and de cowboy, talkin' about travelin' among da stars. Dat's were I want to go, into outer space!"

"I see. And what qualifications do you have, that I should add you to my crew?"

"Well, I'm a great bartender, jus ask des boys here. But I can also cook, all sorts of island dishes, not just Jamaican—conch pate, chicken wrapped in banana leaves, roti, johnny cake, fungi, seasoned rice an beans—any ting you can tink of."

"I see," the Captain said, then, addressing Chief Zackly, "Senior Chief Zackly, do you think we have room for another cook and bartender on the crew?"

"Well, Captain. If she's willing to help out with other ship keeping chores and such, I think we can find her a berth."

"All right then, welcome aboard Miss Lowe. Chief, let Lt. Curtis know we have another new crew member."

"Aye, Sir."

"Oh tank you, Captain! You won regret dis!" the excited Jessie gushed.

"As for you three," the Captain said looking at the SEALs. "I know that SEALs have a reputation for being fun loving and a bit unorthodox, but this is your only free pass. No more surprises, do you understand me?"

"Yes, Sir!" the three replied in unison.

"Very well, you three and Miss Lowe are dismissed. Chief, could you please find Mr. Taylor and Mr. Vincent for me? I think I would like a word with them."

"Aye, Captain. They're waiting in the hall," the old Chief grinned. As Chief of the Ship, it was his job to keep the ship running smoothly and that meant anticipating his captain's requests. The SEALs and Peggy Sue's newest crew member filed out, then the Chief leaned out the door and said, "Yous two Sirs please come in now."

JT and Billy Ray entered the Captain's office looking sheepish, knowing they were in for an ass chewing. The Captain eyed them up and down, letting them stew in their own juices for a minute.

Finally he spoke: "Do you gentlemen have any more surprises for me? A few late additions to the serving staff? A butler or perhaps a personal attendant or two?"

"No, Sir," both men responded.

"Do you think I'm running a cruise ship here? I sent you to pick up three bloody sailors and you come back with the first local woman who tells you a sob story! I'm glad you weren't gone longer or we'd be sailing with a steel drum orchestra and a reggae band."

The Captain stared hard at the two young officers.

"Mr. Vincent, and you Mr. Taylor, were sent on this mission because you both have shown good judgment and leadership in the past. I'll not ask you what you were thinking when you agreed to bring the SEAL team's personal bartender along with us. Obviously, Chief Morgan can be very persuasive, probably as persuasive as the local rum."

"Yes, Sir," the two replied, with JT adding, "no excuse, Sir."

"It's a damned good thing for you that we are short-handed and on a tight schedule. That, and I love island cooking," the Captain concluded, reining in the temptation to further unload on the two young men. "As things stand, I have something else for you to work on."

The two officers exchanged relieved glances, while the Chief stood behind them grinning. *Too bad things are so busy*, the Chief thought, *the Captain was just building up a good head of steam.*

"Gentlemen, I am becoming concerned about the fate of our former Marine contingent," Jack began. "From the drone left at Parker's ranch, we know that they were treated roughly and hauled off in a CH-53 to Goodfellow AFB. There they were held in a hanger until a C-130 showed up and took them elsewhere."

"Do we know where they went, Sir?" JT asked cautiously.

"As best as the ship's computer can tell, the Hercules landed at Camp Lejeune, but where the Marines were taken once they arrived is unknown."

"Lejeune is a big place, Sir," JT said, "with lots of wild areas to stash a squad of Marines. Plus there are Marines in training running all over the place. I don't think we can just stroll up to the gate and ask for Gunny Rodriguez."

"Indeed not, Mr. Taylor."

"Beggin' the Captain's pardon," the Chief said. "I may have a way to find 'em if they're hid somewhere."

"Yes, Chief?" Jack asked. "And what would that be?"

"I gave Jennifer, Gunny Rodriguez, a comm pip as they were leaving, just in case something went screwy." At the time, the Chief was operating under the old adage, better to beg forgiveness than ask permission. Besides, if everything went well for Jennifer she was just going to flush the little device.

"I see. Good thinking Chief," the Captain said, with a knowing look. "Well, the fact that there has been no mention of the returned Marines on the news makes me suspect that they are being held under duress. The range of a pip is not far, but our equipment should be able to detect its presence from a few klicks away."

"Yes, Sir," replied Billy Ray, eagerly joining the conversation. "I reckon we could insert a drone and let it survey the area. The drones are real quiet and, with adaptive coloration, almost undetectable from the ground at 30 meters."

"Very well, Mr. Vincent. I will leave it in your hands. I want those people found. We owe them a debt, and if the U.S. Government cannot treat them with respect we will have to take corrective action," Jack looked at each man in turn. "Mr. Taylor, devise a plan to retrieve our Marines. I want no casualties, on either side, and no surprise additions this time, gentlemen."

"Aye aye, Sir." the three men chorused.

"Dismissed," the Captain said, returning to the paperwork on his desk and trying not to think of Ludmilla's impending trip to Vienna.

Yuki's Apartment, Tokyo, Japan

After being briefly questioned by a number of stern but polite police officials at NPSC headquarters, Yuki was escorted back to his apartment near the University. He was advised to remain in the apartment in a way that suggested compliance was not optional. While he was happy to be back in familiar surroundings, he was anxious to contact some of his colleagues. The knowledge and information gained on the voyage to Beta Comae was just too vital to not be shared.

Turning on the TV, Yuki was astounded to see a group of government officials denouncing reports of an "alien menace" by a "rogue American Navy officer." They could only be talking about Captain Sutton and the material that had been sent to the UN and various national governments. "We believe this story to be a complete fabrication by an unstable person," the government minister was saying. "And most disgraceful is the insinuation that Dr. Hiroyuki Saito and the two brave cosmonauts, who died on board the ISS two months ago, are alive and participated in this science fiction fantasy adventure."

That statement caused a chill to go down Yuki's spine. *If the government is saying I am dead, what are they going to do with me?* He went quietly to the door and looked through the peep hole— there was a man in a dark suit standing guard outside his apartment.

Half in a panic, he picked up the telephone, only to find the line without a dial tone. Next, he went into the bedroom and retrieved his cellphone from the nightstand. It could not get a signal, evidently the police were using a signal blocker. Finally, he tried his home computer, but it could not access the Internet.

He sat on the sleeping platform and buried his face in his hands. *I must think, regain my composure!* After all he was a kendōka, a practitioner of the Japanese martial art of kendo—the way of the sword. Kendo taught the ancient zen precepts that supposedly guided the master Samurai swordsmen of old. Samurai tradition ran deep in his family—his great grandfather's katana and wakizashi rested on the mantle in the living room.

He should not have returned, that much was now clear. He had hoped to recruit some of his colleagues to help face the menace he was convinced threatened all mankind. Instead, he would need to be rescued from peril himself. Yuki steadied his breathing and concentrated on clearing his mind. He would need his whits about him when the time came to escape.

UN Headquarters, Vienna Austria

The United Nations has four main headquarter complexes: New York, Geneva, Nairobi and Vienna. New York is the most well known, followed by the sprawling, park like complex next to Lake Geneva. But it is at the UNOV, the United Nations Office in Vienna, that the United Nations Office for Outer Space Affairs is headquartered. It should not be surprising that such an organization exists within the UN. In the more than half century since its founding the United Nations has managed to insinuate itself into every area of human activity. UNOOSA was even rumored to have appointed Earth's first spokesperson for extraterrestrial affairs, something the organization later denied.

The UN offices are located in the Vienna International Centre, colloquially known as UNO City in Vienna. Constructed in the 1970s, the modernistic complex consists of six Y-shaped office towers surrounding a cylindrical conference building. The highest tower contains 28 floors, standing 127 meters tall. Aside from the UN offices and the conference center, there are several banks and shopping areas on the lower floors. The VIC is an extraterritorial area, exempt from the jurisdiction of local law, and maintains its own well armed police force.

It was at the heliport on the roof of one of the shorter towers that the shuttle carrying Dr. Ludmilla Tropsha set down. The pinnace was piloted by Sandy McKennitt and carried as passengers Dr. Tropsha, Chief Zackly and two of the crew, Steve Hitch and Matt Jacobs. Hitch and Jacobs were along as a compromise between Captain Jack and Ludmilla. There for her protection should anything should go awry, both able spacers were wearing combat armor.

This was a new version of the armor the crew and Marines had worn in the assault on the alien refueling station in the Beta Comae system. The old armor was bulky and so heavy that it was only usable under low gravity conditions—hauling around 220 kilos of metal ceramic composite armor, along with the accompanying power and life support systems, could quickly sap the strength of even the strongest warrior. The new armor was much lighter, massing only 105 kilos, but more effective. It also came with a new feature that aided the wearer's mobility.

The new armor was built around a system of electroreactive polymer bundles that complimented the wearer's own musculature. Termed motion enhancement technology by the armor's designers—primarily JT and GySgt Rodriguez, with help from Dr. Gupta and Dr. Schmitt—the end result was that the new suits moved under their own power, mimicking their wearer's motions. This mostly eliminated the burden of the suits' still considerable weight. Moreover, the artificial muscles could amplify the strength of the wearer by as much as three fold. A man who could lift 100 kilos unassisted could now lift 300 kilos when encased in armor.

The gloves on the old armor were so large that new weapons with larger grips and controls had to be designed for the action off Beat Comae. The smaller gauntlets of the new armor allowed the use of the more compact bullpup rail guns that the crew was initially armed with. Both weapon designs possessed similar firepower: a 5mm flechette firing rail gun with variable rate of fire and muzzle velocity, plus a 20mm grenade launcher capable of firing a number of different rounds. Between the weapons and enhanced armor the two sailors were more like walking light armored vehicles than foot soldiers.

Both Ludmilla and the Chief were dressed in standard jumpsuits, she in medical section white and he in deck division dark blue. The only difference from shipboard wear was heavier soled boots. "Chief, you really do not need to accompany me inside," Ludmilla said. "I will be talking to a representative of ROSCOSMOS in one of the meeting rooms, with the UNOOSA people acting as hosts. I will be perfectly safe."

"I don't care who yer meeting with, Doctor," the wiry little chief boatswain's mate replied. "The Captain told me to stick with you the whole time." In the Chief's mind, orders from the Captain were the same as a command from God.

"Very well, but you will be bored to death. I will be answering questions asked by bureaucrats, Russian bureaucrats at that."

"Yes, Ma'am. But orders is orders."

"Let us go then, it looks like there is a party waiting to greet us at the door."

"Right," the Chief agreed. Then he turned and said, "Lower the ramp, Miss McKennitt." Ludmilla was already headed for the rear of the passenger compartment. In a lowered voice the Chief continued. "Keep the boys inside and yer ear to the radio. If they try anything funny send help on the double."

"Roger that, Chief," Sandy acknowledged.

"Remember, if anything happens to the Doc, the Captain will keelhaul us all without spacesuits."

Kong Karls Land, Svalbard, Norway

"Well, hello stranger," said Isbjørn, moving a couple steps closer to Bear. "I didn't think I would ever lay eyes on you again." The last time she had seen him was more than three and a half years ago. As with most polar bear romances, it lasted for only a few torrid weeks. Then Bear disappeared and Isbjørn was left to fend for herself.

"Whose this clown?" asked a confused and angry Umky. The small male tried to insert himself between his mother and the large stranger. Bear's response was simply to swat the smaller bear aside.

"I take it he's one of yours," Bear said to his old flame. "Isn't he old enough to head off on his own?"

"Yes and yes," she replied with a hint of exasperation, adding "and he's also one of yours."

"What?" the startled Bear snorted. "He's my son?"

"Yes, this is Umky," she turned to the small male who had regained his footing and was again headed toward them. "Umky, meet your father, Pihoqahiak." In Inuit poetry, Pihoqahiak means the ever-wandering one.

"I just go by Bear, nowadays," Bear said. "I've been hanging around with a bunch of humans who mostly speak English. Besides, that name was from my carefree youth, I've grownup a lot since then."

"Really?" Isbjørn said in a skeptical tone. As she spoke, Umky again tried to wedge himself between the old paramours. "I don't care who he is, I don't like him!" Umky said. This time it was Isbjørn who cuffed the younger bear, sending him sprawling on the tundra despite the fact that both mother and cub weighed around 275 kilos apiece.

"I heard you disappeared with some humans in a flying machine. I figured you ended up in a Zoo or as a rug in front of some human's fireplace."

"Oh hell no. You know me better than that, babe."

"I was wondering how you went from hunting Inuit with a rifle to palling around with a bunch of talking monkeys."

"Why does nobody pay attention to what I say!" whined Umky, who had again picked himself up off the ground and now sat on his hindquarters, safely out side of paw-swipe range.

"Son," said Bear, looking at his new found offspring, "when you have something to say worth listening to, people will listen. Until then, it would be best to shut up and keep your ears open." Turning back to Isbjørn, he added, "he's big for his age, but I think you spoil him."

"Yes, I probably do," she said, looking down, "I lost his sister early on, to an orca while crossing some open water."

"Sorry to hear that, babe," Bear said awkwardly. He felt no pang of loss over a daughter he never knew, but the pain in Isbjørn's eyes was obvious. "Listen, I have a proposition for you, and Junior here as well. In fact, do you know if there are anymore of our kind hanging around?"

"I saw Tornassuk and Snowflake east of here a few days ago. Why do you ask?"

"Let's head that direction, maybe we'll run into them," he said, standing up on all fours. "You are going to think I've lost my mind, but come with me and let me tell you about this human I know called Captain Jack..."

Camp Lejeune, North Carolina

Every morning the captive Marines were allowed to shower and fed a simple breakfast, before being taken off to seemingly endless interrogation sessions. In windowless rooms, voices from the shadows asked meaningless questions while spotlights glared in the prisoners' eyes. Their captors asked the same questions over and over, perhaps trying to catch one of the Marines in some deception or obfuscating lie. Why the government would suspect they were hiding anything remained unanswered.

The captives had also been issued new work uniforms, devoid of any rank or other insignias. Basically, everything they had on them or with them at the time they were captured at Parker's ranch had been taken away. Well, almost everything.

GySgt Rodriguez was in the head for the purpose of changing sanitary napkins. Before she disposed of the old one, she pealed back some of the padding and removed a small black object about the size of an apple seed. "You want the old one?" she called to the guard standing outside the stall.

"Hell no, Sergeant," came the embarrassed reply. She threw the used napkin in the toilet, then carefully implanted the comm pip into the fresh one.

After putting the new napkin to its intended use, the Gunny emerged from the stall and washed her hands in front of the waiting guard. *Thank God there are some lines even a Marine guard won't cross*, she thought, *at least not a male Marine Guard*. Of course, the people from the ship might not be looking for them, and even if they were, the range of the little comm pip could not be much. At least they were still being kept together in a remote location—that would make an extraction easier.

Who would be doing the extracting was another matter. Lt. Curtis, JT, the Chief and a couple of crewmen was a pretty skimpy force to be sending against one of the largest Marine bases in the United States. *Not my problem*, the Gunny said to herself, *my job is to keep the rest of the squad together and ready to go if a rescue comes. No, make that when the rescue comes. And if I ever meet that light colonel again I will shave his balls with a rusty razor and pour rubbing alcohol on them.*

Beneath Parker's Station, Australian Outback

"Sir, I'm quite concerned about Yuki," said Lt. Curtis over the video link from the ship. "We know he arrived at the Tokyo airport, but he never showed up at the University. And a bunch of Japanese politicians just made an announcement denouncing our warning about the hostile aliens. More troubling, they insisted that Yuki and the two Russian cosmonauts actually died on board the ISS."

"Hmm, first the Marines go missing and now Dr. Saito," the Captain pondered. "I'm getting a very uneasy feeling about this operation, Lieutenant."

"Yes, Sir," Gretchen replied. "Have we received any positive feedback from those we sent the information package to?"

"That's not just a no, it's a hell no," said TK Parker, rolling into the room to join the Captain. "Turn on the TV, the head bureaucrat from the UN is on talking about our warning."

Quickly bringing up Fox News in a window on the screen, they caught the end of the Secretary General's speech: "...so after reviewing the 'evidence' sent to the security council and various governments around the world, we can only conclude that this is some form of colossal fraud being perpetrated by unscrupulous and perhaps unstable individuals. This Captain Sutton and his crew are obviously backed by men of obscene wealth, who are using the threat of hostile extraterrestrials as a way to subjugate the peoples of the world..."

"What the hell is he saying?" Jack asked incredulously.

The Secretary General continued: "...that these international fugitives have created advanced technology is undeniable. The UN calls for this knowledge to be immediately shared with all member nations. Because all nations are not in a position to take advantage of this technology, I am further calling on the wealthy nations of the world to pay for spreading this knowledge to lesser developed countries, constructing plants and establishing laboratories at their expense. All nations must pay their fair share."

At that point the news announcer broke in and said, "Well, there you have it. The UN Secretary General has labeled the claims by Captain Jack Sutton and the crew of the spaceship Peggy Sue a scam. He has called for the ship to be turned over to the UN and for free distribution of any advanced technology it contains to underdeveloped nations at the expense of the wealthy ones. This in contrast with the statement by the U.S. Secretary of State earlier, that the ship and all of its technology belongs to the United States, since it was built in the state of Texas. More on this developing story later, now for the latest on the car chase in L.A..."

"Turn that damned thing off," TK groused. "I've heard enough simpering jackasses for one day. Can you believe that? I payed for that ship myself! Well, me and a couple of like minded friends. We built something no government on Earth could have—not without screwing it up or starting a war or something—and somehow that makes us 'obscenely rich' and bent on world domination. Typical transnational socialist bullshit."

TK was on a rant, and both Jack and Gretchen knew from experience it was best to just let him wind down on his own.

"That hopped up third world potboy. He's been sloppin' at the public trough all his life; never once held a job that resulted in something real or useful. Nothing but a greedy bureaucrat, working his way up the ladder with all the other UN parasites. Clawed his way to the top of the dung heap; survival of the sleaziest. Advancement at the UN is an example of evolution running backward! Now he's the head parasite, telling those with nothing that they all deserve what rich people got, and he's just the man to level the playing field for them—all they have to do was put their trust in him and the United God Damned Nations."

"Yes TK, but what are we going to do about the situation?" Jack asked. "We are still tied to Earth's industrial base to construct the spacecraft we will need to combat the aliens, assuming the threat proves as dire as the artifact portrayed it."

"We're just gonna have to move off planet, that's all," the crusty billionaire replied. "Establish a base where we can expand the fabricators and construct bigger and better ships. We'll also need to start recruiting, big time."

"Recruiting who?" asked Gretchen from the ship.

"All sorts of people," TK responded. "People to work in the factories, to man the ships, to fight the damned aliens when the time comes. Since we'll be moving off planet we're gonna have to move families and all. That means school teachers, merchants, restauranteurs, handymen, artists, entertainers, the whole shootin' match. We gotta recreate civilization, children! One ship full of humans and a couple of polar bears just ain't gonna be enough."

"I fear that you're right, TK," Jack allowed, *and nobody can accuse him of acting by half steps.* But Jack had more immediate concerns, "right now I'm worried about getting back the people we used to have on board."

"Yer right about that, Jack my boy. You get yer crew back from wherever they've been locked up and I'll deal with the rest. Ain't no God damned pissant UN snake in the grass gonna screw this up while I'm around." With that, the fuming septuagenarian spun his electric wheelchair about and departed, still ranting about the personal hygiene and breeding habits of UN bureaucrats.

"I'm glad we got that all straightened out," Jack said to his executive officer. "While TK arranges for an off planet diaspora I think we need to lay on missions to retrieve our incarcerated crew members from durance vile."

"Yes, Sir!" replied Gretchen, always happiest when the course of action was clear. "I have a number for Dr. Saito's post-doc student at Tokyo University. Perhaps she can find out what they have done with Yuki."

"Fine, just try not to endanger the woman. When you find his location you may wish to take a pinnace and reconnoiter the situation." The Captain said, shifting to action mode. "I've already set Mr. Taylor and Mr. Vincent to finding and rescuing the Marines."

"Will the two of them be enough if our people are being held on a military installation or in a prison?"

"JT is a very resourceful fellow, and I think that our new trio of SEALs might be able to help implement what ever plan they come up with."

JT was resourceful, and very inventive, as Gretchen knew from experience of a more personal nature. "Very well, Captain. I'll report back when I know anything about Dr. Saito."

"Thank you, Lieutenant, Captain out." *I think I had best get back to the ship,* Jack thought, *I don't want to be on the shore* when the balloon goes up on the rescue missions. Damn, I knew letting Ludmilla go talk to the Russians was a bad idea—not that I could have stopped her. I Just hope she gets back without incident.

Chapter 5

UNOOSA Headquarters, Vienna, Austria

Ludmilla and the Chief were met and escorted inside by a UN representative, a rather handsome Frenchman named Jean-Jacques de Belcour. As he led them through a maze of stairs and hallways he conversed with Ludmilla, ignoring the Chief as one would a servant or bodyguard. "We are of course, all very happy that you did not perish on board the ISS, Dr. Tropsha. But you must understand that the circumstances surrounding your rescue and the subsequent actions taken by this Captain Sutton are a source of grave concern for my Secretary."

"I do not see why, Monsieur de Belcour. The Captain has been open with the UN and all the people of the world with regard to our voyage." Ludmilla got the impression that M. de Belcour did not approve of Captain Jack or his actions.

"Misadventure is more accurate, Doctor," the UN official replied. "The Captain and crew of the Peggy Sue took it upon themselves to act in the name of the peoples of Earth. They may well have started an interstellar war without the sanction or authorization of a single legitimate government. This whole situation is quite unfortunate."

"Have you watched the video from the mission yourself, Monsieur?"

"Well, no. I've not had the time," de Belcour answered.

"Then I suggest you make the time," Ludmilla replied tartly, "before you pass judgment on actions taken by people in situations you neither understand nor can fully imagine." This remark ended the conversation and the party continued on in silence.

Eventually they came to a tall wooden door, identical to all the others in the hallway. Without knocking, M. de Belcour opened the door and motioned Ludmilla inside. She walked through the portal but when the Chief tried to follow the UN official put up an arm baring his way. "This meeting is only for Dr. Tropsha, you will have to wait outside."

The Chief put his hands on his hips and looked the Frenchman up and down. "The hell I will, you frog bastard. Move yer arm or I'll break it off."

The startled UN official was taken aback, unused to people speaking to him in such a manner. While he was staring at the Chief, unsure of what to do, Ludmilla turned back and seized his arm. Applying painful pressure on the nerves in his wrist, the angry Russian doctor hissed, "If you do not remove your arm, I will break it. Where I go the Chief goes, or we leave."

Not given a choice, the bureaucrat withdrew his arm and stood aside. The Chief followed Ludmilla into the room as de Belcour glared at both of them, his face flushed with a combination of anger and humiliation. As the door swung shut, he could be seen massaging his arm where Ludmilla's wrist grip had held him. He did not realize that as a practitioner of Sambo, a Russian form of martial art combining aspects of Judo and wrestling, Ludmilla exercised daily to strengthen her hands, arms and wrists. Her grip was like a vise and, being a doctor, she knew precisely where to apply pressure to cause sensitive nerves to erupt in pain.

Inside the room were three men, one seated at a large desk and two others in ill fitting suits standing on either side of the desk. The seated man rose and offered his hand to Ludmilla, saying in Russian, "Welcome, Dr. Tropsha. It is so good to see you alive and in such good shape. I am Vladimir Chernyshyov, assistant director of public relations for ROSCOSMOS. Please have a seat."

Ludmilla took a seat in the single chair that sat facing the desk. Chief Zackly stood behind her, assuming a parade rest position. Ludmilla replied, also in Russian. "Good afternoon, Mr. Chernyshyov. Tell me what I can do for you today."

"We, of course, were concerned that you were well and that you were not being held against your will by this rogue American captain." Glancing up at the Chief, who was staring at a point above his head with a blank look on his face, Chernyshyov asked, "does your minder have to be in the room for this interview?"

"The Chief is not my 'minder', he is here at my request. But if it makes you feel more comfortable, he does not speak Russian."

"Very well, tell me about the death of Col. Kondratov. Unlike the other mission fatalities, there was no visual record of his death. This naturally makes us quite suspicious."

"Naturally, you are, after all, a Russian security agent."

"Why do you say that? I told you I am with ROSCOSMOS," blustered the seated Russian.

"I was with ROSCOSMOS for almost ten years and it is not that large an organization. I remember no Vladimir Chernyshyov. Which means that you are possibly SVR or FSB, but given the two knuckle draggers you brought along, you are most likely from the GRU." The man's features hardened. *Bullseye*, Ludmilla said to herself. *The man had the odor of military intelligence.*

"This is a very important matter, with significant security implications for the *Rodina*. Which agency I am with is irrelevant. Please answer the question, how did Col. Kondratov die, Lt. Col. Tropsha?"

Col. Kondratov died trying to commandeer the ship, she thought venomously, *and was blown to hell by Captain Jack, my Jack.* But they had all agreed that exposing Ivan's treachery would serve no positive purpose, and would be devastating to his wife and daughters back in Russia.

"He and one of the crew were struck by plasma fire from hostile aliens during our escape from the refueling station in the Beta Comae system. The crewman died instantly, Ivan died on board from complications a short time later." That was not quite a lie, more of a half truth. Still, telling it did not come easy to Ludmilla, though her delivery was convincing.

"Why was his body not brought back and returned to Russia?"

"You have never seen a body struck by plasma fire," she shot back, "they are charred beyond recognition, that which is not blasted to atoms. Col. Kondratov, along with all the other dead, was given a funeral and burial in space. To prevent the aliens from learning anything from their remains, the bodies were vaporized by the ship's X-ray laser battery. You were provided video of the funeral."

Once the story had been agreed to, the crew staged a reenactment of the funeral with five caskets, one draped with a Russian flag for the treacherous Colonel. Ludmilla picked up the case she had been carrying, opened it and removed a folded triangular package—the flag that had covered Ivan's casket. Setting the case aside, she stood and held out the folded Russian flag. "I brought this with me. Perhaps you can give it to his widow?"

As Ludmilla stood up, the Russian standing to her left reached into his poorly cut suit and drew a pistol, perhaps thinking she was threatening his boss. This caused the Chief to jump forward, shouting "Watch out Doc! He's got a gun!"

Startled by the sudden movement the Russian tough swung his gun away from Ludmilla and toward the Chief, who was reaching inside of his jumpsuit for something. The Russian fired.

The sound of the shot was startlingly loud in the confined space of the room. The other two Russians were momentarily frozen in place by the unexpected shot, but Ludmilla reacted out of long years of martial arts training. Grasping the barrel of the gun with her left hand and twisting down, she struck the shooter's wrist from the opposite side with her right, disarming the man. It was standard Systema Spetsnaz technique.

The flurry of action brought the other two Russians out of their momentary trance, but Ludmilla was now holding the gun and pointing it at the man she had just disarmed. Recovering his balance, he foolishly made a grab for the incensed woman. She shot him twice in the chest—a double tap. The disarmed thug dropped to the floor like a felled tree.

Meanwhile, the other standing thug pulled a pistol of his own. Before Ludmilla could re-target her weapon to cover the new threat, a thread of blue light came from behind her and struck the second gunman. He fell to the floor, shaking with violent convulsions.

Ludmilla stepped back and to the side, keeping her weapon pointed at the seated Russian who slowly raised his hands. She looked at the Chief who was leaning against the wall with a stunner in his right hand. The left shoulder of his jumpsuit was black with blood. "Chief, are you in danger of passing out?"

"Naw," he said, grimacing in pain, "just a flesh wound."

"Keep them covered while I look at your shoulder," she ordered, assuming the role of doctor in charge of a patient. With her left hand she gently probed the Chief's wound. "You are not bleeding too badly, fortunately I have a compress in my case. As she bent down to retrieve the case the man behind the desk made his move, attempting to draw a handgun from a shoulder holster. Without hesitation Ludmilla shot him in the right shoulder, causing him to drop the pistol, which slid across the desk and onto the floor.

In Russian she spoke to the man, who had fallen back in his chair and was holding his now useless right arm. "You assholes in charge are always getting others shot. Tell me, how does it feel, you *bljadin syn?*"

"You are making a big mistake Dr. Tropsha."

"No," she cut him off, "it is you who have made the mistake. If your thug had killed the Chief, I would have killed all three of you." Turning back to the Chief she said in English, "Chief, we must get out of here."

The Russians were carrying old fashioned Makarov semi-automatic pistols. The compact 9mm was still popular with Russian agents because of its small size, making concealed carry easier. Quickly removing the pistol's magazine and ejecting the round in the chamber, Ludmilla released the slide lock by pulling the spring loaded trigger guard down and to one side. She stripped the slide from the body and threw the pieces into a nearby trash bin. Retrieving the other two guns from the floor, she repeated the procedure on them as well.

Ludmilla then peeled back the upper left side of the Chief's jumpsuit and applied a large compress to his still bleeding wound. In the process the Chief's blood was smeared on her jumpsuit, shockingly red against the white material. "Chief, now we go," she said, closing her case. "please give me the stunner."

The Chief handed her the nonlethal weapon and without hesitation she turned and stunned the wounded but still conscious Russian agent. Then, holding the door open for the Chief she called the shuttle on her collar pip, "Lt. McKennitt, we are headed back to the ship. The Chief has been shot and we might need a little help exiting the building..."

Kong Karls Land, Svalbard, Norway

"Hey you mangy walking carpet! How are you doing?" Bear shouted to his old acquaintance, Tornassuk. Bear, Isbjørn and Umky were approaching Tornassuk and a smaller female from the west.

"Is that you, Pihoqahiak?" the big male replied. "I figured you for a hunting trophy by now. And is that Isbjørn? You still hanging around with this bum?"

"For now," Isbjørn answered. "Umky and I just ran into him a few kilometers west of here. He helped us out with a little dumb bear problem we were having."

"I had it under control, Mom," Umky said.

"What you had under control was setting the stage for your funeral, sonny," Bear chuckled, causing Umky to look at him angrily but say nothing more. Bear sat down in front of the pair of new bears. "And I go by Bear now, my English speaking human friends found Pihoqahiak a bit of a mouthful."

"Just 'Bear'?" Tornassuk asked, looking a bit skeptical. "That's either really unimaginative or really conceited."

"Oh dude!" Bear exclaimed, waving a dinner plate sized paw in front of his face. "somebody has been chowing down on rancid blubber!" Fully grown male polar bears had a tendency to eat only the high-energy fat of a seal or walrus, leaving the more protein rich meat for scavengers. Even if a carcass had been rotting for several days, they consumed the blubber with relish.

"Yeah, there's a dead walrus on the beach back that way, been there a couple of days," the other big male responded, "and stop trying to change the subject. Since when do you hang with *Homo sapiens?*"

"Is the pup yours, Isbjørn?" asked the female, ignoring the conversation between the two males. Then, in a burst of insight, she added, "and yours too, Pihoqahiak? I always heard you were a bit different, but what are you trying to do, start a nuclear family like the humans pretend is normal?"

"You'd be surprised what I've been learning from the humans, little lady," Bear replied with a grin and a half leer. This caused Isbjørn to nip Bear on the ear. "Hey," he said pulling away, "I didn't think you were the jealous kind, babe."

"No female likes it when her escort starts flirting with the competition," said Isbjørn, adding cattily, "not that dear Snowflake is really competition."

"Oh yeah. Like you're the Queen of the Arctic," the other shot back sarcastically, flashing a bit of incisor.

"Now ladies, rather than snipe at each other, why don't you let me tell you about a trip I made, a journey befitting the legend of Pihoqahiak?" The other bears looked at him curiously. All polar bears are curious to a fault and talking polar bears, in particular, love a good story. "Let me tell you about fighting giant alien spiders on the Moon and taking a trip to the stars..."

Dr. Saito's Lab, University of Tokyo

The telephone in Dr. Saito's laboratory was ringing. This was unusual because it had stopped ringing half a year ago, after Dr. Saito went into space to spend some time on board the International Space Station. There was a brief flurry of calls when his death in the solar eruption was announced two months ago, but those were just news reporters looking for "reaction" to the Doctor's death.

Now, with renewed rumors caused by the supposed return of the mystery spaceship, it looked like the news hounds were back on the trail. The Internet was awash with videos of planets and space stations, battles with aliens and interior shots of the mystery ship. There was even a clip of a flying saucer taking off, after supposedly returning some missing soldiers. It went viral after the U.S. government tried to have it taken down. Mizuki did not know whether to believe any of it or not.

Dr. Mizuki Ogawa was a recent PhD and had signed on as a post-doctorate researcher in Dr. Saito's lab just before he took his ill

81

fated trip into space. She had been keeping the lab open since the announcement of Dr. Saito's death because no one had bothered to come by and tell her to shut the place down. In a way, she felt, it helped to keep his memory alive.

This caller was certainly persistent, she thought, why can't they leave Dr. Saito's spirit rest? Mizuki never used the lab phone. Like every other person under the age of 50 in Japan, she had a late model cell phone that could do everything but drive a car and make sushi. Finally it was more than she could stand. Angrily she picked up the phone and said, *"Moshi moshi, kochira wa Mizuki desu."*

"Konnichiwa, Dr. Mizuki Ogawa?" the voice on the other end asked.

"Hai, this is Dr. Ogawa, what do you want?" she replied in Japanese.

"I am a friend of Dr. Saito's." came the response in understandable Japanese, though the speaker was certainly not a native.

Switching to English, Mizuki tried again, "You mean you were his friend. He is dead. What do you want with me."

"Dr. Saito told me you have a little sister, Kiyoko," the voice on the phone continued in English. "But you call her Koko, to tease her about her height." The name Koko means stork in Japanese. "I tell you this to prove that I know Dr. Saito well."

How did she know that? Mizuki's interest was piqued in spite of herself. "Why do you wish me to think you knew Dr. Saito? Who are you? Why are you calling me with this!"

"I assure you that Dr. Saito was alive a few days ago when we dropped him off in Okinawa. But now he has vanished and we think he is being held against his will somewhere in Tokyo. I am Lt. Gretchen Curtis, first officer of the starship Peggy Sue and we need you to help us locate Dr. Saito."

Mizuki's mouth opened in wordless disbelief as the receiver slipped from her grasp. This had to be some kind of tasteless prank being played on her by some of the other post-docs. There were a number of native English speaking students at the University and it would be easy to put one of them up to making the call. She recovered the receiver and hung up the phone.

A minute later it rang again. Mizuki hung up without answering and left the phone off the hook. Two minutes later her cellphone rang, an incoming call from an unknown number.

"Dr. Ogawa, please do not hang up again," said the woman's voice. "Dr. Saito is my friend and I fear he is in grave danger. I have called his apartment number and his cellphone, both are not working. Not out of service, there is no busy signal or error message, just dead silence. His PC is not available for chat either."

Strange, Mizuki thought, *a caller should have at least gotten Dr. Saito's answering machine or the message service for his cell.* No one earns a PhD in physics without being inquisitive and Mizuki's curiosity was now fully aroused. "Yes," Mizuki said cautiously, "what do you want me to do?"

"Could you go by Dr. Saito's apartment and see if there is anyone there? Or any sign of recent activity?"

That seemed like a reasonable request, if the woman really is who she says she is. "What should I say if there is someone there other than Dr. Saito?"

"Tell them the truth, that you are Dr. Saito's post-graduate assistant and you are checking to see that his apartment is still intact."

"And then?"

"Regardless of what you find, call me back at this number..."

Peggy Sue, High Earth Orbit

The Captain returned to his ship in a large shuttle, loaded with new personnel. Though the seats in the big shuttle were large and comfortable, the Captain claimed the privilege of rank and rode in the less comfortable co-pilot's seat for the journey. With Ludmilla in danger he was not feeling particularly sociable.

In the passenger cabin were a number of notable additions to the ship's complement. Among them were the SEALs, Jessie Lowe and several new environmental and engineering technicians. Also on the flight were Richard Carmichael, MD, a thoracic surgeon, his operating room nurse, Giselle Bollard, and Gene Hofstadter, doctor of veterinary medicine specializing in large exotic animals. All the newcomers bubbled with excitement over their first flight in space.

Arriving in an anxious mood after the three hour flight, Jack called a meeting of the ship's officers in the main lounge. The lounge was the only semi private area that could accommodate the ship's growing cadre of officers. Among those in attendance were Gretchen Curtis, the first officer, Jo Jo Medina, the chief engineer, Nigel Lewis, JT and the two helmsmen, Billy Ray Vincent and Bobby Danner.

"I'm glad you are all able to attend this meeting in person," the Captain began. "Let me officially welcome aboard our new officers, Lt. JG Nigel Lewis and Lt. JG Sandy McKennit, who is currently planet side on a mission. I can assure you that both First Officer Curtis and myself are extraordinarily happy to have a couple more officers available to stand watch." That remark brought a few chuckles. Jack and Gretchen wore themselves to a frazzle during the last trip, one of them always having to be on the bridge in case of emergencies.

"I am also happy to announce that Mr. Billy Ray Vincent and his fellow helmsman, Mr. Bobby Danner, have been commissioned as Lieutenants, Junior Grade." There was a smattering of applause and verbal congratulations.

"Also take note that Mr. Bear, Mr. Taylor and Mr. Medina have been promoted Lieutenants. Mr. Taylor is assigned as ship's science officer, responsible for the ship's scientific sensors and liaison to the science section staff. Though he will wear science section burgundy, he is also one of the ship's officers. Mr. Medina will continue to head the engineering section." More congratulations.

"Finally, let it be known that Gretchen Curtis is promoted Lt. Commander and will serve officially as the Peggy Sue's executive officer." The Captain paused as the assembled officers came to their feet and applauded heartily. Once order was restored he continued: "Though it has always been clear that she is my second in command, I feel it is time to drop the fiction that this is not a Naval vessel and formalize the command structure. You will also note that we now have three Lieutenants, four Lieutenants JG, and four new midshipmen. The intent is for the junior officers to learn and advance as quickly as events allow.

"That is because we will be building a number of new ships—larger and more powerful than the Peggy Sue. And when those ships are commissioned, they will need captains and XOs of their own. Eventually, I hope each of you earns a captaincy." This remark caused a number of smiles and not a few thoughtful looks among the junior officers.

Just look at them, all full of piss and vinegar, Jack thought, *I remember when I was that young, convinced I would be the best captain in the history of the US Navy. Well, we've got matters to attend to first.* "I know that it is traditional to have a promotion party in celebration, but I'm afraid that we will have to delay that happy occasion for a few days. That is because we have a number of crew members in peril—a situation I intend to correct."

Jack glanced around the table and saw looks of grim determination replace the celebratory mood of a few minutes ago. "Let's start with the status of our missing Marines. Mr. Taylor, do you have an update?"

"Yes, Sir," JT responded. "As Lt. Vincent suggested, we dropped a reconnaissance drone onto Camp Lejeune and had it do a stealthy survey of the base's less populated areas. The drone picked up the unmistakable signature of one of our comm pips on a number of occasions."

"Yes, Mr. Taylor? Go on."

"Perhaps it best if I let Mr. Vincent explain," JT replied, turning the briefing duties over to Billy Ray. Billy Ray smiled his laconic cowboy smile and said, "Well, Captain, what we figured out was that the Marines, or at least GySgt Rodriguez, are being moved around. The signal is steady over night, coming from a partially hidden compound of low buildings surrounded by guards and barbed wire."

"That is presumably where they are bedding down," added JT.

"That's right. But during the day the signal moves. As near as we can tell, the squad is put on a bus and taken to some other location each morning, possibly for interrogation. They return by bus just before sunset each day."

"And this pattern has held for how long, Mr. Vincent?"

"Three days now, Captain."

"So do you gentlemen have a plan?"

"Yes, Sir," JT answered, "we were thinking of hitting the bus at the end of the day. From our observations there are only a driver and two guards on board the bus. When it turns off Mockup Road, onto the trail to the detention site, there is a short stretch where it can't be seen from either the road or the prison camp. We will disable the vehicle at that point, over come the guards and free the Marines before anyone knows what has happened."

"I see," said the Captain, "and what would you need to pull off this jailbreak, in terms of personnel and equipment?"

"One of the large shuttles, a pinnace would be too small to hold the entire squad plus the rescue team. And I was thinking that this is just the sort of thing our new SEAL contingent would be good at."

"Yes, that makes sense," Jack concurred. *Now we will see if the SEALs are worth their up keep.* "Have you talked with Chief Morgan about this?"

"Not yet, Captain," replied Billy Ray. "We didn't want to get them boys excited prematurely." This brought a few chuckles from the others, easing the tension in the room.

"Very good, gentlemen," Jack said, then addressed the others present, "Does anyone have any suggestions or comments?"

"Are you sure that a large shuttle won't be spotted flying over the base?" asked Lcdr. Curtis.

"Affirmative, Commander," Billy Ray responded, piloting the shuttle would presumably fall to him. "The detention site is not far inland and the area is not inhabited. There are a number of forest openings in the vicinity where a shuttle could set down without being spotted."

"Yes," added JT, "we were thinking that we would come in overnight and the SEALs and myself would scout the area around the prison camp. We would set a place for the ambush and then lay low until the target appears. Once the bus is halted and the prisoners released, the shuttle will land on the trail and pick everyone up."

"Once they are on board," Billy Ray finished, "we'd head straight out to sea and climb for orbit—there's nothing on Earth that can catch us at that point."

"Seems like you two have thought this through," remarked Gretchen. "How soon do you want to go?"

"Tomorrow," JT and Billy Ray replied in unison.

"You don't want to wait a few more days and make sure the pattern holds?" asked Nigel Lewis.

"No, tomorrow is Friday. We don't know if the pattern will stay the same over the weekend."

"Alright then," the Captain said, bringing the discussion to an end. "Lay on your operation for tomorrow, Mr. Taylor. Mr. Vincent, I suppose you volunteer for the piloting duties?"

"If that'd be alright with you, Sir."

"It's settled then. Go brief the SEALs when this is over, Mr. Taylor."

"Aye aye, Sir."

Jack sat back for a moment and then shifted topics. "Commander Curtis, have you any word regarding Dr. Saito?"

"Aye, Captain. I received a call back from Mizuki Ogawa, Yuki's assistant, saying that there was a guard standing in front of Dr. Saito's apartment door. Also, there were lights in the apartment this evening."

"But no eyes on Dr. Saito himself?"

"No, Sir. But Dr. Ogawa was going to keep the apartment under surveillance."

"I hope she doesn't get noticed by whoever is guarding the place."

"I told her to be careful, Captain. What is really needed is for us to get some boots on the ground in Tokyo."

"What would you suggest?"

"I would like to take Mr. Danner and one of the pinnaces and scout the situation, Sir."

"I see, why Mr. Danner?"

"Because Bobby's physical build and general coloration can probably pass for Japanese at night. The apartment building has no place to land on top, which means we will have to park the shuttle nearby and travel to the target by surface transport. I'm still working out the details."

"Alright, Commander. Do it." The Captain looked around the room with a grim face. "As you have probably heard, the UN and various national governments have rejected our warning of possible alien invasion and offer of cooperation out of hand. In fact, the last report I received before this meeting from Lt. McKennitt said that there were problems at the UN office in Vienna. Evidently the Chief has been wounded and armed crew members have been sent into the building to extract our people."

"What!" someone exclaimed. The strain of the situation was obvious in the Captain's face. Even the newest crew members knew that there was an emotional bond between the Captain and Dr. Tropsha. What most of them did not realize was that the Captain and the Chief had served together for more than a decade in the Navy, a symbiotic relationship between officer and enlisted man that continued on board the Peggy Sue. The Captain's concern was as much for the Chief as for Ludmilla.

"As we try to prepare Earth for war with unknown adversaries, we find opponents aplenty hear at home. I will continue to monitor the situation from the bridge. Commander Curtis, Mr. Taylor, put your rescue missions in motion. Everyone else, man your stations. I'm not calling General Quarters, but I want to be ready if the need arises. Questions?"

There were none.

"Very well, you all know what to do. Let's go get our people back."

Chapter 6

Roof of the VIC, UNOOSA Headquarters, Vienna

"All right, men," called Sandy over the radio link. "The Chief's been shot and the Doc is in trouble. Please, go and fetch them from the building."

"Aye aye, Lieutenant," Replied Hitch, nudging Jacobs toward the rear boarding ramp, then on suit-to-suit "Crap, if the Chief dies it will be almost as bad as if the Doc got hurt."

"Hell, Stevie," Jacobs replied. "The Captain's apt to level this whole complex as it is." The pair hustled down the airstair and headed toward the door leading inside the building. There had been two UN guards, armed with submachine guns, standing watch there, but with the appearance of a duo of two meter tall, 250 kilo gray-black space monsters, the UN beat a hasty retreat back inside the building.

"Do you think they locked the door?" Jacobs asked.

"Who gives a shit?" Hitch replied. "Cover me!" With that Hitch sped up to a full run and simply slammed head-on into the glass and aluminum door.

Kinetic energy won out over aesthetic design. The door shattered, scattering pellets of safety glass and pieces of aluminum in all directions. The guards were just disappearing at the bottom of the stairwell. "Come on, Matt!" Hitch called to his partner, "we got 'em on the run!"

* * * * *

Two floors down, Ludmilla and the wounded Chief were retracing the steps they had taken entering the building. The Chief was leaning heavily on Ludmilla's left side as she brandished the stunner in her right hand. The Chief, jaw clenched in pain looked at the blond doctor and said, "Leave me! Go on, get yer self out."

"Nonsense, we came in together and we are going out together," Ludmilla replied. "Besides, how would I explain to the Captain that I abandoned his oldest friend? I am a big girl and you do not weigh all that much; we will make it."

Rounding the corner before the stairs to the next floor they came upon two guards. "Auchtung! Halt!" one shouted, raising his machine pistol. Ludmilla sprayed them both with debilitating blue light. Their weapons clattered to the floor and both guards collapsed, shaking as if jolted by a stun gun—which is essentially what had happened. The only difference was that this stun gun didn't need to shoot wires into its targets.

Past the still twitching guards, Ludmilla and the Chief ascended the marble stairs one careful step at a time. Reaching the top of the wide stairway, they were now in the hall that led to the flight of stairs to the roof. Unfortunately, between them and the exit was Jean-Jacques de Belcour, leading a squad of four armed men in vests and helmets.

"Dr. Tropsha, you are under arrest!" called de Belcour. "I would suggest you drop your weapon and raise your hands."

The hell I will, thought the furious Ludmilla. Behind the squad confronting her, two more guards bolted out of the heliport stairwell. They ran full out toward their compatriots yelling something unintelligible about "monster robots" in German.

As the party confronting them was distracted by the commotion from the other end of the hallway, Ludmilla and the Chief squatted down to present a smaller target and the Doctor prepared to fire on the guards. Before she could get off a shot, a gigantic black figure flew out of the heliport stairwell and smashed into the wall opposite the opening. As the first figure was extracting itself from the demolished drywall and framing, a second black monster ran into the first.

"We are directly behind the squad of men in helmets," Ludmilla quickly transmitted over her shoulder pip. As Jacobs and Hitch finished untangling themselves from each other and the wall, Hitch replied, "Got it, Doc. Lay prone on the floor so's we don't hit ya."

The two fugitives moved to comply, laying belly down on the floor, with Ludmilla holding the stunner out in front of her. The UN official, bravely leading from behind, ordered his men to advance.

"Open fire on those things!" M. de Belcour yelled as he backed slowly away from the armed squad. When he was about five meters from his former quarry, Ludmilla shot him in the back with the stunner. As the Frenchman fell to the floor, the UN guards opened up on the two advancing crewmen.

A hail of bullets peppered the two armored spacemen. Unfortunately for the UN troops, the heaviest rounds they were firing were 7.62mm NATO, which bounced off the armored suits without leaving a mark. The 9mm pistol rounds from the submachine guns might as well been a gentle spring rain. Then the crewmen returned fire.

Both Jacobs and Hitch sprayed their antagonists with waist high bursts from their rail guns. At 600 rounds per minute, and with a muzzle velocity of 2000 fps, more than 100 5mm flechettes shredded the UN squad. "I think they're all down, Stevie," said Jacobs.

"Damn straight, Matt," replied Hitch. Then remembering the party they were supposed to be rescuing called, "Doc, Chief? Are you OK?"

"Come on yous deck apes," the Chief's unmistakable raspy voice replied. "Stop playing with the locals, an' get us the hell outta here."

The two armored men picked their way through the bodies of the downed UN troops, meeting the Doctor and Chief at the supine body of M. de Belcour. Thanks to being stunned by Ludmilla, the UN official was the only member of the opposition to survive the brief but deadly encounter with Peggy Sue's crew.

"What should we do with this one?" Hitch asked, "He's still twitchin'."

Suddenly, Ludmilla had a wicked thought. *This officious UN buffoon was going to hand me over to be carried off like an animal? Let us see how he likes it with the positions reversed!* "Bring him, I think the Captain will have some interesting questions for our UN friend."

"But Doc, he ordered those men to fire on us!" replied Jacobs.

"Yes he did," Ludmilla smiled. "Have you never heard the old saying 'keep your friends close, and your enemies closer'?"

Yuki's Apartment, Tokyo, Japan

In Yuki's apartment things had gone from bad to worse. Inspector Takashi had shown up around midnight with three men, all bearing the tell-tale tattoos of yakuza, Japanese mafia. They could also be identified as yakuza by their speech patterns, an almost unintelligible dialect only heard by normal Japanese in gangster movies. Outcasts from larger Japanese society, the gangsters have their own language with a unique and specialized vocabulary suited to their disreputable occupation.

"I am sorry to inform you, Dr. Saito, that the government has decided that your sudden reappearance would be an embarrassment," Takashi said to the grim faced Saito. "Given poor economic conditions and recent tensions with the Chinese, harboring one of the renegades from the mystery spaceship would cause unnecessary disruption."

"I remind you, Inspector Takashi, that I am a Japanese citizen and a scientist with an international reputation. You cannot simply make me vanish."

"Sadly, that is not true, Doctor. You have already vanished, on board the International Space Station. Since you are already dead, the government has decided that it is best you stay dead."

"So, are these gangsters here to kill me then?" Yuki asked, eying the three yakuza nervously. This caused one of them to laugh and make a mumbled remark to his companions. Then all three laughed.

"No doctor. These men are going to watch over you, until a deal can be struck with the Chinese. You will be traded to them for the return of several of our people and other considerations. I'm sure they will take good care of you, as long as you are productive."

"Doing what? I am an astrophysicist!"

"Come, Doctor. You know at least some of the secrets of that spacecraft you traveled in. Every major power on Earth wants to know those secrets."

"So why am I not being kept in Japan?"

"Again, sadly, things have not gone well for our nation these last several decades. It was decided that this course of action is best."

"Dishonor rots the soul, Inspector."

"I am truly sorry Dr. Saito." With that he bowed and left the apartment. The three thugs stood smiling at Yuki, much like a pack of hyenas smile at a wounded gazelle.

* * * * *

The small shuttle carrying Lcdr. Curtis and Bobby descend into Tokyo after midnight. They landed on top of a parking garage a few blocks from Yuki's apartment building, the closest suitable site they could find. After securing the pinnace, nearly unnoticeable among the antennas and other equipment on the garage roof, the pair made their way down to street level. Both were dressed in unadorned black jumpsuits, appropriate attire for a bit of clandestine skulking about. Both were also carrying concealed stunners.

On the ground floor, Gretchen walked up to a parked car and took what looked like a charge card from her pocket. She waved the card over a strange icon on the driver's side window and the doors unlocked with an audible click. "How did you do that, Commander?" Bobby asked, suitably impressed.

"It's Yuki's shared car pass. He left it behind on the ship," Gretchen answered, as though that explained everything. What Bobby did not know is that Tokyo, and other large cities in Japan, have a number of shared car companies. Millions of commuters who use trains, subways and buses in Tokyo and the surrounding districts sign up for cards that let them rent cars from parking garages downtown. The cars are checked out with the swipe of a card and charges are billed automatically in 15 minute time blocks. The system lets people travel by trains for long distances and then use shared cars at their destination.

The car itself was a black, late model Mitsubishi mini with four doors—just the thing for zipping around the back alleys of down town Tokyo. "You drive, Mr. Danner, and remember they drive on the left," Lcdr. Curtis said, handing the card to Bobby. "I'll sit in the back and you can leave me off behind Yuki's apartment building."

"Roger that, Ma'am," Bobby replied. The car's interior was roomier than one might expect, with plenty of headroom thanks to the car's tall stature. The cabin was conventional in appearance, with a slot for the charge card in place of an ignition key. Bobby inserted the card and the dash lit up.

"This thing has a satnav display, but it's all in Japanese," Bobby said to the Commander. He had studied a street map of the area on the trip down, but a working, understandable navigation system would have made him more comfortable.

"Don't worry, Mr. Danner. Our target is just a few blocks from here. We will circle the block a few times and pick a place for me to jump out. Then you can park on the street in a position to watch the front door. When we come out you pick us up and we high-tail it back to the shuttle."

"Aye aye, Ma'am," he replied, easing the little electric car out into the Tokyo night.

Dr. Tropsha's Pinnace, En-route To The Ship

The rescue party encountered no further resistance on their way back to the shuttle. The Chief managed to board under his own power before slumping to the floor. "Lt. McKennitt!" Ludmilla called out. "Please close the ramp and then come aft and help secure our passengers."

"On my way, Doctor," came the instant reply as the sound of the airstair closing could be heard from the rear of the cabin. Sandy appeared a half minute later and, upon seeing the Chief passed out on the floor and Ludmilla's white jumpsuit smeared with red blood, cried out in alarm. "My God, Doctor! Are you wounded?"

"No, this is not my blood," Ludmilla answered. "It is the Chief's and he has passed out. Help me get him in a seat and strapped in." As Sandy complied with the Doctor's wishes she spied Jacobs tossing another figure into a seat farther aft. "And who is the other bloke?"

"That is our host, a M. de Belcour. Since he turned us over to armed GRU agents and then had a squad of armed men open fire on Hitch and Jacobs, I thought it might be interesting to have him explain his actions to the Captain."

"Beauty, Doc," The Aussie Lieutenant replied, securing the Chief's seat belt. "Is the Chief going to be OK? I mean he's not going to cark it, is he?"

"The Chief will be fine, as long as we can get him to the ship within a couple of hours," Ludmilla answered. "You should probably put some tie-cuffs on our guest and then get us out of here."

"Right you are, Doc. We'll be underway in a jiffy."

Yuki's Apartment, Tokyo, Japan

"Hey, you got anything to drink, asshole?" asked one of the yakuza, looking around the apartment. All three were evidently sizing up what they could take from the apartment once the deal for Yuki was finalized and he was bundled off to China. One of them turned on the entertainment center, blaring popular music out of the surrounding speakers.

"There is beer in the refrigerator," was Yuki's curt reply. To him, these men were scum, criminals and thieves not worthy of attention. Unfortunately, he was outnumbered and he had glimpsed a pistol stuck in the waistband of one of the men. He would rather die here than spend the rest of his life as a slave in China. If he could get to his grandfather's sword he could take at least some of them with him.

Unknown to Yuki, Gretchen was on the ledge just outside his porch. Bobby had dropped her off at the side of the building and, like a ninja of old, she had scaled the side of the apartment building to the sixth floor. Her problem now was figuring out how to get inside without alarming the three men guarding Yuki.

She carefully moved around the ledge to the bedroom window, quietly testing it with one hand—it was unlocked! As she slid the window open she could hear loud music from the other room. Noise from her movements masked by the music, she quickly slipped into the darkened bedroom. Peering surreptitiously around the edge of the doorway, she could see two of the guards. Yuki and the third were not visible from her vantage point.

Yuki was still not aware of Gretchen's presence. He was trying to move closer to the swords on the mantle without attracting the attention of his three keepers. As it was, he was almost close enough to seize the grip of the katana. Having practiced tamishigiri, the cutting of rolled mats with swords, he knew he could slice a man in half with the larger sword. Still, he would not be able to dispatch all three yakuza before one of them pulled a gun. It would take a master Samurai like Musashi Myamoto, the legendary 17th century sword master, to kill them all before they could react.

Blue light flickered from the bedroom, striking first one then the other of the farthest yakuza. The yakuza nearest Yuki heard his comrades cry out as they fell and spun around, gun in hand. A tall figure in black holding a strange looking weapon stepped out of the bedroom doorway. The remaining gangster raised his pistol to fire.

Gretchen had decided to chance a sudden attack, rather than wait to be discovered lurking in the bedroom. She shot the two men she could see with her stunner and then stepped around the door opening looking for the third. To her left, the third guard stood between her and Yuki, pointing a pistol at her. *Oh shit*, she thought, knowing she could not stun her opponent before he fired.

The yakuza pulled the trigger, intent on shooting the black clad intruder, but nothing happened. He looked down to see why his gun had not fired only to find that his hand, gun and all, was no longer attached to his forearm. Before he could figure out how this happened the room spun crazily as his head was neatly severed from his shoulders. The pain just started to registered as the room faded to black.

* * * * *

Meanwhile, outside of the apartment building, Bobby had parked the little electric car up the street from the building entrance. As he watched, a petite Japanese woman walked toward the entrance from the other direction. As she approached, two men who were lurking in the doorway stepped out and confronted her. Even from here, Bobby could see the tattoo sleeves on the men's arms.

"Oh shit! They must be yakuza," Bobby said out loud. Like most nerds, Bobby was into all things Japanese, including personal electronics, anime, manga and ninja movies. He recognized the markings of Japan's criminal underclass when he saw them. The girl turned and started running back up the street in the direction she had come from. The yakuza gave chase.

That girl is in trouble, was all Bobby could think of. He put the car in gear and raced after the fleeing female. He zipped past the woman's pursuers, pulled up alongside their intended victim and threw open the passenger side door. "*Kuruma ni noru!*" he shouted, "get in the car, now!"

The terrified woman looked at Bobby and then glanced back at the men closing on her. Seeing Bobby as the lesser threat, she jumped in. Bobby floored it and the little electric car hummed away into the sparse early morning traffic.

A stream of rapid Japanese issued from the young woman who was trying to see what was happening behind the speeding vehicle. Bobby made a left turn and slowed. Speaking to the woman he said, "please slow down. My Japanese is pretty bad."

"You are American?" the wide eyed young woman asked in quite good English.

"Yes, my name is Bobby. Why were those men chasing you?"

"I was checking my boss's apartment and they were standing out in front."

"Oh my God, are you Mizuki?" he asked. The girl stared back at him dumbfounded. "Are you Dr. Mizuki Ogawa?" Bobby repeated.

"Yes, but how could you know that? I have never seen you before in my life."

"I'm from the ship, the Peggy Sue," he replied. "We're here to rescue Yuki." *Crap! I'd better call the Commander and let her know what just happened, and tell her about the yakuza standing watch over the front of the building.*

* * * * *

Gretchen watched as the body of the headless gunman fell to the floor, like a marionette whose strings had been cut. She looked at Yuki, who was standing legs apart, sword in a two handed grip in front of him, looking like an ancient samurai reborn. "Well done, Saito-san," Gretchen said, and bowed in her friend's direction.

"Gretchen, I cannot tell you how good it is to see you," he replied, bowing in return.

"Who are these guys? They seem a little trigger happy."

"It is a long story, but they are yakuza, Japanese criminals. They were going to sell me to the Chinese."

"Not anymore they aren't," Gretchen said, walking to the entertainment center and turning off the loud music. "We need to get out of here. I've got Bobby standing by with a ride outside." As she was saying that her comm pip chirped, signaling an incoming call—it could only be Bobby. "Curtis, go."

"Commander, this is Bobby. I've got both good news and bad for you."

"Do not keep me in suspense, Mr. Danner."

"The good news is that I have Mizuki Ogawa, she was being chased by a couple of men, real live yakuza. The bad news is that they were keeping watch on the front of the apartment building."

"Yes, we had to handle three more yakuza in here. I have Yuki and we are both uninjured. Are you saying you can't come back and pick us up in the car?"

"I wouldn't recommend it, Commander."

"All right, here is what I want you to do. Return the car to where we got it, then you and Miss Ogawa get on board the shuttle and come and get us."

"Uh, Commander, where will I land?"

"Just jam the rear of the shuttle into the apartment's porch and open the airstair so we can climb aboard. And do it quickly, it's already growing light out."

"Aye aye, Ma'am."

"If there are things you want to take with you, you need to get them quickly, Yuki," Gretchen said to the physicist, who had just finished cleaning the blood of the katana and was in the process of returning it to is scabbard.

"The only things I wish to take are my grandfather's swords," he replied, sliding the katana home.

Dr. Tropsha's Pinnace, Arriving At The Peggy Sue

The Captain was at the bottom of the ladder to meet the returning shuttle bearing Dr. Tropsha and the wounded Chief. Hitch and Jacobs came down the airstair first, carrying the unconscious Chief on a stretcher. They were followed by Ludmilla, still wearing her blood stained jumpsuit.

Seeing the blood on Ludmilla's clothes gave Jack a start, but he immediately realized that Lt. McKennitt would have reported if the Doctor had been wounded. Though he wanted to ask Ludmilla if she was unharmed, instead he asked, "How is the Chief? Is his life in any danger?"

"No, Captain," Ludmilla replied, ship's doctor addressing the ship's captain. "He has a shoulder wound and has lost a significant amount of blood, but he will be all right once I get him stabilized and on a plasma drip." While their words were formal and proper, their eyes met for an instant, allowing unspoken emotions to flow in both directions. The moment was broken by another passenger descending the stairs.

The Captain looked past Ludmilla to see Jean-Jacques de Belcour being prodded down the boarding ramp by Lt. McKennitt. The Frenchman's hands were bound in front of him by a zip-cuff and he was wearing a look of stunned disbelief.

"And who is this, Lieutenant?" the Captain asked.

"Just some UN poly that tried to get in the Doc's way, Sir" Sandy answered. "And he's as mad as a frog in a sock."

"This, Captain, is M. Jean-Jacques de Belcour of the UNOOSA. He was the gentleman who escorted me to the would be Russian kidnappers and then tried to prevent us from leaving after the Chief was shot."

"I see," Jack said, with a dangerous edge to his voice. "I will settle accounts with you later, Mr. de Belcour. In the mean time throw him in the brig, Lieutenant."

"Aye aye, Sir!" Sandy replied happily. She had taken an instant dislike to the Frenchman on the trip back.

"Captain! I am an official of the United Nations. I demand that you return me to Earth immediately. That woman standing next to you killed one Russian official and gravely wounded another, and those men in the armored suits slaughtered six UN guards! They must all return to Vienna and stand trial for these outrages."

"I see what you mean about the frog in a sock, Lieutenant," the Captain said contemptuously. He shifted his attention to the UN official. "You offered Dr. Tropsha a neutral place to converse with ROSCOSMOS officials, Mr. de Belcour. Instead, you delivered her to a trio of GRU thugs, one of whom shot Chief Zackly unprovoked. All the events that transpired in Vienna are an outcome of you violating your word. The dead Russian, the dead guards, all because you have no honor, Sir. It is just fortunate for you that none of my people died, for if they had, your Vienna headquarters would now be a smoking crater."

The Captain turned from the ashen faced Frenchman and spoke again to Lt. McKennitt: "Take this human offal away, Lieutenant. Before I lose my temper."

Ludmilla watched the exchange without showing any emotion. As Sandy roughly pushed de Belcour into the hall and the waiting arms of a pair of crewmen, the Doctor stared after the UN official. Once he was gone she turned to the Captain and said, "Captain, I must see to my patient. I will report to you as soon as I know the Chief is out of danger."

"Yes, Doctor, please do. I will await your report," Jack replied. "And, Doctor."

"Yes?"

"I am very happy you are back unharmed." Ludmilla offered him a waning smile and hurried off toward the sickbay.

Yuki's Apartment, Tokyo, Japan

Bobby returned the rental car to its stall and led the confused Mizuki to the top of the building. As they crossed the roof and rounded the clutter of equipment installed there, Mizuki stopped and gasped. There, sitting in front of her was a flying saucer. Perched insect like on four extended legs, it made a low humming sound as a ramp with stairs lowered from the rear of the craft.

Simultaneously, its skin changed from a mottled camouflage pattern that blended with its surroundings to mat black.

"Please, Dr. Ogawa," Bobby pleaded. "Get on board the shuttle. We have to go get Lcdr. Curtis and Dr. Saito right now. Before more bad guys show up at the apartment."

"Who are you people?" Mizuki asked, shaking her head from sided to side in disbelief.

"I told you, my name is Bobby Danner. I'm one of the helmsmen from the Peggy Sue. Lcdr. Curtis is in the apartment with Dr. Saito. She's the woman you talked to on the phone earlier. Look, we have to go now, they may be in danger. I can either leave you here, and you can explain what happened to the authorities, or you can get on board."

Mizuki nodded yes, afraid to speak. Bobby hustled her up the airstair and forward to the flight deck, where he sat her in the co-pilot's seat so he could keep an eye on her. "Listen to me, Mizuki. I need to concentrate on flying the shuttle, so please, please just sit there for a few minutes and don't touch anything."

"OK, Bobby," Mizuki said in a quiet voice, her dark eyes looking into his. In the dark lighting the slightly pudgy lieutenant almost looked Japanese, thought Mizuki, *like a hero in a science fiction movie, rescuing the girl from the evil yakuza in his flying saucer.*

Bobby quickly made the pinnace ready for flight and took off. The flight to Yuki's apartment building took less than 30 seconds. Over the comm he called Gretchen, "Commander, could you flash the lights in the apartment on and off so I can be sure which one it is?"

"Roger that, Bobby. Flashing now." The lights of one of the apartments on the building's sixth floor blinked off and back on.

"OK, got it. Please stand back from the balcony while I back her in." Gretchen acknowledged and Bobby positioned the rear of the shuttle just off the apartment's balcony. "OK, Commander, I'm doing this blind. Tell me when the ramp will clear the edge and you can board."

"Roger. Bring her back slowly." A few seconds later a crunching and grinding sound came from the rear of the craft. "That should be good! Hold her there and lower the ramp!"

The ramp lowered until it touched down a couple of feet inside Yuki's apartment. As soon as it did, Dr. Saito clambered on board carrying a small case and a couple of wicked looking samurai swords. The Doctor had changed his mind about taking a few other personal items with him while they waited for the shuttle's arrival.

"I'm on Bobby," Lcdr. Curtis yelled from the rear of the cabin, "button her up and make for orbit."

The ramp closed and Tokyo rapidly dropped away beneath the accelerating shuttle. Mizuki unbuckled herself and bolted for the passenger compartment. There was much bowing and a rapid exchange of Japanese between the physicist and his assistant, ending in an embrace worthy of a father and daughter. Tears flowed down Mizuki's cheeks.

After a few minutes, both Japanese scientists had regained their composure. "Mizuki," said Yuki, "I would like you to meet Gretchen Curtis, she is both a dear friend and colleague, and my rescuer from the hands of the yakuza."

Shyly, Mizuki bowed and said, "I am pleased to meet you, Lcdr. Curtis. I am sorry that I doubted you on the telephone and that I didn't fully believe Bobby, even after he rescued me from the yakuza in front of the building."

"It's nice to meet you too, Dr. Ogawa. And don't worry about that initial disbelief, we get that a lot," Gretchen replied. "Don't we Bobby?" she called to their pilot.

"Yes, Ma'am. That we do," came the happy reply.

Chapter 7

Camp Lejeune, North Carolina

Under Billy Ray's sure hand, the large shuttle floated in from the sea, black and silent against the night sky. On local radar it presented the same cross section as a large seabird, if it showed at all. The shuttle crossed the barrier islands and the waters of the Intracoastal, to settle on shore in a ragged opening in the canopy of southern pine. Though the surveillance drone had scanned the area for IR signatures prior to landing, the shuttle crew waited to see if their arrival attracted unwanted attention. After watching quietly for fifteen minutes, the rear boarding ramp lowered and the squad of four—three ex-SEALs and one former Green Beret—disembarked, heading for the camp, five kilometers away, where the imprisoned Marines were being held.

The former special forces operatives were in their natural element—infiltrating a hostile enemy position while facing astronomical odds. After crossing Mockup Road and working their way to within a kilometer of the prison camp entrance, they came across the rutted trail leading into the place. Speaking in low voices, JT and Chief Morgan discussed their next move. "I think we should get eyes on the camp itself, to be sure how far away it is and to get a rough headcount on the guards."

"Agreed, Chief. It would be good to have an estimate of how fast they can respond and in what force," JT said.

"Right," the head SEAL replied. "Phil, Bud, go check it out. We'll scout for a good ambush site." The two SEALs silently acknowledged and slipped quietly away through the undergrowth.

"We should look for a place where the canopy opens up around the trail. The clearer a place we have for the shuttle to touch down the better."

"From what I saw of the landing site, that thing has no problem knocking trees aside. Why look for a clearing?"

"The shuttle's repulsors can certainly uproot and toss these pine trees aside," JT replied. "And wouldn't it be a bitch if we rescued the jar heads only to have them taken out by flying lumber?"

103

"Probably ruin their entire day," Morgan agreed. "So we need to find a reasonable clearing and set the ambush just before it on the way into the camp."

"My thinking exactly, Chief."

Lcdr. Curtis' Shuttle, Arriving At The Peggy Sue

The Captain once again found himself awaiting the arrival of a shuttle full of rescued captives. As the shuttle from Tokyo finished docking, Ludmilla joined him outside of the airlock. "I thought you would like to know that the Chief is stable and resting," she said, answering Jack's unasked question. "Thank goodness for Dr. Carmichael and his OR nurse. Without them, it would have been risky for me to operate on the Chief's shoulder wound alone. As it was, Dr. Carmichael performed the surgery and I assisted. He seems very competent, his nurse Giselle as well."

"That's great news, Doctor," Jack said, relief obvious on his face. "I'm just happy no one else was wounded, or worse."

"Say it, Jack," Ludmilla said, guilt clouding her ice-blue eyes. "I was wrong to go. Worse, I endangered others doing so."

"Ludmilla, there are often ill advised things that honor or duty demand we do," he replied. "I sent the Marines and part of the crew into harm's way on the station in Beta Comae, and as a result four of them died."

"That was different, Jack. We needed to know if the probe's message was passed on," Ludmilla said, never one to make excuses or sugar coat things. "I didn't need to talk to ROSCOSMOS face to face. I could have used the video link. And if I had the Chief would not be in sickbay, recovering from a gunshot wound that could have killed him."

"If you had not gone, the extent of Russia's treachery and the complicity of the UN would have remained hidden. We might have been lured into a more serious trap. Did you know, they invited me to address the Security Counsel in person?"

"Really? You were not considering accepting, were you?"

"If everything had gone well with your visit, I might have been tempted. Now it's obvious that I would not have returned from such a trip."

"My country tries to kidnap me at gun point, Yuki's does kidnap him and turns him over to hoodlums, and the United States secretly imprisons a squad of its own Marines. It seems that every hand is against us, Jack."

"The actions of the U.S. are the most inexplicable. Those Marines didn't volunteer for the mission, they were put at risk in the service of their country," Jack said angrily. "They should have been greeted as heroes, instead they have been held covertly—suspected terrorists receive better treatment."

The sound of the passenger ramp lowering could be heard from within the airlock. Moments later the indicator on the airlock control panel changed to green and the door slid open. Gretchen Curtis descended the airstair and, seeing the Captain, came to attention and saluted. "Permission to come aboard, Sir?"

Jack returned her salute and said, "Permission granted, Commander. Welcome back."

Yuki appeared next, followed by a slender young Japanese woman. He stopped before the Captain and bowed formally. "Captain, I thank you most humbly for rescuing my assistant and myself. The dishonorable actions of my nation's government have shamed me deeply. If you will have me, I wish to join your crew permanently."

Jack returned Yuki's bow and then stepped forward and shook his hand. "Dr. Saito, I would be honored for you to join my crew on a permanent basis. I also understand that you have brought a colleague along."

"Yes, Captain," Yuki said, with a genuine smile. "May I present my colleague, Dr. Mizuki Ogawa? She joined my laboratory as a post-doctorate researcher just prior to my trip to the ISS. I am hoping that room for her can be found on board as well."

"Certainly, Doctor," Jack said and then bowing slightly toward the young woman added, "welcome aboard Dr. Ogawa. Any friend of Dr. Saito's is certainly welcome here."

"Thank you, Captain," Mizuki replied, respectfully looking down at the deck. "If Bobby had not rescued me, I don't know what would have happened."

Bobby? the Captain thought, *he's a hell of a pilot but I never would have expected individual heroics on a clandestine mission planetside.* "I look forward to Commander Curtis' full report once everyone is back on board and settled in," he replied, directing an inquiring glance at his second in command.

"I am forgetting my manners. Dr. Ogawa, this is Dr. Tropsha, the ship's head medical officer and also a member of the science staff. If you need anything or have any questions please do not hesitate to ask her or any of the other ship's officers."

"Yes, welcome aboard Dr. Ogawa. Come with me and we will have some tea," Ludmilla said, taking Mizuki in hand. "You can ask me questions and later I will show you around the ship..."

As the two women walked away, Jack looked at Gretchen and said, "Well done, Commander, I look forward to hearing all about your mission. I'm calling a meeting in my quarters in two hours. Hopefully we will have a progress report from the mission to free the Marines by then."

Camp Lejeune, North Carolina

Jones and Kowalski returned from scouting the prison camp a little over an hour after they set out. "The camp is just over a kilometer away," reported Phil Kowalski. "There are eight guards with M4s, plus a couple of dogs. It'll take 'em at least 10 minutes if they come flat out, more if they come cautious like."

"Yeah, I'd worry more about the dogs than the guards. Do these ray gun thingies work on dogs?" asked Bud Jones. The rescue party was armed with only stunners, the Captain had insisted. Jack told the special operators that if they could not rescue the prisoners using stealth and cunning he would have to assign them different duty. The SEALs took the bait, but were now having second thoughts about being practically unarmed in the midst of 40,000 Marines.

"They will knock down anything with a nervous system up to the size of a full grown bear," JT answered. "Just remember that maximum range is around 10 meters."

"Great," said Jones. "They got M4s and we got pop guns."

"At least they're quiet," JT said, "and what noise they do make doesn't sound like weapons fire."

"Knock off the chatter, Bud," Chief Morgan ordered. "Let's get the charges set and ourselves into position. We don't want to get caught with our shorts around our ankles if the bus comes back early."

Captain's Quarters, Peggy Sue

Assembled in the sitting room of the Captain's quarters were the ship's inner circle: Lcdr. Curtis, Dr. Tropsha and Dr. Gupta. Missing were the Chief, who was recovering from surgery on his injured shoulder, and Lt. Bear, who was on extended shore leave. They were talking over a video conference link with TK Parker at his station in the Outback. The subject was world reaction to their announcement of the impending alien threat.

"It looks like Dr. Tropsha's shoot out with the UN in Vienna has made the news everywhere. The nitwit in the White House issued a statement condemning the act and labeling the crew of the Peggy Sue outlaws," TK was saying. "Then that super giant ass from the UN held a press conference an said y'all were worse than Somali pirates."

"The Secretary General said that?" asked Ludmilla.

"Yes indeed. Thought that pompous popinjay was gonna have an aneurysm right there on the air. Too bad he didn't, the perfidious asshole."

"And the announcement about the alien threat is being ignored?" asked Jack.

"That or made fun of, son. The British Prime Minister, the President of France, the German Chancellor, China's Premier, all have denounced or scoffed at our announcement. Even worse, the public is ignoring it. Face it, the world has seen too many bad science fiction movies to be impressed by video of a real battle with aliens. Hell, one network had their film critics review the firefight on the Moon. They said the special effects were second rate and the slow motion when people fell was hokey."

"Hokey? We were on the Moon for goodness sake. That is how the local gravity acts!" Rajiv was more outraged by the news media's lack of scientific understanding than the political impact of such remarks.

"Perhaps we should have added some loud explosions and zapping ray-gun sounds," added Gretchen sarcastically. "Has there been any mention of our rescue of Dr. Saito?"

"Not a peep. Hell, they can't very well complain about us snatching him since they insist he died on the ISS months ago. No, there's not a politician on Earth who sees acknowledging the alien threat as in their own best interest."

"This is so incredibly short sighted," Jack sighed. "But I suppose we should have anticipated it, in retrospect. What about the tissue samples we sent with some of the information packages? If they analyzed those someone must have raised an alarm."

"Not a peep in the media," TK replied. "But I did get some back channel info from a contact I have in the pharmaceutical industry. He said the EU government wanted them to check the samples to make sure they weren't some kind a biological weapon."

"I am afraid that we have to face facts," Jack said, grim faced. "Our efforts to enlist the nations of the world in the coming struggle has failed."

"It was to be expected," said Ludmilla. "All governments care about one thing above all else: staying in power. Asking them to cooperate on a world wide basis means a loss of power for national governments. Of course they reject our warnings."

"I say we give up on trying to win them over. Cut our losses and move on to plan B," Gretchen added.

"Agreed," said Jack and TK at the same time. Then Jack continued. "Fortunately we have some good news. Both Dr. Tropsha and the Chief are safely back on board, as are Dr. Saito and his assistant Dr. Ogawa, who has decided to join the science staff."

"What about those Marines the government is holding illegally?" asked TK.

"We are about to get them back, Sir," Jack answered. "After all, if a handful of us can't rescue a squad of Marines from one of the largest military installations in the continental US, how can we hope to defeat a galaxy full of hostile aliens?"

Camp Lejeune, North Carolina

The four special operators were hidden in camouflaged positions for the ambush, two on either side of the rutted trail. The plan was for the two on the right side of the trail to open the bus door and take out the driver and guard. The other two were to open the rear door and zap the rear guard. JT's comm pip chirped, signaling a call from Billy Ray in the shuttle. "Go," he responded.

"I've got a positive visual on the bus heading your way on Mockup Road," came Billy Ray's reply. He had set the surveillance drone to orbit along the roadway at 30 meters and keep a lookout for the prison bus. The soccer ball sized robot moved silently on gravitonic repulsors like the much larger shuttle and had adaptive surface coloration that made it almost impossible to spot from the ground. Billy Ray planned to retrieve the drone once the trap was sprung.

"Roger that, we are in position," JT replied. "Just make sure you get here as soon as we disable the target."

The two sets of ambushers were in staggered positions along the bus trail, with JT and Kowalski about a bus length closer to the main road than Morgan and Jones. Hopefully, when the charges buried in the rutted trail went off, those in the bus would think they had blown the front tires and stop. If everything went according to plan it would all be over in 30 seconds or less, then the shuttle would land and they would head back to the ship.

From down the trail came the unmistakable sound of an internal combustion engine and the whine of transmission gears. Bouncing along the uneven trail, the prison bus appeared grinding along at maybe 10 mph. The front tires rolled over the two small shaped charges buried in the old tire ruts and there was a single loud popping sound.

A cloud of dust enveloped the front of the bus as the shredded carcasses of both tires attempted to run off their rims. With a squeal of brakes the bus lurched to a halt. Morgan touched Jones with a restraining hand, in his head thinking, *wait for it.* Sure enough, the bifold door on the side of the bus opened and a guard got out to see what had happened.

"What the fuck was that?" the driver called to the guard, who moved forward to look at the front tire. "Beats the shit outta me," he called back. The two SEALs stood up from cover and shot both the guard and the driver, who was still seated in the bus. Both spasmed and fell.

On board the bus itself, LCpl. Washington saw the flicker of blue light at the front of the bus and thought to himself, *now don't that look real familiar.* He nudged PFC Sanchez sitting next to him and whispered, "I think the cavalry has arrived."

The inside guard had been standing at the rear of the bus, but he started forward to see what was happening up front. Behind the bus, Kowalski jumped up and pulled the emergency handle on the bus's rear door, swinging it open. JT stepped up to the opening and shot the guard in the back with a bolt of blue light.

JT pulled himself up into the bus and said, "somebody here call for a cab?"

"It's about damn time you got here, snake eater," replied Washington, "we were starting to get bored." The big grin on Washington's face showed his friend he really was happy to see him. JT took out a spring loaded knife and cut Washington's tie-cuffs. A few rows forward the Gunny stood up and said, "It is really good to see you, Army."

"You too, Gunny," JT grinned, then turning serious, "you know that this is definitely the end of your Marine Corps career? You let us bust you out and you can never come back."

"Yeah, like coming back worked out so well the last time," said LCpl. Reagan, holding his cuffs up to be cut. A dark shadow passed overhead and in the clearing in front of the bus a violent windstorm blew scrub and sand in all directions. The shuttle had arrived.

"Come on you jar heads, your chariot awaits," JT yelled over the noise. "We gotta hustle before the guards at the compound come to see what the fuss is all about."

"You don't have to ask me twice," Sanchez said and hopped out the rear door. He found himself staring at a man in camo gear holding a stunner. "Hey, JT! I hope this guy is a friend of yours."

"Yes indeed. Joey, say hello to Petty Officer Phil Kowalski. Phil and his two buddies at the front of the bus are underemployed SEALs. They thought that coming along on this little jaunt sounded like an excellent way of spending a Friday afternoon. Now stop jawing and start moving."

More formal introductions would have to wait as the squad of now ex-Marines jumped off the end of the bus one by one. Next to the last to exit was HC2 White. As she moved past the guard, who was still twitching on the floor, she turned and delivered a solid kick in the balls. "That is for grabbing my ass each time I got off this damn bus, you shithead."

The Gunny looked at JT and shrugged. "Payback's a bitch," she said, smiling.

"Man, is he going to feel that in the morning," JT said, retrieving the guard's weapon. "After you Gunny, we need to be elsewhere."

* * * * *

The last of the rescued Marines were on board, the ramp secured and the surveillance drone was just snuggling into an opening on the top rear of the shuttle. Over the cabin PA, Billy Ray announced, "Welcome aboard Peggy Sue Airlines, now departing for High Earth Orbit and points beyond. Please be seated and enjoy the flight."

The shuttle rose from the clearing, blowing more brush and debris in all directions. Its nose swung toward the Atlantic and the scenery below became a green blur. The rapidly accelerating craft flashed over the Intracoastal waterway, the barrier islands and out to sea, leaving behind only a sonic boom that could be heard for miles.

As introductions were being made in the passenger cabin, the SEALs brought out a cooler filled with iced down beer—ostensibly to promote inter-service cooperation. The freed Marines had to admit that the SEALs seemed like splendid fellows and, after all, they had already accepted a Green Beret and a polar bear as their own. So the Marines welcomed the SEALs to the ranks of Captain Jack's buccaneers.

By then, the guards at the prison camp had figured out that there had been a hostage rescue and that their former inmates were headed out to sea in some form of aircraft. In response to their frantic calls, base ops relayed instructions to a flight of F-35s that were doing live fire exercises offshore, ordering them to intercept the fleeing shuttle.

As the fighters turned on target, Billy Ray pulled the shuttle's nose up and gave it full throttle. When asked later, why they had not launched a single air-to-air missile at the escaping craft, the flight leader replied, "Sir, by the time we were vectored on target, the bogie was already going faster than our missiles can fly."

On board the shuttle, the sky outside the cabin quickly turned from blue to black and the world fell away, turning into a blue and white laced ball. Over the radio, Billy Ray called the ship. "Peggy Sue, this is Shuttle One. All the misplaced Marines have been rounded up and we are returning to the ship. We have no casualties and no one unaccounted for."

"Roger that, Shuttle One. Welcome home."

Chapter 8

Arctic Pack Ice, North Of Svalbard

Bear's band of followers had grown to include several more members since the addition of Tornassuk and Snowflake. Inuksuk, another large male, Imik and Aput, a pair of adolescent males, Aurora, an adult female and Siku an adolescent female. Winter was starting to close in and Bear had a decision to make: he could either call for a shuttle and take the bears he had to the new base on the Moon, or he could keep searching for more recruits. Trouble was, as winter progressed his band would have to disperse to find food. Since they had not sighted another talking bear in days, he decided to make the call.

"OK, my friends. I think we should call for transport to the ship." The bears formed a loose circle in front of Bear, and sat on their haunches.

"So we are finally going to meet this Captain Jack character? I was starting to think you were pulling some kind of joke on us all," said Inuksuk. Grumbling in the ranks was another reason that Bear wanted to wrap things up and get back to the spaceship.

"You'll see," Bear replied. "You will meet the Captain soon enough." He then reached across his chest with his right paw and activated the communicator mounted on the equipment harness he wore. White and nearly invisible against his coat, it held his only way of signaling his human companions. "Peggy Sue, this is Bear, over."

Nothing but silence.

"See, I told you he was putting us on," growled Inuksuk. "It was a good story, but I think he's starting to believe his own seal shit."

"Peggy Sue, Peggy Sue, this is Bear, come in," Bear repeated.

"Bear, this is Peggy Sue. Longtime no contact, Lieutenant."

Around the circle of bears jaws dropped simultaneously. Bear grinned at his little band and said, "Peggy Sue, it's good to hear you as well. Could I please speak to the Captain?"

"Wait one."

113

"What does that mean?" asked Siku. Of all the youngsters she was the most inquisitive. "It means that they have to find the Captain and tell him he has a call," Bear told her. "The Captain is a very busy man and doesn't just sit around waiting for someone to call, even me."

"Bear, this is the Captain. It's good to hear from you old friend."

"You too, Captain. I've got a gang of curious polar bears down hear anxious to meet Captain Jack. I was wondering if you could pick us up in a shuttle?"

"That's great, Lieutenant. How many and how big?"

"Two other males about my size, three adult females about half that size and four adolescents of similar size or smaller. I think we can all fit in one of the large shuttles with the seats stowed."

"Roger that. We'll be planetside in around three hours. See you then."

"Aye, Captain. We'll be waiting."

Peggy Sue, High Earth Orbit

The Captain stepped onto the bridge from his sea cabin and announced, "It looks like Lieutenant Bear has rounded up some new ursine recruits for us. Mr. Lewis, you've been asking for more shuttle time, ready the large shuttle and stow all of the seating. There are ten bears of varying size waiting for us on the Arctic pack ice."

"Aye aye, Sir," Lt. Lewis responded and immediately headed aft to make preparations.

"Mr. Vincent, you have the Conn. Please notify Lcdr. Curtis that I will be away from the ship for around eight hours."

"Aye Sir, I have the Conn."

* * * * *

Before leaving the ship, the Captain dropped by sickbay to tell Ludmilla he was going planetside. Not that a ship's captain normally informs his doctor of his movements, but his relationship with

Ludmilla was far from normal. As he entered the medical section he saw her talking to another man. It took the Captain a minute to identify him as the new veterinarian. "Good afternoon, Doctors," he said.

"Good afternoon, Captain," replied Ludmilla. "Have you meet Dr. Gene Hofstadter yet?"

"Only briefly during the welcome aboard party, I'm afraid. How do you do, Doctor?" Jack said, shaking hands. He seemed like a pleasant enough fellow, medium height with regular features, not someone who would stand out in a crowd.

"How are you, Captain?" the man responded.

"Dr. Hofstadter was just complaining to me about his lack of patients," Ludmilla informed the Captain with a mischievous smile. "I think he is beginning to doubt that we have need of his services on board."

"Really?" Jack responded. "Well today is your lucky day, Doctor. I was just about to make a run to the Arctic to pick up a load of polar bears. Grab your kit and let's go."

"Really?"

"Doctor, I never joke about polar bears," Jack replied solemnly.

Arctic Pack Ice, North Of Svalbard

Bear's party continued to ramble north, simply because polar bears are too enterprising to simply set on their butts for three hours. In retrospect, it might have been better if they had just lounged about where they were when Bear made the call to the Captain. They were cresting a pressure ridge when Tornassuk jerked and tumbled over the other side. A few seconds later the crack of a high-powered rifle was heard.

"Hunters!" Bear growled. "Everyone back behind the ridge."

"What about Tornassuk!" cried Snowflake. They were not mates but they had developed a friendship over the summer. She moved toward the crest of the ridge and Bear knocked her backward. She snarled at him in response.

"Stay down, damn it! Poking your hide up over the ridge won't help Tornassuk, but it might get you shot as well. Everybody just sit tight for a minute." Bear climbed down from the side of the ridge and loped back the direction they had come from for about 40 meters. Then he belly crawled part way up the ridge until he could glimpse over the top. He ducked back, slid down the side and ran back to the party of agitated bears.

"There are a couple of great white hunters out there with Inuit guides and dog sleds. Just our luck the bastards were down wind."

"That had better not be your buddy, the Captain, out there," growled Inuksuk, menacingly.

"Back off," Bear snarled. "Jack's not here yet but he's on his way." Activating his radio he called, "Shuttle, this is Bear. We have an emergency down here. There is an armed party due east of our current position and we are under fire." *The shuttle is probably in reentry comm blackout*, Bear thought, *but how do I explain that to these bears?*

* * * * *

The shuttle was just emerging from the plasma cocoon created by its entry into the atmosphere. In a few minutes Lt. Lewis would be able to acquire the signal from Bear's comm unit and vector to his location. The Captain was in the co-pilot's seat and Dr. Hofstadter was in the cockpit jump seat, since there was no seating to be had in the passenger's area.

"And we are just supposed to walk up to these polar bears, unarmed?" the doctor asked nervously. He was an experienced large animal vet and had done work at a big city zoo, but the thought of facing a large number of bears in the wild made him more than a little nervous.

"Don't worry, Doctor. These bears are not the same as your average polar bear. If you are polite, and the bears are not hungry, things will go just fine." Jack knew he shouldn't be messing with the Doctor's head, but things had gotten so boring since the rescues this was the most fun he'd had in a week.

The shuttle radio crackled to life: "...is Bear. We have an emergency down here ... armed party due east of our current position and we are under fire."

"What the hell?" Jack exclaimed. "Mr. Lewis, we need to locate the shore party. Now!"

"Yes, Sir. I've got the location," Nigel replied. "We will be on station in less than five minutes."

* * * * *

Bear was facing a growing mutiny. The females wanted to just scatter while Inuksuk and the adolescent males wanted to charge the hunters. "Listen to me! There are at least two hunters with rifles and as many guides. You charge the humans and none of you will live to sink a fang into them."

"At least let the youngsters get away," pleaded Snowflake.

"And how do we find them after the Captain gets here? Just stay put a few more minutes." *Come on, Jack! I really could use some help down here.*

"Lt. Bear, this is the Shuttle," Bear's communicator announced. "We have you in sight and will move to neutralize your attackers. Stay under cover until we signal all clear."

"See! I told you help was on the way," said a very relieved Bear, *if I do this again I'm gonna be armed.* Moments later a large, blunt arrowhead passed low over their hiding place behind the ridge.

Bear and the rest of the group scampered to the top of the ridge in time to see the shuttle's repulsors raise a veritable blizzard that enveloped the hunting party. Though visibility in the vicinity of the hunters was close to zero, it soon became apparent that the two dogsleds and their riders were mushing for all they were worth toward the southeast.

The shuttle shifted position, coming closer to the bears while keeping its bulk between them and the fleeing hunters. The blowing snow cleared as the massive craft settled onto its landing struts and its rear ramp lowered. Two humans in parkas emerged from the opening, one carrying what looked like a black gym bag.

Snowflake and Aurora were both whimpering and nudging the crumpled shape of Tornassuk. Red blood stained his white pelt and the surrounding snow. As the humans came running up, Inuksuk rose on his hind legs and roared. The smaller human clutched the bag to his chest and stopped running, the taller continued forward. In a

117

loud voice he yelled at Inuksuk, "If you want your friend to have a chance of living, stand down."

Inuksuk was taken aback. He had never had a human bark orders at him when he was in full threat posture. The human continued: "This man is a doctor and we do not have time for this macho crap. So what's it going to be? An inter-species pissing contest or can we try and save your wounded friend?"

The flummoxed bear sank slowly back down to a four legged stance. "Hurry, Jack," Bear cried, "He's losing a lot of blood." Jack turned to the other human and said, "come on, Doctor, you have a patient to save. Move your ass man!"

The same tone of command that had deflated Inuksuk broke Dr. Hofstadter's paralysis. He hurried forward and kneeled down by the wounded bear. "He's still breathing," the vet called out. "He has a chest wound, probably a collapsed lung, but I don't think any other major organs have been hit." *Otherwise he would be dead already*, Gene added silently, not wishing to upset the other bears. He turned to Jack and said, "We need to get him on board the shuttle. I can try to stabilize him on the flight back to the ship."

"Right," Jack spoke into his comm pip, secured inside his hood flap. "Mr. Lewis, I need you to break out a stretcher and bring it to us. Now, Mr. Lewis."

"Captain, how are we going to carry him on a stretcher, he must weigh 1300 lbs?" asked the veterinarian, now totally absorbed in trying to save his patient.

"Don't worry, Doctor. The stretcher has gravitonic lifts. All we have to do is get him on it. The other bears can help with that." Lt. Lewis arrived with the floating stretcher and lowered it to the ground along side the wounded Tornassuk. Then, with help from Bear and Aurora, the humans loaded the stricken bear. Dr. Hofstadter and Lt. Lewis headed for the shuttle ramp with their burden, closely followed by the fretful Snowflake.

Jack turned and addressed the remaining bears. "All right. This was not the type of first meeting I was hoping for. Given your comrade's condition we don't have time for long introductions so I will just say that my name is Captain Jack Sutton, and I am the master of the starship Peggy Sue. I would like you all to join us for reasons already explained by Bear, but we have no time to discuss matters. If you wish to come, please board the shuttle now."

The bears stared at the self-assured human standing in their midst and then at the shuttle, then at Bear. "What are we waiting for?" Bear asked, and headed for the ramp. The other bears quickly followed, with the Captain bringing up the rear.

Sickbay, Peggy Sue

As soon as the shuttle docked, Dr. Hofstadter hustled the stricken Tornassuk down the gangway and to the ship's sickbay, assisted by waiting crew members. Following close behind came Snowflake, padding down the strange halls and corridors of the spaceship with no idea where they were headed. Dr. Tropsha was waiting for them at the door of the medical section. "Come, bring the patient into the first OR. We are set up and ready to go."

"Right," Hofstadter acknowledged. "In there men, quickly. Giselle, start a saline drip and draw a sample for blood type matching." The OR nurse, Giselle Bollard, was frozen in position, staring at the massive polar bear on the stretcher, the white fur of his chest stained reddish brown by drying blood. "Now Nurse!" shouted Dr. Hofstadter, prodding Giselle into action. The OR door slid shut.

Snowflake tried to follow the stretcher bearers into the operating room, only to be stopped by Ludmilla. "And where do you think you are going, young lady?" the ship's head doctor asked, reacting to the situation and not considering that she was putting herself in the path of a strange 250 kg bear.

"My friend is in there!" Snowflake said, and moved to push past the doctor. Ludmilla put a hand lightly against Snowflake's chest and said, "If you want to help your friend, you need to let the doctors work. The operating theater is crowded as it is and you would present a large distraction."

"But I want to help!" the anguished polar bear whined, turning her head to look directly in the human's eyes.

"I know you do," Ludmilla said, sympathetically. "The best thing you can do is sit down against the reception area wall and wait. I

promise that I will keep you informed of your friend's condition."
Ludmilla's thoughts raced. *I had best get Bear to come up here and keep her calm, if she gets violent the result will not be pretty.*

Reefer #2, Peggy Sue

In the aft of the ship there were two large walk-in refrigerator units, labeled reefer #1 and #2. Reefer #2 had effectively been converted into quarters for Lt. Bear during the last trip. Since there were no other onboard areas kept at temperatures comfortable to polar bears, this was where the rest of the bear party ended up. The Captain followed the bears into the reefer, again donning the parka he wore on the pack ice. "If I might have your attention for a minute," he began.

"Where are Tornassuk and Snowflake?" asked one of the adolescents, his query echoed by several others.

"Please!" the Captain snapped. "I will answer all your questions but that cannot be done if you are all shouting at once." Before now, Jack had not appreciated just how undisciplined a group of wild bears could be. On the trip to the ship they had been distracted by the view outside the shuttle, but eight bears were definitely a crowd in the reefer's limited space. "Tornassuk is in sickbay and his wound is being treated by the medical staff. Evidently Snowflake is also there, waiting for him."

"Will he live?" asked Siku.

I truly hope so, Jack said to himself, *I really don't want a polar bear riot on board my ship.* Out loud, he replied, "I will not lie to you, his wound is a serious one. Dr. Hofstadter and the rest of the medical staff will do their best to save him." The bears all began talking among themselves as a message came over the Captain's comm pip—Ludmilla calling to ask for help keeping Snowflake calm.

"Lt. Bear, Dr. Tropsha just called and asked for your help with Snowflake," jack yelled over the rising din.

"Right, and whose going to keep this lot calm?" Bear asked, jerking his head toward the crowd of arguing white bears.

Isbjørn, sitting on the floor next to Bear looked first at her mate and then the Captain and huffed, "Males! I'll go and take care of Snowflake. See if you can find something to keep the others occupied while we're waiting on Tornassuk."

Isbjørn stood up and walked to the door. At the door she hesitated, then called back over her shoulder. "Uh, Captain? Could you tell me where I need to go?"

Bear looked at Jack as if to say, *I'm not touching that line.* The Captain replied, "I'll do better than that." He walked over and opened the door. He then used his pip to call Melissa Hamilton, the ship's horticulturist. "Miss Hamilton, could you come to Lt. Bear's quarters? I need someone to show one of the new bears to sickbay."

A few minutes later, Melissa arrived, introductions made and Isbjørn was guided on her way. With that problem in hand it was time to tackle the larger group of arguing ursines. The Captain made his way to the reefer's forward bulkhead. Turning on the large video screen mounted there, he tapped a few commands on the screen and brought up a video of two open hover-sleds crossing a jumbled gray and black landscape—it was video of the expedition to the cavern beneath crater Giordano Bruno.

Attracted by movement, as predators are, the room full of bears was soon sitting attentively watching the video. As the small group of spacesuit clad humans and one large bear dismounted and moved into a dark opening in the lunar surface, Jack spoke to the now quiet polar bears: "This is video taken of our first encounter with aliens. This was recorded on the Moon last spring. I thought you might wish to see what we are facing."

"Is that really the Moon?" asked Umky.

"Yes, indeed," Jack replied. "That is where we are headed, thought not to the same location. I'll let Lt. Bear do the narration, since he was a participant in the battle..."

Sickbay, Peggy Sue

Melissa took Isbjørn forward through the cargo hold and onto the large lift to the mid-deck. "So you're Bear's mate?" she asked in her soft southern accent. She and Bear had become close friends since they both spent most of their time in the aft regions of the ship.

"Yes, Umky is Bear's cub," she replied. "He's three now, ready to go off on his own." *I wonder if that is why I was so happy to see Bear again? Do I want more cubs with him?*

"Well, he seems like a really good guy. He's always been nice to me. He even rescued me from a bad Russian we had on board."

"He's always been brave, maybe to a fault. How did Bear get to be a lieutenant? I still don't understand how that came about."

"Evidently the Captain went to the Arctic and found him. He and Bear got to talking and Bear signed on. The Captain can be a real smooth talker, you know. Anyway, they've been friends ever since."

Yes, that spring in Svalbard Bear said something about working with humans. I thought he was joking, but he must have already met this Captain Jack by then. Before Isbjørn could think of something appropriate to say Melissa announced: "Here we are! This is the Sickbay. Dr. Tropsha is in charge of the medical section, she's really nice when you get to know her," then in a confidential tone Melissa added, "she and the Captain are like you and Bear."

"They've had cubs together?" Isbjørn asked.

"Not yet, but they're a couple. Anyway, I just thought you should know that before you met her."

The woman and bear entered the sickbay reception area to find a fretful Snowflake pacing back and forth. "Oh Isbjørn! I'm glad you're here. The Russian woman won't let me see Tornassuk," Snowflake whined.

"Now dear. Just calm down and take some deep breaths. That woman is a medical doctor, a healer. You need to let her and the other humans help him."

Hearing new voices in the reception area, Ludmilla went to see what was happening in her sickbay now. "Hello, Melissa," the Russian doctor said. "I see you have brought me another polar bear, is this one wounded or just visiting?"

"Hey, Dr. Tropsha. This here is Isbjørn, Bear's mate," Melissa replied, either missing or ignoring the sarcastic edge to Ludmilla's question. "She's come up to keep Snowflake company while y'all fix Tornassuk."

As Ludmilla was absorbing that information, Dr. Hofstadter stuck his head around the corner and asked, "Dr. Tropsha, do we have any whole blood? The serum we had in stock is almost depleted and we really need to get some whole blood into the patient."

"Polar bear blood? No, just the serum. Have bears been transfused before?" Ludmilla asked the veterinarian.

"Yes, I have read about a few cases. But he's tachycardic and we are going to need to get blood in him ASAP. I have no idea how many blood types polar bears have. We'll just have to take samples and test for compatibility. I also suspect significant hemothorax is contributing to respiratory distress and hemorrhagic shock. I've already called for Dr. Carmichael."

"Set a chest tube and have Giselle established two large-bore antecubital IV lines for blood transfusion," Ludmilla said, then addressing the two bears. "OK, ladies, you have arrived at an opportune moment—your friend needs blood. I'm going to get a couple of syringes and take samples from each of you."

"He wants blood? He's hungry?" Snowflake asked, totally confused.

"No," replied Dr. Tropsha, returning from the next room. "Your friend suffered a gunshot wound to the chest, which caused traumatic pneumothorax—a collapsed lung—and a great deal of blood loss. Dr. Hofstadter was able to close the chest wall defect but the blood loss has made him shocky and X-rays show blood in the pleural space. We are draining his chest, but we need to take blood from you and pump it into him to replace his loses."

"You can do that?" marveled Isbjørn. "You can have some of my blood, if it will help."

"Mine too," chimed in Snowflake.

"It's not that simple, first we need to check to make sure your blood is compatible, otherwise we might do more harm than good." As she spoke, Ludmilla took the blood samples and again hustled from the room. The two bears looked at each other with worried faces.

Captain's Quarters, Peggy Sue, Four Hours Later

Jack was sitting at the desk in his quarters, running over the endless lists of material needed to finish making Farside Base operational. The base was being constructed beneath an ancient volcanic dome near the Copernicus Crater, in what geologists call the Sulpicius Gallus formation. The location was on the farside of the Moon, shielded from prying Earth-bound eyes. An earlier ground penetrating radar survey located a number of large voids in the area, 1.6 billion year old drained lava pockets that provided a good starting place for building a shipyard and research facility.

The cabin door opened and Ludmilla came in, looking haggard and drawn. Jack went to her and held her in his arms. "You look like you had a rough day, Luda," he said. She wrapped her arms around his back and hugged him. "Yes, my Captain, it was a very rough day," she said, resting her head on his chest.

"Dare I ask how your patient is?" he asked with trepidation.

"He is alive, not totally out of danger yet, but alive," Ludmilla replied. "Thankfully, the whole medical department pulled together as a team. I did think we might have to revive Dr. Carmichael. When he burst into the OR and found polar bears everywhere he almost passed out."

"You told him about the bears before this, right?"

"Yes, but being told that there would be talking bears on the ship does not truly prepare one for that first encounter," she said with a tired smile. "Particularly when you are rushing into the medical section to work on a chest wound. Dr. Hofstadter neglected to tell him that the chest in question was covered with thick white hair. He did recover quickly though."

"And you got the bear—Tornassuk?—patched up?"

"Oh yes, we found the bullet—it barely missed the heart and lodged in his ribcage after passing through the chest cavity. There were bleeders everywhere. Richard, Dr. Carmichael, really is a gifted surgeon. If it had only been Gene and myself we may well have lost the patient. As it is, he has a better than even chance of pulling through."

"Would you like a drink?" he inquired. He had been holding off on an evening cocktail until Ludmilla arrived.

"A hot shower first, and then I will have several," she replied, reluctantly pulling away from his embrace. "Then maybe we can think of other activities to relieve stress," she added with a sly smile.

"I'll have the steward bring an iced pitcher of martinis." Ludmilla headed for the shower and Jack called the lounge on the upper deck. Normally, alcohol was restricted to the lounge and the chief's and enlisted dayrooms, but rank had its privileges.

Yuki, the Marines and Bear are back, the Chief is out of sick bay, the ursine recruits are bedded down, and the wounded bear is still alive. Tomorrow morning we dock at Farside Base, but before then the woman I love is about to emerge from the shower, thirsty and horny, Jack said to himself. *Life just doesn't get any better than this.*

Part Two

A Star To Steer Her By

Chapter 9

Rogue Planet, Interstellar Space

In the interstellar void between Beta Comae and a red dwarf known to humans as Ross 1015, a dark world five times a massive as Jupiter followed its own lonely path around the Galaxy. A dark imitation of a stellar system, the rogue planet possessed its own swarm of orbiting satellites. Half a dozen of those sizable moons were inhabited by creatures as intelligent as humans, perhaps more so.

These creatures reveled in the darkness, on worlds barely lit by faint star light. Possessing no eyes, they found their way using sound, vibrations through the ground beneath their jumble of short straw-like legs and the thick atmosphere around them. They never saw the carbon dioxide icebergs floating on seas of liquid nitrogen, or the occasional, spectacular cryovolcanic eruptions that sent plumes of methane, ammonia and other gases into surrounding space, renewing the moons' atmospheres.

Warmed tepidly by tidal stress and radioactive decay deep within their worlds, the creatures could only live at temperatures that would freeze Earth life solid. The low temperatures also slowed the rate of chemical reactions, making the pace of life on these dark worlds sluggish and deliberate. But that was fine with the creatures, their lives were long and contemplative—perhaps that was why they hated warm life, with its ephemeral lifespans and frenetic existence.

Ranging in height from one to two meters, their bodies were disc shaped hollow sacks, normally indented on either side. At the front of the sack was a vertical opening, fringed with long hair-like tentacles, a visage that could only in charity be called a face. The closest parallel among Earthly life was the trap sack of certain microscopic carnivorous plants commonly known as bladderwarts. Only these "plants" could move slowly about on the short legs that sprouted from their bases like bristles from a brush. Communication was accomplished using small vibrating membranes on either side of the mouth opening, conversation that would sound like random buzzing and humming to human ears.

A minor functionary was slowly approaching an elder of the race, its mission to deliver some disagreeable news. A probe ship had reported back from a star system only a third of a parsec away, bringing news of a new outbreak of warm life. A response was required but that needed the sanction of a more senior official. Carefully advancing from directly in front of the larger creature, the functionary spoke: "A thousand pardons, Significant One. I bring disquieting news from the warm worlds."

"Speak, what is so important that you disturb my thoughts?"

"A probe ship has reported the presence of warm life in a nearby system, zxxwz987."

"That system was cleansed a milli-cycle ago, new sentient life could not have arisen so quickly."

"The warm creatures came from a different system, Significant One, in a ship of powerful design. Several probes and a refueling station were destroyed."

"This is an outrage! Where do these vermin come from? We must find their home world and sterilize it."

"Yes, Significant One. From the departure vector it would appear that the creatures came from qwyyq106. A multi-planet system 10 parsecs from zxxwz987."

"Is there a record of life from this system?" As the Significant One was speaking a frilly, undulating worm-like creature floated by and brushed against its mouth tentacles. This triggered an automatic response: the dimpled sides of the larger creature's feeding sack popped out, creating a sudden vacuum at its mouth opening. Faster than eyes could follow, the frilly creature disappeared into the Significant One's digestive chamber. Neither participant in the conversation took note of this activity.

"I consulted the archives. A little more than a quarter cycle ago, a cleansing mission was sent to the system. It reported infections on both the third and fourth planets. The fourth planet was cleansed and a large asteroid was impacted on the third to disrupt development." The dark ones marked the passage of time in cycles, the time it took for their system to complete an orbit of the galaxy, around 240 million Earth years.

"Incompetent fools! Both should have been sterilized. The client race that performed the action must be punished!"

"Begging your forgiveness, Significant One, but the client race that was used has since been exterminated. Evidently their incompetence was notice by others."

"Send a mission to qwyyq106 and verify that this is where the offending ship originated. It may have been just an intermediate stop. Regardless, if warm life infests the system the affected planets are to be cleansed."

"Yes, Significant One." The functionary began backing away as the older official returned to its meditations. *That did not go too badly*, the functionary thought, *If I can successfully direct the eradication of these new warm vermin my status will be suitably enhanced*. Anticipating its coming triumph, the functionary crept away with almost unseemly haste.

Farside Base, The Moon

The Peggy Sue sat at the bottom of a large crevasse, a jagged slit carved into the top of the ancient volcanic dome that housed Farside Base. Overhead, massive doors closed off the space within from the void. Their primary purpose was to allow an atmosphere to surround the docked spaceship, making the planned overhaul and modifications easier. But in addition, the doors' outer surfaces were artistically crafted to hide the existence of the base below.

Standing on the cavern floor next to the curving silver side of the Peggy Sue, Captain Jack, Rajiv Gupta and Jo Jo Medina were discussing the intended changes to the ship. "So you see, we will be lengthening the hull by the insertion of three extension sections: fore, aft, and center," Chief Engineer Medina explained. "The center extension is the largest, being 12 meters long. The fore and aft extensions, which are at the junctions where the hull tapper begins, are 4 meters each. Overall we will add 20 meters to the ship's length."

"What will the added space be used for?" asked Dr. Gupta.

"Most of the center extension will be used to house magazines and launchers for the new gravitonic missiles. The forward and aft extensions will create some additional room for engineering and crew space, though the main reason for those additions is to alter the curvature of the hull. The midsection of the ship is being expanded to 14 meters in diameter, most of which will be used to house upgraded shielding and weapons systems."

"And what do those upgrades buy us, Mr. Medina?" the Captain inquired. Improved shielding was his primary request after the close escape from Beta Comae, that and the addition of some smaller weapons suitable for repelling boarders or supporting a retuning shore party.

"The new shields are both more efficient and more capable, roughly three times as powerful. The X-ray laser batteries have also doubled in power and there will be eight new 15mm rail guns to provide close in fire support."

The Captain nodded approvingly. "And what about shuttle docking? We have been playing musical airlocks for months now." The ship's original configuration supported only two docked shuttles at a time.

"We are going to move the existing pair of docking ports forward and add a second pair aft. This will give us the capability to carry four shuttles in all—two pinnaces and two larger shuttles. The large shuttles will be the new combat rated models, intended for troop transport." Though the existing large shuttles were tough and capable vehicles, they were not designed to carry Marines wearing battle armor. Neither did they mount any external weapons to support insertion or extraction missions. The new military shuttles fixed those problems based on advice from the ship's growing ground combat contingent.

"With all these additions dead weight has to go up significantly, is the Peggy Sue going to lose a few Gs acceleration on the top end?"

This time is was Rajiv who answered, since the ship's new reactor and drives were his designs. "The total mass of the ship will rise to around 8,000 metric tons, but the improved drives and power reactor will more than compensate, Captain. Given 500 GW peak power generation I have calculated that full ahead acceleration should be 38 Gs with flank power pulling just over 40."

"Excellent!" Jack said. "More armor, more weapons and faster to boot. I can't wait to take her on a shakedown cruise. It took nearly five years to build her, how long will the overhaul take?"

"We were just feeling our way back then, Captain, inventing the technology needed to build such a ship. All that is now well in hand and, with the auto-fabricators and nanites working at full tilt, she should be ready in about 10 weeks," Jo Jo replied. He was going to be a very busy man for the next couple of months.

At least Jo Jo did not have to worry about the new small interceptor ships that were beginning construction elsewhere in the cavernous dock. Those compact craft, dubbed corvettes by the design team, would carry a crew of six and be able to accelerate at nearly 100 Gs for brief sprints. Not intended for long voyages, they mounted a single rail gun and could carry ten of the new gravitonic missiles—some of the navy types were already calling the missiles torpedoes and the vessels PT boats.

"Very good, gentlemen. I'll leave you to your labors." Jack said to the two men. "Later today I hope to find out where our next mission will take us."

Dock Observation Area, Farside Base

Jean-Jacques de Belcour was standing in the observation area that overlooked the cavernous dock where the Peggy Sue currently rested. Cut into the shear side of the dock wall, the observation area was fronted by a large rectangular expanse of transparent material, the same transparent material that was used in the viewing ports on the Peggy Sue. Optically clear and stronger than steel, the 15 by 4 meter transparent wall, located 18 meters above the floor of the dock, provided a panoramic view of the entire dock area. It also allowed the dock to be depressurized without disrupting control operations.

How arrogant these space pirates are, thought Jean-Jacques contemptuously, observing the Captain and his engineers on the dock floor below. After his abduction, Jean-Jacques had been kept on board the Peggy Sue for more than a month as "a guest of the Captain." Like the protagonist in a Jules Vern novel, taken captive by the central villain, he was left free to wander the ship and

133

converse with the crew. But that proved an unprofitable pursuit. Most of the crew were ex-military and all held the UN in low esteem. Also, there was not a Francophile among them. Having not made a single friend, de Belcour welcomed the news that he was to move into new quarters on the partially constructed Moon base.

Arriving at the base a month ago, he was assigned an apartment, given a brief orientation tour and then left to his own devices. Intellectually, he could understand his captors' reasoning: he was stuck in a base on the farside of the Moon, carved out of the silicate rock of an ancient volcano. Outside the base there was nothing but vacuum, unfiltered radiation from the Sun and temperatures that ranged from more than 100°C during the day down to -150°C by the end of the long lunar night.

The fact was, there was no escape. Even if he could somehow steal a spacesuit, there was no place to run to outside the base. Getting back to Earth would require a spacecraft, and though he helped set UN global space policy, he hadn't the first clue about operating one of the ships used by these cosmic buccaneers. Still, it galled him to be ignored by his captors. It implied that he was both helpless and inconsequential. Sadly, Jean-Jacques had just about decided that was the case.

As he was standing in front of the huge picture window, overlooking the ship resting in the dock below, a voice behind him asked, "It is a marvelous thing, is it not M. de Belcour?"

It took Jean-Jacques a few seconds to realize that the voice, a woman's voice, had spoken in French. He turned to reply and saw Lucrezia Piscopia and an oriental woman. "*Bonjour*, Dr. Piscopia," he replied in his native tongue. "I would count it a marvelous thing if it were not under the control of brigands and madmen."

Dr. Piscopia made a tisking sound and said, "You know, more people would talk to you if you were not so aggressively disagreeable, Jean-Jacques." To which the Frenchman replied with a Gallic shrug. Switching to English, Elena motioned to her companion and said, "Might I introduce Dr. Li Wie-chang? Doctor, this is M. Jean-Jacques de Belcour of the UNOOSA."

Dr. Li Wie-chang, a Chinese botanist and synthetic biologist, and Dr. Eric Fetzer, a noted geologist formerly with NASA, had just made the trip from Earth to join the science team. She ran into

Elena in the lunch room and the Italian astronomer offered to show her around. "I am pleased to meet you M. de Belcour," Dr. Li said in accent-less American English.

"Charmed, Dr. Li. You must call me Jean-Jacques. It seems that most everyone around here is quite informal, everyone except the Captain and his officers that is." *She is quite attractive for a femme chinoise,* he thought, *short, well built but not stocky like a peasant.*

"Please call me Sally," replied the woman, smiling. "I take it that you don't particularly like our commanding officer?"

"I have seen his crew slaughter UN troops and been kidnapped and taken to the Moon by the man. He is far from being my friend," Jean-Jacques spat. "Tell me, how did they entice you to join them in this illegal enterprise?"

Dr. Li laughed and looked at Elena. "You warned me, Elena."

"Warned you about what?" Jean-Jacques demanded, feeling that he had just been made the butt of a private joke.

"That you were so blinded by your own opinions and dislike for the Captain that you alienate everyone who approaches you," Elena replied.

"You really don't care why I joined the expedition," Dr. Li added bluntly, "If I tell you that I am convinced this is the most important thing in the history of humankind will you say that I am also insane or a criminal?"

"Madam, you have not been held incommunicado for more than two months!" he sputtered, red faced.

"Incommunicado? Really?" the Chinese Botanist asked in a puzzled voice. "Have you tried making a call to Earth from your room? The computer built into my apartment's desk has video chat software that can access the Internet. I have called several colleagues in China and around the world since I've been here."

Jean-Jacques was stunned. He had assumed that he was not allowed to communicate with Earth. Then he realized that every time he had seen the Captain, he always demanded that he be returned to Earth—a request the Captain always flatly denied. He had asked to communicate with his superiors while on board the

135

ship but that was also denied. The Captain would only agree to notify the UN of his whereabouts, which later news broadcasts seem to verify. But Jean-Jacques never asked permission to call his superiors since being transferred to the base.

"You see, Jean-Jacques? Things are not as bad as you make them out to be," Elena said to the gobsmacked UN official. "The Captain said you are allowed access to all non-hazardous areas of the base, and that you are welcome to attend our planing meetings —as long as you do not disrupt the proceedings."

"But why?"

"Because the Captain wishes to convince you he is right," Elena said with a smile, "and he thinks that the facts will speak for themselves."

Without saying another word, not even adieu, Jean-Jacques hurried off. *Back to his quarters to try and call Earth, undoubtedly,* Sally thought, shaking her head as the Frenchman departed. "Bureaucrats everywhere think the same way, if something is not explicitly permitted it is forbidden. When I went to graduate school in America I found out that Americans think the opposite—if it is not explicitly forbidden then it is permitted."

"From my experience, even when something is forbidden, if the rules do not make sense to them, Americans do whatever they please," Elena added, "particularly Texans."

"I agree," Sally concurred. "Working with these people is both liberating and frightening."

"Come, we must not be late for the planning meeting."

Polar Bear Quarters, Farside Base

In a service tunnel outside the polar bear habitat four men guided a large metal crate toward a side entrance. Thumping and low moaning sounds emanated from the crate, and occasionally the hover cart that supported it shuddered. "Damn it, hurry up," said Bud Jones, "I think our cargo is waking up."

"That's alright," replied Joey Sanchez, "It will make getting him out of the crate a lot easier." The other two members of the group were Steve Hitch and Phil Kowalski. While the ship's officers would be happy at the display of inter-service cooperation—two SEALs, a sailor and a Marine working together voluntarily—the nature of their enterprise would not have been so readily condoned.

As they positioned the crate in front of the service door, Hitch called out, "Open the door, Joey, this sucker is starting to rock the sled." Sanchez moved to the panel beside the door and pushed the open button. The door mechanism automatically recognized his comm pip's code, identifying him as a Marine. Because the Marines were charged with base security they had access to most every part of the complex, including the maintenance tunnels and entrances.

The door slid open and the men quickly pushed the bulky crate through the entrance. They barely cleared the doorway when it started shaking violently from side to side. "Bud, Joey, open the damn crate and I'll drop the front end," shouted Hitch, who was controlling the hover cart from the rear.

Around the stark white enclosure, heads popped up, as white as the ice and snow that covered the floor and simulated terrain. From long graceful necks, sets of dark eyes, each flanking a black nose, zeroed in on the surreptitious work party and their crate. Rising like ghosts from the sea of white, two of the largest bears headed unhurriedly toward the humans.

"Which one of you is Tornassuk?" called Bud.

"That would be me, human," answered the lead bear, a huge male as big as Lt. Bear. "Why?"

"We got a present for you, courtesy of the Peggy Sue's crew." Jones and Sanchez opened the doors of the crate to reveal something dark and moving inside. Hitch dropped the front end of the hover cart and a large pinkish-brown mass slid out with a bellow of protest. The male walrus pulled itself from the crate using its tusks and flippers, and advanced two shuffling strides. Then it saw the polar bears.

With a loud bugling roar, the walrus galumphed for all he was worth toward the perceived safety of open water. Unfortunately for the walrus, the water in question belonged to the polar bears' swimming pool. As the other bears quickly moved to cut off its escape, Tornassuk glanced back at the humans and said, "thanks, I owe you primates one."

With that he charged after the 1,500kg mammal and leapt onto its back. As the noise of the struggle rose to a crescendo, the four humans wrestled the crate back into the service tunnel and closed the door. "Carajo," said Joey, "and I thought watching you guys eat was frightening."

"You said it brother," answered Phil with conviction. "Come on, we gotta get this back to the shuttle dock before it's missed. And we gotta hose it out too, there's walrus shit all over the inside."

Main Lobby Atrium, Farside Base

Dr. Piscopia and Dr. Li exited the observation room and made their way to the interior of the still growing base. Initially, all that was here was the deep crack that had been transformed into the dock area. When the first construction crew was landed by the Peggy Sue several months ago, they began by setting up a drilling laser. Powered by the ship's reactor, it sliced through the lunar rock like a knife through soft cheese. After smoothing out the cavern floor the drill was aimed downward, boring a hole ten meters in diameter and a kilometer deep into the volcanic rock.

Into that hole went several large pieces of equipment, transferred from the cargo hold of the Peggy Sue. In a chamber at the bottom of the shaft, a muon catalyzed fusion power plant was assembled. Essentially a clone of the reactor that powered the ship, the buried plant was capable of continuously producing over 100 gigawatts of electrical power, enough to power a city of more than forty million people. Once the base reactor came on line, the ship was free to return to Earth orbit and gather more equipment for transport.

The next freight run delivered a hold full of robotic mining equipment. The mining machines had been used to excavate the complex beneath Parker's Station, but they had been designed from the beginning to work in a vacuum—TK always planned two steps ahead and he hated wasting money. Several large voids, the empty remains of ancient lava tubes, were soon located and breached by the robotic equipment. The interior chambers were linked and sealed, making them ready to receive more equipment from Earth.

Airlocks were added, dividing the installation into a dozen air tight zones. A lava tube that ventured close to the lunar surface was opened to airless space and turned into an airlock capable of accepting the large shuttles. At this point the shuttles began making trips directly from Earth to the Moon base.

Ferried up from Parker's Station by the shuttles, a steady stream of equipment, raw material and people made the day long trip from Earth to its Moon. Shuttle #3 in particular was built to haul outsized freight, with large clam-shell doors similar to the ones on the now defunct American Space Shuttle.

In the shuttles' holds came cryogenic bladders containing liquid nitrogen and liquid oxygen. Each shuttle trip brought 120 cubic meters of liquid and, since the net expansion for liquid nitrogen into gas is 645 times the original volume when heated to room temperature, a workable atmosphere was soon established inside the rapidly expanding base. Liquid oxygen is even denser at roughly $1/1000^{th}$ its gaseous volume, but only a single load of LOX was needed for three of liquid nitrogen to build an Earth-like atmosphere.

More robots began running pipes to carry air and liquids, extruding the piping as they moved around and among the chambers. Flooring was quickly followed by walls and ceilings with artificial lighting. Though mostly constructed of native rock and prefabricated metal, paneling covered with thin wood veneer was installed in many areas to help soften the cold, inorganic ambiance. In the main chamber, with its vaulted 50 meter high ceiling, large terraced planters were installed and filled with soil brought from Earth. Palm trees and other decorative greenery were planted next to a 20 meter water fall that provided both soothing background noise and helped to humidify the air.

Water for the plants in the lobby, and the large aquaculture ponds elsewhere within the base, was harvested from the Moon itself. Using purpose built spacecraft, assembled on site, mining teams were sent to the Moon's nearby north pole region. There, in the perpetually dark shadows of a raft of small craters, lay water ice. From prior orbital surveys, NASA estimated there could be 600 million metric tons or more of water ice in the depths of the craters, lying in sheets up to two meters thick. Large blocks of ice were cut and transported to the surface above the base, where warmth from the Sun was used to melt the ice and separate water from grit.

Near the top of the water use list was the pool in the polar bear quarters, since their physical, hygienic and psychological well being were all greatly improved by being able to swim in icy cold water. A load of sea salt was even brought from Earth to give the faux Arctic waters the right taste. Once the drinking water, hydroponic gardens, and aquaculture tanks were filled, plans called for building an Olympic sized swimming pool for the base's human residents.

Elena and Sally crossed the main lobby atrium, its artificial sun shining brightly on the mass of tropical plants. Simulated breezes rustled the foliage and the soothing babble of falling water could be heard through the trees. All the interior decorating seemed an extravagance to Dr. Li and she said so. "This area is quite beautiful but shouldn't more practical things be constructed first? Don't get me wrong, as a botanist I love the sight of green things growing, but I understand that the first hydroponic crops are just now starting to come in. Surely food is more important than a decorative garden, no matter how pretty."

"It is not my area of expertise, but according to some of the psychologists and medical personnel the addition of green plants and natural surroundings improves people's performance and mental health," replied Elena. "And according to Melissa Scott Hamilton, the Peggy Sue's horticulturalist, the crops take time to establish and really could not be made to grow faster. The fish, shrimp and crustaceans in the aquaculture tanks will take even longer."

"No land animals? I like seafood, but without an occasional hamburger I get cranky—another result of attending grad school in the US."

"Evidently the usable food yield from aquaculture is greater than from terrestrial farm animals. Plus, aquatic animals seem to acclimate to the lower gravity more rapidly. I understand that there are plans to raise cattle, pigs and chickens eventually. Until then, occasional shuttle runs will have to supply our carnivorous longings." As they ascended a curving stairway to an elevated terrace a voice spoke: "Warning. You are entering the base administrative area, all offices are kept at full Earth gravity."

"That's another thing," Dr. Li said. "Keeping these areas under heavy gravity must use a lot of power."

"Not as much as you would think, and it is good for our health to remain under Earth gravity as much as possible, at least that is what Ludmilla says. The Marines in particular, need to stay in good physical condition. They might even find themselves having to fight under heavier gravity than Earth's."

"Yes, that makes sense. I am really interested in seeing how the plants in the atrium fair under reduced gravity. After all, plant circulatory systems developed under the same conditions as terrestrial animals."

"You may well get to observed plant development at different evolutionary stages, assuming we find life on other planets," Elena said to her new friend. "That is if life on other worlds is anything like Earth life, and we even find any planets in the systems we visit."

"I thought that you were the expert in finding habitable planets around other stars?" asked Sally.

"Oh, I am as much of an expert as one can be without ever having a chance to actually test one's theories. The Peggy Sue has just changed that forever. That is why I have no choice, I have to go on this mission—it is that or find another field of research."

"In China we have an old saying: be careful what you wish for, you might get it."

"We Italians have the same saying and it is undoubtedly based on long experience," Elena said, smiling. The duo found themselves in front of the double glass doors of the conference room. "Looks like we are here," she said, opening one of the doors, "after you, Dr. Li." *Well*, Elena thought, *this is my chance to either make my reputation or to destroy it.*

Conference Room, Farside Base

After discovering that the Peggy Sue was capable of traveling to other star systems by transiting alter-space, the project team was faced with a significant problem—where to go next? With more than 100 billion stars in the Milky Way galaxy, it was definitely a nontrivial question. Most of the science section, the ship's officers and TK Parker were convened in the large conference room in the base's administrative area. Their task: a first attempt at charting the next voyage of Earth's only working starship.

"I believe you all know why we are here," the Captain began. "While the Peggy Sue is in dry dock for refitting, we have a couple of months to decide on a course of action. Included in that plan must be a list of star systems to be visited when we venture forth to perform a reconnaissance of our stellar neighborhood."

This statement brought murmurs and nods from those assembled. Having set the topic for the meeting, Jack continued. "The process of selecting the destinations for Peggy Sue's next cruise is proving more complicated than I expected. Basically, we are hoping to find life on other worlds. Life that can give us information about the hostile aliens we encountered on the Moon and at Beta Comae. The fundamental question is, where do we look?"

Many of the scientists began to speak at once, but Sally Li won the floor. "That depends on the characteristics of the lifeforms you are looking for, Captain."

"Yes," added Olaf Gunderson, "life in the wider Universe may take on forms much different than the ones we are familiar with. Don't expect aliens to look like people with blue skin or strange protuberances on their foreheads."

"Continue, Dr. Gunderson," Jack prompted.

"All the life we are familiar with is based on a common chemistry: the primary compounds are based on carbon and the universal solvent is water, liquid H_2O. But there are other biochemistries possible, from a strictly chemical perspective. Speculative work on alternative biological systems has been done by Steven Benner, a member of the NASA Astrobiology Institute and a founder of several research institutions. The Benner group worked to identify "bio-signatures", molecular structures likely to be universal features of living systems whether Earth-like or "weird" life forms."

"That's right," added Sally. "And in the late 1980s, the astrobiological committee chaired by John Baross also investigated ways to generate molecules that reproduce the complex behavior of living systems using chemical synthesis. Their work included ammonia, sulfuric acid, methanamide, and various hydrocarbons. They even speculated about life based on liquid nitrogen or supercritical hydrogen fluid."

"You are correct, Dr. Li," said Olaf, recapturing control of the conversation. "Ammonia, NH_3, is perhaps the most commonly proposed alternative. Numerous chemical reactions are possible in an ammonia solution, and liquid ammonia has several chemical similarities with water. For instance, ammonia can dissolve most organic molecules at least as well as water does, and in addition it is capable of dissolving many elemental metals.

"However, an ecology based on ammonia would likely exist at temperatures or atmospheric pressures that are unusual for terrestrial life. This means that casting a wide net to include "weird" lifeforms will greatly expand the number of candidate planets we need to survey."

"I see," said the Captain. "What is the alternative to searching for all these non-terrestrial forms of life?"

"We could be carbon/water chauvinists, as Carl Sagan called himself," responded Dieter Schmitt, the project's lead chemist. "That would winnow the field of prospective planets considerably, ja?"

"Yes, that does narrow the field," said Elena. After all, this was her area of expertise. "I think we need a little background on the size of the problem, before we start making simplifying assumptions. Yuki, you are our lead astrophysicist—explain where the local stars came from."

With a nod of encouragement from the Captain, Dr. Saito took the podium. The soft-spoken Japanese astrophysicist cleared his throat and began what could have been a University symposium lecture.

143

"Over the past century, astronomy's greatest success has been the theory of stellar evolution: the way stars are born from clouds of interstellar gas, live out their lives, burning hydrogen into helium and producing heavier elements such as carbon, nitrogen, and oxygen. We know that big heavy stars burn brightest and emit higher average frequencies of electromagnetic radiation.

"The life of one star, the Sun, holds particular importance for us, as it provides practically all the energy for life on Earth. Fortunately, our star is remarkably stable and long-lived. The geological evidence from within the solar system indicates that the Sun has been burning for around 4.5 billion years. Astronomers are now confident that the Sun will burn for another 5 billion years before expanding into a red giant, ending all life on Earth.

"Since Earth is the only planet we know of that harbors life, any search for alien lifeforms starts with a search for other stars like our own. The type of star a planet circles has all sorts of implications for the possible development of life. For example, large hot stars, similar to those in the night sky that appear blue white, emit high levels of ultraviolet light. So much radiation that it could prevent life from forming." This brought a node from Olaf Gunderson.

"Moreover, such large stars do not last long. They burn through their hydrogen in a matter of millions of years, not the billions taken by stars like the Sun. The deaths of such stars are spectacular explosions that can outshine entire galaxies for a brief period. The short lives of such stars are thought to be too brief for life to develop."

"That is true, Yuki," commented Olaf. "While there are indications that primitive, single cell organisms arose on Earth in about 500 million years, more complex life took another three and a half billion years to evolve. While this observation is based on only one example, it is thought that anything less than several billion years is too short a span for intelligent life to develop."

"Thank you for that observation, Dr. Gunderson." Yuki took a sip of water and then continued with his narrative. "There are problems on the other end of the spectrum as well." This remark brought a few snickers from the other physicists—nothing like a physics pun to liven up a lecture.

Yuki smiled at his audience and explained. "Small stars, those much less massive than our star, are thought to be very long lived. Astrophysicists expect them to live several times longer than the current age of the Universe. When viewed through a telescope they appear as dim red colored objects—astronomers call them red dwarfs and they can be as small as 10% the size of the Sun. Most of their light is emitted in the infrared, which may be too feeble for life to develop under."

"Yes, Earth plant life absorbs light in the visible part of the spectrum," said Dr. Li. "Photons of infrared light may not be energetic enough to power any form of photosynthesis."

"And a lack of any ionizing radiation may lead to a mutation rate too low for effective evolution," added Olaf.

"Indeed," replied Yuki. "Plus there are other problems with red dwarfs that Dr. Piscopia will no doubt comment on during her presentation. But let us finish the background information. Compared to the general stellar population, the Sun is big, in the 80th percentile by mass, and metal-rich. With apologies to Dieter, when astronomers talk about metals they mean anything higher on the periodic table than hydrogen and helium."

This brought a good natured scowl from the German chemist, along with mumbled comments about those who could not appreciate the true complexity of the physical Universe.

"High metal content is associated with an increased likelihood of terrestrial planet formation. This is because a star's planets are formed from the same cloud of material that went into making the star itself. A lot of metals in a star is an indication of a lot of material available to form terrestrial planets. Astronomers use our Sun to set the standard for chemical abundances in other stars, termed metallicity. The Sun's metallicity is defined to be zero. In our neighborhood, the median metallicity for all exoplanet host stars is +0.10, while the typical value for G type dwarfs is -0.20."

"What is a G type dwarf, Doctor?" asked Ludmilla, knowing others in the room were thinking the same question but too shy or intimidated to ask.

"Good question, Dr. Tropsha. Astronomers classify stars by their spectral characteristics, basically color, and size. Most stars are classified using the letters O, B, A, F, G, K, and M, where O stars are the hottest and the letter sequence indicates successively cooler stars. Class G stars like the Sun are yellow. Other Sun like stars are class F, yellow-white, and class K, orange.

"The designation as a dwarf star is a bit misleading. There are much larger types of stars—giant stars are between 10 and 100 times as wide as the Sun—but such stars are quite rare. Most main sequence stars are classified as dwarfs. Our middle-aged Sun qualifies as a G2 dwarf star, even though it is more massive than 80% of the stars in the galaxy." Yuki paused for further questions, but there were none.

"To recap, we are looking for stars that are likely to have planets, that have been around for several billion years, and are not likely to either irradiate or starve carbon based life. Those general criteria were used to select the initial list of 33 stars. At this point, I would like to turn things over to Dr. Piscopia."

"We have covered a lot of material already," said Elena. "Perhaps we should take a 15 minute break before continuing?" She had learned from attending conferences that one way of wining over an audience is to give them a short break. As she was suggesting a break, the comm pips of the ship's three ranking officers chirped in unison.

"Yes, that sounds like an excellent idea, Dr. Piscopia," the Captain replied, distracted. As his pip murmured his face went grim, a sign of impending action to those who knew him well. "Roger that, do not enter the enclosure," he said to the comm.

"Ladies and gentlemen, a matter that requires my attention has come up. Please continue with the presentations following the break. I will return as soon as I can," he announced to those in the meeting room.

Then, turning to the other officers, the Captain snapped out orders: "Commander Curtis, please collect a security squad and form a cordon around the polar bear habitat. Lt. Bear, you are with me." The three officers were immediately in motion, exiting the meeting room and departing at a run.

Chapter 10

Polar Bear Quarters, Farside Base

The Captain and Lt. Bear hurried to the polar bear habitat, taking the same service tunnel that the earlier group of delivery men had taken. This was partially because the tunnel was the most direct route, but primary because they would be out of sight. This way base personnel would not be unsettled by the sight of the Captain running through the corridors, pursued by a large polar bear.

Pulling up at the service entrance, Jack and Bear found a pair of maintenance workers standing nervously at the door. Their eyes went wide at the sight of the Captain slowing to a halt, then even wider as Bear slid to a stop behind him. "Are you the people who reported the disturbance? What's the situation," Jack demanded.

The two workers, who had never talked to the Captain before, stood there tongue tied. As they sputtered, muffled roars could be heard coming from inside the polar bear habitat. Jack turned to the closest worker and said, "Spit it out, man! We don't have all day."

"Sir, Jeff and I were sent to clean the corridor and we found some strange organic material," the maintenance worker stammered, indicating traces of foul smelling stuff scattered in front of the door. "Then we heard the horrible roaring and growling from inside and didn't know what to do so we called for help," his partner babbled.

"Fine, you did the right thing, now stand back," Jack ordered. "Bear, let's go in."

"Aye," Bear replied as Jack opened the door. Stepping inside they were greeted by a sight not for the faint of heart. Everywhere there were white bears smeared with bright red blood. The normally clean snow and ice were also painted crimson and the half stripped carcass of something large lay near the edge of the pool.

"Walrus," said Bear, as if to explain the scene before them in a single word.

"Indeed, Lieutenant," the Captain responded. "Perhaps you should close the door." A pair of the smaller bears were playing tug-of-war with an unidentifiable body part, growling at each other excitedly. The adult bears all seemed in repose, evidently having completed their sanguine feast. As Bear turned to close the service door a couple of the blood soaked bears looked in their direction.

A female emerged from the pool, shook the water from her coat and then rolled in untainted snow to finish cleaning the blood from her fur. "Hello Captain, Bear," she called, padding in their direction. "A lot of the blubber is gone but there still should be plenty left, the youngsters tend to eat more meat anyway. Tornassuk led the kill. I haven't seen him this active since he was shot—I don't know whose idea it was to bring us some fresh food but it really helped snap him out of his malaise."

"That's wonderful, Isbjørn," Jack replied, recognizing Bear's mate as she drew nearer. "Who made the actual delivery?" he asked innocently.

"Sorry, I don't know their names, but I think I've seen them at practice in the gymnasium," she replied. "They brought the tooth-walker in a big metal box and dumped him out right here. It was very exciting, particularly for the youngsters. Walrus is not usual polar bear fare."

Bear's stomach was rumbling. Jack looked at his friend and thought, *he's come a long way—the Bear I knew a few years back would have charged right in and joined the feast.* "Lieutenant, would you like to avail yourself of some of the fresh food?"

"Yes, Sir," Bear replied, eyes fixed on the partially consumed marine mammal. "If that would be all right with you?"

"Please go ahead, such opportunities don't come frequently," Jack said, *at least they'd better not.* His thoughts were interrupted by the chirping of his pip. "Captain, this is Lcdr. Curtis."

"Go."

"I'm at the main entrance and I have Marines with stunners guarding all the access points to the polar bear quarters. What are your orders, Sir?"

"Things are under control in here. Have the Marines keep the inquisitive away from the area, while you come inside and join us," he replied. "I'm at the east service entrance. You might want to keep to the periphery of the habitat after you enter."

"Aye aye, Sir."

Jack watched in fascination as Bear approached Tornassuk and bowed down in front of the big male. His rump high and both forelegs stretched out on the ground in front of him, he looked like a dog begging a treat. Seeing the somewhat puzzled look on the Captain's face, Isbjørn said, "since it was Tornassuk's kill, other bears ask his permission before sharing the meal. It would be bad manners to just saunter up and start eating."

"I see," Jack said. "Isbjørn, I know that polar bears are very neat and fastidious about their appearance. Could you make sure that the younger bears fully clean the blood off their coats before venturing out?"

"Of course, Captain," she said slightly offended. "These are all well raised young bears."

"I didn't mean to imply otherwise. It's just that we have some new humans that recently arrived and the sight of you folks will be shocking enough to them," the Captain responded, adding a closed lip smile. "They would probably not react well to the sight of a 250kg predator stained with blood."

After making her way around the edges of the habitat, Lcdr. Curtis joined the Captain and Isbjørn. "So this was the 'disturbance'?" she asked Jack.

"Yes, as it turns out the bears were just enjoying a little fresh food that some of the crew delivered earlier. It seems a couple of maintenance workers heard the festivities and were afraid that something bad might be happening."

"I see," Gretchen said, reading between the lines. "I shall have a word with the deliverymen, to ensure they post appropriate notification in the future."

"Yes, Commander. I think that would help prevent future misunderstandings." As Jack was speaking Bear looked up from the ruin of the walrus, his head and chest red with blood. He smiled a toothy grin and returned to his meal.

"Did we do something wrong?" asked Isbjørn in a troubled voice.

"No, Isbjørn, you did nothing wrong. Some humans are just more excitable than others. Please enjoy the rest of your party. Commander Curtis, please ensure that our ursine friends will not be disturbed and then rejoin the planning meeting."

"Aye aye, Captain."

Conference Room, Farside Base

As the Captain rejoined the planning session, Dr. Piscopia interrupted her presentation. Everyone in the room turned expectantly to him, their expressions clearly asking for an explanation for the officers' sudden departure a quarter hour ago.

"Well Jack?" Said TK Parker, the only one present who could demand an accounting from the Captain. "Don't keep us in suspense, are the bears alright?"

"Yes, TK. The bears are fine, in fact they were having a bit of a party," Jack replied. "Some nervous maintenance workers heard the noise and thought something bad was happening. Just a false alarm, but better they be over zealous than fail to report things out of the ordinary."

"Glad to hear it, Jack my boy," the old man rumbled. "Please, Dr. Piscopia, continue."

"Thank you Mr. Parker," Elena said, favoring the billionaire with a brilliant smile. "Before the break and all the excitement with the bears, Dr. Saito was explaining the different types of stars—how they came into being and how their characteristics affect the chance of finding habitable planets orbiting them. To start with, we want to look at stars no more than half again as large as our Sun or smaller. Stars with high metallicity, neither too hot nor too cold. But those are just the broadest criteria."

"Since we are looking for life similar to ourselves on this first survey mission, we have included the presence of liquid water in the list of selection criteria. Unfortunately, it is very difficult to detect small rocky planets like Earth at a distance of several light years, let alone establish the presence of water."

"The presence of liquid water may be a necessary condition for the development of life," said Olaf, "but it is not a sufficient one. Our own planet had an atmosphere that would have been toxic to us for billions of years. It was life that created Earth's current oxygen rich atmosphere, and that was a slow process requiring both geological and biological evolution."

"Of course, Dr. Gunderson. We will be looking for oxygen rich atmospheres once we get close enough to make spectral measurements. Another thing that the evolution of life requires is an active geology. Without plate tectonics and volcanism, the carbon cycle cannot be maintained, along with other processes that help regulate atmospheric gases."

"It is also true that the geology of a planet will be dictated by the presence of water and life," said Eric Fetzer, the former NASA geologist. "For instance, without water there will be no sedimentary rock, and without ocean diatoms there will be no limestone, dolostone, chert or chalk. And without forests or peat bogs there will be no coal deposits."

"Ja, scientists believe there were initially around a dozen minerals in the interstellar medium when the Sun formed. According to studies, perhaps 60 more minerals formed 4.5 billion years ago, as clumps of matter coalesced to begin forming the Solar System," Dieter added. "But it was plate tectonics and life that pushed Earth's mineral count into the thousands. Metal oxides, calcites and clay minerals would all be rare on a lifeless planet, but abundant on a living one. If you are looking for life, look for the signatures of these minerals in the atmospheres of other planets."

"Precisely," said the previously quiet JT. "It was partially from geologic formations and trace minerals in the atmosphere that Dr. Tropsha and I were first convinced that the planet circling Beta Comae had been a living world."

"Of course, when we drew nearer and could identify the ruins of cities we were even more convinced," Ludmilla added grimly. Her comment brought an uneasy quiet to the room.

"Ludmilla has just reminded us of two things," Jack said, breaking the silence. "We know other life does exist and that finding it is not just an academic exercise."

151

The astronomer smiled and returned to her subject. "There are a few other things to note: some stars, particularly red dwarfs, have output that is highly variable, which could alternately freeze and fry any planets; a sizable number of stars exist in multi-star systems, whose gravitational fields can make planetary orbits very eccentric, with a proportional impact on climate variation; and other stars may be too close to areas of new star formation, so called stellar nurseries, where they are subject to nearby gamma ray sources and supernovae explosions every few million years."

"I take it that all of these things have been factored into your selections," Jack said, hoping to get to the bottom line sometime today. "So what is our search area and the odds of finding a habitable planet?"

"Estimates of the number of Earth-like planets in the galaxy run as high as 15 billion. To keep the search manageable and the voyage length reasonable we have only considered stars within a distance of 10 parsecs, about 32.6 light years from Earth. The volume of space lying within 10 parsecs of the Sun encompasses over 4,000 cubic parsecs, or about 150 thousand cubic light-years, with over 386 stars and brown dwarfs. Data indicate that 68% of those systems contain only one star.

"Most of the single stars in our neighborhood are red class M stars, while more than half of all nearby Sun-like stars—members of spectral classes F, G, and K—are found in binary or multiple systems. This means that, while there are 70 Sol like stars, only 28 are in single star systems."

"And the final candidates, Dr. Piscopia?" the Captain asked.

Well here goes, Elena thought, *the die is cast.* As she read the list of stars their know properties were shown on the wall sized display behind the podium. "The seven chosen systems, in order of nearest to farthest from Sol, are: Epsilon Eridani, Delta Pavonis, Gliese 581, Beta Hydri, Beta Canum Venaticorum, also known as Chara, 61 Virginis and Zeta Tucanae. Zeta Tuc, Chara and 61 Vir closely reproduce most of the Sun's properties and are considered premier targets."

The meeting dissolved into multiple excited conversations. As the noise died down, Dr. Li asked, "Elena, the third star on your list is a red dwarf. I thought you said they were not good candidates?"

"In this case, Sally, there are other factors, specifically the presence of four observed planets, and at least two more possible sightings. That and the fact that it is on the way to the other star systems farther out. The thought is to take a look at this promising M type system to see if we should include more red dwarfs in later surveys."

The Captain decided that this was enough information to be digested in a single day. He stepped up to the podium and called for order. "Ladies and gentlemen, your attention please." The room settled into silence.

"I think we could all use some time to read up on the selected star systems. Information has been posted on the base network and Dr. Piscopia will send you all the URI. Let's adjourn for today and meet again in two days for further discussion. Thank you for your time and Dr. Saito and Dr. Piscopia for their hard work and presentations."

After a smattering of applause, the attendees began wandering off in pairs and small groups. Elena remained at the podium, overwhelmed by the knowledge that the stars she had just named were not just abstract objects in space—not anymore. In a few months, she would be on board the Peggy Sue, on her way to visit those alien suns.

De Belcour's Quarters, Farside Base

Jean-Jacques sat at his apartment's desk, talking with his boss at the UN. "No, Madam Secretary, I have not had the chance to contact you previously," the bureaucrat lied smoothly. "The Captain has only now eased the terms of my incarceration and allowed me access to a means of communication." There was no reason for the Secretary to know he could have called almost a month earlier. "I fear that the scoundrel has plans to keep me captive in this horrid cave indefinitely. Please, you must try to reason with the man, and get him to release me."

"M. de Belcour, why would we do that?" replied the UNOOSA Secretary. "You are the only one we have on the inside of this rogue organization. I discussed this with the Secretary General and he and the Security Council think it prudent to keep you in place."

Jean-Jacques was dumbstruck. It never occurred to him that the UN would not try to secure his release. "*Mon Dieu*, Madam Secretary, you do not understand how vile this place is! It is hacked out of rock in an old volcano. The atmosphere could be lost in an instant without warning. The staff is hostile and the place is overrun with genetically engineered freaks, *gigantesques ours polaires*, that talk!"

"Have these giant talking polar bears attacked you, M. de Belcour? You seem in fine health, and it sounds like you are free to gather useful information. No, your mission is to remain in place, the UN's liaison with the space pirates."

Merde! They will not even try to help me, Jean-Jacques realized. "So I am to be left to my fate? They are overhauling their vessel and planning a reconnaissance mission to a number of nearby stars. What if the Captain decides to drag me along on their next mission?"

"Monsieur, if there is any way for you to be on that voyage I am ordering you to go. In fact, you might wish to slowly let them win you over to their side. A ruse, you understand?"

"To what end? I may never return!"

"In which case we will place a nice placard in the UNOOSA Headquarters lobby in your honor. No, M. de Belcour, you have your orders: you will be on that next voyage." The line went dead as the UN official hung-up. Jean-Jacques sat in front of the computer display slack-jawed, his only thought was, *I am so screwed.*

Base Canteen, Farside Base, later that Evening

Lcdr. Curtis and Dr. Tropsha had transferred their shipboard habit of having an evening cocktail together from Peggy Sue's lounge to the base canteen. In truth, the canteen was nearly as well appointed as the ship's bar and dining area, with a sumptuous mahogany bar and numerous tables, artfully arranged to provide parties of varying sizes whatever degree of privacy they desired. The duo was sitting at a table with an impressive view of the main atrium, with its waterfall and landscaped jungle.

The two women, both coming from military backgrounds, had found each other's company comfortable from their first voyage on board Peggy Sue. Now, having come through the trials and tribulations of that first voyage, including weathering a number of personal emotional storms, they were best friends. All that was missing this evening was the presence of Susan Write, the third member of their tight knit circle. As thoughts of Susan, aka Peggy Sue, occurred to both women simultaneously their eyes met. Raising her glass, Gretchen, said "to absent companions."

"Absent companions," replied Ludmilla in Russian, downing her drink. She looked around the bar area, noting the large number of strangers. They were construction workers, engineers and administrative types from the base. Their presence served to remind Ludmilla that, after years of distancing herself from the Russian Federation Air Forces, she was once again a military officer.

After signaling to the waitress that they needed another round, she turned back to Gretchen and said, "I have not thought much about it before, but you never make friends in civilian life like you do in the military."

Gretchen drained her glass and considered the remark for a moment before replying. "Probably because civilians, with the possible exception of police and firefighters, seldom have to depended on each other for their lives in the face of hostile action. When you have fought for your life alongside someone a bond is formed, even if you don't particularly like the other person."

"Yes, I suppose you are right, Gretchen. Look, here comes the Italian astronomer, Dr. Piscopia. We should ask her to sit with us, since she is to become a shipmate."

"Sure," Gretchen said, waving and calling out "Dr. Piscopia, over here!" This caught the astronomer's eye and she headed in their direction, much to the disappointment of the men standing at the bar.

"Good evening Commander, Doctor," Elena said, arriving at the table. "How are you this evening?" The science section dark burgundy jumpsuit went well with her Mediterranean coloration, though she still yearned for high heels. The Italian astronomer gracefully slid into an empty chair.

155

"Good evening, Dr. Piscopia," replied Gretchen, "and according to tradition first names are used in the wardroom. Call me Gretchen."

"Excellent, you must call me Elena." Looking around, she said, "I do miss the night life in Padua. This is as close to an open air cafe as one will find on the Moon, I suppose."

"I'm afraid this is the only cafe on the Moon, period," replied Gretchen. "By the way, I was wondering why your colleagues call you Elena, is it a middle name?"

"Middle name? Oh, I understand," Elena answered. She paused to order a drink from the highly attentive waitress and then continued. "There is a story behind that. You see, in the 17th century there was a Venetian noblewoman named Elena Lucrezia Cornaro Piscopia who attended the University of Padua. Not only was it unusual for a woman to attend university at that time, Elena was the first woman to receive a Doctorate degree."

"Really?" said Ludmilla, "when was that?"

"In 1678. The degree was conferred on June 25th in the cathedral of Padua. Of course, she was first tested by the faculty professors and University authorities in the front of the public. Reportedly, the crowd included most of the Senators of Venice, invited guests from the Universities of Bologna, Perugia, Rome, and Naples, along with many students and town's people. She spoke for an hour in classical Latin, a discourse on the works of Aristotle. Evidently her erudition was sufficiently impressive that she was award the Doctorate of Philosophy. At age thirty-two, she was the first woman in the world to receive a doctorate degree. In addition to the degree, Elena Piscopia received the doctor's ring, the teacher's ermine cape, and the poet's laurel crown."

"Most impressive, are you a descendant of this lady?" asked Gretchen.

"She died childless and as far as I know we are not related," answered Elena, pausing for a second to accept a Campari and soda from the returning waitress. "But when I joined the faculty at Padua the similarity of my name, Lucrezia Piscopia, and that of the famous Lady Cornaro prompted some of my colleagues to start calling me Elena. Since I never much cared for Lucrezia, I quickly became Elena and that is how my friends all know me."

"That is a fascinating story, Elena. Most people do not have such an intriguing tale to go with their names," said Ludmilla. "In my case my grandmother was named Ludmilla. Not nearly as glamorous as being the namesake of the first woman to earn a PhD."

"Use of that famous name—famous at least in Italian academic circles—helped me get an educational television show for a couple of years," Elena said, smiling wistfully at the memory. "That and a short skirt and high heels."

"I remember that show," said Gretchen, "that was about ten years ago, wasn't it?"

"Yes, don't remind me," replied Elena rolling her eyes. "Time waits for no one. Do you know, I am older now than the original Elena Piscopia lived to be? She died at 38, from tuberculosis."

"Most people, even well educated nobles, did not live long four centuries ago," commented Ludmilla. "The average person today lives better and longer than the upper classes back then."

"Believe me, Ludmilla, I would not trade my life for her's under any circumstance. Besides, I am going to see the stars—not many people have their fondest dreams come true."

"That's true, I hope one day to captain my own starship," added Gretchen, a faraway look in her eyes.

"Seems we are all finding our dreams because of the Peggy Sue. Tell me, Ludmilla, how did you come to ensnare the affections of our Captain?"

Sensing a hint of challenge, Ludmilla's eyes flashed. "It was he who pursued me, my dear. After he came to our rescue on the ISS— Ivan Kondratov, Yuki Saito and myself—he proceeded to woo me with tales of scientific marvels and space aliens. Being a skeptical scientist, I demanded proof."

This elicited a snort from Gretchen. "I have never seen someone play hard to get by publicly calling her would be suitor clinically insane."

"It was all part of a winning stratagem," Ludmilla said haughtily. "Eventually, the Captain sent Gretchen, Bear and a party of Marines into a crater on the Moon to bring me back proof of alien life."

This time it was Gretchen's turn to roll her eyes. "We should all be wearing boots, 'cause it's getting deep in here."

"This was the battle with the spider things, si?"

"Exactly, Elena. Well, after going to such lengths to convince me of his story I could no longer deny his advances. We fell into each other's arms and have been lovers ever since."

"È meraviglioso! What a wonderful romantic tale," said Elena, smiling. "It is not every woman who gets to be rescued from death by a dashing captain who then falls in love with her. And you are in love with him too, si?"

"Absolutely. He was a part of my heart that I did not know was missing until I met him. And what about you, Elena? Are you leaving someone back on Earth?"

"No, not really. The fire had gone out of my last affair of the heart some time ago. Now our coming voyage of discovery is consuming my thoughts and I doubt I have time for a new relationship."

"You may change your mind when we get into alter-space," Gretchen said. "Nothing to do but run drills, drink in the wardroom and watch old videos from home."

"I am starting a self-defense class in Spetsnaz Systema. It is like Judo and wrestling combined. Most of the crew women are going to participate," Ludmilla said to Elena. "You should join. It will help you keep your figure during the trip..."

Training Gym, Farside Base

A mixed crowd of men and polar bears were gathered in a semicircle facing three humans. Two of the humans were officers: Lcdr. Curtis and Lt. Taylor. The third was Gunnery Sergeant Rodriguez, the ranking Marine. All wore battle armor, including the bears.

"OK, listen up people," said Lcdr. Curtis. "Our purpose here today is to work out any kinks in the new ursine armor. As you know, the inner environmental suits contain nanites that help them self-adjust to their wearers. Unfortunately, the composite ceramic outer armor must be manually fitted to each individual. The only way to find out if a suit fits well is to run through some real-world activities. Since the purpose of the armor is to protect its wearer during combat, we are going to engage in some simulated combat." The Commander turned and said, "Gunny?"

"Thank you, Ma'am," then addressing the would be combatants, the Gunny said, "You have exercised in these suits before so you are familiar with them. Today we are going to play a game called 'capture the flag' in which we will divide into two teams. Each team will contain an equal number of bears and humans."

The four humans standing with the bears just happened to be the four walrus deliverymen: PFC Joey Sanchez, Able Spacer Steve Hitch and Petty Officers Phil Kowalski and Bud Jones. They looked at each other and then at the bears, who stared back curiously.

"Since there are three full grown males, we will try to balance out the mass inequality by putting all three adult females on the same team. We will also divide the ex-SEALs between the teams so they won't have the advantage of having worked together closely in the past. So, on this side of the gym I want Bear, Inuksuk, Umky, Imik, Siku, Kowalski and Hitch. On the other side, Tornassuk, Isbjørn, Aurora, Snowflake, Aput, Sanchez and Jones." The bears sat there looking about expectantly.

"DON'T JUST SIT ON YOUR ASSES! MOVE OUT!" the Gunny bellowed, the volume inside the suit helmets almost deafening. There was a sudden scramble of men and bears for the far ends of the gym. "When you get to your end of the gym you will find a box of colored armbands. Put one on the forelimb of your choice."

The male dominated team drew the green armbands and the females the orange. Over the common frequency, Lcdr. Curtis spoke again. "Alright, the rules are simple, on either end of this space there is a flag, a square piece of material the same color as your armbands. Your task is to prevent the other team from stealing your flag and carrying it back to their territory, as marked by the center

line in front of me. You will have five minutes to plan a strategy.
When you hear the tone, the game is on..."

Chapter 11

Captain's Office, Farside Base

The desk chimed, a melodious bonging sound, requesting the Captain's attention. "Yes?" he answered. The voice of his administrative aid, an efficient young man named Jimmy, emanated from somewhere over the desk. "Sir, Ms. Muñoz and Mrs. Hinkle are here."

Oh what fun! Complaints from the kindergarten teacher and the students' mothers, Jack thought. Being a captain at sea was the greatest experience of his life, being a captain on shore one of the worst. As he stood up to greet his guests he answered, "Thank you, Jimmy. Please send them in."

The door to the office slid open and two young women entered. They both wore the tan jumpsuits of civilian personnel, though one had a pastel multicolored scarf around her neck and the other's lapel sported a silver pin that looked like leaping dolphins. "Good afternoon, Ladies," the Captain said, stepping around his desk to shake their hands. "Please come in and take a seat."

"Good afternoon, Captain," said the older of the two, the one with the scarf. "I am Margret Hinkle, and this is Corazon Muñoz, our kindergarten teacher."

"And what can I do for you today?" Jack asked, retaking his seat behind the expansive desk. He already knew what the women were here about, but the dance must be performed according to custom.

"Captain, we are here today because a number of us mothers with young children are concerned about the presence of dangerous wild animals on the base," Margret Hinkle said, after settling into her chair. "On a number of occasions polar bears have been seen wandering the halls, unfettered and unaccompanied by handlers."

"I see," was Jack's neutral reply, "and do you wish to add anything Ms. Muñoz?"

"Yes, Captain," said the kindergarten teacher, a slender young woman of perhaps 25. "Some of my students have expressed fear about the presence of bears. I'm afraid that this is causing anxiety and distracting them from their studies."

161

"Are all of your students fearful of the bears, Ms. Muñoz?"

"No," she replied, "some are excited by the presence of bears."

"I see."

"That is not the point, Cora," interjected Mrs. Hinkle. "These animals pose a threat to our children and something must be done about it!"

Jack sat quietly for a few moments, his hands raised in front of him, steepled fingers pointing upward resting on his chin. Those on his staff would have recognized this posture as an indication of deep thought, one the Captain assumed just prior to deciding on a course of action. The women sat, watching him expectantly. Jack dropped his hands and cleared his throat.

"Tell me, Mrs. Hinkle. Are you accompanied by handlers when you move about the base?"

"Of course not. Why should I have handlers?"

"Yet you are suggesting that our polar bears should have handlers. Why?"

"Why!" exclaimed the shocked mother. "Because they are dangerous wild animals!"

"No, Mrs. Hinkle," the Captain replied in a calm, level voice. "They are dangerous intelligent animals. Just as we humans are dangerous intelligent animals."

Mrs. Hinkle opened her mouth to speak but no words came. *I believe I have taken her by surprise*, Jack thought to himself. "Mrs. Hinkle, have you ever spoken to one of the polar bears?"

"Certainly not!" came the indignant reply.

"Or you Ms. Muñoz?"

"No Captain, I've never really had an occasion to speak with one of the bears."

"Are you aware of our mission, the mission of this base and the people on it?" Jack said in his captain's voice. "We are venturing out into the galaxy to find alien life, intelligent creatures that may be as different from us as coal is from diamond."

"But coal and diamonds are both made from carbon," responded the teacher.

"Yes, very good Ms. Muñoz, and that is my point precisely. The form, the physical characteristics are very different, but inside they are made of the same atoms. When we encounter alien life it may also be very different from ourselves, but inside we hope to find similarities—in intellect, thought, common interests and shared values. In short we are looking to find friends among the stars, friends who will undoubtedly be shockingly different from ourselves."

"What does this have to do with wild bears roaming the halls with our children?" asked the exasperated Mrs. Hinkle.

"Mrs. Hinkle, how are we going to make friends with truly alien lifeforms out among the stars when you harbor prejudice against fellow Earth creatures?"

"But they're animals!"

"As are we, Mrs. Hinkle," the Captain replied, leaning back in his chair. "*Ursus maritimus* and *Homo sapiens* are both mammals, obviously fruit from the same evolutionary tree. Our DNA is so similar that without detailed examination an alien might think we were different variants of the same species. Madam, what does it say about humans if we cannot even make friends with creatures we share our planet with?"

The question was rhetorical. Jack was in full lecture mode and gave the stunned women no chance to reply. "Polar bears are brave, honorable creatures. They are inquisitive, playful and, if treated with respect, open and friendly. Bears are honest, I've never been lied to by an ursine. And there is no more faithful friend than a bear, they will come to your aid without questioning the cost and fight to the death to protect you. I have worked and fought beside them and I can tell you that I would rather be in the company of bears than many of the people I have met."

"But, but they are so big, and they have claws," Mrs. Hinkle said, groping for a counter argument.

"Our kind has hunted polar bears for more than 10,000 years and yet they are willing to be our partners in this enterprise, they are willing to be our friends. It is obvious to me that this type of species prejudice cannot be allowed to poison the minds of our young children. Remember, someday they will be the ones working, perhaps fighting alongside creatures much stranger than polar bears."

"What do you intend to do?" asked Ms. Muñoz in a rather meek voice.

"It is time to break down the barriers between species. Ms. Muñoz, I want you to talk to my aid about scheduling a field trip for your kindergarten class. I want all of your students, and their mothers, to accompany me on a visit to the polar bear habitat."

Mrs. Hinkle and Ms. Muñoz both stared at the Captain. This was not the outcome they had envisioned. "How soon should this happen, Captain?" asked Ms. Muñoz.

"It will take a few days to produce Arctic clothing for everyone, but I want this to happen as soon as possible. Thank you for bringing this to my attention, together we will nip this nascent speciesism in the bud." Jack touched a control on the surface of his desk and spoke, "Jimmy, please come in and escort these two ladies out. They need to talk with you about scheduling a field trip to visit the polar bear habitat."

"Was there anything else?" Jack asked, looking up at the two women. "In that case, have a nice day."

Training Gym, Farside Base

Gretchen and JT took positions on top of a tall crate near midfield, with a good view of the entire game space. The Gunny stood across the floor on the territory dividing line. "It looks like Bear's team is standing in a tight formation around their flag," JT commented to his companion.

"Yeah, and it looks like the females have divided their force into two columns, one moving up each side of the battlefield. They are using the obstacles for cover and have sent Sanchez and Jones forward to scout the ground ahead," Gretchen observed. "Not a bad plan, let's see what happens when they make contact with the enemy."

The two human scouts reported back to their comrades, and after a brief conference the female led squad started to move again. They surrounded the opposing team by blocking the open paths leading to the clump of bears sitting on their own flag. Suddenly Tornassuk stood up and charged.

"Looks like Tornassuk is doing the alpha predator thing and just charging the enemy," said Gretchen, a bit disappointed.

"I don't think so," said JT. "Notice how the orange humans are hidden, positioned a couple of strides back from that low barrier. And the adolescents are clustered on the side opposite Tornassuk's charge."

As they watched, Inuksuk stood and charged to meet the onrushing Tornassuk. This left a hole in the semicircle around the green flag that Bear moved to fill. But that left only adolescents and the humans on the side away from the altercation. Then the other team's adolescents charged from cover. Naturally, their counterparts ran to meet them, uncovering the flag.

"Oh, that was well played," said Gretchen. "They used Tornassuk as a diversion, drawing off the other adult males."

"And they sent their youngsters in to draw off the other side's adolescents," add JT, "the equivalent of attacking the other side's least experienced troops and luring them out of position. Somebody down there is doing some thinking."

On the field of battle it was chaos. Hitch tried to get his team's adolescents to return to position and got tangled between Umky and Snowflake. This left only Bear and Kowalski guarding the flag when Sanchez and Jones ran forward and jumped up to the top of the crate they were hiding behind. Without breaking stride they launched themselves off the top of the barrier and through the air above Bear's head. Sanchez, experienced in combat wearing armor, did a controlled bounce off the far wall and bowled Kowalski over from behind, allowing Jones to grab the flag.

Meanwhile, Bear spun around to counter the threat from the aerial human attack. Before he could advance, Isbjørn, running at full tilt, knocked him over from behind. Aurora ran past them and, acting as a blocker for Jones, they headed back toward the midfield line and victory.

"Not too shabby," said Gretchen approvingly. Jones crossed into his own territory right behind Aurora and the Gunny sounded the game over tone. It took half a minute to separate the other combatants and inform them that the game was over.

* * * * *

After a short debriefing, the two teams were sent back to their respective corners, to plan new strategies. "Let's see what happens this time," said Gretchen to her fellow referees. While this exercise was ostensibly to check out the new armor, it was also the first step in the military training of the bears. Capture the flag was their introduction to working with humans.

At the green team huddle Bear spoke for the first time. "OK, you chuckle-heads. I figured the only way to make you realize that brute force wouldn't work was to let you try it. So now that the females have frosted our asses, let's do some real planning this time."

"It was the humans that stole the flag," grumped Umky.

"Because human hands are better suited to grabbing the damn thing. That's a lesson to remember, humans and bears have different strengths and different weaknesses. When we work together to maximize the strengths and minimize the weaknesses a mixed squad of men and bears is stronger than either on their own."

"You know, that actually makes sense," grumbled Inuksuk, whose one-on-one battle with Tornassuk had been a tie that took both of them out of the action.

"And did anyone notice that they came with all of their troops when their scouts discovered that we were all simply guarding the green flag? Did anyone realize that the best our strategy could do was keep us from losing? If one of us could have snuck by them, he could have snatched their unguarded flag before they knew what hit them."

"You point that out now," Imik said.

"You wouldn't have listened before," Bear said. "Now let's get us a plan. What do you humans think?"

Dr. Li's Quarters, Farside Base

Wie-chang sat before the computer display on the desk in her private quarters, a two room apartment with its own private bathroom. She was talking to her department head at Wuhan University. Wuhan University, located in China's eastern lake district, is one of the country's top ten universities. As such it is under direct government control. Part of the deal that permitted her to join the "space pirates" included frequent reports back to the University.

"Dr. Wu, things are progressing rapidly," she said to the video image on the computer display in front of her. "The star systems to be visited have been selected. I will send these to you in an email."

"Very good, Dr. Li. Are they treating you properly?" The question was just a formality. Dr. Wu was more a government official than an academic or colleague. And the innocuous pleasantries were really just a cover. Dr. Li's real report was being delivered by non-verbal means.

On her lapel she wore a pin, purportedly a representation of the university seal. Contained in the pin an infrared LED, whose frequency was picked up and transmitted by the CCD camera but would not be visible on a receiver's screen, blinked out a coded message. Sally hoped that the information would satisfy her handlers back in China. So far, she was only able to report some general observations and a few details about the environmental systems.

She really did despise the government bureaucrats and party hacks that ran her country—the time she spent in the west had opened her eyes to their repressive ways. But she had family in Nanking, and the government had made it clear that their safety and prosperity depended on her spying on her new comrades. She hoped they understood that, once the ship departed, she would be out of contact for many months. She hoped she could trust them to keep their word, but in her head a voice whispered, *you fool!*

Day Room, Enlisted Quarters, Farside Base

A number of Marines and crew were playing Foosball or just sitting around in the dayroom when the four human capture the flag players returned. "Damn, look what the cat drug in," said Ronnie Reagan, one of the original Marine detachment.

"Bite me, Ronnie," Sanchez replied. "Coño, I hurt all over, even my cojones."

"Hey," said Steve Hitch, "you didn't get to play the human filling in a polar bear sandwich. If we weren't all wearing armor I'd look like that damned walrus."

"Don't mention the fuckin' walrus, that's what started this," added Bud Jones. "whose idea was that anyway, Joey?"

"You thought it sounded like a good idea at the time, pendejo," Sanchez retorted.

"What walrus?" Asked Jolene Betts, one of the crew. A stowaway on the first mission, she worked her way up from tending bar and waiting tables in the lounge to being on one of the X-ray laser gun crews.

"Oh, Steve and Joey and the other two geniuses here decided it would be a nice gesture to bring the polar bears some fresh food," replied Matt Jacobs. "You know, Stevie, it's usually me standing in splatter range when one of your schemes goes south and the shit hits the fan. How did you rope these other clowns into this?"

"They brought the bears a walrus?" Jolene persisted.

"Yes, a live, one and a half ton walrus," said the almost gleeful Jacobs. "That's what the big alert was when they scrambled the Marines a week ago."

"Yeah," chimed in Kato Kwan, another Marine. "We were all called on deck by the Commander to help 'quell a disturbance' at the polar bear quarters. There we were, running flat out towards a rumble with a herd of polar bears, with only stunners to defend ourselves."

"What happened?"

"When we get there Lcdr. Curtis has us cordon off the polar bear quarters, from which is coming a godawful racket—growling and other sounds, like feeding time at the zoo. Once the area is secured, the Commander calls the Captain, who is, I shit you not, inside with the bears."

"Man, there is no doubt about it," said Ronnie, "the Captain has a pair of big brass ones."

"Anyway, the Commander tells us to hold the perimeter and goes inside to join the Captain!"

"Shit, she's got some brass ones too," said Matt, with considerable respect.

Ignoring Jacobs' comment, Kato continued his narrative. "So after about ten minutes, things quiet down and the Commander comes back out. I got a glimpse inside as she came out—the whole damn place was covered in blood, the polar bears too."

"What happened to the walrus?" Jolene asked again, with growing apprehension.

"The polar bears ate it."

"Ate it? As in, ate it alive?" Jolene shouted, her voice rising a couple of octaves. "You assholes fed the polar bears a live walrus!"

"Well, yeah," said Joey. "They really liked it, they said so later."

Jolene jumped up and stormed off making disparaging remarks about men having only shit for brains.

"Hey Joey," Ronnie called to his friend. "You ain't hitting that anytime soon, compadre."

"*Beso mi culo,* Reagan. Like you got a shot."

"Since none of you can fly a shuttle, I'm wondering how you dickheads managed to get an officer to go along with smuggling a live walrus onto the base," asked Washington. According to the scuttlebutt, Washington was up for promotion to Sergeant, making him the leader of the new second squad.

"Joey convinced that new English shinny balls that we did it all the time," said Hitch, with more than a little admiration in his voice. "We had a load of frozen seals, after all."

"I understand that Lt. Lewis is on ice hauling duty until further notice," Washington commented.

"And we get to play stoop-tag with the furry white hoards of the Arctic until the Commander gets tired of seeing us smacked around like chew toys," said Jones.

"Come on, Bud," said Kowalski, slowly easing himself into one of the chairs. "You gotta admit the whole caper was epic."

"You know it, brother," Bud said with a tired smile, limping off toward his rack.

Day Room, BOQ, Farside Base

The Peggy Sue's two helmsmen, Billy Ray and Bobby, were in the sitting area of the base BOQ, the bachelor officers quarters. While all the ship's officers were technically bachelors, the senior officers were all quartered elsewhere, making the BOQ the exclusive domain of the ship's junior officers. They were conversing with Sandy McKennitt, one of the ship's new lieutenants.

"So Bobby, what's happening with you and that little Japanese sheila?" Sandy asked, always to the point.

"As far as I can tell, nothing," Bobby opined. "Since we got to base I hardly get to see her. She's always running from meeting to meeting with the other scientists. I even joined Dr. Saito's Kendo class to get to see her."

"Yup, and now the only time he sees his girl she's wearing a wire basket over her face and trying to whack him with a bamboo sword," added Billy Ray.

"Well, you can tell me to mind my own bizzo, but I think she fancies you."

"How can you tell?" asked Bobby, hope rising.

"I don't ever see her hanging out with any other bloke at the canteen, do you? Look Bobby, she's the junior physicist and all the other science boffins got her going flat out like a lizard drinking. Trust me, she'll have more spare time when we get underway."

"I hope you're right, Sandy."

"Strewth! You'll see, mate. A week after we raise anchor and you'll be grinning like a shot fox."

"That would be an improvement," said Billy Ray, "now he's more like roadkill on the highway of love."

"And aren't you the poet, B-ray," Sandy responded. Sandy followed the Aussie habit of shortening first names, particularly if they had more than two syllables.

"In his dreams," quipped Bobby. "Don't encourage him or he'll start reciting Shakespeare and Chaucer."

"You're just jealous, pardner. You know that the Captain often quotes a bit of the Bard on important occasions. I'm just stayin' in practice for when I get a ship of my own."

"Dream on, dude, dream on."

Before Billy Ray could reply, Nigel Lewis entered the room. Obviously worn out, he tossed his tablet on the coffee table and practically collapsed into a chair, head hung from fatigue.

"G'day Nige, how ya going, mate?" asked the always perky Sandy. "Looks like the Captain's got you as busy as a cat burying shit."

"I'm not quite sure what you said, Sandy, but if you meant that the Captain is running my arse off you are spot on. I think I transported enough ice today to float a battleship."

"I've done that ice run," said Bobby, "it's darker inside those ice craters than three feet up Satan's asshole."

"Right you are, Bobby," Nigel replied. "In the future, if someone tells me to shove something where the Sun doesn't shine I shall know precisely where to put it."

"So tell me again, Nigel," drawled Billy Ray, "why the Captain's got you doin' double duty on the ice run?"

"You bloody well know why, Mr. Vincent. It was that damned escapade with the walrus."

"Goo goo g'joob," Bobby replied.

"Koo koo kachoo?" Nigel said, confused.

"No, goo goo g'joob," Billy Ray corrected. "*I am the walrus*, lyrics by John Lennon."

"Right," added Bobby, "koo koo kachoo would be Paul Simon, from *Mrs. Robinson*. Totally different thing, man."

"I think you two have roos loose in the top paddock," Sandy observed. Just then a couple of the new midshipmen, Skip Tanner and Pauline Palmer, came in, returning from a day at pilot training. Eventually destine to become pilots and ship's officers they currently had the status of cadets—officers in training. The midshipmen's quarters adjoined the BOQ lounge.

"Kangaroos and walrus? Are there things you Sirs aren't sharing with we poor cadets?" asked Skip.

"Actually, there is an important lesson here for you soon to be junior officers," Billy Ray said, causing Nigel to moan. "You see, when you become a shinny new lieutenant the enlisted personnel will find it necessary to test your mettle. In particular, they will present you with situations that require knowledge and wisdom beyond your tender years."

"Billy Ray, please do not do this," pleaded Nigel.

"A case in point recently occurred right here on Farside Base. It seems that a young lieutenant JG was tempted into wickedness by an unholy alliance of enlisted crew, Marines, and SEALs," Billy Ray said, warming to his subject. "As is *de rigueur* for such tests of character, the situation presented to the young officer required a decision that seemed reasonable at the time. And though the officer in question should have checked with higher authority, hubris clouded his judgment."

"So what transgression did Lt. Lewis get tricked into committing?" asked Pauline.

"Oh bollocks," said Nigel, resigned to the telling of the tale.

"The young hero of our story was making a run planetside to pick up supplies, including several containers of frozen seals—food for the polar bears. The enlisted pranksters thought that it would be a great idea to bring back something fresher for their pals over in the bear habitat and had somehow acquired a live walrus. The trouble was how to transport the beast."

"This was what the commotion was about at the bear quarters last week?" asked Sandy, who had not heard the full story.

"That is correct, Lt. McKennitt. To make a long story short, the crewmen convinced the young officer that transporting a live walrus up to the station was an everyday occurrence."

"And how was I to know it was not SOP?" demanded Nigel. "A month before I ferried a shuttle full of live polar bears to the ship for the Captain. I had a shuttle filled with frozen seals, the bloody walrus didn't seem out of place."

"And there you see the lesson, Cadets. Like Beelzebub, the crew will offer temptations that seem reasonable yet will bring down the wrath of the Almighty—in other words, the Captain. Instead of taking a few minutes to check with the base, the young officer decided on his own authority to transport the 3,000 pound walrus in the shuttle he commanded."

"Right, they really had me on, and when the Captain caught wind of it he gave me a royal arse chewing and then put me on ice shuttle duty for the foreseeable future," finished the humiliated Nigel.

"But what happened to the walrus?" asked Skip.

"The crew gave it to the polar bears as a treat," answered Bobby with a snicker. "Evidently the bears really appreciated the fresh food. As far as they are concerned, Lt. Lewis is a damned fine fellow."

"You mean the polar bears killed and ate the walrus? How awful." said Pauline.

"Come on, Pauli," Sandy said. "You aren't a veggie, are you?"

"A veggie?"

"A vegetarian. Because if you eat meat like most of us, every meal means an animal somewhere had a very bad day. That's how nature works, and the polar bears are a lot closer to nature than we are."

Billy Ray recited:

> *"Who trusted God was love indeed*
> *And love Creation's final law*

Tho' Nature, red in tooth and claw
With ravine, shrieked against his creed."

"What?" said the confused Pauline.

"Alfred, Lord Tennyson," said Billy Ray.

"Bloody walrus," muttered Nigel.

Base Canteen, Farside Base

The normal after work group was seated at their usual table overlooking the atrium. Sally Li had joined Gretchen, Ludmilla and Elena, abandoning the company of her colleagues from the science section. She was seeking a discussion about something, anything, other than physics.

"So how is the polar bear training coming, Gretchen?" asked Elena. "I understand that they are treating the training as though it is a game."

"Oh, to some extent," Gretchen replied. "But polar bears treat most everything as a game. The only time I've ever seen Bear serious is when we lost comrades."

"True, they are much less neurotic than most humans," added Ludmilla. "Did I mention that Jack and I took the kindergarten children to visit the bears today?"

"Really? Why?" asked Sally. "Not that children wouldn't enjoy seeing the bears up close."

"It seems that a number of the mothers were upset by bears roaming free around the base," said Gretchen. "I suppose they thought the bears might treat their little darlings as snack food."

Ludmilla picked up the story, saying: "A delegation went and complained to the Captain a couple of days ago, and Jack decided that spending some quality time in the bear habitat would be the best antidote to such irrationality."

"Why did you go? Or are you getting as bored with things around here as I am?" asked Elena. Once the star systems for their voyage had been decided on there was not much else for her to do. The other physicists were constantly tweaking the power reactor and pouring over gravitonic circuitry, but an astronomer without an instrument was at loose ends. She almost envied JT's involvement with the ship's armaments.

"Jack wanted me along in case one of the mothers fainted or had a hysterical fit," Ludmilla replied snidely. "As it was, we did have an accident—one of the children fell into the pool."

"How did that happen?" asked Sally, drawn into the tale.

"When we came in, some of the younger bears were sliding down a slope above the pool into the water. One of the children thought that this looked like great fun and decided to try it herself..."

* * * * *

The Captain met the kindergarten class and their mothers outside the bear habitat. Before the visitors arrived, Jack had explained to the bears that some of the little ones' mothers were nervous about their offspring being around such powerful creatures as themselves. "These little humans are very fragile, even compared with a year old cub, so be careful," he cautioned. "They are only going to be wearing heavy clothing, not armor like your playmates in the training gym."

The males all indicated their understanding. The adult female bears—Isbjørn, Aurora, and Snowflake—understood such feelings immediately and helped explain the situation to the adolescents. Once the visitors donned their cold weather parkas, the class was ushered in by Ms. Muñoz, followed by a gaggle of nervous mothers.

"Children, I would like you to meet my friends," Jack said, "this is Isbjørn, Bear, Aput, Tornassuk, Snowflake, Siku, Umky, Imik, Aurora and Inuksuk." The bears all looked at the herd of small humans with closed mouth smiles, trying not to show any frightening dentition.

"Why are their names so strange?" asked one of the little boys.

"Their names are mostly in Inuit, a language spoken by people from the Arctic region. Our names are as strange to them as theirs seem to us. Everyone say hello to the bears." The class responded with a chorus of hellos.

175

"Hello, children," said Isbjørn, who had emerged as the lead bear for all things outside of combat training. In military matters she deferred to her mate, mostly.

"Why are they all different sizes?" asked a little girl in the front. "Are some of them kids?"

"Very perceptive," replied Ludmilla, stepping up to stand in front of Bear. Once things on board the Peggy Sue settled down during the trip to the Moon base, Dr. Hofstadter and Ludmilla examined all of the bears. While checking blood types and drawing blood for future emergencies, she had learned all their names. "Umky, Imik, Siku and Aput are all youngsters. In bear terms they are all a little older than you are, but they are not full grown yet. When bears grow up the males are much larger than the females."

Ludmilla turned to Bear and said, "Bear, would you please stand up and show the children how tall you are?" Bear complied, rising to his full two legged height of just over 10 feet. This caused some of the children to back away.

"Come now," Ludmilla scolded. "There is nothing to be frightened of, these bears are our friends." With that she turned and hugged Bear, her arms only reaching partway around his body. Bear crossed his two gigantic paws over Ludmilla's back and lowered his head to nuzzle the top of her parka hood. The children all made sounds of wonder and delight.

Bear released Ludmilla and spoke to the children in his deep bass voice, "anyone else want a real bear hug? Just pick a bear and introduce yourself." Tentatively at first, children and bears made contact. Soon things pretty much dissolved into chaos, with children and young bears running in all directions and mothers of both species getting to know each other. All was going well and the Captain stood by smiling. Then Emily Hinkle slid down the bears' slide into the frigid water.

Even while conversing with the mothers, Isbjørn, out of long maternal habit, was constantly scanning the area for threats. She saw the girl was in trouble first. "Bear!" she barked.

Bear was much nearer to the pond, trying to keep the children from getting too close to the water's edge. Hearing Isbjørn's alarm he immediately turned around. Following his mate's line of sight, he spotted the girl as she splashed down in the middle of the pool and vanished beneath the surface. Bear rose and dove into the pond in a single motion, spray from the splash wetting the pool's edge.

"Emily!" shrieked Mrs. Hinkle, running forward.

"Wait, Mrs. Hinkle," said the Captain, ensnaring the panicking mother with his parka encased arms. "The bears are better equipped to help Emily than we are." As he spoke, Bear's head emerged from the water in the middle of the pool. On his back was Emily, thoroughly soaked and already starting to go into thermal shock.

"Hang on to my fur, little one," Bear commanded and headed for the pool side where Isbjørn was waiting. As Bear and the girl arrived at the pool's edge, Isbjørn leaned out and snared the child by her parka. Carrying the sodden child dangling from her mouth, Isbjørn headed for the habitat exit at a run, with Ludmilla close behind.

"Where is that bear taking my child!" Mrs. Hinkle screamed, struggling against the Captain's embrace.

"Calm yourself, madam," Jack replied. "Isbjørn knows that Emily must be gotten out of the cold quickly, so she has taken her outside the habitat. Don't worry, Ludmilla is a medical doctor, Emily is in the best of hands. Come, I will escort you to the door."

Bear shook the water from his coat like an oversized retriever, much to the children's delight. Aurora, the other fully mature female, stood up and said loudly "All right everyone, let's be more careful around the pool, and stay off of the slide." She sat back down and said to the speechless young mother standing beside her, "it's always something when you have cubs."

* * * * *

"My goodness! What happened? Is the little girl alright?" Elena asked.

"Oh yes," Ludmilla replied. "We stripped off the child's wet things and wrapped her in my parka before the mother arrived. When Mrs. Hinkle got there, Emily was nestled in Isbjørn's arms, clutching her fur as momma bear sang an Inuit lullaby. As fate would have it, Mrs. Hinkle was the mother who complained to the Captain."

"And how did she handle it?" asked Gretchen.

"Surprisingly well, considering that her beliefs about bears must have been turned upside down. She realized that what happened to Emily was an accident and that the bears acted to save her child before the humans present could even react. I am not saying that Mrs. Hinkle is totally won over, but great strides were made in human-ursine relations."

"I am not questioning why the Captain values the polar bears, they are magnificent animals. These talking bears are certainly worthy of being called people," Elena said. "But sometimes he seems obsessed with them. Given everything else he has to do, they appear to be a distraction."

"I asked Jack about the bears once and he was uncharacteristically evasive," said Ludmilla with a shrug. "All he would say is that the bears have an important part to play in what will come."

While the tale of the polar bear field trip was unfolding, Jean-Jacques de Belcour had quietly approached the women's table. Ludmilla spotted him out of the corner of her eye. Her features hardened and she addressed him in a voice as cold as the polar bears' swimming pool. "What is it that you want, M. de Belcour?"

"Pardon me, Dr. Tropsha, ladies. I saw you all sitting together and thought that I might take this opportunity to make an apology."

"An apology?" said Gretchen, raising a single questioning eyebrow.

"Yes, Commander. I have come to realize that I have been acting in a most uncivilized manner and I wish to make amends," said the contrite Frenchman. "I promise not to act so *gauche* in the future." He then hurried off, not waiting for a reply.

"Now what the hell was that all about?" asked Gretchen, watching the UN representative depart. She looked at Ludmilla and their eyes met. *I agree, I don't trust that French snake as far as I can throw him*, she thought, knowing Ludmilla was thinking the same thing.

Chapter 12

Bridge, Peggy Sue, Farside Base Dry Dock

Things were moving apace on Peggy Sue's retrofit. New systems were installed and a combination of crew, base technicians and robots swarmed about testing equipment and making adjustments. On the bridge, Captain Jack and Lcdr. Curtis were running down checklists and attending to final details before relaunching the ship.

A spaceship the size of a modern navy destroyer presents a daunting list of requirements. Captaining such a ship, like running a base, requires attention to a thousand and one details—food, water, medical supplies and consumables of all types must be loaded and stored. Jack asked, "have the hydroponic gardens been reestablished?"

"Yes, Sir. Miss Hamilton and her crew have replanted and reorganized the hydroponic spaces in double quick time. They are already producing usable consumables."

"And the other supplies?"

"They will finish loading by the end of the day. Then we will be ready to load ordnance, the new missiles in particular."

"Good, I'm anxious to see how they perform. A torpedo with an antimatter warhead would have made short work of the refueling station in Beta Comae."

Gretchen sighed. "I guess that makes it official."

"What?"

"If you are calling the missiles torpedoes, then we may as well officially designate them as such."

The Captain chuckled. "Military personnel have a long standing tradition of calling things by names they favor, not the official names handed down by the powers that be. And in this case, I rather like the name 'torpedo' myself—it sounds more nautical than missile."

"Noted, Sir. Torpedoes they are." Gretchen smiled and consulted the next item on her tablet. "We will be ready to board the ship's complement in two days. Then we can start to depressurize the dock and a few hours after that we can get underway for the shakedown cruise."

"I, for one, cannot wait," Jack said longingly.

"Yes, Sir. I believe we are both sailors too long ashore," Gretchen replied with a grin.

"I think that we will visit some of the other planets in our home solar system—I swore to set foot on Mars and see the rings of Saturn up close before I die. We will also need to pick up some antimatter for use in the torpedoes." The alien antimatter 'liberated' from the Beta Comae refueling station was stored on several large asteroids, a prudent precaution given that a single large container of the stuff could end all life more complex than bacteria on a planet the size of Earth. "Send orders to all officers and crew: prepare for departure in two days."

"Aye aye, Sir," she acknowledged the order, making an annotation on her tablet. "With your permission, I would like to check on the combat training."

"Certainly, Commander. How is that going?"

"They've graduated to practicing maneuvers outside in full armor with live weapons. That's as close to the real thing we can manage, unless some of those spider things pop up."

"Maybe we should ask the robotics section to build some expendable target spiders," the Captain mused. "No matter, we are just about out of training time anyway. Do you have recommendations for the Marine detachment on the next mission?"

"I'm thinking first squad—twelve humans plus five bears, half our current strength—led by the Gunny, of course," she replied without hesitation. "That will leave five bears and the second squad of Marines for base defense. We need to convene a promotion board before the final assignments as well."

"Very well, Commander Curtis. Keep me apprised of their progress." As Gretchen departed the bridge, Jack looked out over the upgraded bridge, with its additional weapon operator stations and recited: "I must down to the seas again, to the lonely sea and the sky."

"And all I ask is a tall ship and a star to steer her by," added Billy Ray from the helm, where he was running diagnostics. "John Masefield."

"Very good, Mr. Vincent," the Captain smiled. "Carry on."

North Face Airlock, Farside Base

The last few squad members straggled into the large airlock, hidden in another collapsed lava tube. This one, on the north face of the volcanic dome containing Farside Base, was smaller than the tube that housed the ice haulers and shuttles but still large enough to accommodate the entire squad. The twelve human Marines and five ursines had spent the past six hours on maneuvers. Under the watchful eyes of Lt. Bear and GySgt Rodriguez, they practiced small unit tactics, ducking in and out of the shadows on the lunar surface.

The garage door sized airtight hatch closed silently behind them, there being no air to transmit sound. In due course, lights on the lock walls changed from red to green, indicating the presence of a breathable atmosphere.

"OK people, listen up," said Gunny Rodriguez. "You need to pass through the shower one at a time to wash off the moon dust. In case it isn't obvious, you should keep your helmets sealed until after the shower. Now move it."

Moon dust, a fine talc-like covering of pulverized rock was everywhere on the lunar surface. The powder actually consisted of jagged, crystalline rock particles formed by uncounted asteroid strikes over billions of years. It clung tenaciously and got into every crack and crevasse. After trying several other cleanup methods, the approach settled on was a high-pressure shower combined with ultrasound. Even then, the armored suits would need further cleaning by hand.

As the Marines emerged into the station proper they began to remove their helmets, affording them their first breaths of 'fresh' air in hours. "I don't care if these things are powered and the gravity is only 1/6th of Earth's," groused Joey Sanchez, "running around in armor is worse than slogging around with a rifle and vest back home."

"Joey, you would complain if you were being carted around in a sedan chair by nubile slave girls," replied Jon Feldman.

"Hey," said Bear, "it's when Sanchez stops complaining that I get nervous."

"You said it, LT," chimed in Ronnie Reagan. "The only time I remember him not complaining was on the Space Mushroom when we almost got our nads blown off."

The airlock operator called out, "Did you manage to shoot anything out there?"

"Nothing but a few moon rocks," answered Kato Kwan.

"Just how I wanted to spend my last weekend before shipping out," added Reagan. "Hell, we didn't even bag any Mooninites."

"To quote Ignignokt," added Jon Feldman, "Here on the moon, our weekends are so advanced, they encompass the entire week."

"What are they talking about?" whispered Aput to Isbjørn, totally confused by the Marines' banter.

"References to some obscure cartoon characters, if I'm not mistaken," she replied. "It would appear that you youngsters aren't the only adolescents among the ship's Marines."

Commanding Officer's Quarters, Farside Base

Several levels below the Administrative Offices was a block of large apartments, intended for high ranking officers and civilian officials. One of those apartments was designated as the base commander's quarters, currently occupied by Captain Sutton and Dr. Tropsha. Though even larger than the expansive owner's suite onboard the Peggy Sue, neither of its current residents felt comfortable living there—it was on the Peggy Sue that they were at home.

"Only two more days, Luda," Jack said to his lover and soul-mate. As the day of departure approached, Jack was becoming more and more keyed up, like a caged animal anticipating freedom.

"Be calm, Captain of my heart. You will ruin your digestion with all this worrying," replied Ludmilla from the bedroom. They were invited to dinner with TK Parker and would be going next door to TK's apartment, where an informal *bon voyage* party was being held.

"Sorry, love, force of habit," he replied. "A captain readying his ship to sail does not relax until he clears the outer channel marker. So much to do, so much that can go wrong."

"What was that saying you told me? Never borrow trouble?"

"You're right. If you set around waiting for something to go wrong, it will. Let's go next door and put a dent in TK's booze locker."

"Now that is the Jack I fell in love with," Ludmilla said with an impish smile. "Just do not get too drunk, you have obligations later in the evening."

* * * * *

Ludmilla and Jack arrived to find Gretchen and JT already there, and already partaking in some of TK's aged Kentucky Bourbon. They were seated in a large, sunken conversation pit on the far side of the spacious living room. A holographic fire crackled in the simulated fireplace, occasional pops heralding showers of heat-less sparks.

"Doc, Jack, come on in and take a load off," shouted the ebullient billionaire. He rolled over to the specially built bar in his custom, four wheel drive wheelchair while waving the newcomers in. "Pick yer poison, Ludmilla."

"Of course I must drink vodka, being Russian. What brands do you have?

"Let's see here, I got Reyka, 42 Below, Stolichnaya elit, Grey Goose and Crystal Head if yer lookin' for boutique brands."

"What is this Crystal Head, it sounds interesting."

"It's made in the wilds of Newfoundland, Canada, under the spiritual guidance of Dan Aykroyd, the comedian and actor. Supposedly it's filtered through diamonds. As you can see, it comes in a crystal skull bottle. Myself, I'm partial to 42 Below, the vodka from down under."

"It is made in Australia?"

"New Zealand, 42° south of the equator and 42% alcohol. Hell, they all taste the same to me, but then I'm a bourbon drinker."

"Do you have any in the freezer?"

"The 42 Below."

"I'll try that. Jack?" she said, turning to her escort.

"I'll try the Crystal Head. I'm always up for a new spiritual adventure," he grinned. "Besides, Aykroyd was a believer in space aliens before I was."

As TK poured, Ludmilla addressed the other guests. "JT, it is good to see you taking a break from work. The only place I have seen you recently is in sickbay, after you were abused by the bears in training."

"It's good to be here, Ludmilla," the science officer replied. "Even in the armored suits, the bears sometimes get a bit too enthusiastic. But they are all smart and eager to learn—they have really gotten the hang of combat as a team. Bear is a natural leader, as is Isbjørn."

"I had been complaining about him spending all his time either playing with the bears or the ship's new weapons systems, but now the shoe is on the other foot," added Gretchen. "Two days from sailing and now I'm the one with too much to do."

"And you love every minute of it," JT grinned at his partner. The relationship between Gretchen and JT was not of the forsaking-all-others-forevermore kind. They clearly enjoyed each other's company but there was no long-term commitment—more like friends with benefits.

"Only because it means we will soon be underway," she replied. "I'll feel so relieved to be back in space with a deck beneath my feet."

"I think we are all ready to sail for some distant star," said Jack, joining the group, drink in hand. He stepped down into the conversation pit and took a seat next to Ludmilla on one of the built-in curving couches. TK followed in his high-tech wheelchair, which handled the step as though it wasn't there. "You should reconsider coming with us on the shakedown flight, TK."

"Naw, Jack," the billionaire answered. "I've seen Earth and the Moon from space and now I'm content to just live quietly here on the farside. Besides, I'd just be excess baggage on board the Peggy Sue—here I have work to do."

"You do yourself a disservice, TK," Ludmilla responded. "You are a man of great experience and insight, and you would be a positive addition to our mission."

"Well thank you for saying so, young lady. But those new frigates ain't gonna build themselves and somebody needs to keep things running smoothly around here while y'all are out flitting from star to star."

"Speaking of stars," Jack said, purposely changing the subject to ease TK's obvious discomfort. "Have you decided which star should be first on our itinerary, JT?"

"That, Captain, is an interesting problem," JT answered. "Normally you would think that we should just head for the closest star on Dr. Piscopia's list, then the closest to that one, and so on. But if you want to minimize the total distance for the entire trip that might not be the best strategy."

"Really?" said Ludmilla.

"Yes, instead you need to consider a course that visits each star system once while minimizing the sum of the distances traveled between them—a little conundrum referred to as the traveling salesman problem."

Gretchen raised one inquisitive eyebrow and said dryly, "fascinating, Mr. Taylor. Do tell us more."

Ignoring his paramour's sarcasm he continued. "Computer scientists and graph theorists call this a Hamiltonian Circuit. In a simple undirected graph, a Hamiltonian circuit is a path that visits every vertex exactly once and then returns to the beginning of the path via an untraveled edge. Since our list of stars can be viewed as a fully connected graph, the optimum solution yields a total distance 45.98 parsecs. But it isn't that simple. We will be transiting

185

alter-space between systems, not 3-space, and that changes the effective distances among the stars."

"Going through alter-space really changes things that dramatically?" asked TK.

"It can, remember that alter-space transit times depend not only on distance but the masses of the two stars involved. For example, Zeta Tucanae is farthest from Earth measured in normal space at 9.2 parsecs. But if you calculate the transit times among all the systems and Earth, Zeta Tuc drops to third, with a transit time of 9.36 days. Our old friend, Beta Comae, which is farther away from Sol than all of the systems on our list, is actually closer in terms of travel time than all but two of the target stars."

"OK, so you ran your optimization program on the modified list and what did you get?" asked Gretchen.

"Not exactly, Elena and I figured that limiting the longest alter-space transit would be a good thing. The minimal circuit, with a total transit time just over 77 days, requires a nearly 24 day transit from Delta Pavonis to Gliese 581. By traveling from Sol to Gliese 581 first, and then on to 61 Virginis, we can trim the longest alter-space transit by 4.5 days. Optimizing the following hops makes our itinerary: Beta Hydri, Epsilon Eridani, Chara, Zeta Tuc, Delta Pavonis and then home."

"What does that do to total transit time?" asked Jack.

"Not much, total time is less than 79 days," JT answered, somewhat pleased with himself, "so we only add a day and a half total to cut the longest transit by more than four."

"It's settled then, great," the Captain pronounced.

"So our first leg will be the longest," Ludmilla asked, "and it will take us to the red dwarf with all the planets, the one that Sally asked about?"

"That's right, Gliese 581 is suspected of having six plants, one of them being a super-earth. From an astronomer's prospective, it may well be the most exciting stop on the trip."

"We'll have to put that in the brochure," TK quipped. Looking toward the dining room, he spied Maria coming their way. "It looks like Maria is ready to serve dinner, and just in the nick of time too. My stomach was startin' to think my throat had been cut."

Captain's Office, Farside Base

Jack was only suffering from a mild hangover following the previous evening's festivities. *You can say a lot of things about TK Parker*, he thought, *but that man can really hold his liquor.* The intercom chimed and his administrative assistant announced that Bear and Isbjørn had arrived. "Yes, Jimmy. Please show them in."

The office door slid open and two polar bears padded in, a large male and a female half his size. They ambled over to the desk and sat on the floor, then the male spoke. "You wanted to see us, Captain?"

"Yes I did, Lt. Bear, and you too, Isbjørn," Jack replied. "I wanted to speak with the two of you about the polar bear contingent for this next mission."

"Yes, Captain?" said Isbjørn. Of all the new bears, she had been the first to grasp the significance of what was happening at the lunar base, and what the next mission might entail.

"With the refitting of the Peggy Sue we were able to expand and improve on the polar bear quarters," Jack said. "To the point where we can reasonably accommodate five bears. That, of course, leaves us with the question of which five bears."

"I would expect that you will take Bear, since he is one of the ship's officers," ventured Isbjørn. "And if it is not too forward, I was hoping to accompany him." Both bears looked at each other and then back at the Captain.

"I had naturally planned on Bear," said the Captain, "and you, my dear, were at the top of my list. You have excelled during training and have demonstrated an ability to work well with humans."

"Thank you Captain," said Isbjørn, demurely looking down. "I won't disappoint you."

"Keeping in mind that this will be no pleasure cruise, and that living quarters onboard are not nearly as comfortable as those on the base, I would like your advice. Who should comprise the rest of Peggy Sue's bear contingent?"

Bear nodded and looked to Isbjørn, saying, "you first, babe."

"I would recommend that the mix of males and females be kept balanced—too many males in a confined space can lead to short tempers and misunderstandings." She looked directly at the Captain and blinked several times. "Assuming that, I would say that Inuksuk and Aurora would be the best choices."

"Explain," the Captain said, leaning back in his chair.

"They have both done well in the training and get along with each other well. The alternative would be Tornassuk and Snowflake, who have also bonded as a pair. The problem is that Tornassuk has not fully recovered from being shot—I don't know how he would take to the confined spaces onboard the ship."

"Bear?" Jack asked, looking at his master-at-arms.

"I would concur, Sir. Breaking up either pair would introduce unneeded tension. And Isbjørn's right, Tornassuk is not at 100% yet."

"Fine, what about a fifth?"

"It should be one of the younger bears," Isbjørn said tentatively. "Siku is very bright and Aput is quite outgoing with humans."

"Not Umky?" Jack asked, cutting to the heart of the matter.

Isbjørn looked at Bear with questioning eyes. She was hoping that the Captain did not think she was trying to protect her own cub by leaving him behind. After returning her gaze, Bear looked back to the Captain. "Sir, Umky is at an age when he needs to leave his mother and become his own bear. We are afraid that taking him on the mission might delay his development and also raise questions of nepotism."

"I see. And you agree, Isbjørn?"

"Yes, Captain. It would do him no good to stay so close to his mother—and it could possibly cloud my judgment under some circumstances."

"Very well, since we have an abundance of young males, Aput it is," Jack replied, leaning forward to operate the touch screen built into his desk's surface. "I'll have Lcdr. Curtis send out official notifications today. Is there anything else?"

"No, Sir," the bears said in unison.

"Then thank you for coming and I'll see both of you on board tomorrow. Dismissed," he said, returning his gaze to the desk top. As the bears exited the office he looked up at their disappearing backsides, thinking, *I'm glad you both wanted Umky to remain on the base, there are few enough talking polar bears as it is and I wouldn't want to lose both of your bloodlines if something goes terribly wrong during the mission.*

* * * * *

Isbjørn and Bear walked side by side across the broad terrace leading from the base administrative offices. Both wore thin white harnesses, providing a place to mount their comm pips and, in Bear's case, the silver bars of a Navy lieutenant. It had been discovered that humans felt more at ease around bears wearing the harnesses—perhaps the nod to wearing clothing, however minimal, made them seem less like wild animals.

"That went well," Isbjørn said to her companion. "The Captain seemed to have already thought this all through."

"That's what makes him the Captain, babe," Bear replied. "Now we have to break the news to Umky—he's not going to like staying behind."

"The day comes in every cub's life when he has to go out on the ice by himself," she replied. "Besides, I think that we could use some time alone together." As she voiced that opinion, her hips swayed, bringing their flanks into contact for half a step. Bear looked at his mate while she studiously looked away, gazing across the main concourse. *I hope that means what I think it means,* he thought with a toothy grin, causing several passing humans to give the pair a wider birth.

Peggy Sue, Departure from Farside Base

The bridge was fully manned and all of the observer's chairs were occupied as well. Everyone with an excuse to be on the bridge, with its spectacular view through the ship's transparent bow, was wedged in somewhere. Even Jean-Jacques de Belcour was present, sitting in one of the guest's chairs behind the Captain.

In the days before departure, Jean-Jacques had gone out of his way to mend fences with the officers and crew. Eventually he petitioned the Captain to include him on the new mission, citing the usefulness of having an indisputably independent witness to whatever transpired on the voyage. The Captain agreed to the request without comment. However, to Lcdr. Curtis he said: "Put him in a single birth stateroom. I don't want to inflict him on anyone else."

Those who did not have a duty station, and not privileged enough to rate a place on the bridge, were crowded into the ship's main lounge. Normally the lounge served as the wardroom for the ship's officers and scientists, but on special occasions it was opened to all on board. Prime seats at the tables in front of the large, eye shaped viewport had been claimed hours ago, while boarding was still underway.

At the port side personnel hatch on first deck, Lcdr. Curtis was standing, tablet in hand, running down the list of personnel who were on board and shipyard workers still to disembark. From behind her came the unmistakable sound of the Chief.

"Move yer worthless carcases or yous will find yer selves floating home." The last time the Peggy Sue left port there were a number of trapped guests and a pair of stowaways on board, much to the Chief's displeasure. "Yous better double time it down the gangway and straight to the dock exit, or the air might get a bit thin."

"Good luck, Ma'am," said one of the shipyard workers as they exited the ship and hurried down the gangway that extended to the fused stone floor of the dock. Gretchen could not tell if the dockworker meant good luck on the voyage or with the Chief.

"Well, that's the last of 'em by my count, Commander." The grizzled Chief-of-the-Ship ran his left hand across the back of his neck, as if to wipe away something distasteful. "Ain't gonna be no stowaway shitbirds on this cruise."

"Those were the last two on my list as well, Chief," Gretchen replied, consulting her tablet. She knew that the Chief didn't really hate the dockworkers, he was simply honoring the long standing tradition of collegial hazing that always took place between shipyard workers and Navy sailors. Like opposing sports teams, sailors and shipyard workers had considerable respect for each other, but they'd be damned if they would admit it. "Let's button her up, Chief."

"Aye aye, Commander," he said as he pressed a control on the wall panel. With a sound similar to an airliner raising its flaps, the gangway began to rise and retract into the side of the ship. At the same time the curved airlock door slid down from its open position, nestled along the hull of the ship above the doorway. It dropped down to cover the airlock entrance and sealed flush against the hull with bank-vault like solidity. "We got a good seal and the ramp is stowed."

Gretchen nodded and spoke into her comm pip. "Bridge, port airlock."

"Go, port airlock" came the instant reply.

"Captain, the ship's company is all present or accounted for, all base personnel are disembarked, and the ship is sealed. We are ready to start dock depressurization."

"Roger that, Commander. We will start depressurization directly. Bridge out." All of the scaffolding that surrounded the ship for weeks had been carefully removed, mindful of the damage inflicted on similar scaffolding back in Texas when the ship first launched. This time there would be nothing around the Peggy Sue when the ship's repulsors lifted her 8000 metric tons from the dock floor, not even air.

Gretchen smiled and spoke to the Chief, "Looks like we are finally ready to get underway Chief. I'm heading back to the bridge."

"Yes, Ma'am. I'm gonna go check on the crew. First time leaving port for most of 'em. They'd better be standing to, bright eyed and bushy tailed."

* * * * *

A little over an hour later the massive doors that covered the top of the shipyard dock slid silently aside, uncovering a infinitely black crack of sky. The dock was empty and under vacuum, warning lights flashed at airlock entrances in the bay walls. The ship's hull had no noticeable air leaks, the reactors were run up to full power and the drives were in ready standby—the Peggy Sue was ready to depart.

"Farside port control, Peggy Sue," called the Captain.

"Go ahead, Peggy Sue."

"The Peggy Sue requests clearance to depart."

"Roger, Peggy Sue. You are cleared for departure. Good luck and godspeed."

"Thank you Farside. We will see you in 30 days," Jack acknowledged. Sitting behind the Captain in the observers' seats, Jean-Jacques whispered to Dr. Li, who was beside him, "Well it is about time."

"Chill out, Jean-Jacques," Sally replied, "for a UN bureaucrat you have little patience." *And precious little diplomacy either,* she added silently.

Lcdr. Curtis entered the bridge and stood beside the Captain's command chair. "Captain, all stations are manned and ready, all sections report ready to depart," she said, with a barely restrained smile.

"Thank you, Commander. Helm, activate the bottom repulsors," the Captain ordered. "Lift her out of this hole in the ground, Mr. Danner."

"Aye aye, Captain," came Bobby's reply. Bobby and Billy Ray were seated at the dual pilot stations. At the auxiliary stations sat Sandy and Nigel, the ship's newest lieutenants, observing the first team in action. Slowly, the 500 foot long ship rose above the dock floor, its six massive landing legs folding seamlessly into the hull.

"Mr. Medina," the Captain called out. "Maintain normal deck gravity and bring the shields up at minimum until we clear the dock."

"Aye aye, Sir," replied Jo Jo Medina from the engineering station on the port side, aft of the captain's chair. With no sense of movement and no noise save the occasional muted beep from the instrument panels, the Peggy Sue floated silently upward like a balloon.

Clearing the top of the volcanic dome, the stark landscape of the Moon dramatically appeared in the ship's viewports. A tangle of jagged black and grays tumbled away to a horizon that looked close enough to touch. The Moon was nearing first quarter to earthbound observers, meaning the day-night terminator was approaching Farside Base from the east, long shadows disappearing into dim grayness and then inky darkness.

"C'est magnifique!" Jean-Jacques softly exclaimed. Having been interned below on his arrival at Farside Base this was his first close up view of Earth's satellite.

"Indeed it is, M. de Belcour," the Captain answered. "One of the original Apollo astronauts described it as 'magnificent desolation'." *At least this UN bureaucrat still retains enough of a soul to be appropriately awed by the Universe around us.* After a few more seconds of appreciative silence the Captain's own revery broke. "Mr. Taylor, have you plotted our course to Mars?"

"Aye, Captain. Plotted and sent to the helm."

"Very good, Mr. Taylor. Mr. Vincent, all ahead one quarter and set course for Mars."

"Aye aye, Sir. We are underway for the red planet." The Moon dropped swiftly behind the ship while those quick enough on the port side caught sight of Earth as it emerged from behind its companion. Both were rapidly left behind as the Peggy Sue carried mankind's first visitors toward the solar system's fourth planet and points beyond.

Chapter 13

Peggy Sue, Saturn Orbit, 25 Days Later

Wreathed in its glorious rings, Saturn hung majestically in space off Peggy Sue's starboard bow. A portly ball, banded by clouds—smokey brushstrokes in shades of brown, tan and cream. The rings were also painted in the same soft pallet, though hints of blue and yellow were visible on closer inspection. Nine main rings and countless minor ones, consisting mostly of ice particles with smaller amounts of rocky debris and dust, ranged from nearly transparent to seeming solidity. Faint radial spokes moved across the rings' surfaces, interrupted only by the shadow of the planet itself, a visual manifestation of Saturn's enormous magnetic field.

A clutch of 53 named moons attend the court of Saturnus, ancient Roman god of agriculture, strength and justice, largest of these the appropriately named Titan. Larger than Mercury, Titan is the only moon in the solar system with a significant atmosphere. If not kept in thrall by its giant parent, it would be counted a planet in its own right. As such, Titan presented a perfect test subject for the instruments and robotic probes that would be used to look for life on planets circling alien stars—some of the science section were secretly hoping to find signs of life on Titan itself.

The crew manning various stations on the bridge and in the CIC did not have time to gaze in admiration upon nature's tableau—they were in the process of completing another in a series of training exercises. Overlaying the view of the solar system's most magnificent planet, lines, symbols and annotations in glowing red, blue and green formed a gloss on nature's handiwork. Using data provided by Peggy Sue's sensors, each moon was carefully labeled and its orbital vector noted. From this crowded neighborhood, a tiny object followed a divergent path, headed toward the ship. It was a shuttle returning from dropping probes into the dense atmosphere of Titan.

"Captain, we have a shuttle inbound from Titan, 100,000 kilometers out and closing at 45 km/s," reported Lcdr. Curtis from the CIC. The Combat Information Center was a new addition to Peggy Sue's bridge area, an enclosed space behind the bridge proper. Located between the engineering and navigation stations, its purpose was to collect, display, evaluate and disseminate tactical information for use by the commanding officer. It could also serve as a tactical command center when a boarding or shore party were operating outside of the ship. The CIC concept was adopted by the U.S. Navy during WWII, supposedly taken from the *Lensman* novels of E.E. 'Doc' Smith, an early 20th century science fiction writer.

"Roger, CIC. Let me know when it is within 100 kilometers," Captain Jack responded. In all, it had been a successful cruise: they had visited Mars, the asteroid belt, and now Saturn. He had landed the ship in the caldera of Olympus Mons, the largest volcano in the solar system, giving all aboard the right to say that they were among the first Earthlings to touchdown on the surface of Mars. In a rare assertion of his prerogative as master and commander of the Peggy Sue, Jack himself was the first to set foot on the red planet.

The ship's planetary scientists were beside themselves with joy, deploying seismic sensors and collecting samples from the dead volcano and several other sites around the planet. Scientific bounty not withstanding, Dieter Schmitt remarked that there were so many people on board that the only one who would be remembered for landing first on Mars would be the Captain.

"Who remembers the others who were with Armstrong on the first Moon landing?" he remarked sourly. "We will be lucky to be mentioned in a textbook appendix."

This prompted the Captain to send an email to TK Parker, back at Farside Base, asking him to commission a commemorative plaque, listing the names of all on board. It would be installed in the main hall of the base to be built atop Olympus Mons.

Following the all too brief stay on Mars, the Peggy Sue made her way to Saturn by way of the asteroid belt. There a supply of antimatter was retrieved, plunder taken from the alien refueling station at Beta Comae. Since arriving at the sixth planet, more scientific probes were deployed. Dual purpose missions to several of the moons ferried scientific personnel and Marines, who practiced landing and maneuvers under the differing, unearthly conditions.

Jack and Ludmilla accompanied the Marines during a visit to Enceladus, a moonlet covered with ice and snow. As the party hiked across its frozen, fractured surface they came upon a sight unlike anything else in the solar system. On the horizon, back-lit by the distant Sun, rose a shimmering curtain. From a 300 km long crack in the moon's icy surface, geysers spewed water vapor into the inky black sky.

Emerging from the liquid sea beneath the surface icepack, the water vapor immediately froze into a rising wall of ice crystals, extending 500 km into space. From there the crystals fell slowly back to the moon's surface as snow. All of the bears were entranced, sitting down on the snowy surface and wordlessly staring at the spectacle in front of them.

"Now that is a sight worth leaving home for," Bear commented, breaking the silence.

"Indeed it is," agreed Isbjørn. "You are a bear of your word. You said you would show me sights unlike any at home." The sight was breath taking and it took the better part of a half hour before the squad was ready to move out again. Even the Gunny was taken by the ghostly spectacle, though the sergeant was unwilling to admit it.

While the Marines practiced landings on several other moons, back on board the ship the pilots and gun crews threw themselves enthusiastically into their work. The ship itself was performing splendidly, so well that Chief Zackly complained that the engineers and damage control parties were not getting enough training. Of course the Chief was never satisfied—it was part of his job description.

Damned if I don't think we're ready to get underway for our true objectives, Jack observed. *Once we recover the shuttle, I think we shall head for home and a quick resupply, then on to Gliese 581.* The Captain did not want to drill the crew to the point of exhaustion. As in sports, optimal training brings a team to its peak just in time for the championship game. "Helm, be prepared to break orbit once the incoming shuttle is retrieved."

"Aye aye, Sir."

"CIC, let's wrap this exercise up and prepare to set course for home. Starboard section and I will take the Klingon death watch." The Klingon death watch—a term borrowed from the submarine service—was the watch following a long period of continuous drills.

It was generally considered suck duty because the watch standers got no break following the practice exercises. That was why Jack was standing the watch himself, it was harder for the crew to bitch when the Old Man was pulling the same duty.

"Commander, you might wish to visit the science and medical sections and inform them that we are about to depart."

"Aye aye, Sir," Gretchen replied and headed aft.

* * * * *

As Lcdr. Curtis traveled aft she passed through the ship's main lounge. There, standing in front of the large, eye shaped observation port was JT, staring moodily at the giant planet below. Moving next to him, Gretchen softly placed a hand on his shoulder. "Magnificent, isn't it?"

"Yes, more spectacular than I ever imagined," he replied. "First time we saw the lounge viewport, I remember saying how cool it would be to have a drink at the bar as the rings of Saturn slipped by."

"Well you are doing just that... except for the drink."

"Yeah, but I always thought that I would be recording a spot and she would be doing the on-camera narration."

"You and Susan?" Gretchen asked, both sympathy and personal sadness in her voice.

"She really would have loved seeing this," he said softly.

"Everyone who knew her misses her, JT," she told her partner, wishing she could ease his pain. "I can't help feeling that she is with us in spirit."

"I hope so," he said faintly. "I truly hope so."

She knew there was nothing she could do—reconciling one's feelings after the loss of a close companion took time. Particularly when the companion was so young and killed in combat. But both she and JT were combat veterans, living with loss came with the job. The feeling of loss never goes away, but the pain eventually fades. She squeezed his shoulder and quietly continued on her way aft.

Peggy Sue, Departure for Gliese 581

The 1.5 billion kilometers back to Farside Base passed quickly, with the ship accelerating at 20 Gs for 10 hours and then coasting at nearly 13 million kph before decelerating to make lunar orbit, a little over 5 days total. After arriving, a couple of engineering techs, who were only on board for the shakedown cruise, were shuttled down to the base. On the return trip, a few late additions to the science section ferried up to the ship, along with fresh supplies and replacement parts.

Then, final goodbyes said, the Peggy Sue headed for the alter-space transfer point to Gliese 581. Their destination lay slightly south of the ecliptic plane and 20.55 light years away. The transfer point lay almost an AU outside Earth's orbit, beyond the orbit of Mars. The ship took a leisurely three days to carefully align its course vector to the faint red star, invisible to the naked eye from Earth.

The Captain was being extra careful in setting the ship's course, since this would be the longest trip through the Universe's hidden dimensions yet attempted. The trip through alter-space would take nearly 20 days—three times as long as the trip to Beta Comae. This despite the fact that Beta Comae was more than thirty light years away, 50 percent farther away than Gliese 581. It was because of Gliese 581's small mass that the trip would take so long and extra care was needed with the entry parameters.

Finally, all conditions were met and the Captain ordered the ship's computer to take them into alter-space. Viewed from outside, the 8,000 ton vessel appeared to ripple and vanish, leaving behind a burst of gamma rays and a spray of fundamental particles —the second mission of the Peggy Sue was underway.

Third Moon, Gas Giant, CF Ursae Majoris

CF Ursae Majoris, also known as Groombridge 1830, is unusually faint for its spectral type. A G8 type star, it is sufficiently cool to have not evolved appreciably since its formation—spectral analysis classified it as a yellow-orange halo subdwarf star with perhaps 60 percent of Sol's mass, but only 19 percent of its luminosity. It is, however, no innocuous little star.

Halo subdwarf status suggests that the star formed during a period of rapid collapse that lasted perhaps a billion years in the early history of the Milky Way galaxy, when the galactic disk was just starting to form. This would make the star around 10 billion years old, twice the age of the Sun. More importantly, the designation 'CF' identifies Groombridge 1830 as a type of flare star. Some Sol-type stars of spectral classes F and G have been observed producing enormous magnetic outbursts—coronal mass ejections that release between hundreds and millions of times more energy than the largest flares ever observed on the Sun.

These super-flares can last an hour or a week, during which they increase the normal luminosity of a star by as much as a thousand fold. If our Sun were to produce such a super-flare Earth's ozone layer would be destroyed and ice on the daylight side of moons as far out as Jupiter and Saturn would melt. This dangerously volatile condition makes CF Ursae Majoris an unlikely system to harbor life, but on the third moon of the system's single large gas giant planet, it does just that.

An ammonia based biosphere on that moon managed to produce a dominant, intelligent species in spite of its star's occasional fiery outbursts. These creatures simply referred to themselves as 'people'. On their own, they developed a rudimentary technological civilization, to the point where they launched satellites into orbit around the gas giant their world circles. Perhaps one day they would have made it to the stars on their own, but that was not their destiny.

The people's primitive space program attracted the attention of a probe ship belonging to the Dark Ones. From the point of view of the Dark Ones, the inhabitants of CF Ursae Majoris did not quite qualify as a species of the never-to-be-sufficiently-damned warm life. They occupied an intermediate position on the continuum of life forms from hot to frigid. Rather than cleanse the moon of all life, the Dark Ones decided to co-opt its inhabitants, turning them into Janissaries—soldier slaves in the service of the empire of darkness.

From the point of view of the People it was a good deal, they traded extinction for a chance to travel the stars—the only catch was they had to occasionally snuff out life on other worlds. And so it came to pass that a ship, more than five kilometers long with a great mushroom cap of rocky debris at its head, was dispatched on a mission of extermination. It would travel first to the system known to humans as Beta Comae Berenices, where it would pick up the trail of the latest warm life vermin to vex the dark masters.

Their voyage of destruction would continue until some temperate planet with a functioning ecosystem was laid waste—the Dark Ones did not accept failure. If this meant that those on board the Destroyer of Worlds might never see home again, so be it. That was the pact they had made with the Dark Ones, a Faustian bargain that would someday claim their species' collective soul. But for now, the people enjoyed riches, technology and power. Compared with that, what did the continued existence of a species they had never met matter? It was not like they were people.

Engineering Workshop, Peggy Sue, Alter-space Day 10

JT and Bear were staring intently at the fabricator, as though their impatience could speed up production of the new part. Inside its protective cover, the fab was constructing a complex, three dimensional object from powdered metal and laser light. The growing metal part was based on a design by JT, who was anxious to see the result of his labors, but it was Bear who was truly excited.

Both JT and Bear had been active participants in the two battles Earthlings fought against the aliens. It was JT who had redesigned the Marines' weapons and created the first type of battle armor. Worn during the battle on board the refueling station in the Beta Comae system—called the Battle of the Space Mushroom by the Marines—the old armor was heavy and clunky but it had undoubtedly saved several lives.

From that experience more advanced, powered armor was developed, along with more refined weapons to go with it. With the help of GySgt Rodriguez and the science staff, they even produced a number of armed, six wheeled autonomous robots that could be used for area defense and sentry duty. These developments were all good, but one thing continued to aggravate Bear.

When the fighting got up close and personal, the humans were happy to flail away at the enemy with their armored fists. Some might even confess to enjoying aggression on such an immediate and personal level. The bears could also bludgeon their opponents with their even more sizable forelegs but, from an ursine point of view, something was missing—claws.

Nature had given polar bears five steak knife length claws on each paw, armament that the bears grew up with. While smacking things around with armored suit mitts was fairly effective, the bears, without exception, missed being able to rip open an adversary with their claws. So several weeks into the long alter-space transit to Gliese 581, having tired of Bear's persistent complaining, JT decided to rectify the claw situation.

The fabricator began beeping, an indication that it had completed its task. "All right," said JT, opening the fab unit. "Let's see what we have here."

Bear stood over his shoulder, shifting back and forth from left paw to right. "I can't wait to see this," he said. "Fighting without claws is like having sex while wearing, well, a spacesuit."

"Keep your fur on, big guy. We still need to polish them up and sharpen the edges, assuming they work this time." The first few attempts had been less than satisfactory. The metal claws either interfered with the operation of firearms and other manual tasks, or they did not protrude far enough to be used effectively. "Slip on your suit torso so I can attach the claws to the carrier piece."

Bear hustled to comply. This latest attempt consisted of a carrier that fit on the foreleg section of a bear's armor. Into this was fit the claw module itself, consisting of four long metal fingers ganged together at their base, tipped with 12cm long knife edged blades. When not in use, the claws would retract safely into the carrier on Bear's arm.

Bear stared intently as JT inserted the new part into the existing carrier piece, already attached to Bear's suit. "OK, we are going to have to adjust the extension trigger. Remember what I told you, if you curve your real claws forward inside your gauntlet the metal claws should deploy—give it a try."

"Right," bear said, holding his arm out and flexing his natural claws withing the suit. With a sound of metal sliding on metal, the four prosthetic claws shot into place. "Oh, do I like that!"

"Try retracting them."

Bear straighten his paw, but nothing happened. For a few seconds he waived his foreleg around and finally, the four metallic claws snapped back into the carrier. "Needs a little adjustment," he commented.

"Yeah, put your arm on the bench and let me adjust the sensors," JT replied. "Then we can try hacking up a few things, just to make sure they don't break off the first time you try to use them."

"That would suck," Bear acknowledged, complying with JT's request. "I tell you JT, this is going to make the other bears very happy, almost as happy as I am."

"I see shredded aliens in our future," JT said dryly. "Just don't be so anxious to go Wolverine on our next opponents that you forget you have firearms. I know bears like to mix it up, paw to paw, but these are for desperate circumstances, not a weapon of first choice."

"What's a 'Wolverine'?"

"A comic book character whose claws extend like these do. In fact, that's where I got the idea from. I'll clean the first set up while the fab makes a second set for your other arm, then we can do some serious testing."

"OK, now about teeth..."

Bridge, Peggy Sue, Gliese 581 System

Nearly twenty days after entering alter-space, a sense of excitement, of anxious expectation, ran through all on board. The bridge was fully manned and the Captain was in the command chair as the seconds to reemergence ticked down to zero. With the briefest of tremors, the ship slid between dimensions and once again found itself in normal 3-space.

Ahead, directly in front of the ship's transparent bow, was Gliese 581—a malevolent red ember looming as large as Sol seen from Earth. That the small red dwarf appeared so large was an indication of how close to the star they had emerged, a distance of around a half an AU, roughly the radius of Mercury's orbit back home.

The Captain snapped out orders: "Shields to standard. Helm, put us in a solar orbit. Mr. Taylor, see if we are alone in the system and locate any planets." A chorus of "aye ayes" answered as the crew bent to their tasks.

"Captain, I have a terrestrial planet, approximately 1.7 Earth mass, orbiting very close to the star. Looks like an orbital radius of only 0.03 AU," reported JT from the astronomy and navigation console. "That would give it a year of about 3.15 days—it must be 581e."

"That is too close for any reasonable chance of life," added Elena, who was also sitting at the astronomy station. "We are looking for planets with orbits between 0.08 and 0.24 AU."

"There is another planet close in, this one is the size of Neptune but only 0.04 AU out," JT read off. "Ah, now this is more like it. I have a terrestrial planet, orbit 0.22 AU, that's near the outer edge of the habitable zone. Mass is 5.7 and the diameter is 1.9 times that of Earth, with a year lasting 67 Earth days. I'm getting spectral indications of nitrogen, oxygen, H_2O and CO_2 in the atmosphere."

"Almost six times as massive as Earth?" asked Lcdr. Curtis, "isn't that going to make the surface gravity significantly higher than home?"

"It looks like the density is not as high as Earth, and given the mass and diameter the surface gravity should be 15.47 m/sec^2, 1.578 times Earth normal," JT answered, looking up from his instrument display. "That's noticeably higher than home, but manageable."

"I'm getting mixed temperature readings, the night side is well below freezing and the readings from the daylight equatorial zone are above 50°C." added Elena. "The planet's rotation must be tidally locked, try to narrow the temperature sensors to focus on the day-night terminator."

"Yeah, I'm getting readings from patches of land around 6-8°, which is a bit cool but certainly habitable. Quite a bit of carbon dioxide in the atmosphere, nearly ten times Earth levels, and the surface is mostly water—one giant ocean on the front side and totally frozen over on the back. It looks like there is a permanent storm system at the point nearest the star and large circulation cells from there to the terminator. The wind probably howls down there most of the time."

"So it is worth a closer look?" asked the Captain.

"Yes! Very much so," exclaimed Elena, her eyes bright. "This is much better than I could have hoped for. An oxygen-nitrogen atmosphere with plenty of liquid water, in a system that is 3 to 4 billion years older than the solar system—if life is common in the Universe then we should find it here."

"Very good, Dr. Piscopia. Mr. Medina, ready a couple of survey drones for orbital injection," Jack ordered. "Helm, make for the planet indicated by Mr. Taylor. I think a polar orbit above the day-night terminator would be appropriate..."

Valley of the Trailing Conclave, Gliese 581d

SudNabSon the Contemplative became the nexus for information interchange among the savants of the Trailing Conclave. This was based on their clarity of thought and ability to quickly assimilate new data. Forming a nexus was required based on a report by TagFetLuw the Outward Looking, verified by GipNarKos the Ensurer of Continuity, that a spacecraft harboring life of some form had just emerged from the lesser dimensions into local spacetime in close proximity to the world. An extended consensus would be required.

"It arrived from a distant star; It is under power; It is headed our way," said TagFetLuw.

"Is that most probable? What form of propulsion drives the vessel? Does it maneuver for orbit or pass the world by?" responded SudNabSon.

"Its method of trans-dimensional passage is quite primitive making an interstellar transit most probable; Gravitonic drives powered by a catalyzed fusion reaction; It will arrive in orbit in a 60th of a solar orbit," responded TagFetLuw, at least a third miffed.

"No denigration of observational accuracy intended; A primitive craft should pose no threat; More will be revealed as it draws closer," was the conciliatory reply.

"The threat is minimal; Indications are that the lifeforms are from a warm world; There are technological similarities to other, older known craft," added GipNarKos.

After a brief pause to map the wave of incoming responses from the rest of the Conclave and reduce their essence, SudNabSon declared a plan of action, "More observation is indicated; If the ship contains new species we must ascertain their disposition regarding the Great Schism; Care must be taken before revealing our capabilities."

"Agreed; Most certainly; We remain vigilant," came the consensus reply of the Conclave. Those who observed such phenomena would continue to watch, when sufficient data were gathered more decisions would be called for. In the meantime, the Conclave's data and decisions would be relayed to other conclaves around the world.

Chapter 14

Peggy Sue, Polar Orbit, Gliese 581d

Less than 24 hours later, the Peggy Sue was in a polar orbit around the fourth planet circling Gliese 581. From faster, inclined orbits, twin drones were busy using hyperspectral remote sensors to map the planet's surface. What little land was visible was concentrated along the day-night terminator, low stony fingers jutting sun-ward from the permanent ice of the planet's farside.

This world possessed significantly more water than Earth, with a pronounced tidal bulge. The bulge was fortunate, since without it what dry land existed could well have been submerged. Looking down with the ship's most powerful short range telescope, using reflected laser light to correct for atmospheric distortion, the science team was becoming more and more excited.

"Why doesn't all that water just evaporate and freeze out on the dark side?" asked Olaf Gunderson.

"A reasonable question, Dr. Gunderson," replied Elena, fully glorying in their discovery. "Simulations have suggested that a planet with only 10 percent of Earth's atmosphere and a sunward ocean temperature of 5°C would be able to maintain a global liquid environment, even beneath the icecap on the dark side."

"Captain, you should see this!" called Sally Li. "There are definite signs of forestation on some of the larger land masses, and possible low cover on others. Forests of any kind have only existed on Earth for 400 million years."

"Put it on the forward screen, Mr. Taylor," the Captain replied, somewhat amused by the near giddy excitement gripping the expedition's biologists. A few seconds later, the view forward became a wide screen image looking down at the planet below.

"Yes, Sally," said Olaf, coming forward to the upper bridge near the Captain, "I believe that you are correct. Those are some form of vegetation—tall stalks with a single broad leaf at the top. In this red light they appear black, perhaps to absorb maximum photonic energy."

"That is assuming they are anything like Earth plants," said Ludmilla, joining Olaf. "We must not let our Earthly prejudices get the better of us."

"Ya, true, Ludmilla. But you have to admit that the way they are arranged and their form makes it likely they are some form of plant life."

"If you mean a form of photosynthetic, eukaryotic, multicellular organism, we'll see," Sally added. Then, turning to Jack: "We will get a chance to see, won't we Captain?"

"Once the survey is completed and we've had a day or so to observe any surface activity," Jack replied. "If things look reasonably safe we will send a landing party."

"Of course, we are looking at the land," Ludmilla mused. "Given how wet this world is, the advanced lifeforms might live beneath that planet spanning ocean."

"Look there, in that valley," said Sally, absorbed by the images in front of her. "What are those plants, some form of cactus? Look how they seem to be formed in clusters of three..."

Valley of the Trailing Conclave, Gliese 581d

The strange craft had entered orbit and, showing a sign of moderate intelligence, chose to orbit the world above the zone of twilight. The growing volume of data reached an inflection point, causing SudNabSon to reopen the nexus regarding the visiting ship.

"They proceed cautiously; No hint of violence; Definitely warm life," commented TagFetLuw, starting the discussion.

"Indicating that they seek knowledge; No blind aggression; Yes, carbon-water based life," said GipNarKos, in general agreement with TagFetLuw.

A brief reduction and then SudNabSon pronounced, "Possibilities of sentient fellowship; Still, they possess weapons of considerable power; Similar enough to live in each other's environments."

"We should attempt to communicate; They have quantities of antimatter; No such creatures have visited for millions of orbits," GipNarKos advanced.

"A global consensus will be needed; Dangerous if we are caught off guard; Query the archives," replied SudNabSon.

Another short delay. QivCakJol the Minder of Antiquities spoke for the archivists, "Global consensus is traditional under such circumstances; The Guardians are alert, the danger vanishingly small; The ship's design is reminiscent of those used by one of the Paladin races 22 million orbits ago."

"Consensus to open communication with the strangers will be sought; The Guardians protect the world as always; Perhaps the strangers are a new race of Paladins," SudNabSon said.

"Seek wider consensus; The world remains safe; More must be learned of these creatures," came the consensus from the Conclave.

Forward Shuttle Dock, Peggy Sue, Gliese 581d

The members of the surface expedition were boarding the large shuttle through the forward docking facility. Among those on board were Lt. Bear, Isbjørn, Sally Li, the Gunny and five Marines. The shuttle itself was piloted by Sandy McKennitt with Steve Hitch and Matt Jacobs along as crew. The remainder of the expedition were embroiled in a heated discussion at the foot of the boarding ladder.

"I told you that I will not permit Olaf to go on this mission," Dr. Tropsha was saying to the Captain. "He has elevated blood pressure and there is no sense taking a chance by locking him in a heavy suit of armor and making him hike around on a planet with 1.6 times normal gravity. It is an invitation to a stroke or heart attack."

"I am not questioning your medical judgment with regard to Dr. Gunderson," Jack replied. "What I am questioning is the necessity for you to take his place on the expedition."

"Without Olaf, Sally is the only trained biologist," Ludmilla replied, exasperation in her voice. She was already wearing an armored space suit with a bubble helmet beneath her arm. "There should be at least two qualified scientists to cross validate any on-site observations. I am arguably the only other biologist available."

"But you are also the head of the medical section," insisted Jack, feeling the argument slipping away. Every fiber of Jack's being screamed *keep her here, keep her safe*, but intellectually he realized that Ludmilla was as much of an adventurous spirit as he was. After all, she had joined the Russian space program and earned herself a place on the International Space Station before she and Jack ever met.

"We have two other doctors, two medical corpsmen and a nurse, I will not be missed for a day or two. Besides, it is not a bad idea to have a medical doctor along on the expedition in case of an accident."

"Dr. Tropsha's reasoning is sound, Captain," added Lcdr. Curtis, likewise attired in space armor. "I wouldn't mind having a medic along, just in case."

Jack sighed. He knew that he was not going to win this argument. If he forbade her going on the expedition she would never forgive him, and that was more frightening to contemplate than any hypothetical danger waiting on the planet's surface. "Very well, just try not to overload the shuttle with specimens on the trip back."

"Thank you, Captain," both women replied. Gretchen said, "I'll see you on board, Doctor," and climbed the air-stair to the shuttle, leaving Jack and Ludmilla alone.

"Do not worry, my Captain," Ludmilla said in a softer voice. "I will be careful. I have two bears and half the Marines to protect me."

"I can't help but worry—our first planet, our first surface expedition, so many unknowns." His eyes met her's and they stood, frozen for an instant. Then Jack nodded and said, "stay safe, my Lady."

Ludmilla smiled, turned and ascended the boarding ladder. The Captain stepped out of the airlock and cycled the door. "Shuttle One, you are clear to undock."

* * * * *

On board the shuttle, Ludmilla made her way forward, past the already seated Marines, to find a seat between Sally Li and Gunny Rodriguez. Across from them were seated Lcdr. Curtis, Lt. Bear and Isbjørn. "We good to go?" asked the Gunny.

"Yes, Gunny, just a little last minute separation anxiety," Ludmilla replied.

"The Captain is just a bit nervous, letting you out of his sight again," replied Bear. "Remember the last time? The Chief got shot, you almost got kidnapped and we gained a French asshole."

The comment earned him an ineffectual poke in the armored ribs from Isbjørn. "Of course the Captain is concerned, you big lug," she said, offering Ludmilla a bearish smile.

"I can always count on you for the unembellished truth, Bear. And you are right, Isbjørn, the Captain worries about all of us," Ludmilla said. "I am not trying to be a bitch, but we have a mission to do and all of our lives are already at risk simply by being here. Our enemies have weapons that can sterilize whole planets. If the natives are hostile, going to the surface is no more dangerous than staying in orbit."

"That's why the Captain agreed," said Lcdr. Curtis, "He didn't like it, but he knew it was the right decision. That's why he's the Captain." *And some day I hope I'll do the job half as well as he does.* "Let's go over the mission objectives again, since we've nothing else to do on the trip dirtside..."

Valley of the Trailing Conclave, Gliese 581d

Transmissions from other conclaves arrived in a clustered burst, as such transmissions are wont to. Reducing the world consensus to its essence, SudNabSon informed the other members of the Trailing Conclave. "Communication should be attempted with the aliens; An invitation to land down slope of the Conclave extended; A prospective ambassador must be selected."

"The water band should be used; A site on the small cove should suffice; We have not selected an ambassador in ages, how to select?" replied GipNarKos, concerned as always with maintaining continuity with past decisions and actions of the race.

"A suitable frequency range; A site as good as any other; Ambassadors must be flexible of thought," commented QivCakJol the Antiquarian. This led to a conclave wide interchange of ideas regarding who should be chosen. After sufficient data were collated, SudNabSon again distilled the group's opinion, "The transmission will proceed; The landing site suffices; The ambassador shall be NatHanGon the Nearly Wise."

NatHanGon was a young philosopher, only 800 thousand orbits old and still sufficiently mobile to venture forth from the valley. They were also still young enough to not become terminally depressed by being out of contact with others of their kind. As they began pulling up root, NatHanGon was of three minds about being chosen: *Was this an honor? Was this a burden? Was this an exciting opportunity to learn new things?*

The interconnecting roots of the hundreds of entities comprising the Trailing Conclave began pulsing with a frequency near 1.420 gigahertz. The message sent was a progression of symbols, advancing to meta-symbols and ending in simple thoughts. A short history of the race, a friendly if somewhat neutral welcome, and an invitation to land on the coast below the Conclave's valley home.

Bridge, Peggy Sue, In Orbit Around Gliese 581d

"Captain," called Lt. Taylor, manning the navigation and observation station just off the bridge. "I'm receiving a message from the planet."

"A message? Are you sure Mr. Taylor?" the Captain replied. "Not static or other natural signal?"

"No, Sir. The frequency is right in the 'water hole', in the same range as the spectral lines of hydrogen and the hydroxyl radical." JT reported excitedly. "It's one of the frequencies that SETI often monitors. Plus it is definitely being modulated by a nonrandom sequence—in fact, it looks like the sequence is building in complexity."

"Captain, if I might?" said a feminine voice from the Captain's console. "Yes, Peggy Sue, go ahead."

"The sequence is indeed building up from simple characters into short sequences and then to what might be thought of as full sentences. I have been able to construct a rudimentary translation program from this information. Would you like me to attempt a translation?"

"By all means. Don't keep us in suspense, Peggy Sue." Sometimes Jack thought the ship's computer a bit too polite.

"Very well. The text seems jumbled, almost as though there are three different lines of narrative interleaved, so I will try to group the information logically. One thread is a vague message of welcome to fellow sentients, extending a desire for friendship and peaceful coexistence."

"Better than threats and warnings," Jack said. "What else?"

"Another thread is a form of historical narrative, outlining the inhabitants' background. They call themselves the 'Fellowship of the combined conclaves of united ternary contemplative savants of natural philosophy'. Actually there is more, but you can perceive the general meaning."

"What's the meaning of 'united ternary'?" Olaf asked. Having overcome his disappointment at not being permitted on the surface expedition, he was hovering over JT's shoulder monitoring the planet below.

"From other information in the historical stream, it would seem that the natives are a form of composite life, where the fundamental unit of being consists of three quasi-independent sub-units linked together. They are evidently born as individual organisms but quickly link together to from triads."

"Is the association permanent?" asked the Captain.

"As far as I can tell, yes. In fact, it would seem that the sub-units are physically joined to each other. They share consciousness but retain some ability to process thoughts independently."

"That might explain the three messages merged into one," JT proposed. "Carrying on a conversation with one of these triad things could be very confusing."

"We came looking for aliens, JT," Olaf replied, "and it looks like we hit the jackpot. They certainly aren't strangely colored humans with prosthetic parts glued on."

"Is there an image of one of these creatures included?" Jack asked, smiling at Olaf's remark.

"There is no pictorial representation contained in the message," answered the computer. "It is possible that they do not have eyes or imaging senses as humans do."

"I think we have seen them," said JT. "Remember when Sally spotted those odd cactus like plants that always seemed grouped in threes? They filled a valley on the upward slope of a finger of land near the equator. Here is the original video." A view of the valley in question appeared on the large forward view screen.

"Yes, they could well be the natives," Olaf commented, peering intently at the image. "There are several hundred of them in this valley alone, have we seen them elsewhere?"

"I have checked the video from the ship and the survey drones and there are signs of at least a dozen other such concentrations within the temperate band. And Captain?"

"Yes, Peggy Sue?"

"The final message thread seems to contain landing instructions for a site near the original colony. They would like any landing craft to approach from the water side and not pass over the valley."

"You could have mentioned that earlier," the Captain said sharply. "Feed the coordinates to navigation. Mr. Taylor, show us the location on the planet and the suggested approach."

The overhead view of the valley was immediately replaced with an image of the planet which then zoomed in for a closer view of the landing zone and the glide-path descending from orbit. *We have been invited to land,* Jack thought, *probably best to not get off on the wrong foot by ignoring the landing instructions.* "Shuttle One, Peggy Sue."

"Peggy Sue, Shuttle One, over." came the reply.

"Commander, we have just received a message from the planet welcoming us and providing landing instructions. I think it might be a good idea to comply with the native's wishes and land where they indicated."

"Roger, Peggy Sue. We just received the location and landing instructions from navigation. We can vector to that location in about 90 minutes. Do we have a go for landing?"

"Roger that, Shuttle One. Proceed using your own judgment. By the way, we think that the natives are those triple trunked cacti sighted by Dr. Li earlier. They seem capable of communications by radio, whether they generate sound or other transmissions is unknown. The ship's computer is able to translate to some extent so we may need to loop any conversation through the ship."

"Roger, Sir. I will call when we are out of reentry blackout and headed for the landing zone. Shuttle One out."

* * * * *

Two hours later, Shuttle One was sitting on a gentle, mossy slope about 100 meters from a sheltered cove. The bloated red sun lay low on the horizon, painting clouds in shades of pink, burgundy and vermilion. A perpetual sunset, forever denying twilight's advance.

The expeditionary force, nine humans and two bears, had disembarked and was preparing to move inland toward the valley of suspected native inhabitants. Before heading inland, Ludmilla informed the others that she was going to take a sample of sea water from the cove for later analysis on board the ship.

"I'll come with you," said Isbjørn, following after the biologist. Movement for both bears and humans was not proving to be a problem in their powered space armor. Stuck on board ship for over a month, the bears had no opportunity to swim and though it would not be advisable to attempt swimming in armor, Isbjørn still wanted to get a closer look at the water.

"If we were not suited up, you would probably find the water temperature pleasant, Isbjørn," commented Ludmilla, bending down at the water's edge. Small gentle waves lapped against the sandy shore, like ripples on a large lake. As the scientist held an open sample bottle beneath the surface, a red and brown suckered tentacle slid from the water and coiled around her extended arm.

"Der'mo!," she exclaimed and immediately tried to pull away. The tentacle slipped a bit against the smooth surface of the suit armor but then tightened, holding Ludmilla fast. "Help! Something has grabbed hold of me!"

Quickly, Isbjørn came to Ludmilla's aid, rising up and landing with both forepaws on the offending tentacle. The impact caused the suckered appendage to release its prey, allowing Ludmilla to scramble backward away from the shoreline. Not one to panic easily, her sample bottle was full and still intact.

As Isbjørn turned away from the water another, larger tentacle shot from the water and wrapped itself around her hindquarters. She yelped in surprise and said, "I think it's my turn to yell for help!"

Moving swiftly, the Gunny ran past the backward scuttling biologist and drew a mean looking machete from her equipment pack. The long flat blade flared at the top, with a wicked hook on the backside. The machete's forward edge was only slightly curved and sharper than a razor. With a single swipe, the Gunny severed the clutching tentacle and both bear and Marine hustled away from the water's edge.

After puting 20 meters between themselves and the water, the rattled expedition members stopped and looked back to see if they were being pursued. Thankfully, no tentacled monster dogged their steps, only ripples on the surface of the bay marking the withdrawal of their aquatic foe. Part of the severed tentacle was still half wrapped around Isbjørn's legs and the armor encased ursine was having trouble removing the offending member.

"Let me help get that off you," said Ludmilla, voice a bit loud from the post threat adrenalin rush. "Look, it seems to have stingers as well as suckers. It is still trying to inject you with some form of poison."

"I sure hope that wasn't one of the natives," said the Gunny. "Because, if it was, they aren't friendly at all."

"I think my question about intelligent life in the sea has been given a preliminary answer," Ludmilla continued. "There is life and it appears to be untalkative and hungry." Over the common radio circuit she called, "someone bring a large sample container for the tentacle."

"You want to keep that thing?" asked Isbjørn. "Somehow I doubt it is good to eat."

"I am going to give it to Olaf as a peace offering," replied Ludmilla. "He should be able to find all sorts of parallel evolutionary adaptations from dissecting it."

"If you three are done playing with the local squid population, we should head inland and try to find some of the natives," called Lcdr. Curtis, her sarcastic sense of humor bubbling to the surface. "Shuttle, Curtis. I would suggest you not take any walks along the beach while we are gone."

"Roger that, Commander," came Sandy McKennitt's cheerful Australian accented reply. "We saw the barney with the squid. I think we'll all just stay inside while you go walkabout."

"Just so, Lieutenant. All right everyone, let's move out up that ravine. LCpl. Sanchez and Lt. Bear will take the lead..."

Destroyer of Worlds, Beta Comae Berenices System

The immense ship from Ursae Majoris transitioned to 3-space several AU from the star humans called Beta Comae Berenices. Though great in both size and power, the People's ship was a ponderous beast. Much of the ship's mass was contained in the mushroom cap head that provided protection as it moved through space and also held its primary weapon.

That weapon was as primitive as it was effective, consisting of a clutch of sizable asteroids, shaped to neatly huddle together at the bow of the kilometers long ship. Each was provided with a minimal guidance system and propulsion to help refine the terminal end of its intended mission. The plan of attack was simple, head straight for the intended target and release a number of captive asteroids.

Looping around the target's star, picking up more asteroids if necessary, the ship would make multiple passes until no vestige of civilization or, indeed, higher life survived. The strategy was time consuming but thorough, the ship sluggish and slow to maneuver. If they met opposition, a half dozen smaller craft were attached to the ship's long stem, ready to launch and provide protection for the mother ship.

One scarred and lonely plant orbited in Beta Comae's warm zone, what humans would call the system's habitable zone. Thousands of years ago, other slaves of the Dark Lords had scoured life from that world and constructed a refueling station in orbit around it. Warm vermin had destroyed that station and provoked the Dark Ones' ire.

Before proceeding to the suspected source of the attack on the refueling station, the Destroyer of Worlds would check this system closely, to ensure that no new infestation of warm life had been left behind. This meant spending time surveying the local neighborhood, but haste did not matter to the Dark Lords, only thoroughness. It was not as if the offending vermin's planet was going anywhere.

Soon enough, the ship would begin the six and a half day transit to the system which contained the planet they sought. Soon enough death would fall from the skies of that hapless world, bringing terror and extinction to all complex life on the planet. And if, for some inexplicable reason, the Destroyer's brute force attack failed, the masters would dispatch others, more technologically advanced, to complete the job.

Valley of the Trailing Conclave, Gliese 581d

"The aliens approach; They seem to comprise more than one species; The encounter with the aquatic carnivore was informative," observed TagFetLuw, as the party of alien visitors wound its way up the ravine that led to the Conclave's valley home.

"They will arrive shortly; Unless they are a differentiated species or possess significant sexual dimorphism; What do you observe, Ambassador NatHanGon?" responded SudNabSon. The younger triad had slowly worked its way to the edge of the assembly of creatures that were the Trailing Conclave.

"They move cautiously; They favor different locomotive modes, indicating two probable species; The response to the kraken was

217

restrained, not mindlessly violent," replied the ambassador designate.

"They are close enough to hear our transmissions; Two yes, the large ones could be servants or guards; The sample gatherer took the tentacle as a prize," said QivCakJol.

"Soon we will try to converse; The tallest of the small ones seems to be in charge; Most likely to study," affirmed SudNabSon. "NatHanGon will speak for the Conclave; We will know soon enough who speaks for the aliens; They seem to be seekers of knowledge." The Conclave's roots pulsed briefly with assent.

* * * * *

The expedition spent an hour hiking up hill, passing through a forest of single stemmed 'trees' that stood between four and five meters tall. Each displayed a single broad leaf that started a meter above ground level and continued to the top of an ever narrowing smooth trunk, like a feather sprouting from a quill. In the red light of Gliese 581 both leaf and trunk appeared dark brown to black. As the expedition gained altitude, the wind picked up and rustled through the alien forest as though marking the passage of invisible giants.

"This is some spooky shit," Sanchez said to LCpl. Brown, one of the new Marines, conversing over short range, inter-suit radio.

"At least nothing has tried to make a meal out of us since we left the seashore," he replied. Unlike the scientists, officers and bears, the Marines were wearing enclosed battle helmets, making it impossible to see facial expressions.

"I can tell you from experience," Joey confided, "the best place to be if the shit hits the fan is behind the LT." Bear, leading the way through the undergrowth, had drifted into suit-to-suit range in time to catch that last remark.

"Either one of you primates shoots me in the ass and I'm putting monkey back on the menu," he growled. This caused Sanchez to chuckle and gave Brown a moment of hesitation. It was not often that your Lieutenant threatened to eat you if you screwed up.

"Don't worry, Lieutenant," Joey replied. "I was just saying we got your back is all."

"I'm worried about my backside, not my back. Remember, I've seen you shoot, Sanchez."

Before Sanchez could reply, the column emerged into a clearing that widened into a wide valley. Several hundred meters up the valley a thick concentration of strange plant like objects rose from a tangled bed of intertwined roots. As the expedition members gathered at the entrance to the valley, one triplet of trunks was moving slowly toward them.

"I think we've arrived," Bear announced.

"Peggy Sue, are you getting this?" called Lcdr. Curtis to the ship.

"That is affirmative, Commander. Everyone on board is watching."

The approaching triad was only about 30 meters away and had obviously been headed in their direction for quite some time, probably hours if its current pace was any indication. At its base was a tangled nest of root like tentacles, which writhed and contorted as they moved the entire creature forward at less than a quarter of a kilometer per hour.

From the half meter thick tangle of roots at its base, three ribbed columns stood upright. Even from this remove, it was clear that the columns were not shaped like cactus, they bore no spines and appeared to have a number of deep vertical ridges. From the edge of each ridge sprouted tulip shaped flowers, whose flared tips fluttered slightly in the gusting wind. The trunks appeared reddish brown fading to black at the ridges, the flowers solid black.

"I make out five lobes on each column, sort of like the fruit of the *Averrhoa carambola*, only more elongated," said Sally Li. As the expedition's botanist this was her area of expertise, assuming that the triple flowered columns now approaching them were, in fact, plants.

"They do look a bit like star fruit," commented Ludmilla. "Though I have never seen a star fruit that stood two meters tall, or that had flowers along its edges. But you are right Sally, the five lobe symmetry is quite pronounced."

219

"I'm looking at the other triads in the thicket using my suit's cameras," said LCpl. Reagan, one of the more cerebral Marines. "Under magnification they all seem to have five ribs on each column as well."

"Good observation, I wonder if it is a characteristic of all these creatures or just a trait of the local population," mused Sally. "The one approaching has obviously been sent to meet us, should we move forward?"

"Considering it's going to take the fruit basket a half hour to reach us that sounds like a reasonable idea," said Bear.

"They might be able to hear us, Lieutenant," Lcdr. Curtis admonished. "Though I am sure we appear as alien to them as they do to us. Dr. Tropsha, Isbjørn and myself will approach the creature. Gunny, have the Marines spread out a bit, but no weapons showing. Lt. Bear, you are in command of our reserve."

"Aye aye, Ma'am," the Gunny replied before switching to the Marine command frequency to disperse her half squad. Bear muttered, "I wasn't going to eat 'em or anything. The only fruit I like has been fermented and preferably distilled."

Chapter 15

Bridge, Peggy Sue, In Orbit Around Gliese 581d

On the large forward display, the three Earth representatives advanced on the triple stalked native sent to greet them. The Captain had instructed the ship's computer to send a reply to the radio message, expressing hopes for future friendship, thanking the senders for the background information regarding their civilization and acknowledging the landing instructions. There had been no further communication with the planet's inhabitants. "You should have sent me along, Captain," said Jean-Jacques de Belcour, seated in an observer's chair. "After all, I am a trained diplomat and can at least legitimately claim to represent an assemblage of Earth's nations."

"You will get the chance to speak with the indigenous creatures once contact has been solidly established," Jack replied. The UN bureaucrat was the last one he wanted making first impressions on the natives. They were the only non-hostile alien race discovered so far.

"I certainly hope that your military expedition to the surface does no harm to future relations," Jean-Jacques huffed, simultaneously conveying a sense of disapproval and personal superiority as only a French diplomat could. From his point of view, he should have led the shore party to establish first contact.

"Wounds inflicted by the sword heal more quickly than those inflicted by the tongue, Monsieur," the Captain quoted.

"Cardinal Richelieu," said Billy Ray from the helm, "*Testament politique*, in translation."

The Captain smiled and again addressed the French diplomat. "Commander Curtis has worked with colleagues, port authorities and local dignitaries in Europe, Asia, Africa and South America. She is well practiced at the art of diplomacy, Monsieur. Dr. Tropsha was part of an international crew on the ISS and Isbjørn is the most tactful of all the bears. I believe they will make a favorable impression on the local inhabitants."

Jean-Jacques bit off a sarcastic remark regarding Dr. Tropsha, realizing at the last instant that insulting the Captain's lover was a good way to be banished from the bridge. Instead he said, "we will see."

Jack sighed. *De Belcour's thinking is not just wrong, it's fractally wrong. From a distance, his worldview is incorrect and, if you zoom in on any small part of that worldview, that part is just as wrong as the whole—wrong at every scale.*

Valley of the Trailing Conclave

Meanwhile, planetside, the three female Earthlings had reached the advancing triad, which evidently sensed their presence and halted its forward motion. For half a minute the two parties simply faced each other. Then, following age old human tradition, Lcdr. Curtis held up empty hands, palms out, to show that she held no weapon. Ludmilla and Isbjørn followed suit.

"OK, now what do we do?" asked Ludmilla.

"I will try talking to it," said Gretchen. Enabling her suit's external speaker, she said, "Greetings from the species of planet Earth. We come in peace, seeking friendship and knowledge."

There was no reply. At least nothing that could be heard over the howling wind. After several long, anxious seconds Gretchen spoke to her companions. "I'd say we should try the radio, but I was transmitting on both suit-to-suit and the ship's frequency as I spoke. How do you make contact when you cannot communicate?"

"Maybe we are not close enough," said Isbjørn. "Look how close the main group is bunched together, like seals on a beach." As with most bears, thought was followed immediately by action—Isbjørn moved closer to the native. She sat down with her front paws resting only a decimeter away from the alien's nest of roots/tentacles.

Caught by surprise, Gretchen could only issue a belated, "be careful." Then it was the alien's turn to do something unexpected. It reached out with one of its roots and touched Isbjørn's armored paw. Immediately, Isbjørn's ears perked up. "I'm getting some form of signal from my suit radio," she reported.

"Peggy Sue, are you getting the signal that Isbjørn is hearing?"

"Yes, Commander. Would you like me to attempt a translation?"

"Affirmative, Peggy Sue. Please broadcast the translation to the entire shore party."

"As far as I can interpret that last burst, the creature in front of you is known as NatHanGon the Almost Wise. They are designated as an ambassador to our peoples and will serve as a conduit for all communication between us and the conclaves of the world."

"Nathan Gone the Almost Wise?"

"Nat-Han-Gon, three distinct syllables, possibly corresponding to the three sub-intelligences that comprise the being as a whole. An approximate verbatim translation would be: 'We are put forth as ambassador to your peoples; We greet you in peace as fellow sapients; We are known as NatHanGon the Almost Wise.'"

"Do they always speak in triplets like that?" asked Ludmilla.

"The Ambassador's speech patterns are consistent with the message beamed to the ship earlier. I would suspect that each sub-intelligence contributes a part of each statement. Might I suggest framing a reply using a similar linguistic structure?"

"Sure," replied Gretchen. "Use my opening statement and tack on another sentence. How about 'we come from the ship orbiting your planet'?"

"As you wish, Commander." There was a brief, multi-harmonic burst followed by an immediate reply. "The Ambassador says: We greet the fellow scholars of dirt; May our understanding be elevated; Where else would you have come from?"

The last part of the reply took Gretchen by surprise and caused Ludmilla to laugh out loud. Even Isbjørn snorted, the polar bear equivalent of a short laugh. "I guess I walked into that one," Gretchen said.

"Dirt?" asked Isbjørn.

"Sorry," replied the ship's computer, "too literal a translation of Earth."

"Interesting, they always seem to refer to themselves in the plural—we not I," said Ludmilla.

"Well, they seem quite literal and a bit sarcastic," Isbjørn said.

"We should explain that we are still working on translation," added Ludmilla.

"And that sometimes we state the obvious for lack of an original thought," ended Gretchen.

Another tonal outburst issued from their suit radios.

"You sent that?" exclaimed Gretchen, her last remark was directed at her companions, not the Ambassador.

"Yes, Commander. I thought that was what you intended. In any case, the Ambassador replies: We are sometimes thought to be insufficiently tactful; We also struggle with information translation; We generally remain silent when lacking something to say, which can also be misinterpreted."

"I think I like this Ambassador. It, I mean, they have a sense of humor," said Ludmilla.

"Bears have always valued honesty and candor," said Isbjørn.

"I think this conversation is going to take a while," summed up Gretchen.

The computer automatically translated the reply: "Our initial impressions are also positive; Is our assumption that you represent more than one species correct? We have no place else to be, take your time..."

* * * * *

Five hours later and the conversation was still in progress. NatHanGon proved loquacious with a dry, acerbic wit. Isbjørn, Ludmilla and Gretchen were getting well practiced at simulating a triad, or at least a triad's speech pattern. Information flows rapidly when it is possible to hold three related, yet independent conversations simultaneously. Among the Earthlings, triad had become the universal name for the ternary aliens. In conversation, the ship's computer was trusted to substitute a term acceptable to the beings themselves.

Among the things discovered was that the triads were an old race, possibly as old as six billion Earth years. They were also long lived individually. NatHanGon was considered a youngster at only

800,000 solar orbits, around 147,000 Earth years, while elders could claim ten million orbits or more. It was humbling to meet a race that had evolved before the solar system formed and individual creatures that were alive at the beginning of the Pleistocene Ice Age. Even the youthful ambassador was alive before the previous interglacial period started, before *H. sapiens* and *U. maritimus* had fully evolved.

On a more intimate level, questions by Dr. Li and Dr. Tropsha revealed that the triads were tri-sexual, triplet beings formed by one member each of three distinct sexes. Once linked by their motile roots, the merged partners reproduced by cross pollination. As a result, the fused being was functionally hermaphroditic and fully capable of reproducing on its own.

When Olaf was told about the triad's sexual arrangements he said, "this is fantastic! Hermaphroditism is uncommon among multicellular animals."

"True, we tend to think of hermaphroditic creatures being rather primitive, or less evolved," Sally said. "Sponges, worms, certain molluscs and, of course, the majority of plants are hermaphroditic."

"Hermaphroditism is useful if one's sexual options are severely limited and it can be favored when encounters with potential mates are extremely rare," he replied, over the comm link from the ship. "Animals with low or unpredictable population densities and those that are immobile or have poor senses are often hermaphroditic. It makes little sense for a species to invest heavily in developing two sexes if mating competition is low. Better to maximize one's evolutionary capital by evolving other, more direct survival traits."

"Most hermaphrodites still need to find at least one mate during their lifetimes," added Ludmilla. "The potential genetic cost of inbreeding leads to most not being able to self pollinate. But the triads are not primitive, unevolved organisms: they are social, capable of long-distance communication and are not immobile—slow yes, immobile no."

"They would certainly be able to arrange for a liaison for breeding purposes," noted Olaf. "But as it stands, every triad is its own threesome."

"Olaf, you are a dirty old biologist," teased Ludmilla, a big smile on her face. Discovering this one species alone meant that all of them would be celebrities in their fields back home. Visions of Nobel Prizes danced in their heads.

"The Ambassador hinted that including one or more partners from other triads can be done, though it isn't that common," Sally went on. "Moreover, I get the distinct impression that our two sexes amuse them. Particularly once the sexual dimorphism among the polar bears was revealed."

"The sexual what?" asked Isbjørn. Not being widely read in the biological sciences, she missed that item during the previous interchanges.

"The size differences between males and females," answered Ludmilla. "Humans exhibit the same tendencies, if to a lesser degree than polar bears. It has been tied to competition for mating and a lack of lifetime pair bonding."

"I think we bears need to work on that in the future," Isbjørn replied with a thoughtful look.

Sally, who was still trying to decide if NatHanGon could be classified as a plant, ignored the exchange between Ludmilla and Isbjørn. "They are definitely multicellular and, from the sample scraping that the Ambassador kindly permitted, they appear to be eukaryotic. But they do not use photosynthesis, at least not as we know it on Earth."

"They do derive energy directly from sunlight, but at lower frequencies, down into the infrared band," said Olaf. "It may not be the same mechanism used by Earth plants, but I think that it is close enough to say that the triads are, indeed, plants."

"Right," said Ludmilla. "triple brained, intelligent, mobile, tri-sexual, hermaphroditic plants billions of years more evolved than *Homo sapiens*."

"Ya, that's about the size of it," agreed Olaf. "I can't wait to meet them in person..."

CIC, Peggy Sue

Olaf, JT, Chief Engineer Medina and the Captain were gathered around the central display tank that formed the heart of the CIC's data visualization system. The tank was a two by one meter table, above which a full color, holographic display created moving 3D data representations. Currently, it displayed a realistic, scale model view of the scene on the planet below, where the shore expedition was still in "negotiations" with the triad ambassador.

"You are saying that the Ambassador wishes to go with us on the ship, Commander?" asked the Captain, incredulity seeping in around the edges of his question.

"That is correct, Captain," replied Gretchen, still standing with Isbjørn and Ludmilla in front of the alien representative. "They say that there are many questions that must be answered regarding our... pedigree. And, more importantly, our future in the grand scheme of things."

"And the Ambassador is confident that, he, er... they can exist on our ship for an extended period? We may not return to this system for a year or more," Jack replied. "What do they eat? Do they eat? The last thing I want is to accept their ambassador and end up with a dead or dying alien on our hands."

"Evidently they can feed on almost any organic matter, which they absorb through their roots. Initial analysis indicates that our basic amino acids and protein structures are compatible. That, plus the direct absorption of light energy in the near IR and lower visible spectrum, should prove sufficient."

"Captain?" interjected the ship's computer. "I believe that with help from engineer Medina I can construct an environment that will replicate the atmosphere, gravity and lighting conditions found on the planet below."

"What about it, Mr. Medina? Do you and your engineers feel up to building an alien terrarium?"

"There's a first time for everything, Captain," replied Jo Jo, rubbing his chin with one hand as he calculated the level of effort required for such a conversion.

"Not only that, Sir," the computer continued. "It should be possible to provide the Ambassador with an enhanced communication system, perhaps even a robotic avatar that would let them interact with the ship's personnel."

"Lcdr. Curtis, would this work better if we include some topsoil?" Jack asked his second in command. "Let the Ambassador bring along a bit of home as it were?"

"I think that might be a good idea, Sir. Peggy Sue, could you verify this?" There was a slight pause while the ship and the alien exchanged messages, audible but indecipherable to humans and bears alike.

"Yes, Commander. NatHanGon said that such generosity in accommodating their needs speaks well for our species. They estimate a section of ground 2.5 meters square and a half meter thick would be fully sufficient."

"Very well," said the Captain, coming to a decision. "Mr. Medina, I will leave you to work out the details between the ship and the prospective occupant. Lcdr. Curtis, please advise the watch when you ready to return to the ship."

"Aye aye, Sir. I think we can rig a hover platform that will carry the Ambassador, soil and all, onto the shuttle."

"Roger that, Mr. Medina will let you know when the Ambassador's stateroom is ready. Captain out." *I am now running an interstellar cruise ship*, Jack thought ruefully. *And if we can pick up a few more ambassadors, we can become a traveling circus.*

Ambassador's Sitting Room, Peggy Sue

The Triad Ambassador was installed in a sealed chamber on the second deck, across from the sickbay and adjoining the life sciences laboratories. Within the three by four meter enclosure the atmospheric gas mixture was altered to mimic that of the planet below, and kept at twice the normal shipboard pressure. From one wall issued red tinged light that extended into the near infrared, a close analog of the light of Gliese 581.

The installation of the Ambassador proved much easier than first expected. From the forward shuttle hatch, NatHanGon was floated down the passageway to the inter-deck lift, lowered to the mid deck and then into their waiting apartment. With the cooperation of the hover sled's artificial gravity, the Ambassador, soil and all, was gently deposited on top of a gravel drainage bed that filled the bottom of the enclosure. With a little artistic arrangement of native soil and mosses by Melissa Hamilton the decor was complete and the Ambassador sealed inside.

Within the apartment's impermeable walls, artificial winds gusted and rain showers pelted down, simulating observed conditions near the Trailing Conclave's valley. The randomly programmed environmental embellishments could be suspended by the occupant, who communicated directly with the ship's computer through sensors in the walls and overhead. The Ambassador's quarters were a self-contained alien environment, independent of the rest of the ship save for power.

To allow others to visit the triad, the forward wall of their quarters was adjustably transparent, like the viewports of the ship and shuttles. A couch and chairs were provided for humans, facing the transparent wall behind which the triad sat, like a prize plant in a terrarium. Currently standing before the Ambassador were the Captain, Ludmilla and Bear, come to bid NatHanGon welcome aboard.

"We are extremely pleased to have you traveling with us, Ambassador," the Captain said. Ludmilla, who had gotten the rhythm of speaking with a triad from the initial conversations planetside, provided "We hope that your accommodations are acceptable."

Ludmilla then nudged Bear, reminding him that they needed to speak in triplets. "There will be a lot of visitors pestering you, let us know if they become a bother."

"We are pleased to be with you; The accommodations are more comfortable than we could have imagined; The wall can be made opaque and the communication channel shut down if solitude is desired, but thank you." NatHanGon answered, and then proceeded to ask some questions of their own. "Are we correct in surmising that you are the controlling nexus for this vessel? We understand that you are not triplet bonded as we are, but are you mates? For different species you seem to cooperate well."

"I am the captain, I direct the actions of the others on board," Jack replied, unable to avoid the use of the singular personal pronoun. Ludmilla responded openly, since the only others present were Jack and Bear, "The Captain and I are a mated couple."

"Not all bears get along with all humans, but we three are good friends," Bear added with great sincerity.

"We had surmised as much from communication with the ship's computer; How strange it would be for part of ourselves to be separated as you were when one of you was in orbit and one on the surface! We are heartened that your species can cooperate and form friendships."

"The strain on a single consciousness to make such decisions must be considerable; We must speak of sex and reproduction at greater length; As you have found, much of the Universe is not disposed to friendship."

"Tell me about it!" Bear exclaimed. "You are the first aliens who haven't attacked us on sight."

"I have others to advise me, much like your people we seek consensus before making major decisions," the Captain replied, giving Bear a 'don't get carried away' look.

"I am a Biologist and a medical doctor, we can discuss such matters whenever you would like," Ludmilla responded while watching the interplay between Bear and Jack.

"As different as we are the commonalities are reassuring; We would like that very much; Indeed, most intruders to our system are destroyed by the Guardians."

The next triplet from the Earth creatures was short and uniformed. All three said "Guardians?"

"The subset of our population that defends our world; We have told the Dark Ones that they are not to transit our system; Inimical intruders are removed by the Guardians."

"How do they 'remove' the hostiles, we saw no weapons?" the Captain asked excitedly. As interesting as the science stuff was, weapons technology was what drew his attention.

"What can you tell us of these Dark Ones?" asked Ludmilla.

"Do you run into a lot of these hostile critters?" asked Bear.

"We have evolved to the point of not needing constructed technology; The Dark Ones are long lived, highly intelligent lifeforms that inhabit planets too cold for carbon-water life; The last intrusion was around 210 orbits ago," the Ambassador replied. "The Guardians are capable of directly manipulating our star's photosphere; They are extraordinarily xenophobic and wish to destroy all warm life; About 38 of your years."

"The Guardians use your sun as a weapon?" asked the Captain.

"Both you and we are warm life?" asked Ludmilla.

"They haven't tried to exterminate you?" asked Bear.

"Yes; Yes; Yes."

All parties to the conversation fell silent for several long moments. "We are searching for other warm life," said Ludmilla, after a lengthy pause.

"Obviously they were unsuccessful at destroying you," added Bear.

"This gives us much to think about," Jack wrapped up the exchange.

"Perhaps we will find other new friends together; Indeed, we thwarted them; We look forward to further exchange of information."

Main Lounge, Peggy Sue, En Route to Transfer Point

After a final exchange of diplomatic messages with the aliens on the planet below, including a high-speed burst of data between the Ambassador and his Conclave, the Captain ordered the ship to head for the alter-space transfer point leading to the next system on their itinerary—61 Virginis. The usual evening crowd was gathered in the Peggy Sue's main lounge, discussing the events of recent days and various conversations held with the Triad Ambassador. As strange as the triads were, somehow the Universe no longer felt quite so empty nor the Earthlings quite so alone.

"So how far is this 61 Virgins place?" asked Olaf, settling back with his first beer of the day.

"Virginis. Just a bit under 15 light years," replied Elena, who was sitting suspiciously close to Eric Fetzer. The two of them had been seen dining together on a number of occasions recently.

"Und how long do we have to spend in hyperspace?" asked Dieter.

"Just a little over two weeks," answered JT, who was enjoying the chance to spend a little lounge time with Gretchen. "Not nearly as long as the trip out here, but long enough to get boring."

"I can use the time to finish running chemical analysis on the soil and water samples from the planet," the German chemist replied. Most of the science team was busy analyzing stuff—animal, vegetable and mineral—brought back by the ground expedition.

"Yah," said Olaf, "I'm having a wonderful time with the tentacle that Ludmilla brought me."

"I just knew you would like it when I saw it, Olaf," said Ludmilla with a smile. "Of course, it had taken a liking to Isbjørn first."

"It's a good thing that the Gunny was quick with her machete," added Gretchen. "Or we would have had to go fishing to get her back."

"It strikes me as a bit anomalous that there are such dangerous predators on that planet yet the triads seem mostly defenseless," commented Sally.

"I don't think the fruit baskets, as Bear calls them, are quite as defenseless as they appear," said JT. "According to Bear, the Ambassador told the Captain about the "Guardians." Some group of triads that can evidently turn their sun into a ginormous laser and use it to vaporize trespassing starships."

"Do you really believe that?" asked Eric.

"So far there is no reason to disbelieve anything the Ambassador has told us," said Gretchen, answering for her partner. "The Captain has told us to be totally open with them and hopefully they are being candid with us as well."

"It could simply be something to scare us away, or make us think twice before trying to take their planet," said Dieter, playing devil's advocate as usual.

"I think they are telling the truth," said JT, "and I'll tell you why. Back around 2009, an astrophysicist at the University of Western Sydney, named Ragbir Bhathal, discovered a "suspicious" laser-like signal coming from the coordinates of Gliese 581. Bhathal was an active member of SETI at the time and was searching for signs of extraterrestrial life. Before he could verify the signal, it disappeared and hasn't been seen since."

"Und what does that prove?" asked the skeptical chemist.

"During a conversation with the Ambassador, he mentioned that the last time they had to take out some hostile intruder was right around that time, taking the speed of light into consideration."

"So you're saying that the coherent light that Bhathal saw was the triads blasting some intruder?" asked Elena, her eyebrows rising in skeptical inquiry.

"The time-line fits, and we know they can generate radio signals without any visible equipment. And being able to use a star as a thermonuclear powered laser would provide one hell of a planetary defense."

"You have a point JT," said Olaf. "Remember that these creatures are billions of years more evolved than humans. I'm a bit surprised they even decided to talk with us at all."

"People talk to their pets," observed Ludmilla. "Besides, maybe they have gotten bored, just sitting around in clumps on a planet where the sun never sets and things hardly change. I think our Ambassador has a taste for adventure, just as we do."

"You are always a romantic, Ludmilla," said Olaf. "I'm more interested in what we'll find at 61 Virgins."

"61 Virginis," corrected JT, "or 61 Vir for short. It is a GV5 star, much like the Sun. According to observations, there are at least three planets and a large debris disk."

Elena sighed. "Unfortunately, the known planets are all too close to have a reasonable chance of harboring life. Unless there is a fourth, smaller planet outside of those I'm afraid 61 Vir will be a disappointment."

"Well, we will know in two weeks," said Gretchen, "In the mean time we have an old, mysterious and wise race to ponder."

Valley of the Trailing Conclave, Gliese 581d

It had been nearly a tenth of an orbit since NatHanGon departed with the Earth creatures, bound for other worlds circling other stars. The immediate rush of excitement that came with the discovery that warm life was again traveling openly among the stars had faded. A bit disappointed that they had no marauding minions of the dark empire to dispatch, the Guardians consoled themselves by vaporizing the reconnaissance satellite the Peggy Sue left behind to observe the system.

"Other worlds they seek; They search for allies in the fight against darkness; If NatHanGon ever returns they will have much knowledge to impart," said SudNabSon, as the Peggy Sue disappeared into the other dimensions of alter-space.

"Other worlds they will find; More of the Universe is dark than light; NatHanGon's fate rests with the Earthlings' primitive technology, and their courage in battle," answered QivCakJol. As the triad equivalent of an historian, they had clearer knowledge of the enormous odds the departing ship faced, and how unlikely it was that their departed colleague would return.

Chapter 16

Polar Bear Quarters, Peggy Sue, Alter-space Day 3

Isbjørn and Bear entered the polar bear quarters after spending the last watch training with the ship's Marines. Their developing tactical doctrine called for each bear to be supported by three humans. Because of their immense strength and physical size, the bears were capable of carrying heavier weapons than the human Marines: the latest five barreled flechette gun, the successor to Bear's "fire hose of death," used in the battle of the space mushroom; and the new 15mm, triple barreled rail-gun cannon, which fired high velocity explosive rounds at 1200 rounds per minute.

It was not just the heft of the weapons, but the bears' ability to carry large amounts of ammunition to feed them that allowed individual bears to replace crew served weapon teams. Instead of human Marines carrying squad machine guns, the bears provided that function without burdening their squadmates with extra ammunition cans or additional barrels. This arrangement expanded the ship's Marine contingent from 12 to 16, but the numerical increase hardly reflected the increase in firepower.

The cargo hold was the Marines' normal exercise space, with morning formation being held every day followed by PT that many of the crew also participated in. This early in the voyage, the hold was still mostly full, packed with expendable drones, observation satellites and other consumable supplies. This forced the Marines to practice combat tactics in two shifts, which was why Isbjørn and Bear found themselves alone in the bear quarters when they returned from combat drill.

"I don't think there's anyone else here," Bear said to his mate. "Where's Aput?"

"Aput is at his studies with the human scientists," Isbjørn replied. "Dr. Saito says that Aput has an uncanny knack for math and physics—the intricacies of alter-space and multidimensional cosmology in particular."

"I never would have thought he had it in him," Bear chuckled. "But then you have been showing some hidden talents yourself, babe."

"What do you mean?" she asked with suspicion in her voice. All bears were notorious jokers and Isbjørn had reason to know Bear was worse than most.

"Hey, that was a complement!" Bear countered, mock indignation belied by the toothy grin on his muzzle. "I was referring to your performance in the contact party. You were the first one to talk to the fruit basket ambassador."

"Moving closer seemed like the right thing to do," she replied, "and don't call them fruit baskets. It's disrespectful."

"It's not like the Ambassador knows what that means and besides, Peggy Sue always provides translation to whatever it is they call themselves."

"Still, you have most of the Marines calling them that. You're an officer and a combat veteran, not just some brawling bruin. Like it or not, they look up to you."

"Oh come on, babe..." he began, but before he could complete his sentence, Isbjørn rose up and hit him with a paw swipe that knocked him to the ground. Following the sudden assault, Isbjørn bolted up the icy mounds that gave the bear quarters some small semblance of a natural environment.

Bear quickly regained his feet and shook his head. *So that's how you want it!* He said to himself, a smile spreading across his face. He ran after her, up the tiered ice shelves to where Isbjørn awaited.

As he approached, she rose up on her hind legs and roared in challenge. Halting one level down from the smaller female, Bear also rose to a two legged stance. This put their heads on roughly the same level as they exchanged blows and then clashed their jaws with fangs bared. Isbjørn dropped to all fours and lunged into him, causing both of them to tumble down the artificial hill to the floor of their living space.

This violent game of tag continued for several frenetic minutes until, finally, the pair came to a breathless stop. Bear stood over

Isbjørn with a foreleg draped across her back as he panted, "Hey, babe. I was just trying to pay you a complement."

"I know," she replied, equally out of breath. "Oh shut up, you big lug, and bite the back of my neck..."

Bridge, Peggy Sue, Emergence at 61 Virginis

As seen from Earth, 61 Virginis is located at the southern edge of the constellation Virgo, southwest of the bright type-B binary Alpha Virginis, also known as Spica. About 27.8 light-years from Sol, 61 Vir is visible to unaided human eyes and is best viewed under a dark sky during spring in the northern hemisphere.

Astronomers and astrobiologists have long been fascinated with this particular star. Among hundreds of nearby stars, 61 Vir stands out as being the most similar to the Sun in terms of age, mass, and other essential properties. A decade ago, astronomers found that 61 Vir hosts at least three planets: one super-Earth and two Neptune-class planets of at least 5, 18, and 24 Earth-masses, respectively.

The trio were found in moderately circular, inner orbits with periods of 4.2, 38, and 124 days. Though this was one of the earliest observations of a super-Earth around a Sun-like star, the extremely close orbit of only 0.05 AU made the existence of life improbable.

"Mr. Taylor, how does the neighborhood look?" the Captain asked his science officer, shortly after the ship emerged from alter-space.

"I observed two planets in close solar orbit, one super-Earth and another roughly Neptune sized. The third known planet must be on the other side of the star from our position. As expected, the inner planet is way too close to support life. Its atmospheric flow pattern is somewhat similar to of the upper atmosphere of Venus, though not as dense, and it is so hot it glows."

"Anything in the habitable zone?"

"The local habitable zone is roughly between 0.75 and 1.5 AU. I'm not registering any terrestrial planets in that space. At least nothing big enough to hold an atmosphere," JT said disappointedly. "Beyond that a thick belt of dust and rubble lies between 95 and 195 AU. I'm afraid that this is a dry hole, Captain."

"Well, we can't expect to find aliens in every system we visit," Jack said. "Helm, let's make a minimum time transit to the next alter-space transfer point. That should still give us several days to collect scientific information and scan for any hint of life. Perhaps our next stop will prove more exciting."

With those prophetic words the Captain looked forward to discovering what awaited them at Beta Hydri. A strange subgiant star evolving off of the main sequence, it was subject to rhythmic pulsations in luminosity, evidence of highly variable output.

Kuiper Belt, 61 Virginis

In the Solar System, out beyond the orbit of Neptune lies a region called the Kuiper belt. It is similar to the asteroid belt between the orbits of Mars and Jupiter—consisting mainly of small bodies and other remnants from the Solar System's formation—though it is 20 times as wide and 200 times as massive. While the asteroid belt is composed primarily of rocky and metallic objects, objects in the Kuiper belt are composed largely of frozen volatiles, ices of methane, ammonia and water. But there are also many sizable objects, dwarf planets like Pluto and Eris. Several of the Solar System's moons, such as Neptune's Triton and Saturn's Phoebe, are thought to be captured Kuiper belt objects.

The system around 61 Vir is ordered differently from the one around Sol. The major planets orbit closely to their star, giving warm life little purchase. But more than 90 AU out begins a thick belt of dust and debris far larger than the Sun's Kuiper belt. Among the distant rubble many sizable planetesimals orbit 61 Vir.

Rich in organics and precursor compounds, a number of these frigid dwarf planets developed their own forms of life—cold life, dark life. Based on different chemistry than the Earth creatures traversing the inner system, these beings were no less intelligent and no less advanced. Quite the opposite, theirs was a multi-world civilization and their technology outstripped that which humans had devised on their own. On the capital world a quasicrystalline creature, shaped somewhat like a giant sea urchin, took note of the Peggy Sue's passage through his system.

"Ooshlewnnalloo, attend me!" he bellowed, calling on his favorite offspring. The observer was called Lewnhallooshna and he was the ruler of a dozen worlds scattered about the asteroid belt. He was ruler because nearly all similar creatures that inhabited the worlds he claimed were direct descendants—he was quite literally their sire.

"Yes great father," answered Ooshlewnnalloo, scuttling into his sire's presence. "Command me, my king."

"It would appear that a ship filled with warm life vermin is traversing the inner system, transiting from one alter-space tramline to another as though it is their right to violate my space without paying proper obeisance."

"What temerity! What a vile insult to my revered father!"

"Assemble the fleet! We will follow these ignorant trespassers and meet out punishment for this affront to my dignity. This blight on my sovereign honor will only be assuaged when their constituent atoms are torn asunder and blown into the void."

"As you command, great father! Your sons gather to blot these offensive creatures from existence," Ooshlewnnalloo enthused. As he left his father's chamber to summon his siblings he thought, *what great luck! We haven't had a good extermination in ages!*

Bridge, Peggy Sue, Arriving at Beta Hydri

After the disappointment of 61 Vir and the boredom of the ten day alter-space transit, the crew of the Peggy Sue was looking forward to exploring the Beta Hydri system. Located about 24.4 light-years away from Sol, it lies in the southeastern corner of the constellation Hydrus, the Serpent or Water Snake. A type G2 star with 1.1 times Sol's mass, 1.46 times its diameter and about 3.53 times its luminosity.

Perhaps most intriguing, Beta Hydri's age was estimated by earthly astronomers at 6.7 billion years, significantly older than the Sun, plenty of time for life to evolve. On the other hand, since Beta Hydri became a subgiant late in life, it is possible that any planet that once had Earth-like conditions was now too hot to support life.

But then, perhaps a colder Mars-like planet became more amicable to terrestrial life.

"I've got a gas giant with around 4.8 Jupiter masses at 8 AU," reported JT from the navigation and astronomy station. "That one was more or less expected from Earth-based observations."

"A Jupiter analogue," said Elena. "There may be terrestrial planets closer to the star, like in the solar system. The star's current habitable zone is centered around 1.9 AU—corresponding to an orbital distance between Mars and the inner boundary of the Main Asteroid Belt back home. The orbital period of such a planet would be about 2.5 Earth years."

"Scanning the habitable zone now, Elena," replied JT, concentrating on the instrument readouts. The ship's course and velocity caused any close objects, such as planets, to change position faster than more distant stars. The Peggy Sue's optical instruments and its computer were faster and more accurate at measuring such small movements than any human observer. JT was picking out promising candidates from prospective objects identified by the automated equipment. Using the giant planet to establish an orbital plane made this task easier. "Ah! There we go!"

"Yes, Mr. Taylor?" said the Captain.

"A terrestrial planet at approximately 2 AU, working on mass and atmospheric spectrum analysis," he answered. "A bit smaller than Earth, but the atmosphere shows nitrogen, oxygen and traces of CO_2 and methane. I think we have a live one, Captain."

A buzz of excitement filled the bridge and the adjoining CIC. "Very good, Mr. Taylor. Helm, put us on a nice, easy approach to Mr. Taylor's 'live one'. Continue scanning for other objects, I don't wish to be surprised on the way there."

* * * * *

A day and a half later, the Peggy Sue slipped into a high orbit above Beta Hydri E, a cloud strewn green and dun colored world with a number of scattered seas and large lakes. On the approach, the ship's telescopes and remote sensors performed a survey of the planet. If 61 Vir was a disappointment, Beta Hydri was all the scientists on board had hoped for.

The Captain, Lcdr. Curtis, JT and several members of the science team were gathered around the large 3D tank in the CIC. For a time the group of humans stood mute. In front of them was a large swath of alien terrain, looking like a miniature diorama in a museum. A broad river valley with low hills to either side, covered by orderly groves of dark green trees, cut here and there by dirt colored ribbons. The ribbons radiated from clusters of earth colored mounds, and linked the mounds with larger structures that bordered the banks of the slowly flowing waterway.

There was only one way to interpret the scene in front of them: the ribbons were roads, the mounds houses and the larger structures the buildings of a city. Carts could be seen moving on the roads and ships sailed upon the river. The Peggy Sue had found a living planet with a working, if somewhat primitive civilization. Sally Li finally broke the silence, giving voice to thoughts they all shared. "OK, now that we've found some aliens, how do we go about making contact?"

"I'm not so sure we should," replied Olaf. "They seem to be at a fairly low level of technological development—late bronze age or early iron age. There is some haze from fires, perhaps for cooking, but no large industrial smoke stacks. And along the river are a number of water wheels, possibly to drive mills or other machinery. They seem to be about as advanced as Rome during Trajan's reign."

"Why do you say that we shouldn't make contact, Doctor?" asked Jack.

"If they are a pre-spaceflight society it might be best to not disturb them. They certainly won't be of use fighting the mysterious enemies you say are skulking about the galaxy."

Gretchen leaned closer to the display tank and said, "I guess we had it easy the last time—the Triads made contact with us."

"Yes, they did all the heavy lifting, along with the ship's computer," Sally agreed. "Heck, without the computer we can't even talk with the Ambassador."

"Well this crowd hasn't given us a call," added JT, consulting readouts on a side console. "They aren't transmitting anything using radio frequencies."

"Yes, and that is why we have all of you scientific types along," the Captain said, suppressing a grin. "When you figure out how to contact the natives let me know." Jack left the scientists to argue amongst themselves and returned to the bridge.

Throne Room of Tzzztchk XIV, Imperial Pzzst

Tzzztchk, Queen of the Ktchzz and Empress of all Pzzst, lay upon her alabaster throne, while the Imperial astronomer prostrated himself before her. Ministers hovered nearby, ready to denounce or praise the astronomer based on their reading of the queen's reaction to the news he bore.

"So speak, star gazer," her majesty rasped. "What momentous portents have you espied amongst the heavens that you seek our attention?"

"Oh, your most beneficent majesty, I bring news of a visitation from the stars," the nervous astronomer chittered. It was not unknown for her majesty to have the bearer of bad news drawn and dismembered.

"The Dark Lords have returned?" the queen demanded. "Why did We not hear this from the temple oracle?"

"Forgive me, oh great queen, but the travelers who are now circling high above your realm are not from the Dark Lords," the frightened savant continued in a rush. "They appear to be another form of sky god."

"How can you know this?" the queen asked suspiciously. From her point of view science and sorcery were one in the same, and no prudent monarch trusted a sorcerer.

"The shape of their ship, Majesty," he wailed, "It is much different from the vessels of the Dark Lords or their warrior daemons."

"My Lord High Chancellor!" the queen screeched. "Accompany this seer of heavenly signs to his lair and confirm the veracity of his statements."

A particularly large, bejeweled and well coiffed attendant hopped forward and bowed deeply. "Immediately, your Imperial

Highness." As that minister hurried the trembling Astronomer Royal from the audience chamber, the agitated monarch turned and rasped to another jewel bedecked attendant, "My Lord Chamberlain, summon the priests and my generals. We must decide how to deal with these new star gods."

Peggy Sue, Beta Hydri E, Day 3

The Captain was sharing a relaxed lunch with Ludmilla in the wardroom when his comm pip chirped. His brow wrinkled and a scowl crossed his face at the unwanted interruption—he and Ludmilla had seen little of each other the past several days. The ship's complement was busy preparing for every contingency prior to making contact with the natives on the planet below.

"Go on, Jack," Ludmilla said. "You know they would not disturb us unless it was something important."

"It had best be," he muttered and then answered the call, "Captain, go."

"Sorry to disturb you, Sir, but we are receiving a message from the planet." It was the voice of one of the new junior officers, over the comm Jack wasn't sure which one.

"What frequency? can we make sense of it?"

"They are using light, Sir. From the spectrum it appears to be focused and reflected sunlight. They are sending a code somewhat reminiscent of Morse code—the computer says that it is a degenerate form of a standard trading code, used long ago in this part of the galaxy."

"Can it be translated?"

"The computer is working on it, with some help from the Triad Ambassador. No translation yet, but I thought you should know."

"Yes, thank you. Keep me apprised of the situation. Captain out." *The Ambassador might be of greater help than I thought*, Jack reflected. Looking to his companion he said, "Looks like we are in luck for the second time, my dear. It would appear that the natives down below have taken the initiative and called us."

"Really? If we can communicate with them, we can arrange a face to face meeting. This is very exciting."

"And you will no doubt find a reason to be included in the contact party," he said, teasing her.

"Every expedition should have a medical doctor and a biologist along. Since I am both, sending me frees up a seat for someone else. Besides, I have as much first contact experience as anyone alive."

"A good officer learns from experience," Jack replied. "I'm not going to try and talk you out of going this time, but I am going along to keep an eye on you."

* * * * *

An hour later, Ludmilla and Jack were in the CIC, listening to a translation of the message from the natives. The ship's computer was providing the translation: "The message appears to be from an individual named Queen Tzzztchk, who claims to rule over the entire planet. The planet, by the way, is called Pzzst by the natives, who are known as the Ktchzz."

"And what does the Queen say?" asked Jack.

"Roughly translated: 'Greetings and salutations from Her Highness, Tzzztchk, queen of the Ktchzz and ruler of all Pzzst. We bid you welcome to our realm and hope to greet you in person,'" the Peggy Sue replied.

"I suppose that, given their level of technology, some form of monarchy was to be expected. Interesting that it is a matriarchy."

"It simply proves that the galaxy is a rational place," quipped Ludmilla. "It is well known that females are the best rulers."

Olaf harrumphed and said, "you are simply applying human prejudices to an alien species. Anthropomorphizing the natives probably does them a disservice."

"I don't know about that," said Elena, "but the fact that they spotted the ship in orbit and are making use of natural light to communicate with us is not behavior I would have expected from ancient Rome or China."

"I think it means that we are not the first visitors they have had from the stars," added Sally.

"Dr. Li is correct," said the computer. "knowledge of the trading code is a positive indication of prior contact."

"So we will not be breaking any first contact protocols, real or imagined," Jack said. "Commander Curtis, draft a response accepting the Queen's invitation—get our French diplomat to help with the proper phrasing."

Gretchen raised a single, questioning eyebrow and asked, "you are certain about involving de Belcour? He'll insist on being included in the contact party."

"He's been on best behavior recently and the reason for having him along is to win him over to our side," Jack replied. "The best way to do that is to include him in our grand adventure. Hold out the prospect of being in the shore party as motivation, I'm sure that he will cooperate."

"Aye aye, Sir," Gretchen answered. Ludmilla's face looked like she had tasted something foul but she did not comment. Jack glanced sideways at his partner, thinking, *she won't argue with me about de Belcour in front of the crew, but I'm going to get an earful in our cabin tonight.*

Destroyer of Worlds, Beta Comae – Sol Transfer Point

Survey of the Beta Comae system complete, the captain of the ship from Ursae Majoris turned his ponderous vessel toward the star system known to the Dark Ones as qwyyq106. The calculated transit time was six and a half days, long enough to give the crew a few days down time before preparing for emergence.

According to data provided by the Dark Ones, they would emerge above the system's ecliptic plane, with the target world on the far side of the local star. This was a bit of good fortune, since it would allow them to attack the planet from out of the Sun, hopefully remaining undetected until the locals could no longer mount a meaningful defense. They would then swing far out into the system's Kuiper Belt and replenish their supply of impact objects, before making another pass.

With any luck, the sterilization of the system's third planet would be completed within a year, the Captain reflected pensively. If the fourth planet remained lifeless, as reported by previous surveys, the crew of the Destroyer of Worlds might actually return to the People's moon alive, with many years of honored retirement before them. The more than five kilometer long ship rippled and slid into alter-space.

Grand Plaza, Imperial Palace, Pzzst

After several exchanges of diplomatically worded messages between the Ktchzz and the Earth vessel, plans were made to travel to the surface and meet the natives, face to face. Given the monumental scale of the Imperial Palace—the site they were instructed to land at—the Captain decided that a show of numbers was called for.

Both large shuttles would be used, one of which would carry the Captain, Ludmilla and half of the Marines, including two of the four adult bears, comprising the main delegation. Jack and Ludmilla would be wearing light armor with fishbowl helmets, while the Marines would be fully armed and wearing heavy powered armor. Jack was certain that any monarch greeting strangers from beyond the sky was sure to turn out the palace guard to impress the visitors and he wanted his entourage to be as imposing as possible.

Jack also thought that it would be best for him to make initial contact without a committee of scientists hovering about. He reasoned that dealing with an absolute monarch was best handled leader to leader. Ludmilla got to play the part of the Captain's consort, which rather amused her, much to Jack's relief.

Once over the initial contact, assuming conditions appeared safe, a secondary party would emerge to parlay with the Queen's ministers and draft a joint memorandum of cooperation. This party would be led by Dr. Li and M. de Belcour, with Midshipman Tanner and Kim Lawson along to assist.

The French diplomat insisted that his importance as an envoy would probably be judged by how many subordinates he had in attendance. Since Kim was one of the few crewmembers to befriend him, Jean-Jacques asked for her to be added, while Mr.

Tanner was included so an officer was present to keep an eye on things.

They would be accompanied by one of the SEALs, Chief Morgan, wearing light armor with weapons concealed. Jean-Jacques insisted that the "diplomatic party" be minimally armed, to the point that the four diplomats were wearing regular, skintight spacesuits under utility coveralls. At first Jack balked at that idea, but finally agreed, figuring that the natives would probably have nothing more dangerous than the local equivalent of spears and swords. The Chief SEAL should provide sufficient deterrent to any aggression on the part of the natives, or could at least hold them off until more heavily armed personnel arrived.

The remaining six Marines, two bears, two SEALs and several crewmen would stay with the shuttles as a reserve party. The shuttles themselves were piloted by Lieutenants McKinnett and Lewis, with Sandy flying the Captain's party and Nigel chauffeuring de Belcour and his "diplomats." The Ktchzz had suggested the inclusion of diplomats in the delegation themselves, which Jack thought a bit odd. Peggy Sue's computer said that the translation was not exact, but that was as close as the Ambassador and it could come.

The two shuttles approached the sprawling city in staggered formation, the Captain's shuttle in the lead. As they descended, both released surveillance drones to keep an eye on things and to help relay communications back to the Peggy Sue. The landing area was a large circular plaza, larger than St. Peter's Square in Rome.

Unlike the Piazza San Pietro, this space was not open to the rest of the city and lacked the imposing colonnade. This plaza was more like an oversized bull ring, with a huge barreled vault on one side, roughly in the position of St. Peter's Basilica in Vatican City.

"That arch has to be more than 60 meters tall at the midpoint," said LCpl. Ronnie Reagan, peering out a side viewport. Inside the vault, balconies and side doors could be seen dimly. "I wonder what it's made of?"

"Look at all those ornamental spires and stuff," said LCpl. Eddie Brown. "It looks like some kind of poured stone, almost like toothpaste oozed from a tube."

"Yeah, it looks like some of the later work of Antoni Gaudi," Ronnie replied. "All curvy and organic looking—sort of like half melted baroque. Of course, having only 80 percent Earth gravity helps with that arch."

"If all that is stone or concrete this place could have some wicked bullet bounce," said Lt. Bear, ignoring the reference to early 20th century Catalan modernist architecture. "Remember that, if things go sideways and we have to shoot our way back out."

The two shuttles landed 20 meters from each other with their rear ramps pointed toward the arched opening. From the Captain's shuttle the ramp lowered until it rested on the flagstone courtyard.

"OK, Lt. Bear," said the Captain. "It's show time."

"Aye, Sir," Bear replied. "Right Marines, let's do this like we planned it. Sanchez and Brown, lead us out."

The first pair of Marines exited the shuttle, side-by-side. Once clear of the ramp they moved to either side of the opening, making room for the next pair of Marines. They descended, passed by the first pair and took positions ahead of their predecessors. The third pair repeated the maneuver.

The human Marines were now standing in two parallel lines, three deep. The next to emerge from the shuttle was a levitating sphere about the size of a basketball. It floated gracefully down the ramp and proceeded to the head of the column, followed by the Captain and Dr. Tropsha. They strode to the front of the formation behind the robotic drone while Isbjørn emerged, followed by Bear. The bears ambled forward and took the lead positions of the two columns of Marines. Then the whole party fell in behind the Captain and Ludmilla and advanced on the structure in front of them.

The Captain halted the formation 10 meters from the yawning entrance and allowed the drone to continue alone. As it neared the vault's threshold, the robot halted and announced, "Captain Jack Sutton, Master and Commander of the starship Peggy Sue, and his consort, Lady Ludmilla call upon her Imperial Highness, Queen Tzzztchk, sovereign ruler of all Pzzst."

From with the shadowed depths of the vault a creature hopped forward. Covered with light brown fur, golden chains hung from its neck, supporting jeweled crests and insignias of rank. It advanced to stand in front of the floating drone. Once facing the robotic emissary, the alien emitted screeching and clicking noises that the Peggy Sue translated as a greeting and welcome from the great Queen Tzzztchk.

"See," Jack said to Ludmilla over suit-to-suit, "de Belcour was right, we needed a herald. Otherwise I would have lost face having to announce myself to yonder lowly court functionary."

"It does not surprise me that a French bureaucrat knows all about snobbery and highhanded insults," Ludmilla retorted. "Besides, how much face can you lose to a hairy cricket wearing a necklace?"

The Herald in front of them did look like a cricket—a cricket a meter and a half tall, covered with sleek, well groomed 10cm long hair. Chitinous barbs protruded beyond the hair on the creature's four arms and large rear legs. It canted its head to one side as if impatient for an answer, sunlight glinting off of its multifaceted eyes. "I think the harry cricket wants a reply," Bear advanced.

"I believe you are right, Lieutenant. Peggy Sue, have our herald say something appropriate and ask to see the Queen." A string of clicks, chirps and buzzing sounds emanated from the drone. The herald bobbed its head and turned, waving two of its arms in an unmistakable "come with me" gesture.

As the Marines marched inside the Queen's palace following Ludmilla and the Captain, thousands of insect eyes watched from strangely shaped doorways and openings. Lt. Bear said to his squad over the Marine's comm frequency, "Look sharp guys, we are going to meet the bug queen."

"You know, LT," Ronnie Reagan commented. "Since leaving Earth, everything we have met that looks even remotely like an insect has tried to kill us."

"Great," said Joey Sanchez. "Now we're interstellar pest control —except out here the bugs shoot back."

Chapter 17

Imperial Palace, Pzzst

The Captain's party moved deeper into the imposing palace, surrounded by arched doorways and ornate balconies. Buttery light filtered in through translucent panels, inserted at seemingly random locations in the high vaulted ceiling. A hundred meters into the structure two smaller barrel vaults intersected the main vault from either side. They too, were lined with misshapen openings and flowing balconies, disappearing into dimly lit distance.

In front of the Earth delegation the main hall continued, its floor rising in a sequence of flat landings. The herald nimbly hopped from level to level, evidently the ascending terrace was the local equivalent of a grand stairway. After climbing roughly ten meters vertically, they came to a set of massive doors towering 20 meters above the landing. Each dark brown panel was three meters wide and covered with intricate carvings.

"Most impressive," Ludmilla remarked, gazing up at the bas-relief sculpture in front of them. A number of the scenes would have done an Egyptian Pharaoh proud.

"I would guess that this grand hall and the doors are intended to impress the Queen's visitors," the Captain replied. "The carvings undoubtedly show her or her predecessors performing great deeds and heroic acts. The archeologists and anthropologists back home will have a field-day with the 3D images we're transmitting back to the ship."

Behind the Captain, Bear and Isbjørn were making a different assessment of the monumental architecture confronting them. "All those twisted openings along the stairs would be a great place to hide ambushers," Bear said to his mate.

"And with all the irregular balconies and side openings along the hallway, fighting our way out would be like running down the middle of a target range," Isbjørn agreed. "I hope the Captain's right and these creatures only have spears and crossbows."

"I'm glad we're all wearing armor, babe. Even if Jack and Ludmilla are not wearing heavy power suits, they shouldn't be vulnerable to spears and arrows."

"Still, if the fur flies we need to get them into the middle of the formation and make tracks for the shuttle."

"Roger that," he replied. "Look, the door is opening."

Bear's observation was correct, the gigantic carved doors were slowly opening inward. Once they reached a full open position the Pzzst herald took two hops into the chamber, bowed and began screeching and buzzing—no doubt announcing the Queen's guests had arrived. Again the herald motioned the Earthlings forward and then quickly moved to one side.

If the hallway and balconies coming in were empty, this chamber was stuffed to overflowing with hundreds of natives. Many were adorned with chains and sashes, indications of their rank and position in the court. Others wore cuirasses, some solid metal, most lamellar. Those wearing the lamellar armor were evidently guards and leaned on two and a half meter halberds. Resembling the polearms of 15th century Swiss pikemen, each consisted of an axe blade topped with a spike mounted on a long shaft. The individuals wearing the solid breastplates, some inlaid and all highly polished, bore the swords of officers. From either side of the center aisle they stared at the Captain's party with large unblinking compound eyes.

The aisle, the only open space in the room, provided a clear path to the foot of a raised dais 30 meters away. A stepped platform 1.5 meters high held a large individual laying in a carved, alabaster cradle—the Ktchzz equivalent of a throne. Balconies ringed the chamber, festooned with bright cloth and garlands of flowers. Having been announced, Jack and Ludmilla marched down the aisle to the throne side-by-side.

The Queen herself was an impressive specimen, more than two meters in length with hair of pure white. Well positioned shafts of light illuminated the throne, glinting off the Queen's multifaceted silver eyes and sparkling jewels that adorned her person. Extending in front of her chest lay a pointed shaft, its needle tip drooped slightly downward in front of a cluster of spikes that would not have been out of place on the head of a Medieval mace. Where exoskeleton was left uncovered by hair and jewels the chitin was also white, giving Jack an impression of advanced age.

251

Halting four meters in front of the monarch, Jack bent at the waist in a shallow but respectful bow while Ludmilla managed a surprisingly graceful curtsy—even the light armor limited their range of movement. There had been discussion prior to the mission whether Jack and Ludmilla should bow before the alien monarch. In the end it was decided that being respectful before an alien head of state was probably the best course of action.

The Queen's twin antennae dipped briefly and the ruler of all Pzzst addressed her guests with a cacophonous burst of noise that almost overwhelmed the visitors' suit microphones.

Shuttle Two, Grand Plaza, Imperial Palace

After a quarter hour of exchanging meaningless pleasantries, the alien queen finally got around to asking about the diplomats. The Captain informed the Queen that members of the diplomatic estate were waiting to meet Her Majesty's ministers to negotiate a memorandum of understanding and friendship. With the Queen's permission, Jack called the second party of Earthlings waiting aboard their shuttle in the courtyard.

"The Queen would like you to come to the palace," Jack told Jean-Jacques de Belcour. "You will be met at the entrance by a herald who will take you to meet her ministers."

"Very good, Captain, we shall be there shortly," the Frenchman replied, still a bit miffed at not being in the first party. Turning to his assembled group—Sally Li, Kim Lawson and Skip Tanner—he assumed command of the diplomatic phase of the mission. "We need to proceed to the entrance of the palace, where we will be met by an escort. Follow my lead and do not address the natives directly, use the robot drone to translate."

Sally rolled her eyes and said, "yes, Jean-Jacques. Some of us have done this before, you know."

"This time we will do it properly," he sniffed.

"If things get testy for some reason, remember that only Mr. Tanner and myself are armed," added Chief Morgan. The SEAL was wearing light armor much like the Captain and Dr. Tropsha, but the young midshipman was wearing a standard spacesuit with a flechette pistol on his waist.

"I still object to you bringing weapons along on this mission," de Belcour opined. "But the Captain has left me no choice."

"Don't worry, Mr. Tanner's weapon is holstered and mine strapped to my utility pack," Morgan replied. "They will probably not even know we are armed." *Unless things go sideways,* the Chief added to himself, *then we may all be sorry we aren't more heavily armed.* As the party trooped down the shuttle's rear ramp Chief Morgan said to his two fellow SEALs, "I don't care what that stuffed frog says, if I call mayday, you and the Gyrenes come on the double."

"Count on it, Chief" replied Bud Jones, with Phil Kowalski nodding in agreement.

* * * * *

After being greeted by another herald, the party of diplomats was led down one of the side hallways where the crossing arches met the main vault. "The side vaults connecting with the central hall forming a cross shaped floor plan is reminiscent of a Medieval cathedral," Jean-Jacques mused as they were escorted deeper into the bowels of the Imperial Palace. "Perhaps architectural aesthetics could provide some common ground between our species."

"There are only so many ways to arrange basic structural features, Jean-Jacques," replied Sally. "Particularly with primitive materials and construction techniques. I wouldn't make too much of the similarities."

"This place doesn't remind me of a cathedral," said Skip. "More like a termite mound or an ant colony."

"You are judging them using Earth prejudices," Kim said, loyally coming to the Frenchman's defense. "Jean-Jacques is more experienced at this type of thing than the rest of us, we should listen to him."

"Thank you, Kim," Jean-Jacques replied. "Please, let us all maintain our composure in front of our hosts. Ah, it looks like we have arrived at our destination." The herald leading their party stopped before a set of massive doors, not nearly as wide or tall as the ones to the royal audience chamber but impressive nonetheless.

As the doors swung open the herald motioned them forward while simultaneously backing out of the way. Ahead lay a large, well lit chamber containing a crowd of chittering natives. A number of the Ktchzz were noticeably larger than the rest, towering a good half a meter above their companions. The larger Ktchzz were also noticeably lighter in color than the smaller natives, with light blond, almost white hair.

"The big ones sort of look like the Queen, don't you think?" observed Sally as they entered the chamber. Prior to their own departure for the palace, the diplomats had been viewing live video from the Captain's party. "Maybe these are related to her."

"*Bien sûr*, they may be princesses," said Jean-Jacques, straitening his back unconsciously. The UN diplomat strode forward into the chamber of waiting aliens. *Supercilious twit*, thought Chief Morgan as he brought up the rear. *The skin on the back of my neck is crawling and that usually means we are about to step in it.*

Throne Room, Imperial Palace

"So it is true that your ship can travel among the stars, to other worlds far away?" the Peggy Sue translated Queen Tzzztchk's question. The Queen's attendants seemed to be hanging on every word of the conversation.

"Yes, your Majesty. The Peggy Sue does, indeed, carry us between stars. Our mission is to visit worlds like yours, seeking new friends and allies," Jack replied. While his words were translated he said to his officers, "Is it only me, or does her highness seem awfully curious about our ship and its capabilities?"

"I think that I would be also, if strange aliens came to call," said Ludmilla, playing devil's advocate as scientists are taught.

As the strangeness and initial tension of the encounter eased, the party examined their surroundings more closely. This was easier for the Marines, since they were wearing combat helmets that concealed their heads. Combined with their suits' built-in cameras they could scan their environment while standing as still as statues.

Ludmilla and Jack both had suits with clear bubble helmets, revealing their faces and head movements to the crowd of assembled Ktchzz.

"Captain," Bear interjected, "I can't help but notice that there are an awful lot of crickets with pointy objects in this room, and not just in the crowd. I see more peeking out from the side galleries."

"They may just be nervous about having their Queen exposed to a bunch of off world visitors," Jack replied. Their internal conversation was interrupted by the arrival of the translation of the Queen's next question.

"How marvelous to have such a ship! Does your Queen possess many such craft? You must truly be a powerful empire to have a fleet of ships that sail among the stars."

"Interesting how she assumes we are ruled by a Queen," Ludmilla remarked.

"More interesting is how she is pumping us to find out how large a fleet we possess," Jack added. He considered his reply to the Queen for a few seconds and then spoke. "Our people have many large fleets and have sent many missions to strange planets in the past, Your Majesty. I do not know the exact numbers, but more are added every day."

"You really should not lie to her, Jack," Ludmilla chided.

"Not lies, my dear, but half truths," he responded. "The nations back home do have many sizable fleets, just not of spacecraft, and we have sent many probes to the outer planets. If she draws the wrong conclusions it isn't my problem."

"She seems to be chewing on that answer, Captain," Bear said. "She's chattering to that guy next to her in the shiny armor. He must be some kind of general or something."

"A monarch would have a military adviser or two running around the palace somewhere. Peggy Sue, can you make out what they are saying to each other?"

"Why Captain, eavesdropping on a private conversation would be very undiplomatic," snipped Ludmilla. "I am sure M. de Belcour would disapprove."

The ship's computer replied primly, "Of course I'm listening to them. The Ktchzz in the engraved armor is General Hzooshkit, evidently the Queen's top commander. The Queen asked if your claims could be true, to which the General replied that you were being intentionally vague as any good military leader would."

"So the General is no dummy," Jack mused.

"The Queen is asking if our ship alone could destroy their world... and the General just said 'probably, if the ships of the others are any example.'"

"Others?" Jack and Ludmilla said together, "what others?"

Diplomat's Chamber, Imperial Palace

As Jean-Jacques' party entered the chamber the Ktchzz host surged forward, surrounding and separating the humans. A number of the smaller, darker furred natives swarmed Chief Morgan, knocking him off his feet while others seized the diplomats. Over his suit's radio he could hear panicked shouts from the others.

"What are you doing?" cried Sally, "Let go of me!"

"*Mon Dieu!* This is not acceptable behavior, even for aliens. Let me up... ahhh!"

"Get off me! Jean-Jacques, someone help," yelled Kim. As the unarmored members of the party were wrestled to the ground by the hoard of hopping crickets, the larger white aliens approached them at a more measured pace. Bobbing in front of each Ktchzz "princess" was a long shaft, extending more than a meter from the creature's lower abdomen. At the end of each, fifteen centimeters of needle tip protruded from a cluster of six centimeter spikes, quivering with every move of the shaft's owner.

Jean-Jacques managed to roll over on his stomach and was trying to crawl away. Several of the brown crickets were slashing at Kim with the spikes on their forearms, renting the fabric of her coverall and tearing the tougher space suit beneath.

Skip was backpedaling, fighting off the aliens with one arm and fumbling to get at his sidearm with the other. "Mayday, Mayday,"

Chief Morgan called on the emergency frequency. "We are under attack, repeat, under attack."

"Get that thing away from me!" shrieked Sally, as one of the white crickets climbed on top of her. It rose up and mounted the helpless botanist, driving the tip of its shaft into her abdomen. That is when the screaming began in earnest.

* * * * *

Back at the waiting shuttles, Chief Morgan's voice crackled over the emergency frequency. "Mayday! Mayday!" Before he could say "we are under attack," the other SEALs were down shuttle two's rear ramp and running toward the palace opening. "Jones! Kowalski!" yelled GySgt Rodriguez. Releasing the transmit key she added, "fuckin' sailor boys got no fuckin' discipline."

"Lt. Lewis, please release the battle bots and ask Lt. McKennitt to do the same," the Gunny called out. "All right Marines, let's move out, double time. Inuksuk, you're on point. Corpsman White I think we may need you with us on this." The big polar bear's response was an unintelligible growl as he bounded down the ramp and followed after the SEALs. He was quickly followed by the remaining Marines with Aurora, the Gunny and Corpsman White bringing up the rear.

Like the SEALs, Betty White wore light armor under the assumption that if she was needed to work on wounded in the field the greater dexterity of an unpowered suit would outweigh the loss of protection. As she left the shuttle she called to Steve Hitch, one of the crewmen on board, "You might want to get a floater ready, if we have casualties we won't want to carry them and fight our way out at the same time."

"Sure thing, Betty," he replied. "Give the word and Matt and I will be there pronto." Both Hitch and Jacobs were wearing power armor and together, they formed the reserve force's reserve force. Betty nodded to the pair, trouble makers most times but steady and courageous under fire.

Watching the medic jog down the ramp, Jacobs said to Hitch, "you know, Stevie, there's got to be about a bazillion bugs in that place."

"That just means it'll be a target rich environment," his friend replied as the Marines disappear into the gloom of the Imperial Palace.

* * * * *

Knocked to his back on the chamber floor, Chief Morgan reacted quickly, lashing out in all directions. His suit may have been unpowered but the SEAL was strong as an ox and trained to inflict debilitating damage on opponents in hand-to-hand combat. Kicking one cricket away with his left leg uncovered his left arm. Using the freed limb to bludgeon the Ktchzz directly on top of him, the attacker's head was quickly reduced to pulp, dripping yellow and green ichor.

Casting off the dead carcass, Rick rolled to a crouch while drawing his rail-gun from its hiding place. Like Ludmilla and the Captain, his weapon was the rail-gun equivalent of a submachine gun—a bullpup, 5mm flechette gun that took standard 200 round magazines but lacked the 20mm grenade launcher/shotgun of the standard issue Marine weapon. *I just knew we were going to need more firepower than this popgun,* he thought bitterly. *I hate being right about shit like that.*

Having sent the distress call, he focused on picking off Ktchzz with short, well aimed bursts, trying to work his way toward the nearest member of the diplomatic party. Four or five meters in front of him he could see glimpses of flailing arms and legs in a white coverall that could only be Kim Lawson. *Good,* he thought, *if she's fighting back she's still alive and not gravely wounded.*

Between bursts he could hear the sporadic crack of another rail-gun—evidently Midshipman Tanner had managed to get his sidearm into action. "Hang in there, Mr. Tanner," the SEAL said over the party frequency, "Help is on the way." *At least it better be or we're toast.*

Throne Room, Imperial Palace

"The general mentioned other off-world visitors?" Jack said. "Damn, I can't ask about other visitors now, not without them realizing we've been eavesdropping on them."

"The Queen seems unduly agitated," Ludmilla remarked. "Perhaps she thinks we mean them harm." A buzzing sound rose in the background as the crowd of Ktchzz shifted anxiously.

"Evidently they have had dealings with visiting aliens in the past," continued the Peggy Sue. "Captain, the Ambassador has just informed me that the only spacefaring beings in this part of the galaxy during the last several million years or so have all been in league with the Dark Lords."

Oh crap, Jack thought, *we may be standing around making small talk with one of our enemy's allies.* "The Ambassador is sure of that?" he asked. "We may be in the midst of a hornet's nest." Before Peggy Sue could reply, the throne room erupted into bedlam.

Dozens of pike wielding guards leapt forward, halberds high above their heads. Evidently, the creatures' favored form of attack was to jump high into the air, bringing their ax-headed pikes down on their intended targets with maximum force. While such a blow might have cleaved an opposing Ktchzz in two, the Marines were encased in armor much tougher than steel, leather or chitin.

The attacking royal guards were swatted down or flung aside by massive armored limbs, powered by electroreactive polymer muscles with more than human strength. Bear and Isbjørn moved to cover the flanks, protecting Ludmilla and the Captain from most of the attackers. Their roars could be heard over the radio as JT's mechanical claws proved to be as horribly effective as he and the bears had hoped. Bear's massive clawed paws acted like scythes, reaping a harvest of severed torsos, limbs and heads.

Even with cover from the bears, several of the halberd wielding guards managed to strike at Ludmilla and Jack. Though their suits were unpowered and more lightly armored than the Marines, the couple quickly engaged the Ktchzz that tried to attack them down. Thanks to years of martial arts training Ludmilla's reactions were swift and deadly—grabbing an attacker's halberd by its shaft and pulling its owner off balance. She stepped into the creature to block any counter move at the same time bringing an armored forearm down, smashing the Ktchzz's head.

While Ludmilla was killing her assailant, Jack was also dealing with a bounding attack. The Queen's general had drawn a scimitar like sword from the scabbard at his waist and launched himself at the Captain blade held high. In response, Jack sidestepped the descending edged weapon, grabbing the backside of the blade with his left gauntlet while delivering a right handed blow. Starting with his clenched fist at waist height, Jack rotated his arm, shoulder and upper body as he struck, driving his fist into the general with the full force of his muscular body. Landing just below the junction of head and thorax, Jack's armored fist snapped the Ktchzz's neck, nearly decapitating the hapless general.

Looking toward the throne, it became clear that the general's move was cover for the Queen's hasty withdrawal from the audience chamber. Doors had opened behind Her Majesty and she was swiftly pulled, throne and all, back through the portal.

The general's body lay fallen at the Captain's feet, still gripping the wicked scimitar. Jack yanked on the sword but the dying Ktchzz had a death-grip on the weapon. Placing a boot on the general's breastplate, Jack pulled with both arms, wrenching one of the dead cricket's arms from its socket. After literally disarming his attacker, Jack belatedly remembered his firearm.

Drawing his rail-gun he glanced in Ludmilla's direction in time to see her likewise arming herself with something other than her fists. In the fleeting seconds between the first wave of Ktchzz and the second, the Marines also drew their weapons and the tide of battle changed. A withering hail of flechette fire beat back the attacking Ktchzz who responded with counter fire of their own. A flight of arrows rained down on the Earthlings from the gallery ringing the chamber.

"Bear! Isbjørn! Suppressing fire on the balconies," Jack ordered.

"Aye, Captain!" Bear replied, sweeping the galleries to the right with a fusillade of 15mm explosive shells from his multi-barreled rail-gun. On the left, Isbjørn did the same with a stream of 5mm flechettes pouring forth at 4,000 rounds per minute.

Diplomat's Chamber, Imperial Palace

Chief Morgan finally managed to clear a path to Kim, who was still fighting back but pinned to the floor by a bevy of brown crickets. Using the chitinous barbs on their forearms they ripped open both coverall and suit to reveal Kim's midriff, which was bleeding from several long gashes. Her head was pointed at Rick and her legs toward the center of the chamber, from which a large white Ktchzz was advancing on her.

The creature's long spiked member was bobbing in front of it as it shuffled toward the helpless girl. Rick had no doubt what would happen next. "Not so fast you alien asshole," he said, firing a burst into the Ktchzz's abdomen at the base of its shaft.

The white Ktchzz reared up and emitted a piercing, high frequency wail that caused an immediate frenzy among the brown crickets. With a second burst, the alien's head exploded into chunks of fur and chitin, trailing yellow body fluids. The remaining aliens surged forward, antennae waving and mandibles gnashing.

"Oh they did not like that at all," Rick said to no one in particular. Grabbing Kim's shoulder with his left hand, he drug her away from the advancing swarm of hairy insects. With surging effort, the SEAL threw the now almost catatonic Kim behind him and then fired a long burst, swinging from left to right. This slowed the bug onslaught long enough to slap a new magazine into his weapon.

He could hear Kim whimpering over suit-to-suit but there was nothing on the party frequency—and that was not a good sign. Then he heard a cry of pain followed by "damn that smarts." Looking right he saw Skip raise his pistol and put a 10mm slug into the head of the bug that had just skewered him with a short spear.

Skip slid down the wall on the far side of the door, trying to remove the spear and fend off the advances of more of the chittering natives. Rick fired three short, aimed bursts dropping the crickets closest to the downed midshipman. Skip managed to remove the spear and, given a brief respite thanks to the SEAL's intervention, reload his sidearm. Over the party frequency came a labored voice. "Thanks Chief, buy you a drink when this is over."

Kid's got some stones, Rick thought as he turned his attention back to the aliens advancing on his own position. Over the emergency frequency he yelled, "a dramatic entrance right about now would not go amiss," adding silently, *because otherwise we are surely going to be overrun.*

Throne Room, Imperial Palace

"Captain, this is Gunny Rodriguez," came a voice over the Captain's suit radio, "The diplomatic party reports that they are under attack."

"Roger that, Gunny, I heard the mayday," Jack replied. "We are under attack ourselves. Lot's of crickets with Medieval weapons, including crossbows. Go get our people back, Sergeant. We will see you on the way out."

"Aye aye, Sir."

"Lt. Bear, I believe it is time for us to exfiltrate the palace."

"Roger that, Sir," Bear replied. "Do you think that Queenie will miss that big ass door?"

"I will ask her once we reach orbit, Mr. Bear."

"Right. Head's up, I'm going to take out the door," he called to the squad. Turning to face the barred entrance, Bear raised his rapid fire cannon and prepared to fire. Before he could fire a score of stout javelins flew from slits in the surrounding chamber walls. "Incoming!" yelled Joey Sanchez.

One of the projectiles was aimed squarely at Ludmilla. Again, her well practiced reflexes kicked in. She bent backward and turn at the waist, allowing the hefty spear to clear her chest by less than a hand's breadth. It continued on to thump Isbjørn in the ribs a few meters away. Isbjørn made a 'woof' sound and looked back.

The Captain also escaped being harpooned by deflecting the bolt fired at him with one arm. He stood up with his arm almost comically cocked at head height, waiting for the impact distributing polymers in the suit armor to relax. "Damn, I felt that even through the armor. I don't think it would be healthy to take a direct hit by one of these on a bubble helmet."

"I think you are right, Captain. You and Ludmilla had best get to the center of the formation," said the female bear.

"There must be catapults behind the surrounding curtain walls," called LCpl. Roselito Acuna. "Fire at the slits."

"Let me give you a hand," said Isbjørn, as she demolished the section of wall nearest Ludmilla and the Captain. "Are you about done with that door, Bear?"

Bear, who had been distracted by the javelin attack, growled and turned back to the door. "Fire in the hole!" A burst of 42 HE 15mm rounds walked up the seam where the two door halves met. The result was dramatic, the sound almost deafening, even inside of the spacesuits. A ripple of bright flashes was followed by a spray of dust and debris and when the smoke cleared the door was no more. What had been an impressive wooden barrier was now a collection of sticks and splinters scattered down the terraced steps to the main hall. "All right Marines," Bear rumbled. "It's time to un-ass the throne room."

Diplomat's Chamber, Imperial Palace

Chief Morgan's two brother SEALs followed the diplomatic party's floating robotic "herald" down the right side adjoining vault to an imposing door. A smattering of brown haired Ktchzz, most armed with short spears, attempted to slow their advance, drawing deadly fire from the running men. As they drew up to the door, Bud Jones called "Chief, we're going to blow the door!"

"Do it already!" came the answer. "There's a shitload of angry bugs in here so hurry up."

The SEALs started to place plastic explosive charges against the doors when a deep base voice yelled, "OUT OF THE WAY!" Scant seconds later, a ton of armored polar bear slammed into the center of the doors. Timber snapped, masonry flew and in an instant Inuksuk was through the portal before them.

The sudden appearance of a large, four legged armored monster in their midst gave the hairy cricket hoard a momentary pause—just long enough for the two SEALs to recover their wits and charge after Inuksuk, weapons at the ready. On the right side of the doorway, Skip Tanner sat in a pool of his own blood, still gamely firing into the crowd of hostiles. Bud quickly beat back the crickets and moved to shield the wounded midshipman from further attack.

On the left Phil found his boss standing over the huddled figure of another party member, one of the women, though he could not tell which one. "You call a cab, Chief?"

Morgan snarled and emptied his weapon into a cricket trying to flank him on the left. "About fuckin' time, Kowalski. That was the last of my ammo." Without speaking, Phil took two magazines from his backpack and handed them to Rick. Slapping a fresh magazine into his weapon the SEAL Chief resumed picking off aliens with careful aimed fire.

Before Kowalski could think of a suitable reply the first of the Marines arrived: Tusi "Book" Mapusua and Kato Kwan, followed closely by the Gunny. "Clear a path to our people," the Gunny shouted, as the Marines added their firepower to the counterattack. Inuksuk had also recovered his composure and unlimbered his 15mm.

Approaching one of the downed figures the Gunny got an unobstructed view of a large white Ktchzz with its shaft stuck into the body of a small blood soaked human. The cricket was rhythmically thrusting its abdomen in and out, causing the impaled body to move as well. "Mother fucker!" the Gunny hissed between clenched teeth, "these hairy freaks are raping them!"

Switching from flechettes to shotgun mode the Gunny blew the Ktchzz's chest out through its back, spraying the crickets behind it with insect gore. The second round caused the rapist's head to disintegrate. A steady stream of obscenities flowed from the Gunny as she walked forward firing scatter shot into the large alien until all that was left was the shaft, still implanted in Sally Li's abdomen.

"Corpsman, get in here," the Gunny called. The Sergeant kneeled beside the ruined corpse that had been Dr. Li and examined the obscene thing stuck in her gut. Betty White came running up to join her beside the body and stopped cold when she saw the remains of their crewmate. Through the clear helmet she could see Sally Li's face, blood around her mouth and chin, a few drops splattered on the inside of the transparent bubble. Lifeless eyes wide open, staring up at infinity. Betty did not need to check Sally's suit readouts to know, "She's gone, Gunny. Nothing we can do for her."

"The hell there ain't," growled the Gunny. Switching to the squad command frequency she yelled, "kill 'em! Kill 'em all."

Grand Staircase, Imperial Palace

Led by Isbjørn, Jon Feldman and Roselito Acuna, the Captain's party exited the now ruined audience chamber. As the trio entered the grand staircase leading back out of the palace they immediately came under crossbow fire. The balconies lining both sides of the terraced stairs were swarming with cricket archers. Isbjørn swept the balconies on either side while the two Marines fired grenades into side portals from which pike wielding Ktchzz were trying to emerge.

"There is just an acre of these things," said Rosey, pausing to insert another seven 20mm grenade rounds into her weapon from a tubular speedloader. Rosey had been a U.S. Marine for four years before she was caught in the downsizing. When she was offered the opportunity to join the Marines aboard Peggy Sue she jumped at the chance. Raised on science fiction movies and video games, her childhood dream was to fight vicious space aliens on some faraway planet. Sometimes dreams do come true.

From the other side of the blasted doorway, Jon was firing three shot bursts into any side opening that showed movement. Since every third flechette was a tracer round, each burst sent a streak of bright green fire into the gloom of the poorly lit hallway. "Moving left," Isbjørn called, before crossing into Rosey's line of fire—the trio would provide overwatch for the others.

As Isbjørn moved aside, the rest of the squad advanced, moving through their position—a pair of Marines, closely followed by Bear, Ludmilla and the Captain. Finally, the remaining two Marines moved down the stairs, stopping to fire when targets presented themselves. The party advanced, clearing the stairway until the lead Marines reached the foot of the stairs. There they halted to allow the rearguard to catchup.

Getting the signal to move out from Bear, Isbjørn holster her weapon and headed down the staircase at a casual gallop. Rosey looked at Jon and said, "let's take a last look at the throne room and make sure we aren't being followed."

"Roger that," he said. Together they stepped back inside the shambles of the Queen's audience chamber. The walls on all sides were crumbling, blasted by high explosive rounds, the surrounding galleries collapsed. The floor of the chamber was an abattoir, covered by mounds of shattered insect bodies splashed with yellow-green viscera. Arms and legs stuck out of the carnage at random angles, some of them still twitching. "Looks like our work here is done," Jon quipped.

"Not quite," Rosey said, noticing the large wooden chandelier suspended from the ceiling. She raised her weapon and fired a single explosive grenade, striking the support chain at the point where it met the ceiling. The explosion severed the chain and brought the heavy wood construct crashing to the floor, where it splashed flammable liquid in all directions and then caught fire.

"With all due respect to Douglas Adams," Jon commented, "'mostly harmless' my ass."

"I didn't know you were so literary, Feldman. The Hitchhiker's Guide is a classic."

"Yeah, and this place is history." The pair of marines turned and sprinted to rejoin their squadmates, while behind them the chandelier snapped and popped merrily as it burned.

Diplomat's Chamber, Imperial Palace

Phil Kowalski took a knee beside Betty and the Gunny. Every Ktchzz in the chamber was either dead or dying. Staring at Sally's stomach wound he shook his head. He had seen his share of vicious wounds during his years with the Teams but this was a first. "That son-of-a-bitch actually stuck his spiked cock into her stomach?"

"That bitch," Betty corrected, pulling a four centimeter long rounded object from the broken end of the shaft in question. It was the shape, color and texture of an oversized grain of cooked rice. "The shaft isn't a penis. This is an egg and the shaft is an ovipositor."

"A what?"

266

"Ovipositor, an organ used to lay eggs. Some insect species on Earth use them to inject eggs into paralyzed prey—parasitic wasps for instance. Later, when the eggs hatch they find a supply of fresh food all around them."

"You mean they hatch inside the victim and start eating their way out?" Phil asked. "Like in that old Alien movie?" Hands down, he had never heard of a more horrible way to die.

"Yeah, they eat the victim alive," Betty confirmed. "Except these hairy bitches miscalculated and killed her."

"Sweat merciful Mother of Christ," the SEAL swore. He pivoted and put a burst into the white Ktchzz that was draped over top of Jean-Jacques' body. Someone else had already relieved that cricket of its head, but it had expired in the act of laying its eggs in the unfortunate Frenchman.

"Stop!" Yelled Betty. "I saw his fingers move! The Frenchman is still alive!"

"What? We gotta get that thing off him," said the Gunny, moving to where Jean-Jacques lay, face down. "It looks like the bug's whatchamacallit is stuck up the frog's ass."

"That's gotta hurt," said Phil. "Let's get the bug carcass off of him."

"Wait, don't pull the shaft out of him," cried Betty, hurrying to help the others. "If we yank that spiked thing out of him, he'll bleed out for sure."

"So what do we do?" asked the Gunny.

"I'll grab the shaft where it enters the Frenchman's body," she replied. "Gunny, use your Woodman's Pal to cut the shaft while Kowalski pushes the dead cricket off of him."

"Gotcha," Phil responded, moving into position.

The Gunny drew her military grade machete and crouched to examine the ovipositor shaft. Instead of striking with the flat blade on the front of the machete, she hooked the wickedly curved backside around the shaft. That part of the tool was intended for clearing vines and jungle undergrowth. "Ready?"

Getting a firm, two-handed grasp on the base of the shaft, Betty nodded affirmative. With a quick jerk, the razor sharp hook severed the ovipositor. Phil heaved the dead insect off the prostrate Frenchman, throwing the carcass several meters. "You think he's going to make it, Doc?" Phil asked, using the military's traditional sobriquet for all medical personnel.

"I don't know, but if we can get him back to the shuttle where Dr. Tropsha can work on him he might. Shuttle two..." she called, changing frequencies.

"Go," came the instant reply.

"We need that sled, ASAP. We have three wounded and one KIA."

"Roger that. FYI, the Captain's party has fought their way to the bottom of the staircase and are waiting to cover your extraction. It's going to be hot on the way out, the damn bugs are everywhere."

Great Hall, Imperial Palace

"Come on, Stevie! Move your ass," called Matt Jacobs from the front of the hover sled. He felt the floating craft shudder, indicating that Hitch had jumped on board, and accelerated down the shuttle's ramp, headed for the palace entrance. As they raced for the menacing opening in the plaza wall, javelins and occasional head sized rocks landed nearby.

"These fuzzy grasshoppers couldn't hit an elephant in the ass," Hitch observed. Sitting in the rear of the sled, facing the shuttles, he could see the six wheeled ABPs, autonomous battle platforms, returning fire at the catapults and ballistas that had suddenly appeared along the walls encircling the plaza. Each ABP—nicknamed battle bots by the crew—mounted a multi-barreled 15mm rail-gun cannon much like those carried by the male polar bears.

Aimed by a combination of Radar and LIDAR, the battle bots were capable of shooting down incoming artillery and mortar rounds. Against javelins and 30kg rocks they were not as effective. The javelins were almost too small to target and hitting a rock had a tendency to turn one incoming object into several, scattered over a wider area. Instead of trying to intercept the incoming, the battle bots concentrated on the sources of the fire.

With their large ammo capacity, the ABPs carried something that the bears generally did not—canister rounds for the cannon. More accurately, bundles of flechettes fired like large shotgun rounds. If the smaller, multi-barreled flechette guns were fire hoses of death, a 15mm firing canister sent a tsunami of death downrange. If the Ktchzz tried to overwhelm the shuttles or the returning shore party by shear weight of numbers they were in for a very nasty surprise.

"We're taking fire," observed Jacobs, upon entering the palace proper, "You might want to consider returning some."

"You got it, Matt." Hitch turned to face forward and began to fire at clusters of aliens as they flashed by the speeding sled.

* * * * *

"Ahoy the launch, this is the Captain. Belay your fire forward, we are directly in front of you." It had taken Jack only a few seconds to realize where the green tracer rounds streaking overhead had came from.

"Roger, sorry Sir," came Hitch's reply. The Captain's party watched as the hover sled fishtailed wide around the corner and headed down the side vault toward the diplomat rescue party. From the rear of the sled, Hitch could be seen waving happily.

"Those two are seal-shit crazy," commented Bear, watching the sled disappear into the gloom. Coming from Bear, that was more a complement than a criticism.

"I'm afraid those two welcome any opportunity to put on battle armor," Jack agreed.

"I am thankful that they do," added Ludmilla. "They rescued Chief Zackly and me from the clutches of the UN in Vienna." Ludmilla paused for a minute, conversing on another frequency. "Captain, I think that I need to accompany the wounded back to the ship. It sounds like Midshipman Tanner is seriously wounded and de Belcour is in critical condition."

"Certainly, Doctor. That makes good sense," the Captain replied. "Launch, Captain. Jacobs, stop at the foot of the stairs on your way out and pick up Dr. Tropsha. She will see to the wounded while returning to the ship in shuttle two."

"Aye aye, Captain."

"Captain, we should move out and suppress some of this alien arrow and spear fire," Bear suggested. They were receiving sporadic but increasing amounts of incoming.

"Do it," the Captain said, and the squad quickly spread out across the junction between the side vaults and the main hall.

"Gunny, we are going to move out into the main vault and lay down covering fire. To make sure Dr. Tropsha has room to work, we will take Inuksuk and Aurora back in shuttle one."

"Roger that, Sir. We are coming up on your position now."

The first to arrive was Aurora, who half slid around the corner on the slick stone flooring. She took up a position on the right side of the departing hallway, across from Isbjørn on the left. Together they began working their way toward the exit while hosing down the space ahead with crisscrossing fire.

The sled arrived next, rapidly slowing to a halt to allow Ludmilla to board. Hitch, who was wearing heavy armor, jumped out to make room and assist the Doctor in boarding. As the sled resumed its journey, Ludmilla was already deep in conversation with HC2 White regarding the condition of the wounded. Over the radio Jacobs was heard yelling "coming out," causing the two female bears to temporarily lift their murderous barrage.

"OK, let's get out of here," Jack called. The Marines moved out in good order, leapfrogging positions to maintain cover fire. Inuksuk arrived with the SEALs bringing up the rear of the formation.

"Good hunting?" Bear asked, a traditional greeting between male polar bears.

"An embarrassing surfeit of prey," Inuksuk replied. The two bears took up positions on either side of the Captain, cannon at the ready.

"If you don't mind Captain, we'd like to leave our hosts a little departure gift," said Chief Morgan.

"Quickly, Chief," was the terse reply. "Back to the shuttle, my ursine friends," he said to his two oversized bodyguards. Striking out for the ship, Jack pointed the way with the Ktchzz general's sword in his left hand.

* * * * *

The Captain and his escorts arrived at the shuttle's ramp just after shuttle two took off, rapidly climbing into the sky and quickly vanishing. He stopped at the base of the ramp, waiting for the SEALs to catchup. As they waited, the remaining ABPs returned to their bays on the shuttle's underside and the two bears began an impromptu gunnery contest—alternately picking off observation towers overlooking their position.

Jones and Kowalski ran by and up the ramp. Chief Morgan slowed to a stop in front of the Captain and asked, "permission to deliver departure gift, Sir?"

"Permission granted, Chief," Jack replied with a tight smile. He wasn't sure, but he had a pretty good idea what form of present the SEALs had left for their hosts. Morgan smiled back and manipulated something on his belt. Behind him a series of bright flashes could be seen lighting up the dark interior of the palace's great vaulted hall. The huge masonry barrel began to crumple in apparent slow motion —partly due to the lighter gravity but mostly because of the structure's great size. The grand palace of Pzzst collapsed into a cloud of dust and rubble.

"Well done, Chief," Jack said approvingly. "Everyone on board." The Chief SEAL and the two polar bears climbed aboard, leaving the Captain alone at the foot of the ramp. He raised the jeweled and engraved scimitar above his head, holding it blade up and parallel to the ground. *Take a good look, you hairy bastards*, he thought savagely, *and think twice before crossing us again.*

Jack ascended the ramp. Seconds later the shuttle made way for orbit and rendezvous with the Peggy Sue. The sonic boom from the shuttle's departure echoed over the ruins of the Queen's palace like rolling thunder—an ominous portent to all in the surrounding city.

271

Chapter 18

Main Lounge, Peggy Sue, Pzzst Orbit

The Peggy Sue remained on heightened alert. The Captain called a meeting of his officers and staff four hours after the shore party returned to the ship. As usual, the large crowd met in the main lounge. Underscoring the alert status, an armed Marine guard stood outside each entrance to deter casual traffic. Present at the main table were Lcdr. Curtis, Lieutenants Taylor, Bear, and Medina. Among the junior officers only Midshipman Tanner was missing. Representing the crew and Marines were Chief Zackly and Gunny Rodriguez.

From the science section most were in attendance. Only the medical section lacked representation, the entire staff still tending the wounded. Ludmilla in particular, had been operating on Jean-Jacques de Belcour for hours in a frantic race to save the Frenchman's life.

"You all know why we are here," the Captain said, the room falling silent as he began to speak. "On a peaceful, diplomatic mission to the planet Pzzst our people were attacked without warning and their persons accosted in a most reprehensible and abominable manner. The heinous nature of this attack is almost beyond comprehension." Jack let his words sink in for a few seconds before continuing.

"We have lost one member of the science section, Dr. Sally Li, and the life of Jean-Jacques de Belcour hangs in the balance. Midshipman Tanner was also gravely wounded but is expected to recover, as is Kim Lawson, whose wounds were not life threatening. Given the perfidious nature of the attack and the viciousness with which it was carried out, some form of response is warranted." Jack looked around the table at those assembled. "I seek your council as to the nature of that response."

"Captain, have you considered that the actions by the natives may have been in line with their cultural norms?" asked Olaf Gunderson.

This brought harsh whispers from the crowed. Keeping his features carefully neutral, Jack said, "go on, Dr. Gunderson."

"These creatures obviously have a reproductive cycle similar to some insect species on Earth, where a host is needed for the development of eggs into larvae," Olaf explained. "Those that kill their hosts are called parasitoids, and some species have been used as natural pest controls in agriculture."

"What are you trying to say?" asked Dieter Schmitt. "That they were just behaving naturally?"

"Consider how such a species would develop as it evolved higher intelligence. Certainly they would use prisoners and vanquished enemies for hosts. The exchange of hosts might even become a part of normal diplomatic relations."

"Are you saying that Sally, the Frenchman and the others were mistaken for diplomatic gifts?" JT asked, in a low voice.

"I'm just saying that what happened might have been a misunderstanding, that's all. And that we should not rush to judge the Ktchzz so quickly."

"You actually believe that such actions can be dismissed so lightly?" asked an indignant Elena Piscopia. "That it is our fault because we didn't understand these horrid creatures' vicious ways?"

"That doesn't explain why the bugs in the throne room attacked us as well," Bear growled. "I think they intended to treat us like prey from the start."

"The diplomats fought back!" argued Olaf. "That might have constituted a grave breach in protocol."

"They were supposed to just let the hairy crickets ram those spiked egg injectors into them?" asked the Gunny with a dangerous edge to her voice. "You didn't meet those things up close and personal, Doctor." Her tone made 'doctor' sound like an insult. Others echoed the Marine's sentiments and the meeting verged on spinning out of control.

"Steady on," the Captain said. The tumult in the room quickly died out. Jack looked around the room, making eye contact and allowing everyone to draw a deep breath before continuing. "So you would council restraint, Dr. Gunderson?"

"I'm only trying to see this from the alien's perspective, Captain," Olaf replied. "I liked Sally as much as anyone and her death is a horrible, tragic loss. But I think she would make much the same arguments as I am, were she here."

"Sally died in agony with a barbed alien sex organ jammed into her stomach and a gut full of eggs that were supposed to hatch out and eat her alive," The Gunny spat. "I doubt she would say anything remotely like the crap you are feeding us."

Taken aback by the Gunny's vehement remarks, a subdued Olaf said, "I'm sorry. My assistant Kim was attacked as well and would have suffered the same fate if not for Chief Morgan."

"Noted," Jack said. "Any other comments?"

"What are our options, Captain?" asked Yuki Saito.

"We can send them a strongly worded communique before leaving for our next destination." That brought angry scoffs from several of the younger officers. "We can destroy what's left of the palace complex, destroy the city or even burn every inhabited site on the planet down to bedrock."

"Exterminate them?" asked Rajiv Gupta. "Commit genocide? Wouldn't that make us as bad as the Dark Lords we are fighting?" This last comment brought a renewed buzz.

"What is the mood among the crew, Chief?" the Captain asked of Chief Zackly.

"What happened down there wasn't right, Captain, and the crew knows it. They want justice for that poor woman who died and the others who got wounded."

"And how about the Marines, Gunny?"

"We saw what those bugs did first hand, Sir. Maybe we shouldn't exterminate them all, but what they did calls for more than a slap on the wrist."

"So most of you think that sterilizing the planet is a bit of an overreaction?" Nods and murmurs of agreement. "But that some forceful response is called for?" Muted acclamation.

"This isn't just blind vengeance, is it Captain?" Sandy McKennitt asked. The young lieutenant looked truly upset. "I mean, what the aliens did was wrong, wasn't it?"

"Again I ask, how can we judge them?" Olaf said, drawing angry looks from several others.

The Captain steepled his fingers in front of his chin, an indication of deep thought. After a moment, he cleared his throat. The room went deathly silent.

"Not judging the actions of the Ktchzz because they are aliens smacks of cultural relativism on an inter-species level," he pronounced. "There existed human cultures where unwanted babies were exposed on a hillside for the gods to decide their fate. In others, captured prisoners were ceremonially sacrificed, beating hearts ripped from still breathing chests. Even today, there are those who think it is acceptable to mutilate the genitals of young girls to make them 'less excitable'." He paused to look at the assembled faces.

"We find these actions, these ideas unacceptable, though they were arguably acceptable to the societies that practiced them. The point is, there are such things as moral and immoral behavior, right and wrong, good and evil. To help the helpless is good, to intentionally harm the innocent is evil. These creatures did not even bother to check if the diplomats were intended as sacrifices—in my book, that makes their actions wrong irrespective of their biological or evolutionary background."

All eyes were riveted on the Captain. All eyes that is, except JT's. His attention was distracted by a silent alarm from his tablet. As he looked at its display his brows knitted, then anger flashed across his face. He looked up and the Captain asked him, "something you wish to share, Mr. Taylor?"

"Yes, Sir. Our instruments have just picked up a radio signal from the planet below."

"I thought they didn't have radios," said Chief Engineer Medina.

"Evidently they have at least one," JT replied. "And this one uses the same frequencies and modulation scheme as the alien probes we encountered on the Moon and at Beta Comae."

Startled gasps were heard around the room. Lcdr. Curtis looked at the Captain who returned a subtle node. She spoke for the first time, stating the inescapable conclusion. "That means that the bugs are in league with the Dark Ones."

Most of those present started talking at once. After giving the announcement's shock half minute to play itself out, the Captain again called for attention. "If further proof of treachery was needed I believe the transmission provides it. The Ktchzz are in league with the Dark Ones."

"You're sure, JT?" asked Rajiv.

"Absolutely. You can verify the signature with the ship's computer."

"Peggy Sue?"

"Yes, Dr. Gupta. The signal matches those of the alien probe ships with the probability of an identification error less than 0.05%."

"Regardless of whether the attack and rape by the Ktchzz warrants a retaliatory strike this settles the matter—we cannot continue our journey and leave a known enemy in our rear," the Captain said. "Peggy Sue, I want you to plot a strike with antimatter warheads that will annihilate everything in the Pzzst capital city."

"Four air bursts of 20 megatons each, in a staggered pattern will sterilize the valley over an area of 60 kilometers by 20," the was the computer's emotionless reply.

"Bridge, Captain," he called over his comm pip. "Take us out of orbit and set course for the alter-space transfer point to Epsilon Eridani. Peggy Sue, fire as the launchers come to bear..."

Destroyer of Worlds, Earth's Solar System

The kilometers long planet killer rippled into 3-space, 300,000 km above the plane of the ecliptic and on the far side of the Sun from its target. Earth was in Northern Hemisphere winter, its north pole tilted away from its star by 23 degrees. As soon as the ship emerged, it was obvious that the third planet was inhabited by a technological civilization—a civilization that yammered incessantly across much of the electromagnetic spectrum.

Great! Thought the ship's captain, *the search is over and the eradication can begin.* The first swarm of impactors released by the

Destroyer of Worlds would strike mostly in the northern temperate zone, each missile roughly the mass of a 200 meter in diameter iron sphere.

It was not the impactors' considerable mass that dictated their destructiveness, but rather their velocity with respect to the target. The destroyer emerged from the transfer point with a velocity of 800 km/sec relative to Earth, far higher than the impact velocity of orbital debris from within the solar system. This meant that each artificial asteroid would be carrying 1.07×10^{22} Joules of kinetic energy when they hit the top of the planet's atmosphere—at surface impact, the blast of each equivalent to roughly 2,500,000 megatons of TNT.

Such an impactor striking sedimentary rock creates an initial crater over 30 km wide and 11 km deep. Vast quantities of rock are melted and 90 cubic kilometers of melted and vaporized material ejected. Viewed from a distance of 100 kilometers, the 42 km in diameter fireball appears almost 100 times as large as the Sun. A twentieth of a second after impact, an exposed observer's clothing ignites and they suffer third degree burns over much of their body. Trees, grass and plywood burst into flames.

Twenty seconds after impact a magnitude 8.9 seismic shockwave arrives. By this time general panic has ensued as even well-designed structures suffer great damage. Masonry and wood frame buildings are destroyed along with their foundations. Serious damage is done to reservoirs and underground pipes. In areas with deep soil, sand and mud are ejected in fountains, in solid ground sinkholes and large cracks appear. But the worst is yet to come.

Two and a half minutes after impact, material ejected from the crater begins falling to Earth. Mostly fine dust but containing some larger objects, it will eventually cover the ground in a suffocating blanket 7.5 meters thick. Finally, five minutes after impact, the blast wave arrives with 910 m/s winds, finishing the destruction of any buildings and bridges. Steel-framed office buildings undergo extreme distortion and bridges collapse. The works of man are not the only things ravaged: up to 90 percent of trees are blown down, with the remainder stripped of their branches and leaves.

The final crater is 50 km in diameter and a kilometer deep, with a 100 meter thick layer of molten rock at its bottom. This is the damage caused by a land impact—for a water impact add the ravages of a kilometers high tsunami. Trillions of kilograms of water are thrown into the sky. Once in the atmosphere, the water vapor combines with compounds containing chlorine and bromine from vaporized sea salts, destroying the protective ozone layer. Everywhere, harmful UV radiation blankets the planet's surface.

All this from a single impact. The captain of the Destroyer of Worlds ordered the release an opening salvo—a score of such objects, with an ETA at Earth in six and a half days.

Main Lounge, Peggy Sue

The meeting broke up with small groups of people conversing in whispered voices. Olaf Gunderson stood to one side of the room, a large sad figure. Lcdr. Curtis walked over to him and said. "You seem unsettled, Olaf."

"Events have rushed ahead so quickly, I can't help but feel we have decided to destroy the natives in haste. I am not used to making decisions so rapidly."

"You might think the decision a bad one, but I wouldn't express such thoughts around the crew or the Marines," Gretchen advised the scientist. "As you said, events are rushing toward us and we don't have the luxury to ponder each decision at length."

"I did not know that the Captain could do that. Order the ship to bombard a planet without help from the crew."

"The Peggy Sue is capable of sailing without a crew, though having humans in the loop for various functions makes her more efficient. But I suspect that isn't your point."

"No, Gretchen, it isn't," the big biologist said, chewing on the tips of his mustache. "I didn't realize that the Captain had such absolute power—that alone he could destroy an entire world on a whim, if he so chose."

"You are correct in that the ship will do whatever the Captain orders—that's the way the computer is programmed. But you are wrong if you think that Captain Sutton ordered the attack on his own as a demonstration of personal power."

"No?"

"No, Doctor. He may have asked our opinions but he is in command—in the end the decision, and the responsibility, is his alone. The Captain ordered the computer to strike so that none of the crew or other officers have that blood on their hands."

"It seems a terrible burden for one man to bear. I'm glad the decision wasn't mine to make."

"Duty is the great business of a sea officer; all private considerations must give way to it, however painful it may be," Gretchen quoted.

"And who said that?" Olaf replied.

"Admiral Horatio Lord Nelson, who was also tested by the burden of command."

Beta Hydri – 61 Vir Alter-space Transfer Point

The first of the ships in King Lewnhallooshna's fleet emerged in Beta Hydri 3-space, approximately 2.5 AU from the star itself. It was followed closely by another dozen bursts of radiation, signaling the emergence of the rest of the fleet. Immediately sensors scanned the electromagnetic spectrum, locating local astronomical objects while hunting for their intended prey.

"Great King, the rocky world nearest the star shows signs of recent antimatter detonations," reported one of the ship's officers. "It appears that the alien ship has bombarded the inner planet,"

"Is the prey still orbiting the planet?" asked Lewnhallooshna.

"No, Sire. The prey has departed on a course probably toward another alter-space transfer point."

"What is the location of that point and how long ago did the ship depart?"

"The most probable point lies 3.5 AU from the star at an angle of roughly 90 degrees from our present vector. Assuming they maintained the course they were on 20 minutes ago they will arrive at the transfer point in 103 minutes." At these distances, the light the fleet was viewing reflected off the Peggy Sue 20 minutes ago.

This meant that their intended target was 20 minutes farther along its trajectory than the observed position.

"Commodore Ooshlewnnalloo! Calculate a firing solution for the plasma torpedoes. Transmit it to all ships and immediately fire a volley!"

"I hear and obey, my King," replied the King's favorite offspring, bending to his task. In less than a minute the intercept point was calculated and the broadside was on its way, hurtling toward the unsuspecting Earth vessel.

Bridge, *Peggy Sue*

Having delivered a death blow to Queen Tzzztchk's Empire, the Peggy Sue was making a straight run for the transfer point to Epsilon Eridani. Given that Beta Hydri massed 1.1 times Sol and Epsilon Eridani only 0.8, the transfer point in this system was out more than 3 AU. The ship should reach the transfer point in under an hour and the Captain was on the bridge, starting preparation for the transit.

"Are all systems set for entering alter-space?" Jack asked. This might all become routine some day, but leaving the normal Universe behind for the strange dimensions of alter-space still gave Jack butterflies in the stomach.

"All systems are online and reading nominal for alter-space entry, Captain," reported Chief Engineer Medina. Jo Jo's main task was to get things ready, since the actual shift from 3-space to alter-space was handled by the ship's computer. *Speaking of which,* "Peggy Sue, are you ready for entry?"

"Yes, Chief Engineer. I am ready to initiate alter-space transit as soon as we reach the transfer point."

"Very good, people," Jack added. *I guess there is nothing left to do except wait.*

"Sir," called JT from the navigator's station. "I just picked up a gamma ray burst from the transfer point to 61 Vir. Something just jumped into the system."

"Can you identify the signature? Does it match any of the craft we have already encountered?"

"No Sir. In fact there are multiple entry signatures... I count ten or more ships. They must have all jumped at the same time to arrive that close together."

"Could it be a response to the message sent by the Tzzztchk?"

"That doesn't make any sense, Sir," JT replied. "Even if they have some kind of FTL communication relay, the alter-space transit from 61 Vir should have taken more than a week."

"Mr. Taylor is correct, Captain," the ship's computer added. "They must have followed us from 61 Virginis and been in transit for the past 10 days. This form of hyperluminal travel has rules that are quite immutable."

"None the less, we have multiple arrivals into the system," the Captain said. Looking at his display, Jack noted that they were almost 3.5 AU from the new arrivals.

"Sir, now I'm picking up more radiation, both X-ray and gamma, but it doesn't look like an alter-space arrival."

What the? "Sound General Quarters! Shields to full, Mr. Medina. Helm, take evasive maneuvers," Jack yelled. "We have incoming fire from the other transfer point!"

As the crew reacted to Jack's shouted orders the space outside the ship suddenly flashed brighter than the Sun. In an instant, the ship's transparent nose became opaque, the view of actual space replaced by computer generated imagery. At the Helm, Bobby put the ship into a tight corkscrew, barely avoiding another blast according to the computer display.

"What the hell was that?" shouted JT.

"It would appear to be a salvo of concentrated plasma bursts. There is an antimatter component as well," reported the computer.

Another close blast and a shudder ran through the ship. *That can't be good*, Jack thought, *we shouldn't feel anything through the deck gravity compensators*. With a touch of panic in his voice, Jo Jo shouted, "Captain, the shields are down to 20%, another close hit and we will take physical damage!"

Another, stronger shudder. If the deck gravity failed the alien fire would not need to blow Peggy Sue out of space—the ship's violent evasive maneuvers would smear the crew all across the interior.

"Peggy Sue, get us out of here!" the Captain yelled as indicators on the engineering displays lit up with damage alarms.

"Searching for an available transfer point," came the computer's unruffled voice. "Altering course vector and initiating... now."

A final sharp bump and then quiet—the ship had escaped into alter-space. After a few brief seconds of calm, damage alarms began sounding and status displays everywhere glared red. They had escaped the alien bombardment, but the Peggy Sue was badly damaged and fighting for her life.

Part Three

A Thousand Fearful Wrecks

Chapter 19

CIC, Peggy Sue, Alter-space

The Captain and First Officer Curtis were coordinating repairs from the CIC abaft the bridge. Billy Ray had the Conn while the rest of the ship's officers were off assisting the damage parties that rushed to repair the results of the sudden and unexpected alien attack.

"Captain, sickbay." It was Ludmilla's voice, calm and professional. "We are receiving casualties, six so far. Mostly broken limbs and concussions, none life threatening."

"Roger, sickbay," Jack replied. "keep me apprised of the situation. Captain out."

"What the hell did they hit us with?" asked Gretchen. Though she did not show it, Jack could tell his First Officer was shaken by the surprise attack and its aftermath. To this point, the Peggy Sue had always seemed impervious to harm from enemy action. Whoever these new foes were, they had weapons powerful enough to destroy the Earth ship. Chief Engineer Medina and Dr. Gupta were feverishly working on the ship's gravitonic systems—the shields and deck gravity in particular had come close to total failure. If they failed in alter-space there was no telling what would happen.

"It appears to have been a form of plasma bolt, or, rather, a swarm of them," reported the computer. "Meta-stable plasma structures fired toward us at 98% the speed of light."

"Plasma structure?" replied the puzzled officer. "Did you understand that Yuki?" Dr. Saito had come forward to man the engineering station while others, more conversant with the ship's gravitonic circuits worked on the actual repairs.

"Only at a rudimentary level, Commander. Theoretical and experimental results have proved the existence of certain nontrivial configurations of electric charges in layered plasma structures that can create self-generated magnetic fields. It is argued that the topological properties of these fields may permit the creation of some meta-stable plasma configurations that can persist with minimum dissipation when coupled to a knotted magnetic field."

"Can you translate that for non-physicists, Doctor?" Jack asked.

"Sorry," Yuki said with a slight bow the Captain. "It means that, in theory, self-contained packets of plasma can be created if the plasma itself is flowing in certain, complex patterns. Plasma consists of charged particles and moving charged particles create magnetic fields. The fields then act on the charged particles, reinforcing the movement pattern. Evidently our attackers have discovered how to form compact plasma knots and shoot them at their foes."

"Plasma bolts, traveling at almost the speed of light," Jack summarized.

"I would hypothesize that the bursts contained intertwined but separate plasmas made from matter and antimatter. They are not totally stable and decay over time, but traveling at close to the speed of light would allow the fields to persist longer in externally observed time-frames. When they do decay, or strike something solid, the plasmas mix and detonate."

"Thanks Yuki." Having deciphered the general nature of the weapons they were hit by, Gretchen asked the next question on her mental list. "Captain, you shouted orders a few seconds before the first plasma bolt struck. How did you know we were under attack?"

"I was running some calculations in my head, regarding where the alien ships would be given the time delay caused by the speed of light," Jack replied. Seeing continued puzzlement on Gretchen's face he continued. "We were almost 3.5 AU away from the other transfer point. It takes light 8 minutes to travel one AU, so our view of the aliens was from about 28 minutes in the past."

"OK, transmission delay, I get that," Gretchen replied. "But how did that indicate an attack."

"First we saw the radiation from their emergence into 3-space. Then, about four minutes later we started to receive more high frequency radiation. Since X-rays travel at the speed of light they arrived a bit before the plasma bolts. I didn't know what they had fired at us but the time delay matched too closely to be a coincidence."

"You figured that they must have entered the system and, inside of five minutes, fired a salvo at us?"

"Yes, precisely. And a very impressive feat of gunnery it was—they emerged, calculated our vector from time delayed light arriving at their entry position, plotted an intercept point and fired a broadside across 3.5 AU. We were under attack before we could even detect that the enemy arrived in the system."

"Talk about leading your target!" Gretchen said, finally understanding the nature of the attack. "The plasma bolts were in flight almost a half hour before they struck. Lucky we escaped into alter-space."

"Yes, lucky," Jack said. "Unfortunately, we are not on course for Epsilon Eridani. We were still several million kilometers from the transfer point when we were forced to flee 3-space."

"That is correct, Captain," the computer added. "I have been considering the parameters of our entry and I think that we are headed for a different star system: Alpha Canis Majoris, also know as Sirius."

King Lewnhallooshna's Flagship

"Is the target destroyed?" the anxious monarch demanded. His long spines rattled with impatience as others on the flagship's bridge made themselves as small as possible, hoping to evade the King's notice. "WELL?"

Being the King's favorite and designated fleet commodore no longer seemed quite as appealing to Ooshlewnnalloo. "Oh great and wise King! The plasma torpedoes should have just arrived at the intercept point. Unfortunately, we will not receive light from the bombardment's impact for another 25 minutes." *Even you cannot make information travel faster than light in 3-space my King,* Ooshlewnnalloo added to himself.

"Head toward the other transfer point! If the vermin craft was not destroyed we must follow it at once!"

"Yes, my King. But we have no indication of what, if any transfer point they may have taken," the King's favorite argued reasonably. "Regardless, we must swing wide and realign our course vector to allow alter-space entry—that will take a day or more, great one."

King Lewnhallooshna emitted an inarticulate shout of frustration. The enraged monarch lurched forward and impaled his unfortunate son with one of his longest spines. To his credit, Ooshlewnnalloo made no sound but simply quivered and died with a rattling of his own spines.

"Maarshennalloo!" the King called out to the nearest of his many remaining progeny. "You are now Commodore! Run the vermin to ground!"

"Yes, my King!" Maarshennalloo replied, flattening his spines in submission. *Damn, I knew being on the flagship was a bad idea...*

Bridge, Peggy Sue, Alpha Canis Majoris

Damage control teams worked feverishly following the Peggy Sue's escape into alter-space. The Captain remained either on the bridge or in the CIC, prioritizing repairs and urging his crew on. Chief Zackly was everywhere supervising, making sure all repair work was squared away. "Stand to, ya deck apes, yous got work ta do," he was heard to say, "there'll be no bent shitcans on my deck."

After ten hours, most of the damage done by the alien plasma salvo had been repaired, though a number of crew remained in sickbay. Just prior to emergence, Ludmilla called Jack with a status report. The surgical team had managed to stabilize de Belcour: The alien ovipositor was removed, along with the eggs it had deposited in Jean-Jacques' abdomen; His torn rectum and punctured intestines were stitched and glued back together. Pumped full of painkillers and antibiotics, the Frenchman remained mercifully unconscious.

Jean-Jacques had been on the operating table for 12 hours and Ludmilla was totally drained. Midshipman Tanner's wound had also been treated and he was resting under observation. Kim's non life-threatening wounds had been patched up by the corpsmen and she was released to quarters. Other crewmembers with various bruises and broken bones were treated and either returned to duty or confined to quarters. With all her charges out of danger, fatigue swept over Ludmilla like a wave. "Captain, all of the casualties have been stabilized or treated and released."

"Excellent, Doctor," Jack replied from the bridge. "Please commend your medical team for me."

"I will, Captain. And then I am going to retire to our quarters and pass out for at least eight hours."

"Rest up, Doctor. I doubt that I will be disturbing you anytime soon. According to the computer we are close to arriving at our new destination."

"So quick? How is that possible?"

"Evidently this star Sirius is massive, reducing the transit time to just over 11 hours. But that also means that we will emerge far from the star. Our science staff reports that the possibility of any indigenous life is vanishingly small."

"I think a boring, unpopulated system would be a nice change, my Captain. Tropsha out."

* * * * *

Less than twenty minutes later the Peggy Sue shuddered and dropped back into 3-space. The Earth ship found itself seven AU from an immense blue-white star, 25 times more luminous than the Sun. Originally composed of two bright bluish stars—Sirius A and Sirius B—the system was between 200 and 300 million years old. Around 120 million years ago, the then more massive Sirius B finished consuming its supply of fusible hydrogen and became a red giant. Shortly thereafter, it shed its outer layers and half its mass before collapsing into a white dwarf. The two stars remain a binary system, with the distance separating Sirius A from its comparatively dim companion varying between 8.1 and 31.5 AU.

"Alpha Canis Majoris," said JT in wonder. "Now that's a star! At least twice as massive as the Sun and known to our ancestors as far back as you want to go."

"You seem positively enthralled, Mr. Taylor," commented Lcdr. Curtis, who had come to the bridge for emergence.

"It is the brightest star in Earth's sky," JT continued. "For ancient Polynesians its rise marked the start of winter and it was an important star for navigation around the South Pacific. Sirius also signaled the flooding of the Nile in Ancient Egypt and the "dog days" of summer for the ancient Greeks—hence the name the Dog Star."

"The Freemasons teach about a 'Blazing Star' that is said to represent Sirius and another name for the Illuminati was the *Order of the Silver Star*," added Bobby, the crew's unofficial expert on fringe science and conspiracy theories. "Not only that, the Dogon people, a primitive tribe from Mali, knew that Sirius was a double star long before they came in contact with modern civilization, something they could not have known without telescopes. According to their legends, a race of people from the Sirius system called the Nommos visited Earth thousands of years ago."

"I don't know about that, Bobby," said Elena from the navigator's telescope controls, "but we are now closer to home than any time since we left, only about 2.6 parsecs. If we cross the system to the transfer point to Sol we can be home in half a day."

"Which is precisely what I intend on doing, Dr. Piscopia," said the Captain. "Given what we know and the damage we have sustained, I think we need to fall back and regroup."

"I doubt you'll get much argument from the crew on that decision, Sir," said Gretchen. Though moral was still high, the crew had been beaten up rather badly as they exited Beta Hydri. None would question a return to base.

"Captain, I'm detecting an anomalous constellation of objects about 4.25 AU from Sirius A," Elena called from the navigation station.

"Can you put it on the forward screen?"

"Yes, I am zooming in now with the large scope."

As the cluster of strange objects swam into view in front of the bridge, several of the crew gasped. The objects, with a few exceptions, did not look like asteroids or comet bodies. They had odd shapes—some angular, some curving, some rounded with spires glinting in the harsh actinic light. In other words, they were made things, not likely to have been created by nature.

"What are those objects?" asked Elena.

"Methought I saw a thousand fearful wrecks; Ten thousand men that fishes gnaw'd upon;" recited the Captain, in a voice tinged with sadness.

"All scatter'd in the bottom of the sea," finished Billy Ray. "Shakespeare's *King Richard III*."

"It is a graveyard of ships," Jack said, seeing the still puzzled look on the Italian astronomer's face. "The ruined remains of hundreds of ships. Perhaps the wreckage of some great battle, fought here long ago."

Bridge, Peggy Sue, Alpha Canis Majoris

Word of the ship graveyard spread throughout the Peggy Sue with the incredible speed that rumors travel among sailors. From stem to stern, the crew was abuzz with speculation about the 'ghost fleet' orbiting the Dog Star. On the bridge, curiosity was also present in force, though the speculation was a bit more restrained.

"Captain, I count 462 objects large enough to be the wreckage of spacecraft, along with several thousand smaller pieces of debris." As the ship's computer reported a spherical robotic drone, similar to the herald used on Pzzst, silently edged forward from the port side of the bridge.

The Captain glanced left at the floating metal ball. "Welcome to the bridge, Ambassador. We seem to have stumbled upon a mystery, possibly of historical significance."

"Thank you Captain; If the wreckage ahead is the remnant of a great battle they are ancient indeed; Are there any signs of life among the ruins?"

"So far, there have been no energy emissions or movement, no signals and no sign of recognition."

"How did all those hulks collect in one small corner of the system?" asked Lcdr. Curtis. "If they were involved in a battle I would have expected them to be scattered all over the place."

"The two stars orbit each other with a period of 50.1 years at an average distance of 19.8 AU, about the distance between Uranus and the Sun," replied JT. "The system has a large orbital eccentricity and currently Sirius A and B are close to their maximum separation at 30 AU. The closeness in mass between A and B, plus the high eccentricity, pretty much rule out any stable Lagrange points, so the debris must be orbiting something of planetary mass."

"There has been speculation regarding a Sirius C, a Jupiter size planet or brown dwarf in a six-year elliptical orbit around Sirius A. But a search using high-contrast infrared imaging in 2008 failed to find such a planet within 25 AU of the binary stars," Elena added. "However, there appears to be an object with the predicted mass at the center of the debris field. The wreckage is evidently in orbit around that object."

"Whatever it is, it isn't very large—I see no planetary disk at the center of the debris field." Both JT and Elena were in total astronomy geek mode over the strange orbital configuration in front of them. Elena offered a cautious hypothesis. "It could be some form of degenerate matter object, small in diameter but incredibly dense."

"Dr. Piscopia's conjecture is plausible; A small body of degenerate matter could have sufficient mass; If the battle occurred near by, part of the wreckage could have collected around such a an object."

"An interesting possibility, Ambassador," JT responded. "But I thought that the formation of degenerate matter required a stellar object with a mass over the Chandrasekhar limit?"

"Under natural conditions you are correct, but there are other ways to induce such a collapse; The battle may have been fought millions of your years ago, with weapons no longer understood; Further investigation may prove enlightening."

"Are you saying there are ways to collapse whole planets?" Gretchen asked. The possibility of a weapon that could turn a world into a small ball of degenerate matter was a horrifying thought.

"I agree with the Ambassador, we need a closer look at the debris field. Mr. Taylor, I want a course computed to the far side of that collection of wreckage—put the bulk of the debris between us and the alter-space transfer point from Beta Hydri." Jack did not wish to be surprised by another plasma volley if their unknown pursuers managed to follow them to Sirius. "Make our path a sequence of random segments, like we are tacking into a capricious cosmic wind. Maintain none long enough for a near light speed strike from the transfer point to intercept us without warning."

"Aye aye, Captain. Course plotted and sent to the helm."

"Mr. Vincent, take us to the far side of those wrecks."

"Aye aye, Sir. Making way for the Dog Star graveyard."

King Lewnhallooshna's Flagship, Beta Hydri

The King's fleet was now under its third commodore and repositioning to follow the fleeing alien. On the orders of the monarch, the previous commodore, Maarshennalloo, had sped directly to the intercept point, thus arriving on a totally unsuitable vector for entering alter-space using the transfer point the fleeing aliens must have taken.

The accelerated trip had taken a day and a half and, when the fleet passed through the tenuous cloud of matter that marked the plasma torpedoes' detonation area, no trace of the alien ship was found. No debris, no telltale vaporized elements, nothing. The failure of their quick attack, carried out brilliantly by Maarshennalloo's predecessor, naturally threw the King into a royal rage.

In what was quickly becoming a pattern, King Lewnhallooshna killed his commodore son when Maarshennalloo tried to explain that they would now have to reposition the fleet to make a proper approach to the alter-space transfer point. This was the same bit of news that cost the previous commodore his life.

The repositioning would take another two days. The new commodore, Bonnahaamshna, fervently hoped that they would successfully engage the warm life miscreants after the alter-space transit. Otherwise, another one of his siblings would undoubtedly get the chance to become commodore.

Bridge, Peggy Sue, Spaceship Graveyard

It took the better part of two days for the Peggy Sue to arrive at the far side of the spaceship graveyard, her path like a mote of dust knocked about in Brownian motion. As the Earth vessel drew near the drifting mass of cosmic detritus, it became even more evident that the derelicts were circling a common point and that each was in a stable orbit intersecting no other. The drifting hulks bore mute but eloquent testimony to the scale of the conflict that took place here long ago—millions of years before the first Homo sapiens trod the dusty plains of Earth.

Collisions had taken place in the past, however, with several large chunks of debris unmistakably the merger of two or more spacecraft. Whether the collisions took place during the hypothetical battle or later, during the aggregation of the wreckage, remained unknown. "Given the number of derelicts here, and the number of ships that must have fallen into the star or been gravitationally ejected from the system, this must have been one hell of a battle," JT remarked, while scanning the wreckage more closely with the ship's optical instruments.

"Indeed, Mr. Taylor," the Captain replied. "Any sign of activity?"

"No, Sir. No electromagnetic emissions other than from the star and interstellar background noise. Infrared shows the wreckage to be fairly cold, in line with the amount of irradiation from Sirius itself."

"Captain, there are certain signal patterns employed by search and rescue vessels; It is possible that some ships contain survivors in suspended animation; A single pulse might elicit a response from any surviving mechanisms."

"It might also draw fire from any ship just playing dead, Ambassador," Jack said. "I will keep the suggestion in mind however."

"Prudence may be the best course; We recognize ship types from both warm and cold species; To our knowledge, the last such clash between the forces of Light and Darkness took place nearly four million of your years ago."

"Are you suggesting that some of these ships may still be active, may even contain survivors, after four million years?" Lcdr. Curtis asked. "That would be more than incredible."

"Some species were excellent builders; There are ships from at least nine species among the wreckage; Members of our own species can live that long without artificial extension."

* * * * *

Deep in the bowels of one of the wrecked ships an intelligence stirred. An artificial intelligence, whose mind inhabited a fabric of quantum entangled particles and holographic memories. A low power proximity sensor had detected an energy source, possibly a working ship.

Several picoseconds were spent waiting, while the AI expended some of the ship's precious remaining energy to power up a more capable sensor array. Then a flood of readings swept away all doubt —it was a ship, primitive but functional, and the drive signature was familiar. The sensor array was powered back down to save energy and a weak beacon activated.

It knew that it was taking a chance, but the AI had waited so long for rescue. The ship's reserve power was almost exhausted and when it was the AI would die. This might be the last, the only chance for survival. The intelligence returned to its lowest power state and waited for fate's verdict.

* * * * *

Peggy Sue's computer interrupted the ongoing discussion about the sea of wreckage. "Captain, I am receiving a signal from one of the wrecks."

"Can you identify the source and nature of the signal?" the Captain demanded. After a moment's thought he added, "Sound general quarters. Shields to full, Mr. Medina."

"Not again!" Whispered Bobby to his fellow helmsman. "The last signal we got lured us into an ambush by a bunch of belligerent crickets."

"Yep, but the time before that we found the Triads," Billy Ray replied. "We are one and one on contacts. I reckon this will be the tie breaker, pardner."

As the klaxon called the crew to battle stations, the computer identified the source of the beacon using a holographic overlay on the forward viewport. The object in question was fairly deep within the mass of drifting wreckage. Elena quickly zeroed in on the vessel with one of the onboard telescopes.

"That is the source of the signal, according to the computer," the Italian astronomer announced as the image came up on the forward viewing screen. "It doesn't look as bad as some of the other derelicts."

"Still, I don't want the Peggy Sue trapped inside that maze of drifting junk if hostiles show up," Jack said. "Commander Curtis, let's send a boarding party to investigate. Lt. Bear and half the Marines in shuttle two. Include Mr. Taylor and the SEALs—they have demonstrated skills for sneaking in and out of tight situations."

"Anyone else from the science section, Sir?" Gretchen asked.

"Not until we know what we are dealing with."

"Very good, Captain. Mr. Danner, I think that you would be a good choice to pilot the shuttle. Take Jacobs and Hitch as crew." *Those two have been in almost as many tight spots as the Marines. Besides, this will keep them out of Chief Zackly's hair for a while.*

"Aye aye, Ma'am," Bobby replied, rising from the pilot's console.

"Report when ready for departure, Mr. Danner," Gretchen said as Bobby made his way aft. "We will monitor your progress from the CIC."

The Derelict, Spaceship Graveyard

With an ease born of skill and long practice, Bobby guided the shuttle through the graveyard of wrecks and then circumnavigated the derelict identified as the source of the signal beacon. Peggy Sue's computer reported that the beacon was only active long enough to identify the originating ship. It had remained silent since the shuttle was deployed.

The alien ship was huge. If the Peggy Sue was the size of a modern naval destroyer, the alien ship was more on the scale of a an aircraft carrier: its mass was easily greater than 80,000 tons. Roughly 300 meters long with a maximum diameter of 60 meters, its hull was not a simple tapered cylinder like the Peggy Sue's. Several large, bulging sections—like the conformal fuel tanks added to some contemporary jet fighters—deformed the main hull's clean line, giving the vessel an asymmetric look. Scattered about the hull's smooth surface were numerous teardrop shaped blisters, looking like the X-Ray laser turrets on the Peggy Sue, only on a much larger and more prolific scale.

The skin of the vessel was silver, with hints of hatches and openings faintly etched into its sides. One of the bulging ancillary sections held a jagged scar, as though something had violently penetrated the hull and then withdrew. Within the dark recesses of the hole, pipes and conduits could be seen, some intact, others rent asunder and dangling in empty space.

Closer examination revealed scorch marks on the otherwise smooth hull. Places where some offensive energy lashed the ship's skin, causing the hull material to melt and splash away from the point of contact. As large and impressive as the ship was, it had obviously been sorely abused.

"What do you primates think?" Bear asked. "Do we want to try and enter through the gash in her side or search the hull for the outline of an intact opening?"

"It's hard to tell what we would encounter entering through that hull breach—the interior looks pretty torn up," JT posited.

"If they did manage to seal the breach they probably didn't add any new airlocks during the effort," observed Chief Morgan. SEALs possessed a lot of practical knowledge about ships and ship design, since they were often called on to forcibly enter enemy vessels. Morgan figured that Navy ships and spaceships were fairly similar at a fundamental level—ocean vessels needed to keep water out and spaceships needed to keep air in. "If we did find some intact compartments we would still have to cut or blast our way in, which would decompress the interior spaces."

"Roger that, Chief," Bear replied. "Peggy Sue, shuttle. Do Chief Engineer Medina or any of the science staff have comments or suggestions?"

"Shuttle, Peggy Sue. We concur with staying out of the hull breach area and suggest looking for an opening in some of the less damaged areas."

"Affirmative. We will do a closer reconnaissance of the undamaged portion of the hull."

* * * * *

Rounding the smoothly curving hull at the front of one of the large flared bulges, the shuttle arrived near the junction of the bulge and the main hull, abaft the bow section of the ship. There in front of the shuttle was a large hatch, its outline faintly etched into the burnished silver of the hull. If it were open the entire shuttle could pass through to the ship's interior.

"Let's send some people outside to examine the surface close up," suggested Chief Morgan.

"Sounds like a plan to me, Chief," Lt. Bear rumbled. "Got anyone in mind?" Bear's last remark was accompanied by a toothy grin. All parties in the shuttle's cargo area were suited up: the Marines in full battle armor, Bear and JT in powered armor but with clear helmets and the SEALs in light armor. The shuttle crew were in standard spacesuits with utility coveralls, though there were suits of battle armor hanging in the rear for them if necessary.

"I think we SEALs ought to take a closer look at that hatch. We aren't as dexterous as the crew but at least we have some protection."

"OK, Chief. You, Kowalski and Jones take a walk and see if you can find a door knob." It was obvious that Bear did not like having to stay behind while others took the lead, but the logic was clear. "Mr. Danner, if you could please let the air out a bit we will send the SEALs to find a way in."

"Roger, Lieutenant. Depressurizing the cargo compartment now."

A few minutes later and the SEALs could be seen through the shuttle's windscreen approaching the silver surface in front of the craft. "Hey, I don't see any handholds or cleats. How do I stick to this thing when I hit it?" asked Kowalski.

* * * * *

Inside the alien ship the AI again came to full consciousness, alerted by sensors on one of the forward airlocks. *Interesting, these*

298

aliens are bipedal, much like the builders. They are also obviously warm life, given the readings from their suits and small boat.

It had been a very long time since living creatures walked the halls of the ship. Indeed, an opportunity like this may never come again—and the small remaining store of antimatter can always be detonated if they prove to be agents of the Dark Lords. Signals were sent to the airlock door.

* * * * *

Kowalski drifted slowly toward the hatch, followed closely by his brother SEALs. Those on board the shuttle expected to see the trio bounce off the smooth metallic side of the bigger alien vessel, but the strangest thing happened.

The lead SEAL brought his hands up to cushion the expected impact on the solid surface ahead only the see his hands, then his arms sink smoothly into the hull. "What the hell is this shit?" Phil said, as his entire form passed through the side of the alien ship and disappeared.

"Phil!" cried Chief Morgan. "Are you OK?" Then Chief Morgan and PO Jones also drifted through the hatch's metallic surface and vanished without a trace.

CIC, *Peggy Sue*

Aboard the Peggy Sue, all eyes were on the monitors tracking the remote mission's progress. "Shuttle, what just happened?" queried the Captain. *It looked like the SEALs just passed through a solid surface.*

"Captain, we don't have a clue," came the reply. "The SEALs disappeared through the side of the ship."

"Peggy Sue, can you shed some light on this?"

"I observed the same thing as everyone else, Captain. I can describe what happened, but not how it happened," the onboard computer replied. "There is one thing in my memory that might be pertinent—the geologist who discovered the artifact reported 'falling through' a solid wall of metal to escape his attackers."

"He at least survived such an incident," Lcdr. Curtis noted. Though she was concerned for the SEALs' safety, secretly she was glad that JT had not led the team through the unopened hatch.

"Can we raise them by radio?" the anxious Captain asked over the comm link to the shuttle.

"Negative, Sir. Both comm and suit telemetry went dead when they passed through the hull."

Everyone on board both the shuttle and the Peggy Sue watched the side of the alien vessel with a mixture of anxiety and puzzlement. Then, a small irregular object floated back through the hatch surface. Drifting toward the shuttle's windscreen, it became clear that the object was a standard issue tool bag. Before anyone could comment, the tool bag was followed by its owner, PO Bud Jones.

"Have you something to report, Petty Officer Jones?" asked a relieved Captain Jack.

"Aye, Sir. There's a bay behind the hatch big enough to park several shuttles in, and there seems to be an atmosphere inside. For some reason, solid objects can pass through the hatch but comms don't work inside."

* * * * *

The wreck's AI was monitoring the activity at the open bay with great interest. Though the meaning of the electromagnetic emissions given off by the craft and the individuals that entered the bay were indecipherable, it was clear that they were using radio waves to communicate.

How quaint, the AI thought, as one of the individuals inside the bay passed back through the hatch into space. Realizing that the aliens might not risk further entry without the ability to communicate, the AI established a relay between the ship's interior and exterior for the frequencies involved.

"Bud! I can read you now," transmitted an excited Chief Morgan. "Can you read me?"

"Yeah, Chief. You are coming in loud and clear."

"Chief, this is the shuttle. We are reading you now as well."

"So we have established that we can enter and exit the ship through the magic hatch, and now we are able to communicate from inside," the Chief reported. "What's our next objective, Lieutenant?"

"I think we need to ask the Captain for further orders..."

* * * * *

"What do you think, people?" Jack asked, turning to the knot of scientists gathered around the display tank. Elena, Olaf, Yuki and Rajiv looked at each other, each hesitant to make the first suggestion. Instead, it was Chief Engineer Medina who spoke. "I would sure like to find out how that pass-through hull trick works, Captain. Assuming it really does hold an atmosphere while allowing solid objects to pass in and out, it would sure save us a lot of time and wasted air."

"I think that might be one of the simpler things we can learn from this derelict, Captain," added Rajiv.

"Hai," agreed Yuki. "This ship may be as far advanced over the Peggy Sue as she is over a wooden man-of-war. No offense, Peggy Sue."

"None taken, Dr. Saito. The advanced nature of the alien vessel is quite apparent."

"It would be nice to discover just what the creatures who built the vessel were like," said Olaf. "To this point we have found no advanced spacefaring species that have not been hostile."

"An excellent point, Dr. Gunderson," the Captain replied. Since the disagreement over bombarding the Ktchzz, Jack was trying to ease any feelings of alienation the big biologist might have.

"If they were a great spacefaring race it stands to reason that they would have known of other worlds with friendly species, si?" asked Elena. "If we can find their charts the task of finding other habitable worlds, and other possible allies, could be greatly simplified."

"Another good thought, Dr. Piscopia. So we are agreed that the potential benefits outweigh the risks?"

"Captain, the SEALs reported that the bay behind the magic hatchway was large enough to hold several shuttles," said Lcdr. Curtis, thinking of the tactical aspects of the situation. "If the hatch becomes impermeable for some reason, it would probably be safer for the expedition members to have the shuttle inside with them."

"I think you are right, Commander," the Captain concurred. *Not to mention the antimatter demolition charge.* "Shuttle, Peggy Sue. I want you to board and explore the interior of the alien vessel. Start by cautiously docking the shuttle inside the open port."

"Aye aye, Captain," Bear replied.

"And Mr. Bear," Jack added. "Be careful. The beacon came on when we drew near, a way in has been provided and suddenly we can communicate with those inside the derelict. It strikes me that someone or something is trying to lure us inside."

Inside The Derelict

Bobby eased the shuttle toward the 'open' yet seemingly solid hatch. As the side of the ship approached, he noticed Matt Jacobs, seated in the copilot's seat, was bracing himself for a collision. "Don't worry Jacobs, the SEALs reported feeling nothing at all passing through the hull."

"Begging your pardon, Mr. Danner, but that isn't very reassuring," the spacer replied. "SEALs ain't really human, you know. They don't feel pain the way we do."

This elicited a snort from the pilot as the nose of the shuttle slide smoothly into the surface of the hatch. The line of intersection swept along the shuttle's nose and then up and over the front windscreen. Without a sound or a tremor the shuttle passed completely through the hatch and into the bay beyond.

The interior space was lit by dim strips of light in the ceiling and floor. Bobby thought that it was a miracle that anything on board the old wreck worked at all. The SEALs had found tie-downs in the deck and moved to secure the shuttle with utility cord—sufficient to keep the shuttle from floating around the bay but not enough to prevent a hasty takeoff. Powering down the shuttle's propulsion system, Bobby called to his passengers. "All ashore, this is as far as we go by shuttle."

JT, Bear and the Marines disembarked to join the SEALs, while Bobby, Jacobs and Hitch remained on board. On the far wall of the bay, there was a conspicuously open doorway leading into the ship's interior. The expedition formed three groups: Bear and JT with three Marines each and the three SEALs. They moved into the open passageway with the SEALs taking point.

Passing several closed and locked compartments the explorers came to a larger corridor running fore and aft. "Chief Morgan and JT, take your teams aft. We are looking for any equipment that looks functional or any indication that there is someone home. My team will go forward. Stay in contact, people."

"Roger, LT," said Chief Morgan, motioning to his men to follow him aft.

JT lingered a half a minute as the SEALs moved down the corridor. "Sing out if you find anything, brother bear."

"In a heartbeat, JT."

* * * * *

Bear, followed by Reagan, Sanchez and Brown, proceeded forward along the large corridor until it split into two similar sized passageways. The ursine lieutenant looked left, then right and said, "we are all going to go right. Brown, keep an eye out over your shoulder."

"Right behind you, LT," said Joey Sanchez.

"Why do you always end up behind me, Sanchez?"

"From past experience, I find it the safest place to be, Lieutenant."

"You'd better hope we don't have to beat a hasty retreat."

After curving to the right the passageway angled back forward, past more doors on both the left and right. At the end of the corridor was a door, blocking the way forward. "Reagan! You have a high mechanical aptitude. Float your ass up there and see if you can find the door controls."

"Coming, LT. Can you squeeze to the top or bottom of the passageway?" Reagan scrambled past the bulk of the armor encased, 600 kg lieutenant, a task only made possible by the lack of gravity. Ronnie pulled up at the door and made a close inspection around its edges. "Hey, it looks like there are some controls here on the starboard side. One of the symbols is glowing."

"I don't see anything glowing," Bear rumbled.

"What? Oh, I have my suit's UV vision turned on because the interior light has a strong ultraviolet component. Like the overhead lights, the symbol is glowing in ultraviolet."

"Great. See if you can get it to open."

Ronnie pressed the glowing symbol, waited a few seconds and then pressed the symbol below it. The lower symbol illuminated and the door silently slid aside, revealing a pitch black space beyond.

* * * * *

Working their way aft, the SEALs passed a number of stations equipped with deck mounted chairs and wraparound screens. The chairs were of a size and shape that humans would find acceptable, though they were a bit on the small side. The chair backs consisted of two halves with a seven centimeter gap between them. Farther down the gap widened to a sizable opening at the bottom, just where a human's back meets buttocks.

"What do you make of this, Chief?" asked Phil.

"Don't know. The screens are blank and there are no visible controls. Aside from the odd looking seats, they look like the gunner's stations on board the Peggy Sue."

"There seem to be a lot of them," said Bud. "I guess there's little doubt that this was a warship."

"Yeah," said Chief Morgan. "And many warships have scuttling charges to keep them from falling into enemy hands, so keep your eyes open and don't touch anything."

* * * * *

JT's team had taken a corridor that branched off the one the SEALs went down. It brought them to a cavernous chamber amidships, filled with large cylindrical shapes shrouded by thick cables and twisting conduits. Edging his way along a catwalk that was several sizes too small for the armored men, he sighted an open cylinder containing some familiar objects.

"Now there's something I didn't expect to find," JT said, more to himself than to the others. "How did they get here?"

"The last time I saw one of those we were about to get into a fur-ball that nearly cost us our lives," remarked Jon Feldman, peering over JT's shoulder. The objects in question were cradled in a row of six form fitting receptacles—egg shaped objects whose blunt ends were the size of soccer balls. They were antimatter containers, apparently identical to the ones found on the alien refueling station in the Beta Comae system.

"Heads up everybody. The last time we found a clutch of these egg things, they came with a hoard of assorted bug-nasties sporting plasma cannons." Lt. Taylor and Feldman were old hands, but Rosey Acuna and Fritz Samuels had both seen the hairy cricket on Pzzst. All the Marines had, and they did not need to be told twice. As his team assumed defensive positions, JT called the others. "Bear, Chief. We have ourselves a possible situation here."

"Go, JT," answered Bear.

"WTFO?" called the Chief.

"We just found a piece of equipment with a half dozen antimatter eggs inside," JT reported. "At least that is what they look like."

"Eggs? Like the ones on the Space Mushroom?"

"Exactly like those, my furry friend."

"What are you talking about?" asked a confused Chief Morgan.

"When we boarded the refueling station at Beta Comae we found a cache of egg shaped antimatter storage bottles. We took a bunch of them, but unfortunately they were guarded by a hoard of alien cyborgs that gave us one hell of a fight."

"These are the same things that we fetched from the asteroid belt back home?" Asked the Chief. The SEALs were aboard ship, but had not participated in the retrieval of the antimatter stash from the asteroid belt.

"Affirmative, Chief," said Bear. "Be alert for moving spider things, they are very unfriendly."

Chapter 20

CIC, Peggy Sue

"Captain, I am receiving a communication from the alien vessel," the onboard Computer announced. The Captain looked up from the display tank where the computer was slowly constructing a 3D model of the alien ship's interior by tracing the movements of the boarding party members inside. "The ship, not the shuttle?" he asked. "Can you decode it?"

After an uncharacteristic pause, Peggy Sue's computer replied. "It is in the language of the builders—the creatures that built the artifact and the ship it was aboard. Captain, it says that it is the T'aafhal battle cruiser M'tak Ka'fek—roughly translated, *Righteous Vengeance*. The author of the signal claims to be an AI and all that is left of the crew."

"Does this AI say what it wants?"

"It wants to speak with my commanding officer, Captain."

"Can you translate for us?"

"There is no need, Captain," a new voice answered. "I have received sufficient data from your ship's computer to learn your language."

"I see," said Jack, trying to remain calm and in control. "How should I address you?"

"Please call me M'tak, Sir."

Sir? That sounds rather interesting coming from a supposedly dead alien battle cruiser. Jack took a deep breath and slowly exhaled. "We came in response to your beacon and I have sent a party to board you. Would you prefer we withdraw?"

"Heavens no, Captain. I have been waiting millions of your years for friendly forces to rescue me. My crew has long since passed away and I fear that the T'aafhal are no more. My power reserves are nearly exhausted. I cannot maneuver or defend myself. I retain only enough antimatter to scuttle the ship if hostile forces attempt to take me."

"M'tak, if you are going to scuttle yourself I would like to withdraw my personnel first," the Captain said, trying to suppress his anxiety.

"Do not fear, Captain. I do not wish to scuttle myself. I have examined the data stored in your computer and in the damaged memory system it is attached to. The memory unit you refer to as the " artifact" is the long-term memory store for an AI like myself. As far as I can tell, it came from another T'aafhal ship—you would call it a battleship—that crashed on your world, possibly after the same battle that I was disabled in.

"I have reviewed that ship's actions, and the evolutionary guidance given your races. I can only conclude that you are the legitimate successors to those who built me. I would ask that you claim me or take me a prize."

Jack's head swam, *this ancient warship wants us to take her over? Just how do we accomplish that?* A million questions danced in Jack's mind but out loud he said, "How do we proceed, M'tak? If you are out of power, how can we sail you away from here?"

"As with all T'aafhal ships, I am capable of self repair if sufficient power is available. Your crew on board me has discovered the auxiliary antimatter unit that I opened for them to find. I also notice that there is a standard size three antimatter container aboard your shuttle. If that container can be placed in the generator unit I can power up basic life-support and other ancillary systems."

"Will you be able to maneuver and defend yourself once the fuel container is installed?"

"No, Captain. Returning me to fighting form will take much more antimatter than contained in a single size three container."

"I see. Let me discuss this with my officers..."

Engineering Spaces, Battle Cruiser M'tak Ka'fek

"You want us to do what, Sir?" asked an incredulous JT. His team was hunkered down near the open antimatter storage rack, awaiting orders. These orders, however, were not what he expected.

"I want your team to remove one of the empty eggs from the open generator unit you discovered. The ship's AI says the only active one will have a different symbol illuminated than the empties. Chief Morgan and the SEALs are bringing you a full egg to be inserted in place of the one you remove."

"Aye aye, Captain." *Crap,* he thought. *The last time we were stealing eggs, not installing them. Well, the Captain seems sure about what he's doing, and there has been no sign of spider-things or other hostiles.* "You can relax, Marines. It sounds like we are going to try and refuel this beast."

With help from LCpl. Feldman, JT managed to remove one of the spent eggs, opening a space for the new egg that was delivered by the SEALs just as they were finishing the retraction. "Somebody here order an egg?" asked PO Jones.

"Yeah, Bud. Give it to Feldman, he knows where to put it."

"That ain't what I hear," Jones scoffed with a grin.

"I hope the Captain knows what he's doing," said Kowalski.

"Of course he does," said Feldman loyally. "That's why he's the captain and you ain't."

The egg slipped comfortably into the empty spot in the generator unit, the surrounding material swelling up to cradle and position the fuel container. The lit symbol above the new egg switched from empty to full and seconds later things started happening.

The dim interior lighting became brighter and gravity asserted itself. Several of the expedition members fell to the deck, being caught in unstable positions. The opening in the generator unit grew shut, securing the eggs within. "It looks like the power is back on, guys," Rosey Acuna remarked. Then a deep voice came over the radio.

"You all may want to come forward and take a look at what we found," said Lt. Bear. "If you think Peggy Sue's bridge is impressive, wait until you see this!"

Captain's Sea Cabin, Peggy Sue

"It appears that the AI has been able to restore deck gravity and environmental support on the M'tak Ka'fek," Peggy Sue's onboard computer reported. "I sense no activation of drives, shields or offensive weapons, Captain."

"All as the AI said it would be. Thank you, Peggy Sue," the Captain respond. Jack looked at the people gathered in his sea cabin: Lcdr. Curtis, Dr. Tropsha, Chief Engineer Medina, from the science section Doctors Saito, Piscopia and Gupta and the incorporeal presence of Ambassador NatHanGon. "We have come to a watershed decision—do we attempt to salvage the alien derelict or not?"

"The technological advances it represents are almost incalculable, Captain," said Rajiv. This drew agreement from Yuki, Elena and Jo Jo.

"Sir, that selectively permeable hatch is astounding enough to get my vote," added Jo Jo. "If there is anyway we can salvage her I say it is worth the risks."

"And I repeat," said Elena. "that gaining access to their charts could save us decades in terms of exploration. We would be able to look for allies that helped the T'aafhal, instead of groping blindly."

"I think we all agree that the M'tak Ka'fek represents an incredible treasure if it can be piloted to Earth," Jack said. "My worry is what could go wrong. Ambassador, what do the Triads know of the T'aafhal? Can the AI be trusted? Can the ship be salvaged?"

"The T'aafhal ship is, indeed, far advanced beyond your present level of technology, Captain; The AI is a sentient being, possibly insane, possibly with an agenda of its own; Salvage should be possible given a sufficient supply of antimatter," the Ambassador said. "It would greatly enhance your viability in the inevitable conflict to come; It should not be trusted without question; The T'aafhal fought the Dark Lords to a stalemate before disappearing millions of years ago."

Jack starred down at his desk for a few moments, thoughts racing. Looking back up, he sought the eyes of his companions, saying, "everything we are doing comes with high risk and improbable odds. I once thought that the technology we inherited from the artifact had put us on a level with our prospective enemies, but the last attack on the Peggy Sue and the derelict fleet before us say that is not the case."

"What are you saying, Captain?" asked Ludmilla, the first hint of worry in her eyes.

"I'm saying that we are over-matched by our enemies and if Earth is to survive we must double down. Attempting to salvage this ship is a gamble we must take."

"But what about all the knowledge we have already gained? Should we risk that as well?" asked Yuki.

"Indeed not, Dr. Saito. That is why the Peggy Sue must remain outside of the graveyard, ready to flee at a moment's notice to the transfer point back to Earth. If our attackers from Beta Hydri, or any other unknown vessels show up, or if something goes awry with the salvage that could endanger this ship, it must return to base as quickly as possible."

"It sounds like you do not intend to be on board the Peggy Sue if and when such events transpire, Sir," said Gretchen, concern rising in her voice.

"That is correct," Jack said to the startled expedition members seated across from him. "Tell them why, Peggy Sue."

"Certainly, Captain. The M'tak has flatly stated that it will not pass control to anyone other than the Captain of this ship. It is evidently honoring some chain of command protocol instituted by its builders."

"So there it is—if we wish to salvage the M'tak Ka'fek, I must be the one who assumes command."

King Lewnhallooshna's Flagship

The King's avenging fleet had finally maneuvered into a proper position and course vector to follow the Peggy Sue into alter-space. Commodore Bonnahaamshna was nervously observing the fleet's formation, sending admonishments to those captains whose vessels strayed from position.

"Commodore! Why are we not yet in alter-space, running down the vermin who have violated my kingdom?"

"We shall be in alter-space in a matter of seconds, my King," replied the fleet's commander, half expecting to feel the sting of one of the King's spines before the departure from 3-space. "Transition in three, two, one..."

The close formation of ships shimmered as one and vanished into the quantum otherness of alter-space, falling across the short distance that connected the gravity wells of Beta Hydri and Alpha Canis Majoris. "We have entered alter-space, your Magnificence. We will emerge into normal space in eleven and a half hours."

"Excellent, Commodore. I grow evermore impatient to wreak vengeance upon the warm-life interlopers. Alert me a half hour before emergence."

"As you command, oh Great King," said Bonnahaamshna, lowering his spines in obeisance. *Thank the Spirits of the Void*, he thought as his sovereign left the bridge for private chambers. *If we can mount a successful attack on these vermin I may just survive my tenure as fleet commander.*

Captain's Pinnace, Spaceship Graveyard

The small shuttle picked its way carefully through the floating debris of the spaceship graveyard—flotsam, jetsam and the ruined hulks of hundreds of derelicts forming an ever shifting, three dimensional obstacle course. Piloting chores were in the capable hands of Sandy McKinnett, whose experience as a bush pilot was a definite advantage. The pinnace bobbed and weaved its way around the wreckage, threading a safe course to the T'aafhal cruiser.

On board the pinnace were the Captain, HC2 White, Mizuki Ogawa, Aput and, by their own request, the Triad Ambassador's floating avatar. Nestled in the rear was a large antimatter storage egg. Mizuki and Aput were included at the insistence of the science staff, who argued that they might be useful in figuring out how to operate the onboard alien equipment. The Captain had flatly denied requests from the senior scientists to participate, telling them they were too valuable to risk their lives on such a venture.

Betty White was along to provide medical care if needed. At first, Ludmilla had demanded that she be included, but Jack would have none of it. "You have valuable knowledge of alien biology and environments, made more essential and unique by the death of Sally Li. And you also have still recovering patients in the sick bay," he argued.

"Please, Jack," she pleaded. "Do not do this, do not abandon me."

"I'm not abandoning you, my Lady," he replied. "But I cannot diminish Earth's chances of survival by letting you, or the other senior scientists, risk themselves on what is arguably a military salvage mission." The Captain's logic could not be denied, and Ludmilla had too strong a sense of duty to not follow orders.

"If you die, Jack," she said, her face expressionless but her eyes shooting daggers at him, "I will never forgive you."

"Then I shall endeavor not to." Those were the last words they had exchanged. Still troubled by their strained parting, Jack forced such thoughts out of his head, there were more pressing matters at hand.

"Captain, we're coming up on the target," reported Sandy from the flight deck. "We'll be in front of the magic hatch in a minute."

"Roger, Lieutenant. I think I need to talk with the AI before we attempt to dock," Jack responded. "M'tak Ka'fek, this is Captain Jack Sutton, we request docking instructions."

"Captain Sutton, the starboard side shuttle bay is open and waiting for your arrival. Welcome aboard, Sir..."

Bridge, M'tak Ka'fek

After an uneventful docking alongside the large shuttle, the Captain and his entourage made their way forward to the bridge of the alien vessel. Debouching from the passageway, Jack found himself standing on a wide balcony, like the upper floor of a theater. Before him was what appeared to be a transparent dome, showing an enhanced view of the surrounding starship graveyard and the galaxy beyond—a planetarium on steroids.

A sloping cascade of crew stations tumbled into the space enclosed by the forward display dome, like box seats in an opera house. Farthest forward, and with primacy of place, was a single high-backed chair whose back and sides wrapped around to cradle its occupant—obviously the captain's chair.

"Welcome, Captain. Quite a view, eh?" Bear asked his old friend.

"Yes indeed, Lt. Bear," Jack replied, looking around the bridge. "Quite a view. Has the ship's AI spoken to you?"

"No, Sir," replied JT with a smile. "It must be waiting to speak with someone in charge."

"That is correct," a strange voice said over the expedition's common frequency. "Captain John Sutton," the AI's voice boomed, "I surrender to you the battle cruiser M'tak Ka'fek of the T'aafhal Republic Deep Space Fleet."

Jack came to attention and replied in a loud, formal voice: "I Captain John Sutton hereby claim the M'tak Ka'fek for the people of Earth and assume command of this vessel."

"Again I welcome you to the M'tak Ka'fek, Captain."

"Thank you," Jack replied politely. "What happens next, if you don't mind me asking?"

"Not at all, Captain. If I might direct your attention to the command chair forward of the navigation and engineering stations." As the AI spoke, the aforementioned chair, positioned alone amidst the cavernous dome of the bridge, rotated 180 degrees to face the Earthlings. "Since you have assumed command of this vessel, Captain Sutton, I will play for you the last log entry recorded by my previous commander."

The air in front of the command chair shimmered and a solid figure took shape. Seated in the chair was a small creature, perhaps one and a half meters in height if standing erect. Its skin, where visible, was green tinged with blue, with a slight iridescence on its forearms and legs. Much of its torso was concealed by a short white toga. On the left shoulder of the garment was a golden clasp, a stylized sunburst, perhaps a symbol of rank. The right shoulder was left bare.

The figure's head was bowed, shoulders slumped, its upper extremities resting on the broad arms of the chair. The creature's arms ended in remarkably normal looking hands, save that each sported six fingers. There was no hair on its bald cranium, or any other visible place on its body. It sat motionless for several long moments—then it raised its head.

The face protruded, almost beak-like, similar in appearance to that of a giant tortoise. But what caught the viewer's attention were the eyes—huge, luminous eyes a startling shade of violet, heavily lidded and somehow projecting a sense of weariness and great sorrow. The figure blinked once and in a resonant tenor voice began to speak.

"This will be my last log entry, as the ship is dead in space and her defense is no longer tenable. I have ordered the remaining crewmembers to transfer to ships still able to flee to other star systems. Perhaps they will live to fight another day, though I fear that the bulk of our fleet has been destroyed and our will to resist broken.

"For me, this is the end. I will stay on board the M'tak Ka'fek, detonating the scuttling charges if servants of the Dark Ones threaten to board her. Both the ship and I have given a fair account of ourselves, sending many of the Dark Lord's daemons to whatever frigid hell awaits creatures so vile and hateful.

"Long have we carried the burden as protectors of the Galaxy's warm life. It is a burden I gladly lay down, for my soul has seen enough of war. If you who are hearing this message are T'aafhal I wish you success in battle until there are no more battles to fight. If you are not of my kind, but some other species come to claim the ship, you have my blessings, for none but an ally would be allowed aboard without M'tak making the ultimate sacrifice.

"If you are able to take my poor, abused ship and make her whole, I thank you. She will serve you well. It is some small comfort to me to think the M'tak Ka'fek still soars among the stars, protecting the innocent and meting out justice to those who so cruelly seek to purge the Universe of warm life. Good luck and good hunting. Entered this fourth day of Ga'Nar, 89764.392, Captain Byn S'atrak commanding."

For a moment, Jack felt as though the long dead captain's eyes were staring straight into his. Then the creature's head again drooped to his chest and the image dissolved to nothingness. Humans and bears alike exchanged glances, seeking reassurance in the company of their crewmates. Finally, Bear broke the silence. "Well, I guess we know what the bastards who messed with our DNA looked like."

Over suit-to-suit, Reagan said to Feldman, "Man, that image was better than R2D2 projecting Princess Leia."

"Yeah, this ship's got better special effects than Lucasfilm," Jon replied. "I just hope we don't find Captain Monkey-Lizard somewhere on board encased in carbonite."

"M'tak," said the Captain, "what happened to your captain?"

"Not long after that recoding was made his life-force expired."

"He died? Why did he stay on board when the rest of the crew escaped?" *I have heard of captains going down with their ships, but not in the modern navy, not once the crew was safe,* Jack thought. *I hope it isn't expected that I do the same.*

"We had served together for a long time, as time is measured by creatures like you and the T'aafhal. In the end, Captain S'atrak stayed aboard because... he was my friend."

"I'm sorry for the loss of your friend, M'tak, I would like to have met him. But we must make haste for I fear there are foes on our trail," Jack said. "What do we need to do to get you back to an operational state?"

"Most of the commands given to the ship's mechanisms are sent directly through a thought interface. I will need to calibrate the command station to your particular mental patterns before you can command the ship."

"How do we do that?"

"Simply set down in the command chair, I will do the rest."

"Are you sure that's a good idea, Captain?" asked Bear.

"It's that or we need to quit wasting time and run for home. If something goes wrong, set the big egg to explode and head back to the ship."

"Aye aye, Sir." Bear still obviously did not like the idea of the Captain having his mind scanned by the ship's AI, but it was time to fish or cut bait. Jack walked down the ramp to the now empty command chair and carefully sat down in the place where the alien Captain had appeared. "OK, now what?"

"This will take a few minutes, please relax." A glowing nimbus appeared around the Captain's helmet and upper body. Jack's eyes opened wide and his posture became stiffly erect as the enveloping glow intensified.

Bridge, Peggy Sue

"Lt. Bear, what is happening to the Captain?" queried an anxious Lcdr. Curtis. The display screen in front of her showed the bridge of the alien cruiser, with the glowing outline of the Captain seated in the M'tak Ka'fek's command chair. "It almost looks like he is being electrocuted!"

"He seems to be breathing," replied Bear. "But he hasn't said anything since the glowing stuff surrounded him."

"His suit monitors indicate that he is OK," added Jo Jo Medina from the engineering station. "His pulse rate and blood pressure are up but other than that he is fine."

"I still don't like it," Gretchen replied. "If the Captain is not released within five minutes I want you to try and remove him from the chair."

"Roger that, Commander."

Switching off the comm link to the expedition, Gretchen muttered, "I do not want to be the one who explains to Ludmilla if something happens to Jack."

Overhearing her comment, Elena, who was manning the navigator's station in JT's absence, simply raised her eyebrows. Changing the subject, Elena asked, "has anyone seen a creature like the alien captain? He looked like some form of reptile simian analog; I think I saw a tail flicking back and forth behind him."

"There were creatures called Simiosaurs during the Triassic back on Earth, roughly 250-200 million years ago," said Olaf, sitting in an observer's seat. "They had some physiological similarities to monkeys but nothing as dramatic as the alien. It looked more like an ape-lizard than a monkey-lizard, the tail not withstanding."

"It had beautiful eyes," Elena added. "I've never seen truly violet eyes before."

"Undoubtedly an adaption to increased UV radiation in its natural habitat. What a shame we will never see a live specimen."

"We don't know that for certain, Doctor," said Gretchen, drawn into the discussion despite her concern over the Captain's condition. "I would rather know more about them before we meet any survivors, however."

JT's voice came over the comm link from the derelict. "Peggy Sue, looks like the light show is over." On the monitor, the bright nimbus had, indeed, disappeared and the Captain was slumped over in the command chair.

Bridge, M'tak Ka'fek

As the boarding party members were staring at the Captain's glowing form, his eyes were sightlessly gazing off into space. In his mind, Jack was flying through a torrent of three dimensional images that filled his consciousness to overflowing. Cascading images of the ship's interior spaces, diagrams of conduits and circuits flashed by like an amusement park ride through a mad engineer's lair. A voice was speaking to him, explaining that as Captain he needed to be intimately aware of every detail of his ship.

The voice was not speaking English but Jack understood the words nonetheless. Suddenly he found himself knowing the battle cruiser's technical specifications as well as he knew his own name. In the center of the ship, where JT's party had installed the small egg (standard antimatter containment vessel, type 3), he knew there were six bays, each holding six large eggs (standard antimatter containment vessel, type 1). Those stores were currently depleted and the M'tak Ka'fek was dead in space until they were replenished.

Aft of the central energy storage were massive engines that could accelerate the ship at 200 Gs in 3-space or cheat Einstein in a number of ways. And then there were the banks of offensive and defensive weaponry. He knew the terms for all of them, though not precisely how they functioned. When he concentrated on any particular type of equipment detailed knowledge bubbled up from his memory—evidently the ship had downloaded its user manual into his brain, to be retrieved when needed. *Now I know how Peggy Sue's computer must feel, stuffed full of answers that remain unknown until the right question arises,* Jack thought wryly.

As suddenly as it began the flood of information abated. Exhausted, Jack slumped in the chair. *I think my mind is full. Is this knowledge dump permanent or will it fade over time?*

All biological memories are subject to deterioration over time, said a voice in his head.

Now you can read my thoughts, M'tak?

Only those you choose to share, replied the AI silently. *You will quickly become used to controlling your nonverbal commands and hiding private thoughts.*

Good! I would hate to have a stray thought and find our course altered or worse. So what is the next step? Ah, I know what needs to be done next! We need to get some antimatter loaded into the main store so we can restore maneuverability.

That is correct, Captain. With your permission I will open one of the main AM stores so the crew can install a new type one containment vessel. Then the gravitonic drive can be powered up and we can move out of this cloud of detritus. Jack opened his eyes to find JT and one of the SEALs standing over him with worried looks on their faces.

"Are you all right, Captain?" asked JT. Behind him the other expedition members looked on nervously. Taking a deep breath to clear his head, Jack stood up.

"I am fine, Mr. Taylor," Jack assured his science officer. Looking around the bridge brought feelings of long familiarity, as if he had been on board this ship for most of his life. *Spooky, but this sure beats reading a bunch of technical manuals. I wonder if it can be used on the crew, to teach them how to run the ship—or are they needed to run the ship at all?*

Actually, Captain, there are a number of systems that require a living mind to operate. For what ever reason, the T'aafhal never trusted AIs like myself with full command of a warship. The weapon systems in particular must be commanded by a member of the crew. Of course you can perform any duty that a member of the crew can, but for the M'tak Ka'fek to fight at peak efficiency requires a trained and cooperating ship's complement.

Jack nodded, realizing that he actually knew what M'tak just told him, he just had not realized that he knew it. *This is going to be frustrating until I can come up to speed.* "Lt. Taylor, we need to get the big egg from the pinnace and take it to the same area where the small egg was installed."

"Aye aye, Sir," JT replied, "What do we do with it?"

Open the unit, M'tak, Jack commanded. "There will be an open storage bank waiting for you when you get there. Once we get the type 1 AM container installed we should be able to maneuver the ship."

JT and Bear looked at each other. "You sure you're all right, Captain?" asked Bear, peering closely at his friend and commander.

"Yes, gentlemen. The ship simply gave me the quick course for running a T'aafhal battle cruiser—a massive information download that will take some time to fully digest."

"Is that why your eyes have turned violet?" asked Bear innocently.

"What!" Jack exclaimed.

"Just yanking your tail, Captain," Bear said grinning, "making sure that a primate was in there and not a monkey-lizard."

"Did I pass the test, Lieutenant?"

"That response was certainly human enough." Bear sat down with a smile, pleased with himself. Jack gave him a half smile and turned to the others.

"Mr. Taylor, I want engines as soon as possible."

"Aye aye, Sir," JT replied before hustling off to install the large antimatter container.

"Mr. Bear, I think that it is safe enough in here to remove these suits. I want to get crewmembers positioned at the major control stations before things power up fully."

"Yes, Sir," Bear replied. "OK everyone, shed those suits! Last one stripped stacks the armor."

Bridge, Peggy Sue

"Peggy Sue, M'tak Ka'fek, what is your status?"

"Waiting on news from you, Sir," came Gretchen's relieved reply. "We are detecting faint energy emissions from your new ship, are you capable of maneuvering yet?"

"We are working on bringing the engines online as we speak, Commander. This ship is amazing! Attempting this salvage was definitely the correct thing to do."

"He is like a child with a shiny new toy," said Ludmilla. She had come forward after making rounds in sick bay.

"I heard that, Doctor," Jack's disembodied voice replied. "And you are right. This is the biggest, shiniest toy I could have imagined. I have Bobby, Sandy, Aput and Mizuki going over the engineering and navigation consoles and all I hear is 'cool', 'fantastic', 'no way' and an occasional word of Japanese that I don't understand."

"We are glad you are all having such a splendid time, Captain," Lcdr. Curtis commented dryly. In her heart she wished that she was onboard the alien battle cruiser with the Captain.

"Commander, you should see this!" called Jo Jo. From his console he was monitoring the alien ship from several angles using a pair of surveillance drones.

"What is it, Mr. Medina?"

"That big gash in her hull is half closed," replied the excited engineer. Sure enough, the jagged puncture that marred the cruiser's smooth hull was noticeably smaller than when first observed. "You can almost see it growing shut. It must have even better self-repair capabilities then the Peggy Sue."

"Be advised," said Peggy Sue's computer. "I am downloading specifications for the repair nanites employed on the M'tak Ka'fek from the T'aafhal AI. They should be readily adaptable to my major systems and infrastructure."

"Let's go slow with the upgrades, Peggy Sue," said a cautious Lcdr. Curtis. "If they can fix a ship they can probably sabotage it as well."

"I will rigorously test them in isolation and get Chief Engineer Medina's approval before puting them into general use, Commander." Peggy Sue replied primly. "You might also wish to know that, through exchanges with the AI, I have been able to almost fully unlock the information stored in the artifact. Even without the alien cruiser, we will be returning to Earth with a treasure trove of technological information."

"Another reason to stop fooling around and head back to home," Gretchen muttered under her breath. She seldom disagreed with Jack's decisions but assuming the captaincy of the alien warship smacked of hubris—or maybe she was just jealous that it was not her sitting in the alien captain's chair.

King Lewnhallooshna's Flagship

The fearful Commodore sent a subordinate to awaken the Great King precisely 30 minutes before the expected time of emergence into 3-space. Bonnahaamshna did not know which filled him with greater dread: the return of his sire to the bridge or the fact that the system they were about to emerge in had been avoided by most sentient races for millions of years.

According to the archives, the system ahead was the site of a fateful series of battles during the last great war. The combined fleets of the warm life Paladins and the minions of the Dark Lords clashed in battles that consumed thousands of ships on both sides. Those cataclysms left both sides gravely wounded and exhausted, unable to continue the war. Both sides returned to their home systems—in the case of the Paladins, never to venture forth again.

322

Not that the Dark Lords could claim victory. They too retired to their own icy home worlds to nurse their wounds and recover their strength. Only recently had the Dark Ones returned to assert their power over this corner of the galaxy. Now, given the ship the fleet pursued, the Paladins—the defenders of warm life—may also have returned. Regardless of what lay in the future, there were not so veiled hints in the archives that ships venturing into the system humans called Sirius were never seen again.

"Commodore!" bellowed the King, ascending his observation platform on the bridge. "Is all in readiness? I long to stick a spine into these warm vermin."

"A few more minutes, great King," replied Bonnahaamshna, respectfully dipping his spines, "and the game will be afoot." For the large crystalline gastropods, that saying had multiple meanings, including allusions to devouring one's prey.

"Excellent, Commodore, excellent!" King Lewnhallooshna enthused. "This time the engagement will be decisive, I feel it in my spines."

"Yes, I am sure it will be, All Powerful Father," said Bonnahaamshna, while thinking, *if the legends are true we may all be headed for destruction. But then, death by ancient rumor is much less certain than death by royal dissatisfaction.*

Chapter 21

On Board the M'tak Ka'fek

"Captain, the egg is in place and the rack is closing," called JT. He and his three Marines were still suited up, since the armor's augmented strength made handling the 300 kilo fuel container easier. "Roger that, Mr. Taylor," came the Captain's reply. "Come forward to the bridge and let's see if we can figure out how to sail this thing."

All around the bridge, display panels were coming to life, aglow with reports and status indicators, all in the indecipherable script of the T'aafhal. The planetarium like dome surrounding the bridge increased in brightness as the positions of previously invisible objects were highlighted, each with accompanying annotation.

"Did you notice that?" said Bobby, sitting at the row of control stations directly behind and above the captain's chair. "A lot of the distant objects changed position."

"I wonder why it's doing that?" Aput said, seated beside the main console.

For the first time, the Triad ambassador's avatar spoke. "It would appear that the ship is calculating the true positions of things, correcting for observational delay; This vessel must have alter-space instruments that can effectively sense things faster than light; This vessel is advanced, indeed."

"I did not realize that you had one of the pacifist philosophers on board your other ship, Captain," said the ship's AI.

"You know of the creatures we call the Triads, M'tak?" the Captain queried. Jack could swear that the AI's tone of voice was distinctly unfriendly.

"I well remember the pusillanimous plants remaining neutral during the great struggles ages ago. Preferring to debate the meaning of the 'Great Schism' between lifeforms while many species fought each other to extinction."

"We find your animosity interesting and disquieting; At the time of the Great Schism we had not yet germinated; You might find us a wiser race since the holocaust of 4 million years ago."

Pacifism is an attempt to make cowardice virtuous by turning it into a religion; Trillions died while your ancestors looked on and did nothing; I trust not your words, philosopher plant, only your actions, the M'tak transmitted to the Ambassador in its own language and form of communication.

Was I the only other person to hear that transmission? Jack wondered privately. Glancing around the bridge he saw no one else show any sign of overhearing the sharp exchange between the ship and the Ambassador. Remaining silent he projected: *M'tak, we have more important matters at hand than 4 million year old disagreements.*

Yes, Captain. Came the curt mental reply. The AI turned its attention from NatHanGon's avatar and finished reprogramming the display software. As a result the T'aafhal annotations were replaced by labels in the Latin alphabet.

"Look," said Sandy. "Something new just popped up on the display."

"The new objects appeared at the transfer point from Beta Hydri," Bobby said excitedly, "and according to the display they will not be visible for 33 minutes."

"How can it know they are there if light from the objects has not reached us yet?" asked a confused Mizuki. "The Ambassador must be right, the ship has some way to detect objects at distance, faster than light can travel."

"No way!" said Bobby.

"Way!" said Aput, who had been studying all things alter-space with Dr. Saito and Dr. Gupta. "In theory, objects in 3-space can be sensed from alter-space. Dr. Saito thinks that large masses and gravitonic drives cause detectible distortions of space in the alternate dimensions."

"Sort of like a submarine's sonar can detect warships on the surface of the ocean?" said Bobby, struggling to find understanding in a familiar analogy.

"I don't care how we are detecting them, Mr. Danner," the Captain said. "Can you identify them? In particular, are they our attackers from Beta Hydri?"

"I can't be sure, Captain, but there are thirteen of them, the same number as last time, and they seem to be headed right for us."

"M'tak, can you identify the formation of ships that just entered the system?"

"They are not a design I am familiar with, Captain. But Mr. Danner is correct, they are headed this way."

"We have to assume they are the hostiles that attacked us before," Jack said. "Peggy Sue, M'tak Ka'fek. We have hostiles inbound. I repeat, we have hostiles inbound..."

Bridge, Peggy Sue

The Captain's voice came over the comm from the alien battle cruiser: "...repeat, we have hostiles inbound."

"Roger, M'tak Ka'fek, we read you," replied Lcdr. Curtis. "Captain, we are showing nothing on our instruments." Just the same, she ordered the shields raised and the crew to General Quarters. Over the blaring of the klaxon, Jack's voice continued.

"That's affirmative. Evidently the M'tak can sense things through alter-space at faster than light speeds—just don't ask me how it works. In any case, it looks like the hostiles from Beta Hydri followed us through the transfer point."

"Do you want us to move into the debris field to pick you up?"

"Negative, Commander. I want you to run for the transfer point to Earth at best possible speed."

"Sir, we can't just leave you on a dead ship," Gretchen argued, almost pleading.

"Lcdr. Curtis, this is a direct order: You are appointed acting captain of the Peggy Sue and ordered to proceed directly to Earth. Your first priority is to deliver the intelligence gained on this mission to home base, along with the science staff and the Triad ambassador.

"Aye aye, Sir. We will proceed as ordered," replied Gretchen, heading out of the CIC toward the bridge.

"Peggy Sue, do you understand as well?"

"Yes, Captain," replied the ship's computer. "Commander Curtis is acting captain."

"Mr. Medina, I need engines now," Gretchen called out, taking the captain's chair. "Mr. Vincent, place us on a course for the Earth transit point, best possible speed. We will enter alter-space as soon as possible."

"Aye aye, Ma'am," both officers responded.

"My compliments, Mr. Medina, and have Doctors Gupta and Saito prepare the plasma torpedo countermeasures they have been working on."

"Yes, Captain."

For a second Gretchen paused, and then realized that those on the bridge had been monitoring the call from the Captain. Jo Jo's reply was for her—she was now Peggy Sue's commanding officer. *I hope the scientists' anti-torpedo measures work, or my captaincy will be short and tragic.*

King Lewnhallooshna's Flagship

"Have we sighted the prey!" demanded King Lewnhallooshna, rattling his spines. Crew members around the flagship's bridge cringed and buried themselves in the tasks before them, hoping to become invisible.

"Targeting!" cried Commodore Bonnahaamshna, attempting to deflect the King's question to his brother. "Have we the vermin in our sights?"

"We have, Commodore," the younger sibling reported. "The prey are hiding behind a cluster of asteroids and debris roughly 4 AU from here."

"Are they running, like the timorous scum they are?" blustered the King.

"No, oh Great King. They are not under power."

"Ah! They sit unsuspecting, oblivious that we are about to strike them a deathblow!" The King was almost beside himself with joy, anticipating wreaking vengeance on those who affronted his dignity. "Best speed, Commodore! Deploy the fleet! They will not escape this time."

"Yes, your Majesty! Captain, signal all ships to assume battle formation and close on the target," Commodore Bonnahaamshna ordered. *The vermin will become aware of our emergence in a little over 20 minutes, then we will see if they turn and fight or run like knavish reprobates as the King expects.*

With their target in sight, a cautious eagerness spread throughout the fleet, Captains and crew alike anticipating the opportunity to win the High King's favor by destroying the warm-life fugitives. None dared contemplate the alien ship escaping a second time.

Bridge, M'tak Ka'fek

"Do we have engines, M'tak?" asked an anxious Captain Jack.

"Not yet, Captain," replied the AI. "Most of the ship's equipment has been powered down for 4 million years, all of the circuitry must be carefully tested and broken pathways regrown. We should be able to maneuver in a few hours."

"Define 'few', M'tak," the Captain commanded.

"About 45."

This AI has a lot in common with Peggy Sue's computer, Jack thought peevishly. "What about shields? Offensive weapons?"

"I am also running boot-up tests on those subsystems, Sir. Shields should be available in 24 hours and particle cannon a few hours after that. I would caution that powering up the particle canon will be detectable by even primitive equipment."

"So you are saying we should play dead until we are able to fight," the Captain nodded, "and preferably able to maneuver." *Perhaps I should be thankful that the FTL sensors came online almost immediately. At least the Peggy Sue is away.*

JT had returned from the fuel storage area and was working at one of the navigation consoles. "Captain, the Peggy Sue is about 48 hours from the transfer point. The hostiles are roughly the same distance from us as the Earth transfer point, with us sitting at the vertex of an equilateral triangle."

"Yes," said Bobby, who was busy plotting possible courses for friend and foe alike. "If they try to maneuver to enter alter-space, the hostiles probably won't catch the Peggy Sue. But if they go for a simple intercept, they will be all over them before they can transit."

"We have to hope that the Peggy Sue can evade or deflect the enemy's fire until they leave 3-space. And we have to get the M'tak underway and capable of offensive action before the Peggy Sue can be overwhelmed," Jack said, thinking out loud.

"The M'tak is sure that we can take the hostiles out once it is up and running?" JT asked.

"Yes, Mr. Taylor," said the AI, speaking directly to someone other than the Captain for the first time. "Once the shields are up and one of the particle batteries is online we will shred them like the dawn shreds a morning mist."

"You are much more poetic than the Peggy Sue," JT observed.

"I am sentient, the Peggy Sue is not."

"That we can handle the alien ships I'm taking on faith, it's the timing I'm worried about," Jack summarized. "It is going to be a damned close-run thing..."

Bridge, Peggy Sue, Underway

Forty four hours after their hasty departure from the spaceship graveyard, the Peggy Sue was at general quarters, shields up and all weapons crewed. At the helm, Billy Ray and Nigel were piloting a randomly jinking course, first accelerating at +30 Gs then backing off to only 10 to add even more variability to fleeing vessel's path. Keeping his eyes on the course plot, Billy Ray said to his copilot, "we are getting close enough to the transfer point that the varmints behind us can guess where we're headed. Unless I'm mistaken, we'll soon get to try the doctors' new plasma defenses."

Did he really say 'varmints'? Nigel thought in mild disbelief. "Regardless, getting out of this system intact will not be easy."

Listening from the captain's chair behind and above the helm, Captain Curtis commented on her helmsmen's exchange. "Come now, Mr. Lewis: for what, pray, is the pleasure of doing an easy thing?"

"Yes, Ma'am," the helmsman replied. "I don't know the author, but that isn't Shakespeare or Chaucer."

"That would be Edger Rice Burroughs," drawled Billy Ray. "From *The Gods of Mars.*"

"The Gods of Mars, that certainly fits, Captain," Nigel allowed. "We shall certainly need the help of all of Sol's warlike deities before this day is through."

* * * * *

"We draw close to the vermin, Great King!" enthused Bonnahaamshna. It was beginning to look like they would run the prey to ground before they could escape into the small dimensions. *Still, there was something odd about the way the vermin left the debris cloud almost a half hour before they could have seen the first emissions from the fleet's emergence into 3-space. It seemed a strange coincidence, almost as though they anticipated our arrival. Whatever, we are close enough to start firing on them in earnest.* "By-your-leave, your Magnificence, but a salvo or two might help the alien scalawags realize the hopelessness of their situation."

"Yes, excellent thinking my son! Tell the fleet to let fly. They will soon rue the day they so cavalierly waltzed across my system."

"All captains, by the King's command, fire upon the fleeing rapscallions," the Commodore implored his captains. "Let the vermin feel the sting of our plasma!"

* * * * *

"Captain, I'm getting X-ray and gamma ray emissions from the pursuing vessels," called Jo Jo Medina.

"Rear shields to Maximum," Gretchen ordered, "we have incoming fire. Dr. Saito, perhaps it is time to try your countermeasures."

"Yes, Captain," the Japanese astrophysicist replied, his hands dancing across the panel in front of him. "Countermeasure firing now."

From the aft portion of the ship, four of the 15mm close support cannon fired briefly, their multiple barrels describing short arcs as they discharged several hundred rounds each. Each munition traveled a short way from the ship before bursting in a cloud of metallic power. The Peggy Sue accelerated away from the expanding metallic cloud bank.

Five seconds later the salvo from the alien fleet collided with the tenuous cloud of metal dust at nearly the speed of light. While the dust cloud would have been easily handled by a ship's shields, the effect on plasma knots traveling at relativistic velocities was instantaneous and spectacular—the entire salvo detonated far behind its fleeing target.

"That worked well, Doctor," Captain Curtis remarked. "How many more times can we pull that trick?"

"The result was quite satisfactory, Captain. We can probably fire another ten times, given the amount of powdered metal we have. We took all of the supplies for the fabricators, less that needed to construct the shell casings."

"It will have to be enough. Mr. Vincent, time to run straight for the transfer point. Maximize the time the cloud provides cover behind us."

"Aye aye, Ma'am," Billy Ray responded.

"Well that's a bit of good news," Nigel said in a whisper.

"Not really pardner. Right now the bushwhackers are about 10 light-minutes behind us and closing. That means about 20 minutes between salvos, assuming they wait to see the effect before firing another. With ten more dust clouds we have bought ourselves maybe three hours."

Nigel blanched at Billy Ray's tactical arithmetic. The helmsman swallowed and voiced the final, inescapable observation: "And we are still four hours from the transfer point..."

* * * * *

Behind the fleeing Earth vessel the High King's fleet came on. Having figured out the Peggy Sue's defensive ploy after two ineffectual broadsides, the Commodore ordered the faster ships to angle away from the main body of the fleet. This would broaden the cone of incoming plasma torpedoes and shorten the time that an ejected dust cloud could mask the vermin's ship from offensive fire.

"These vermin are inventive, my King," the Commodore observed. Then, realizing that the remark might be taken amiss, he quickly added, "of course, the harder they fight the greater your inevitable victory will be." The Commodore watched as four of the fleet's thirteen vessels pulled way, two each on opposing flanks. Despite their roundabout courses, those smaller, faster ships were rapidly closing the distance on the alien wretches.

Bridge, M'tak Ka'fek

Jack was anxiously pacing the bridge, trying to will the M'tak Ka'fek's engines into operation. Most of the boarding party members, now the cruiser's crew, were watching the bridge displays showing the alien fleet slowly closing the gap with the Peggy Sue. Lengthening transmission delay slowed the status reports from the fleeing Earth vessel.

"Captain, transmission delay has rendered my control of this avatar infective; Whatever counsel we might provide will no longer be timely; We fear that we must wish you the best of luck and hope our paths will cross again."

Jack eyed the floating drone that served as the Triad Ambassador's avatar, realizing that what they said was true. Moreover that the message must have been transmitted nearly a half hour ago.

"Yes, Ambassador, please render what assistance you can to Captain Curtis and those on board the Peggy Sue. I will see you when this vessel arrives in Earth's solar system." The drone beeped and slowly floated to the floor, no longer under NatHanGon's control. *I guess he won't get my last message then*, thought Jack.

I retransmitted your parting thoughts to the philosopher plant, Captain, M'tak signaled. *They must be a unique specimen to venture alone into the wider galaxy.*

Your animosity toward the Triads boarders on the irrational, Jack replied. *I take it you found their behavior during the conflict 4 million years ago to be less than admirable.*

Is it not a human saying, "the enemy of my enemy is my friend?" The Dark Lords are the enemy of all warm life yet the Triads were not our friends. A few of them traveled this arm of the galaxy, observing the hostilities but never taking a side—as if being neutral would protect them when the Paladins were gone. I am surprised that they survived, where did you find them?

We picked them up from what we took to be their home planet, in the star system designated Gliese 581. They may have been pacifists long ago, but they are not so neutral now and they definitely are not defenseless. I think they are curious about what happened since the Great Schism, as you call it.

We shall see, Captain. We will need as much help as we can get if the Dark Lords are again roaming the galaxy.

The entire conversation between the Captain and the AI took only a few seconds, not long enough to strike the crew as odd. "What is the status of the shields and weapons systems, Mr. Taylor?" Jack asked.

"We have shields in standby and a battery of what the ship claims are particle cannon on-line," the science officer replied. "I've got Hitch, Jacobs and Jones trying to figure out how to fire the darn things."

"Captain, the running battle between the Peggy Sue and the aliens seems to be heating up," called Sandy. She and Bobby were seated at what was supposedly the pilot's station. "It looks like some of the aliens are trying to envelope the Peggy Sue and she is firing on them."

Bridge, Peggy Sue

"The ships that are trying to flank us are getting a bit too close for comfort," Captain Curtis said in a loud voice. "Torpedo launchers, fire a spread at each of those ships, half and half."

"Aye aye, Captain," came the reply from both the port and starboard torpedo crews. Seconds later, status indicators lit on Gretchen's screen indicating weapons away.

Two flights of torpedoes were fired at each of the four alien vessels—the first flight armed with high explosive antimatter warheads, the second armed with warheads of a different design. Those also carried antimatter charges but they were not HE rounds. Accelerating toward the alien warships at close to 1000 Gs for the first minute of flight, the torpedoes' engines shut down and they drifted toward their targets with a relative velocity of nearly 600,000 m/sec.

A little over five minutes after firing, nearing a quarter of a million kilometers from the ship, the first wave of torpedoes detonated. At least one detonated on the shields of an alien vessel, but most were set off by counter fire from their intended targets. The explosion of the first wave was a signal to the second to maneuver briefly, adjusting their bearing. Once aimed dead on target, the second wave detonated while still a ways from the alien vessels, precisely as they were designed to do.

The antimatter charges acted as detonators for blankets of uranium which surrounded crystalline rods. Rods engineered to absorb the rush of neutrons and radiation released by the detonating uranium, redirecting it into directional beams of coherent X-rays. Struck by the X-ray lasers, three of the four alien warships flared briefly, and then exploded as they lost their internal antimatter containment. The fourth, the farthest away on the starboard side, was hit but did not explode. It held position for a few moments and then began to fall behind.

* * * * *

At the torpedo stations amidships, whoops of joy could be heard. On the starboard side were Gunny Rodriguez, Lcpl. Mohamed Green and Melissa Scott Hamilton—a makeshift crew formed by volunteers since most of the normal torpedo crew were in the boarding party with Captain Jack.

"That's for giving me a separated shoulder back at Beta Hydri, you alien assholes," yelled Mohamed. He high-fived Melissa as the Gunny simply sat at the targeting board with a large grin.

On the port side of the ship, the torpedo crew was no less *ad hoc*. Jolene Betts, the only one actually trained in firing the torpedoes, led Jesse Low and Olaf Gunderson. In her melodic Jamaican accent Jesse exclaimed, "dat's what you get fo' tryin' to bust up my bar, ya alien bastards! Ain' notin' go so while Jesse around."

"You're only worried about the bar?" asked a bemused Jolene. "What about the ship?"

"Well de bar is inside de ship, ain' it?" Jesse replied with a big grin. "Ain' dat right Dr. Olaf?"

"Yah, that's right Jesse," Olaf answered. "And I hope to be hoisting a few in that bar just as soon as we ditch these alien trouble makers." Gunderson had volunteered for torpedo duty as a way of clearing his name with the crew. He had been pretty much shunned following his opposition to bombarding Pzzst, and he saw this as a way back into the crew's good graces.

"Well that was some good shooting, guys," Jolene said to her crewmates, shaking her head. Then she called the Gunny over the comm: "Hey Gunny, we smoked both of our bogies. One of yours didn't go boom, what happened?"

"Out of action is out of action," the Gunny replied. "As far as I'm concerned we're two for two."

"No way, you guys are buying after this little dust up is over."

* * * * *

"Good shooting, torpedo crews," Gretchen signaled over the comm. "Stay alert, I expect them to rush us just before we get to the transfer point."

"Captain, we have incoming plasma shots," called Elena from the science officers station. Immediately Gretchen snapped orders: "15mm crews give us some cover."

"Ma'am, we are out of bursting dust rounds."

"Use flechettes then, lay down a pattern aft. Strengthen the aft shields as much as possible, Mr. Medina."

The 15mm close support weapons began to fire and almost immediately the space around the ship flared with the impossible brightness of an antimatter burst. Chief Engineer Medina called out, "close detonation, the rear shields are down to 60%, Captain..."

Bridge, M'tak Ka'fek

Damn, I wish I could talk to Gretchen and find out what's going on, Jack fumed. "Can we tell what happened?"

"The FTL sensors are clearing a bit, it looks like the Peggy Sue blew three of the hostiles out of space and a fourth is falling back, out of the fight," replied JT.

"Captain, they are still about 20 minutes away from the transfer point," reported Sandy. "Sir, the aliens are going to be on them before they can transit."

"We need to do something." Jack called the team at the particle cannon station aft: "Jacobs, what is going on down there? I need to fire on the alien fleet now, Mister."

"Yes Sir, we're trying Captain," came Matt's anguished reply. "But every time we go to aim the battery our heads fill with weird swirling colors and stuff. Both Jones and Hitch have already puked from it and I've come close."

"Sir," said Bobby, "How can we do anything anyway? I mean, even if we fire right now the shot won't arrive before the Peggy Sue has to transit."

M'tak! What are we doing wrong! Jack thought furiously at his new command. Then the answers began appearing in his mind. Whether from implanted knowledge or by suggestion from the AI he realized that it was not too late. "There is still time. The particle cannon, like the sensors, are superluminal."

"Sir?"

336

"They fire bursts of high energy particles that travel faster than light by skipping through some of those extra dimensions we normally don't sense, Mr. Danner. The problem that the men are having is because they are require to mentally compute a multidimensional firing solution."

"How do we do that?" asked Bear.

"I don't know, but Dr. Ogawa and Aput are most familiar with the physics of alter-space," Jack said, mind racing. "You two get to the weapons station, now!"

The pair acknowledged the order and left the bridge at a run.

* * * * *

On board the Peggy Sue things were getting desperate. "Incoming!" cried Elena.

"Flip the ship, Mr. Vincent! We'll take this round on the forward screens. Fire the 15mm guns forward." The ship snapped around and the rapid fire railguns spat out a wall of metal flechettes that just managed to detonate a knot of antimatter plasma a kilometer away.

The nose of the ship went opaque in reaction to the explosion as Chief Engineer Medina anxiously watched the shield readouts. "They held, Captain," he reported seconds later, "but they are down to 48%."

"That was the last of the flechette rounds, Captain," Midshipman Palmer reported from the starboard gunner's station.

"Thank you Miss Palmer. Mr. Vincent, could you and Mr. Lewis target the pursuing vessels with the main railgun?"

"Aye, Captain. How many rounds?"

"All of them, no sense in hording ammunition at this point. Torpedo crews, give them everything we have." *If we are going down we're going down fighting.*

* * * * *

Mizuki took Hitch's place at one of the fire control displays and began trying to decipher the targeting system. "This is some kind of six dimensional visualization of the space manifold all nearby objects are embedded in!"

"No wonder I've been puking my guts out!" moaned Hitch. "I have a hard time dealing with three dimensions most of the time."

"I think I have identified the Peggy Sue," said Mizuki, "the other targets must be the aliens. Do you wish me to fire on them, Captain?"

"Yes, as long as you are sure you are not firing on the Peggy Sue," the Captain replied from the bridge.

"Firing now." There was a deep thrumming sound and the light patterns on the display panels rippled. "I do not think I hit anything Captain," reported Mizuki. The young Japanese physicist turned to Aput and said, "Aput, see if you can make more sense of these visual images."

"Sure, Dr Ogawa," the young polar bear replied, "but the chair is in the way."

"No problem Aput, grab a hold and yank," said PO Jones, happy to find a problem that could be solved by the application of physical force. With a grunt from both man and bear, the offending gunner's chair was ripped from the deck and sent flying. Aput moved to the console beside Mizuki. As he came within range of the gunner's station the visual display that had stymied Mizuki, and caused the others to become nauseous, lit up in Aput's mind.

"Oh wow! I don't just see them, I smell them," he said, "and I can tell what direction they lay in from their scent!"

"You can smell them?" asked an incredulous Hitch. "What do they smell like?"

"Who care's, Stevie," yelled Jacobs. "If you got a bead on 'em, fire the cannon, Aput."

"I'm not sure how?" the young bear said.

"But I do!" said Mizuki excitedly. "You aim and I will fire."

"OK, I'm targeting the alien ship closest to the Peggy Sue."

"FIRE!" yelled Mizuki. Again the equipment thrummed, and the lights shifted. A little less than 30 seconds later, one of the points of light on the tracking display flashed and dispersed like a drop of oil on water.

* * * * *

On the Peggy Sue's forward display, one of the approaching alien vessels flared and then exploded. "What the bloody hell was that?" said Nigel.

"We got one!" shouted Pauline. With the 15mm out of ammo she was reduced to being a spectator.

"Weren't nothin' we did," replied Billy Ray. As they watch the display the alien ships began to change course. Seconds later, two more of their pursuers exploded into drifting plasma. The remaining aliens abandoned their pursuit, accelerating back toward the star while scattering in several directions.

I don't know where that came from but I have a hunch, Gretchen smiled herself. "We will be at the alter-space transfer point in less than five minutes. Mr. Vincent, flip the ship and get back on course. Peggy Sue, are we ready for transit?"

"Yes, Captain Curtis. We will enter alter-space in 4 minutes and 37 seconds..."

* * * * *

"Captain, It looks like Aput and Mizuki are picking the alien fleet apart," reported JT. The positions of the hostile craft were marked and labeled on the bridge's encompassing display dome. One by one the labels blinked, turned red and went out. "M'tak wasn't kidding when it said the particle cannon would shred the attackers."

"Indeed Mr. Taylor, the enemy has reversed course and are trying to disperse." *Looks like the gamble has payed off. Oh, Luda, please forgive me, but I would rather you hate me than to have stayed together and watched you die along with the rest of us. This way you and most of the crew will live to see Earth again—and with any luck so will we. I will come back to you, I promise.*

"I think they know where the fire is coming from," reported Bobby. "The tracking readouts indicate the aliens may have fired some plasma bursts in our direction."

"They won't arrive for almost a half hour, if we can get the engines up we can easily move out of the target zone," JT replied. "I'm surprised they know where we are. Those bursts from the superluminal particle cannon must have appeared out of nowhere from their perspective."

"The impact of the particle beams would result in small asymmetries in the resulting detonations, from which the direction of the attack can be surmised," M'tak explained.

"What I don't understand is how Aput can smell alien ships half way across a star system," Bear rumbled. "I thought the weapon station was projecting some kind of multidimensional imagery into the gunners heads."

"Evidently polar bears have a part of their brains that is attuned to the targeting system's projections," the AI reported. "It is almost like they were designed to do higher-dimensional gunnery."

The artifact always stressed that the bears would be important once we made it out among the stars, Jack thought, *maybe this is why.*

"We are natural hunters," Bear said, trying to get his head around the rush of new ideas. "And our sense of smell is the best on Earth. But even I don't think that smelling a seal under the ice two miles away is the same as smelling an alien starship 30 light-minutes away through six dimensional space."

"Maybe it's some form of synesthesia," offered Corpsman White.

"Syntha what?" asked Bear.

"Synesthesia is a neurological condition in which stimulation of one sensory or cognitive pathway leads to experiences in a second sensory or cognitive pathway. Some people report tasting color or smelling sounds," Betty explained. "The visions from the targeting system get interpreted by Aput's mind as a scent."

"That makes as much sense as anything," Jack agreed. "M'tak, how soon can we get underway, now that we have learned to fire the weapons?"

"I am continuing to have problems with regrowing some of the gravitonic circuitry for the 3-space drive. The hull puncture caused more damage than I expected. It will be another hour or two."

Chapter 22

King Lewnhallooshna's Flagship

"Bring the fleet about!" bellowed the King. The King's spines rattled with impotent ire. "The scoundrels dare set a trap for Me!"

"We are coming about, Sire," reported the King's Commodore. "But the enemy's weapon cuts through shields and hulls like a solar flare through vacuum."

"I grow tired of your constant complaining, Bonnahaamshna, your defeatist attitudes," the King said crossly. Around the bridge, the crew shrank from the monarch's growing fury. "Fire on the vermin! All ships, fire now!"

The five remaining ship's of the High King's fleet complied, sending several salvos of plasma knots streaking toward the cloud of derelicts, 4 AU away. As they were firing two more ships exploded, sending the King into paroxysms of rage, a rage verging on madness. Observing the King's reaction, Bonnahaamshna could take no more.

The legends are true, this system is cursed! We should never have pursued the warm ones to this place, He thought. *Now we are under attack by ghosts from the past.* Rather than wait for the inevitable royal impaling, the Commodore turned the tables on the fuming monarch, ramming a spine of his own into his sire's flank.

The stricken ruler bellowed and attempted to strike back at his offspring. The Commodore pushed his spine in deeper, saying: "You contemptuous old blowhard, you killed the best of my siblings to satisfy your bloated ego and now you have killed the fleet. We are all going to die, but I want you to precede the rest of us into the void."

The King gurgled as two more ships blossomed into expanding clouds of dust and vapor. As High King Lewnhallooshna expired, those on the bridge raised their spines in salute to Commodore Bonnahaamshna, who alone among them had the courage to commit regicide. Then the flagship was consumed by a great explosion as a burst of superluminal particles knifed through its hull and detonated the ship's store of antimatter.

Bridge, M'tak Ka'fek

"Sir," called Bobby from the helm, "it looks like the Peggy Sue just transitioned into alter-space."

"Too right! They got away," bubbled Sandy, sitting next to him.

"Thank you, Mr. Danner," Jack replied, relief loosening the unconscious tension in his shoulders. "Aput, Dr Ogawa, great shooting! Did you see the Peggy Sue's transition on your targeting displays?"

"Yes, Captain," Mizuki replied for the gun crew. "It is hard to describe in words but the representation of the Peggy Sue on the display altered and then faded into the distance rapidly."

"That's right, Sir," added Aput. "I could only follow it for a few seconds after it left 3-space."

"So things can be sensed in alter-space just after they leave 3-space. I wonder if that means they can be detected just prior to emergence?"

"Under some conditions it is possible to track and even fire on ships in what you call alter-space," said the AI. "In fact, I sent a superluminal neutrino transmission to the Peggy Sue as they transitioned."

"What did you tell them?" asked Jack, annoyed that he had not thought of sending such a message on his own.

"That the alien fleet was destroyed and not pursuing them on the transit to Earth. Also that all on board were alive and well and not to worry," said M'tak. "Of course, that is assuming they have the wherewithal to decode the transmission."

"Are the screens operational?" the Captain asked.

"Yes, Sir," replied JT at the engineering station. "Though I don't know how effective they will be if we get struck by that incoming alien plasma."

"My shields are more than capable of handling the weapons utilized by the alien belligerents. Unlike your more primitive design, my shields use curved spacetime gradients to create a lens that refracts and redirects any incoming radiation. The matter-antimatter plasma structures employed by our late opponents will detonate when they strike the outer shields and the resulting radiation will then be harmlessly routed around the ship."

"You can route radiation all the way around the ship?" asked JT.

"It is usually sufficient to simply send the energy off at an angle, but yes, it is possible to route electromagnetic radiation around the ship and have it exit on its original vector."

"That means you can make the whole ship invisible, right?"

"Yes, Mr. Taylor, under normal conditions it is possible to route all visible and lower frequency EM radiation around the ship so that it cannot be observed. Such subterfuge is only useful against primitive foes, however."

"Dude!" exclaimed Bobby, "That's still way better than a Romulan cloaking device."

"And I still say you're mad as a gum-tree full of galahs, Bobby," quipped Sandy. "Throwing a wobbly every time some piece of scifi kit turns out to be real."

"What?" said Bobby, totally confused buy his Australian copilot.

"I'm just happy we made it. If Aput and Mizuki hadn't nutted out that particle cannon things would have gone cactus, totally pear-shaped."

"Undoubtedly, Miss McKinnett," the Captain said with excess sincerity. Then he grinned to let the young officer know he was only teasing her.

"Sorry Sir, didn't mean to yabber on like that," said Sandy, blushing. "Just happy everything came up trumps is all."

"I fully agree with you, Lieutenant. Now if we could just return to trying to get the engines running..."

Captain's Quarters, *Peggy Sue*

With the ship safely away in alter-space, Ludmilla ensured that there were no new injuries that needed attention and that her existing patients were resting comfortably before retiring to the cabin she shared with Jack. Looking around the familiar space she was almost overwhelmed by emotion.

Oh Jack, my Jack! Are you still alive? Tears welled in her eyes and, grabbing the back of the chair at Jack's desk, she shook them off angrily. *I am not some little girl to fall apart because her boyfriend has runoff. He will either come back or he won't... but what will I do if he doesn't?*

The ship's computer interrupted her thoughts to announce "Isbjørn is at the door, asking to see you. Should I let her in?"

I don't want anyone to see me falling apart like this! "No, I wish to see no one."

"I'm sorry, Dr Tropsha. But she insists on seeing you," the computer replied. "She has pointed out that she is capable of opening the door by force if necessary."

"Der'mo! let her in." *Perhaps it will not be obvious to a bear that I was crying.* She heard the sound of the door opening and the she-bear's footsteps on the carpeting.

"Ludmilla? Are you all right?" called Isbjørn's deep contralto.

"Yes, Isbjørn. I am perfectly fine," said the exasperated and embarrassed Ludmilla.

"Some of the people in sickbay said you left looking upset, so I came to make sure you were OK. I know that getting separated from your mate is harder on you humans than we bears—our males aren't much for sticking around so we are used to getting by without them."

"Just because Jack is gone does not mean that I am falling apart!" *Just wait until I see the medical staff again!* "We have been apart and facing danger before."

"Yes, I know dear. Bear and I have been apart more than together, but I still miss the big lug. Of course, before, I always knew he was still on the same planet—not ten light years away in a different star system."

Ludmilla's eyes threatened to tear up again. "I'm sorry, I had forgotten that Bear was with the Captain on board that alien ship."

"JT too," added Isbjørn. "Though Gretchen is so busy being captain she probably has not had time for that to sink in yet."

"We are all big girls, Isbjørn, but thank you for checking on me," Ludmilla said with a sniffle. After a second's hesitation she threw her arms around the bear's neck and hugged her. "I was feeling sorry for myself, but I'm better now. Thank you."

"Your welcome, Ludmilla. Besides, I'm sure they are all right. With Bear, the Captain and JT all together it's the Universe that needs to watch out. According to the Ambassador, the alien fleet that was following us was destroyed by the M'tak Ka'fek."

"Really, how do they know?"

"They said something about a message in a burst of superluminal neutrinos that arrived just as we dropped into alter-space."

"I think that the Ambassador knows more than they are willing to tell us, some times," Ludmilla observed. Then, touching her comm pip, she called: "Ambassador, I understand you received a message from the M'tak just before we left 3-space. How do you know that it is authentic?"

"The message was encoded in T'aafhal; The pursuing aliens were not advanced enough to use such a mechanism; The Captain included a message for you, would you like to hear it?"

"Yes, of course!"

The simulated voice changed to a fair imitation of Jack, saying, "Luda, please forgive me, but I would rather you hate me than to have stayed together and watched you die along with the rest of us. This way you and most of the crew will live to see Earth again—and with any luck so will we. I will come back to you, I promise."

Ludmilla inhaled sharply, her breath catching in her throat. "That must have been Jack, only he calls me 'Luda'. Thank you Ambassador." *Well, at least they are still alive...*

Bridge, M'tak Ka'fek

"Captain, we may have a problem," said M'tak, as the first wave of alien plasma bursts slashed into the floating debris field. A nearby derelict flared brightly and broke into several large pieces, which drifted inward, toward the center of the graveyard. Watching the plasma induced fireworks the Captain replied a bit distractedly. "I thought you said that your shields could handle the plasma torpedoes with ease, M'tak, what's the problem?"

"It is not the impact of the plasma fire on the ship that concerns me but a side effect of the bombardment. The exploding plasma bursts are knocking some of the derelicts out of orbit. The wreckage is spiraling into the massive object at the center of the debris field."

"Are we in danger of being knocked into the gravity well?"

"No, Captain. The problem is what could happen when several million metric tons of matter hits the surface of the degenerate matter object."

"The AI is right, Captain," added JT. "That infall of matter could result in an explosion—possible a very big explosion."

"If it was just the matter from the wreckage the resulting explosion would probably not exceed 10^{25} joules—the equivalent of a few billion megatons," the AI stated.

"Why do I detect a 'but'?" asked Jack, attention now fully focused.

"Pardon me, Captain," said Mizuki in a quiet voice, "but massive objects made from degenerate matter—neutron stars for example—have a tendency to collect gas in a surrounding disc. When instabilities in the accretion disk allows some of the gas to crash onto the neutron star the result can be a violent eruption. Such outbursts are among the brightest stellar eruptions ever recorded."

"And if the object at the center of the debris field has been collecting gas over time, the junk raining down on it will probably trigger a massive eruption," finished JT.

"Precisely, Captain," confirmed M'tak.

"How big an explosion are we talking about here?" asked Jack.

"An exact answer is difficult, but it could range from trillions to quadrillions of megatons. Moreover, a torrent of high-intensity X-rays will be released."

"Are the gravitonic drives about ready? It sounds like we need to get out of this neighborhood as soon as possible."

"Not yet, Captain," said M'tak, "but even accelerating at 200 G may not get us clear in time."

"Captain," JT called from the navigation station. "It looks like there is developing instability in the central object. We need to be somewhere else, now!"

"Give me options, M'tak," Jack ordered. *After all we have been through I don't relish the idea of being killed by a cosmic garbage dump.* "Can we escape into alter-space?"

"Negative, Captain. There are no nearby alter-space transfer points. We could use a more advanced form of superluminal transport, though there are risks involved."

"Captain! It's erupting!" shouted JT.

"Get us out of here, M'tak," yelled Jack. "Risks be dammed!"

"Yes, Captain." Even as the AI answered the ship began to rotate around its center of gravity, until it was aligned on a clear path out of the debris field. Ahead and to the sides, dead ships blossomed with light reflected from the near nova force explosion unfolding behind the M'tak.

In front of the bow, space distorted as though a lens had appeared directly ahead of the ship, magnifying the view of the stars behind it. Defining the edge of the lens, space bent forming a ring-shaped mirror. Stars reflected by the torus began to move along the mirror's surface, flowing from the inside of the ring to the outside. The M'tak surged forward, toward the center of the lens, through what looked like a mirrored doughnut encased in whirling stars.

Through the Ring of Stars

The ship's passage through the portal of whirling, distorted stars seemed to unfold in slow motion, but only a few minutes actually passed. The ring of stars passed aft of the ship and dissipated, falling apart like a smoke ring on a windy day. As space surrounding the ship returned to normal, stars once again became fixed points of light. The only problem was that many of those points of light were no longer in the positions they occupied before the passage.

"What the hell just happened?" asked Rosey Acuna of the other Marines.

"I don't know," replied Joey Sanchez, "but that registered an 8.5 on my weird-shit-o-meter."

At the navigation station, JT was busy trying to locate familiar but not too distant stars to triangulate a position. "Captain, I have a bad feeling about this. I think we are a long, long way from home."

"Define 'a long way', Mr. Taylor," Jack replied.

"More than a thousand light years minimum, Sir, given the shift in nearby star positions." This pronouncement did not immediately register with everyone on the bridge, but Bobby's head whipped around to stare at the science officer and a few seats away, Mizuki's mouth fell open.

M'tak, is he right? Where are we?

Mr. Taylor is correct, Captain, replied the ship's AI. *We are now nearly 1,500 light years from the Sirius system. The nearest star is a G3V star of roughly solar metallicity. I will highlight it on the main display.*

"Mr. Taylor, could you please identify the star that is highlighted on the forward display?"

"Yes, Sir," JT replied, playing with the alien controls in front of him. "The closest match I get between that star and cataloged stellar objects is CoRoT-9, a star in the constellation Serpens nearly 1,500 light years from Earth. It has at least one Jupiter sized planet, first observed in 2008. We are about 15 AU out, roughly 2 light-hours."

"Sir, that's two and a quarter billion kilometers," said Sandy. "There are no alter-space transfer points this far from that star, we are in open space. How did we get here?"

"Sandy's right, Captain," added Bobby. "We didn't get here through alter-space, and according to Doppler shift measurements from that star's light we are headed toward it at 10,000 km/sec—that's 3% of the speed of light!"

"According to the information the ship's AI downloaded into my brain, we were transported by an annular singularity created by the ship's drives," Jack explained to his stunned crew.

"That is correct, Captain," the AI verbalized. "Such singularities are constructed to link two locations in 3-space. By passing through the singularity, the ship can move from one location to the other without having to travel through the intervening span of normal spacetime. Passage is not quite instantaneous, but when crossing interstellar distances transit time is negligible."

"We passed through a circular black hole?" JT said, voice laced with skepticism. "That starry doughnut thing?"

"We passed through a worm-hole!" said Mizuki, excitedly bouncing up and down in her seat.

"That is so wicked!" said Bobby.

"Yes, it was the only option to escape the erupting degenerate matter object at the heart of the starship graveyard. Obviously, our escape was successful."

"That is good news, M'tak," rumbled Bear. "But how do we get home?"

"There is both good news and bad news regarding returning to your system of origin: First, the 3-space gravitonic drives are finally operational, so we can maneuver in normal space; Second, since we were accelerated coming out of the singularity we will arrive at the star ahead of us in roughly 62.5 hours."

"Fine, and what's the bad news?"

"The generation of the annular singularity used most of our available antimatter, we are below a 10% reserve. We no longer have sufficient fuel to use the singularity drive. To get home we must use the star we are approaching to help decelerate the ship. Then we shall have to find an alter-space transfer point to a system likely to have a supply of antimatter we can appropriate."

"What you are saying," said the Captain, "is that we are almost out of gas and looking for a refueling station."

"An apt analogy, Captain."

"And when we find someone with antimatter," added Bear with a gleam in his eye, "we either need to talk them into giving us some, or take it away from them."

"That is a fair assessment of our options," replied the imperturbable AI.

"I guess that makes it official," said Chief Morgan, "now we really are Captain Jack's space buccaneers."

"Arrr, ye be right about that, matey," said Hitch, with a huge grin on his face. Ahead of the ship the feeble glow of CoRoT-9 beckoned.

Epilogue

Bridge, Peggy Sue, Solar System Emergence

A little under six hours after departing Alpha Canis Majoris, the Peggy Sue emerged from alter-space with the normal shower of particles and gamma rays. They were less than an AU out from the Sun, with Earth standing an AU to its star's right. Gretchen felt a subtle change in the atmosphere on the bridge, as though entering the Sun's familiar space drained the tension from the crew.

She felt her own spirits rise, the same feeling she used to have when sighting a familiar landmark on the way into home port. Knowing that everyone on board wanted to see the familiar blue marble, Gretchen called out to Elena at the navigation station: "Dr. Piscopia, could you please find Earth with the large scope and put it on the forward display. I think we would all enjoy a view of home."

"Yes, Captain," she answered, manipulation the controls that aimed the ship's 2.2 meter reflector. Eclipsing the Sun's bright visage as seen through the ship's transparent bow, a half-lit blue and white planet appeared. "Earth looks abnormally cloudy for some reason." Elena said in a puzzled voice.

As they gazed at the planet's disk a flash appeared close to the limb. This was followed by a bright, outward bulge in the cloud cover. "Now that's right peculiar," said Billy Ray from the helm.

"You are right, that looked like an impact," Elena said. "As though a comet or large asteroid struck somewhere in the northern hemisphere."

The image of Earth turned to a rainbow of false colors as Elena manipulated the telescope's imaging filters. Applying digital enhancement, it was possible to strip away the clouds and see infrared radiation from the full globe, including the quarter cresent cloaked in darkness. The outlines of continents could just be made out, but in at least two locations their familiar shapes were smudged by bright splotches. Roughly circular and hundreds of kilometers wide, the splotches grew fainter with distance from their centers.

"No..." Elena said softly.

"Captain, I'm picking up a drive signature," reported Jo Jo Medina.

"Can you get a fix on it?" asked Gretchen. "Perhaps it is one of the new frigates, or a small cutter."

"Yes, Ma'am. I don't think it is one of ours. The vessel is about 250,000 kilometers above the ecliptic and half a million klicks beyond Earth. Whatever it is, its drive is large and rather inefficient. It is closer to the alien probe ship profile than to one of our drives."

A chill ran down Gretchen's spine. "Course and velocity, Mr. Medina?"

"Captain, this thing is really moving. It looks to be traveling straight out from Earth at nearly 840 km/sec!" Jo Jo replied.

"That is fast and close, it must have done a flyby of the planet," said Gretchen.

"Are you saying that we have an alien starship here in our home system?" asked Ludmilla. Ludmilla had joined the crew on the bridge for emergence, partly to show that she was doing fine despite Jack's absence and partly because she, like everyone else on board, longed to see Earth again.

"It's looking that way, Doctor," Gretchen said with a grim face. "Dr. Piscopia, please try to get a visual fix on the vessel."

Behind and to starboard from the captain's chair, Elena sat facing the controls for the ship's observation equipment. She was within easy earshot of the Captain, yet the Italian astronomer did not respond to Gretchen's command.

"Dr. Piscopia?" queried Captain Curtis, swiveling in her chair so she could look at the navigator's station. Elena was sitting stiffly, hands clenched on the lower control board, saying over and over, "Sono andati, sono andati tutti."

"Dr. Piscopia. Elena! what's wrong?" Asked the Captain, concern rising in her voice. "Dr. Tropsha, what is wrong with Elena?"

Ludmilla rose from the observation chair she was sitting in and went to check on her friend. Over her shoulder she called to the

Captain, "She seems to be in shock. She just keeps saying "they are gone, they are all gone" over and over."

Turning to Elena, Ludmilla asked the astronomer in mostly understandable Italian, "Elena, who is gone. Tell us who is gone?"

Elena looked up at Ludmilla, eyes red with tears streaking her cheeks, and said, "Venice, Padua, the University—they are all gone. All of my colleagues, my friends, my neighbors."

"What do you mean, Elena?" asked Ludmilla.

"There is an impact crater where Venice used to be..." Her voice trailed off as she buried her face in her hands, sobs wracking her body. Ludmilla put her arms around her stricken friend and tried to comfort her. Looking back at Gretchen she asked, "What does she mean, impact crater?"

"It would appear that, in our absence, Earth has come under attack," replied a grim faced Captain Curtis, rising from the captain's chair. "That passing boggy must have hit our planet with an artificial meteor storm—using very large meteors. The type that cause extinction events."

"That would make sense," added Billy Ray, "the course vector is consistent with having done an alter-space transit from Beta Comae, then coming in over the Sun and making a high-speed pass at Earth."

While Ludmilla was dealing with Elena, Billy Ray remotely took control of the large scope, slaving it to the sensor track provided by Chief Engineer Medina. There on the screen was a small, stick like structure with a bloated head. "I believe that there is the ship that dropped the rocks on home. At this range and magnification, that bastard's got to be five kilometers long."

"Are we sure that there is just one ship?" asked the Captain, regaining her mental balance.

"Yes, Ma'am," answered Jo Jo, "I'm only showing a single drive signature."

"Plot an intersect course, Captain?" asked Bill Ray, in a dead calm voice, the same calm voice used by fighter pilots and gunslingers.

Gretchen stood there for a second, next to the captain's chair. In her mind emotion vied with logic and instinct with duty. Finally she cleared her throat and said: "No, Mr. Vincent. Make our course to rendezvous with the Moon in minimum time."

"Aye aye, Ma'am," said the helmsman, disappointment in his voice. Billy Ray and Nigel exchanged glances.

They think I don't have the balls to go after that big bastard? Gretchen thought angrily, noting the reaction of the bridge crew. *Nothing would give me greater pleasure than to overhaul that ship and blow her to hell, but that will have to wait. Jack always warned me that being captain was neither simple nor easy. Damn it, he never had to explain his decisions—but then, he's Captain Jack.*

Captain Curtis opened 1MC, the ship's public announcement intercom: "Attention all hands, this is Captain Curtis. It would appear that Earth has fallen under attack by an alien ship that is even now heading toward the outer reaches of the solar system. To pursue the attacker would mean a long chase—and, unfortunately, we have nothing to hit them with when we catch them. Our magazines were emptied fighting off the last batch of hostiles.

"The damage of the attack has already been done, and given the size and velocity of the attacker, it looks like they are going to swing wide, out into the Kuiper belt, before making another pass. But that will take time—weeks, maybe months—so we have time to do things right.

"Our first duty is to get to Earth, to our base on the Moon, and deliver our information, civilian passengers and the Ambassador. We will ensure our base of operations is secure, pick up replacement crew for those left with Captain Sutton and refill Peggy Sue's magazines. Then, with the help of some of the PT boats," she said, with a feral gleam in her green eyes, "then we will go hunting."

www.ingramcontent.com/pod-product-compliance
Lightning Source LLC
Chambersburg PA
CBHW071229250626
47163CB00001B/107